Round the Red Lamp

and

Other Medical Writings

ROUND THE RED LAMP

and other medical writings

A. Conan Doyle

Edited with an introduction and notes by
Robert Darby

Kansas City:
VALANCOURT BOOKS
2007

Round the Red Lamp and Other Medical Writings by A. Conan Doyle
First Valancourt Books edition, December 2007

Introduction and notes © 2007 by Robert Darby
This edition © 2007 by Valancourt Books

Library of Congress Cataloguing-in-Publication Data

Doyle, Arthur Conan, Sir, 1859-1930.
 Round the red lamp and other medical writings / A. Conan Doyle;
edited with an introduction and notes by Robert Darby. – 1st
Valancourt Books ed.
    p. cm.
Includes bibliographical references.
ISBN 0-9792332-7-5
 1. Physicians—Fiction. 2. Medical fiction. I. Darby, Robert. II. Title.
PR4622.R69 2007
 823'.8—dc22

                2007006692

Published by Valancourt Books
Kansas City, Missouri
http://www.valancourtbooks.com

CONTENTS

INTRODUCTION

THE reviewers were aghast. To the *Spectator*, the stories in *Round the Red Lamp* were 'worse than nightmares which overwhelm human misery and sin'. Cases such as those described in 'A Medical Document' indicated 'a preternatural imagination of a specially gruesome kind'. The *Catholic World* agreed: 'If we are not easily nauseated we may wade through professional horrors so ghastly in their way as anything that the feverish imagination of Edgar Allan Poe conjured up.' For the *Nation* the stories were merely 'disgusting'. Although most of them dealt with such everyday phenomena as sickness, childbirth, love and hate, tales of medical life were evidently not the sort of fare that readers expected from the creator of the sharp-eyed Sherlock Holmes and his urbane companion.

A more positive note was sounded by a critic in the *Speaker*, who wondered whether 'the tragical and the painful commonplaces of the sickroom and death-bed' ought to be made themes of fiction, but concluded that it was appropriate because Conan Doyle had 'a lightness of touch and an instinctive delicacy of feeling that enable him to deal with even the most gruesome of subjects without offending the most sensitive taste'. Indeed, the reviewer went on to praise the author as 'the first writer of fiction of any eminence since the days of Samuel Warren who has made serious use of the experience of a medical man for fictional tales. *Round the Red Lamp* is ... immensely in advance in power and realism of "The Diary of a Late Physician."'[1] 'Realism' was ambiguous praise in the 1890s, when the word was more likely to imply the obscenity of an Émile Zola than approval of an author's fidelity to life.[2] Conan Doyle's reticence in not naming some of the medical or social issues to which his stories make oblique reference (syphilis, prostitution, adultery and masturbation being the most scandalous)

---

[1] Cited in Alvin E. Rodin and Jack D. Key, *Conan Doyle's Tales of Medical Humanism and Values* (Malabar, Fla.: Krieger Publishing, 1992), Introduction, pp. 3-6. Samuel Warren (1807-87) was the author of *Passages from the Diary of a Late Physician* (3 vols., London, 1832-38). Warren studied medicine at Edinburgh but did not graduate or practise, and later became a lawyer and MP.

[2] Douglas Jarvis, 'Morality and Literary Realism: A Debate of the 1880s', *Southerly* (Sydney, Aust.), Vol. 43, Dec. 1983, pp. 404-420.

ensured that, unlike the English publishers of Zola's novels, he did not face police harassment or prosecution. The hysterical press reaction to Ibsen's play *Ghosts*,[1] dealing ever so decently with the subject of hereditary syphilis, helps to explain why Conan Doyle did not specify the problem which drove Francis Norton to the door of Dr Horace Selby late one rainy London night.

Conan Doyle had sent a number of minor contributions to medical journals while practising as a GP in Portsmouth during the 1880s, but it was only after he moved to London and set himself up as an eye specialist that he began to write stories with a medical setting or flavour. The first, 'A Physiologist's Wife', was published in September 1890, followed by 'A Straggler of '15' in March 1891. By then he was becoming famous as the creator of Sherlock Holmes, and the success of the concept—short stories about the self-contained adventures of a single character, suitable for magazine publication—led Jerome K. Jerome to hope that the formula adopted by the *Strand* might work for his own magazine, the *Idler*. In mid-1892 he wrote to Conan Doyle:

> I want something very strong to follow my 'Novel Notes,' which I will end about February. Now what do you say to giving yourself a rest for a while now, and then taking up for me a complete series of six or eight stories to commence in March and run straight away? ... Then we could advertise this series and make it a feature of the magazine.[2]

The author agreed, and word soon got around that he was at work on a new series of stories in which another central character, this time a medical man, would give continuity. The series was provisionally called 'In a Doctor's Waiting Room', and then 'Tales of a Physician's Waiting Room', though neither of these titles was finally used.

Although Jerome had asked for 'something very strong', when

---

[1] *Ghosts* was first performed in England on 13 March 1891. The *Daily Telegraph* went to town with expressions such as 'positively abominable ... disgusting representation ... infecting the modern theatre with poison ... an open drain; a loathsome sore unbandaged, a dirty act done publicly ... absolutely loathsome and fetid ... literary carrion'. Details in *The Oxford Ibsen*, ed. and trans. James Walter McFarlane (London: Oxford University Press, 1961), Vol. V, *Ghosts*, p. 482.
[2] Quoted in Richard Lancelyn Green and John Michael Gibson, *A Bibliography of Arthur Conan Doyle* (Oxford: Clarendon Press, 1983), p. 82.

the stories were written they proved too strong for him; he published only four of the projected eight, and the concept of a single recurrent character was abandoned. When the collection was finally issued by Methuen in October 1894, under the title *Round the Red Lamp: Being Facts and Fancies of Medical Life*, it contained a variety of stories, not all to do with medicine, and with no continuity of characters. In the preface Conan Doyle replied rather defensively to those who thought it wrong to write about painful subjects by asserting that it was 'the province of fiction to treat painful things as well as cheerful ones', and to remind readers that the darker side of life was the one most frequently presented to the surgeon and the physician: 'One cannot write of medical life and be merry over it.' Not only that: 'A tale which may startle the reader ... and shock him into seriousness, plays the part of the alterative and tonic in medicine, bitter to the taste, but bracing in its result.' The stories, in other words, were valuable because they were astringent rather than soothing. In the preface to the reissue of the collection in the 'Author's Edition' of his complete works he further explained that five of the stories[1] had not previously appeared because they were 'strictly—some would say too strictly—realistic'. Even then he had toned down some of them: in the original version of 'The Curse of Eve', read to general revulsion at a meeting of the Authors' Club, the woman dies.[2] It may well be that the lukewarm or hostile reaction to the stories was less a response to their 'realism' than the result of disappointment that they did not confirm the romantic image of the doctor as miraculous healer and pillar of society that was emerging as the medical profession consolidated its status as a respected Victorian institution. The fact that Conan Doyle, himself a medical man by training and original vocation, did not share this adulatory perspective on his colleagues is a point worth considering further.

In view of the prominence of medical men in the works for which Arthur Conan Doyle is best remembered (one study identifies no few-

---

[1] 'His First Operation', 'The Third Generation', 'The Curse of Eve,' 'A Medical Document,' and 'The Surgeon Talks'. One wonders why Jerome seems to have had no trouble accepting a story as horrific as 'The Case of Lady Sannox'; perhaps the Victorian public found 'strong realism' acceptable if it involved people, and especially a woman, being punished for sexual transgression.

[2] Bibliography, pp. 82-83.

er than 37 doctors in the Sherlock Holmes stories alone)[1] it is a striking fact that very few of them emerge as worthy characters, let alone
as any kind of hero in the battle against human suffering and disease.
The best of them is probably John Watson himself—despite his dull
and imperceptive mind, he is loyal and dependable, the epitome of
decent gentlemanly values. When, in 1886, Conan Doyle got the idea
of creating a detective inspired by Edgar Allan Poe's Monsieur Dupin,
he realised that his character could not report his own adventures, but
would need 'a commonplace comrade as a foil—an educated man of
action who could both join in the exploits and narrate them. A drab,
quiet name for an unostentatious man—Watson would do'.[2] While
he is handy with his fists and sometimes his service revolver, Watson's
powers of observation are not what one might have expected in a doctor trained to draw diagnostic inferences from his patients' symptoms.
That almost magical power, reportedly inspired by the clinical performance of Dr Joseph Bell, one of Conan Doyle's teachers at Edinburgh, was given to the irregularly educated detective; and he is rarely
backward in pointing out his comrade's failings as an investigator:

> Well, Watson, a very pretty hash you have made of it. … I cannot
> at the moment recall any possible blunder that you have omitted.
> The total effect of your proceedings has been to give the alarm
> everywhere and yet to discover nothing.[3]

But Watson's bluff common sense was a necessary foil for Holmes'
forensic acuity, and the partnership proved both enduring and profitable: 'If I irritated him by a certain methodical slowness in my mental-
ity,' he explained, 'that irritation served only to make his own flame-
like intuitions and impressions flash up the more vividly and quickly.
Such was my humble role in our alliance.'[4]

Among the other doctors that appear in the Holmes stories, some
are unfortunate, such as the amorous Dr Ray Ernest, whose affair

---

[1] Alvin E. Rodin and Jack D. Key, *The Medical Casebook of Doctor Arthur Conan Doyle* (Malabar, Fla.: Krieger Publishing, 1984), pp. 376-377.
[2] Arthur Conan Doyle, *Memories and Adventures* (1924; London: Greenhill, 1988), pp. 74-75.
[3] 'The Disappearance of Lady Frances Carfax'.
[4] 'The Creeping Man'.

with Josiah Amberley's wife ends fatally in the husband's improvised gas chamber;[1] some are decent but unsuccessful, such as Dr Percy Trevelyan, author of a 'monograph on obscure nervous lesions'[2] and winner of the 'Bruce Pinkerton Prize', who believed that a distinguished career as a specialist in nervous diseases lay ahead, but who fails for want of capital and must take in a lodger to pay the rent;[3] some are ridiculous, such as the illustrious Camford physiologist Professor Presbury, who acquires a rejuvenating drug and turns into a monkey every time he takes it;[4] and some are outright figures of evil. In 'The Missing Three-Quarter' the formidable Dr Leslie Armstrong is described as 'a man of energy and character', more likely than any other man Holmes knew, should he turn his mind that way, 'to fill the gap left by the illustrious Moriarty'. Perhaps the nastiest of them all is the monstrous herpetophile, Dr Grimesby Roylott, who murders one of his step-daughters and is only narrowly prevented from getting the second, prompting Holmes to remark, 'When a doctor goes wrong he is the first of criminals. He has nerve and he has knowledge. Palmer and Pritchard were among the heads of their profession.'[5]

In fact, neither William Palmer nor Edward Pritchard was particularly eminent as a physician, but they were certainly two of the most notorious of several Victorian serial killers, and both were hanged, in 1856 and 1865 respectively, for having poisoned inconvenient family members.[6] In America Dr Thomas Neill Cream not only murdered his wife, but made a practice of poisoning women who came to him

---

[1] 'The Retired Colourman'.

[2] What these were remains unstated, but in the late Victorian period references to private or nervous diseases usually designated something sexual, most probably masturbation, spermatorrhœa, or impotence.

[3] 'The Resident Patient'.

[4] 'The Creeping Man'. Similar interest in atavism—reversion to more primitive evolutionary forms—is found in 'Lot No. 249', one of the less strictly medical stories in Round the Red Lamp, and in The Hound of the Baskervilles, where Dr Mortimer is introduced as the author of several essays on the subject. Fear of atavism was a common theme in late Victorian cultural commentary. See Robert Mighall, A Geography of Victorian Gothic Fiction (Oxford University Press, 1999), esp. chap. 4.

[5] 'The Speckled Band'.

[6] Simon Dewes, Doctors of Murder (London: John Long, 1962); see also individual entries in Oxford Dictionary of National Biography.

seeking abortions; in London, at the very time when Conan Doyle was writing many of these stories, he was charged with murdering several prostitutes; tried and found guilty, he was hanged in 1892. Pace Holmes, it was not just that a doctor had nerve and knowledge: by the 1890s the rising status of the medical profession meant that doctors were respected as authority figures and generally trusted to do good rather than harm. As the author of a recent study of Cream's career points out, the 'adulation of the doctor' was a significant factor in his ability to despatch his victims so easily; the prostitutes trusted him because he was a doctor and swallowed the pills he gave them, believing that they would improve their complexion or protect them from venereal disease.[1]

Despite these scandals, the fact that a medical man could write so disparagingly of his colleagues in his medically focused stories demands explanation. Very few of the characters in Round the Red Lamp emerge as heroes and many are shown in a far from flattering light: indifferent to patient suffering ('The Third Generation'); willing to mutilate a drugged and helpless woman at the request of a mysterious third party ('The Case of Lady Sannox'); fumbling an operation so badly that the wrong person has his ear amputated ('The Surgeon Talks'); and insensible to the reasons of the heart ('A Physiologist's Wife'). The explanation for Conan Doyle's disenchanted view of a profession that has always attracted more than its fair share of hagiographers may be sought in the course of his own career and in the limitations of Victorian medicine as a curative practice.

Although a natural story-teller, Conan Doyle studied medicine because he believed it was a surer road to a lucrative career, and a more likely means of escaping the poverty into which his father's alcoholism had condemned the family. He hoped, at the same time, to do a little writing on the side; as he wrote to his mother a couple of years before he graduated:

> I have certain advantages which, if properly directed and given a fair chance, might lead to great success, but which it would be a thousand pities to nullify aboard ship or in a country practice. Let me once get my footing in a good hospital and my game is

---

[1] Angus McLaren, A Prescription for Murder: The Victorian Serial Killings of Dr. Thomas Neill Cream (University of Chicago Press, 1993), p. 62.

clear. Observe cases minutely, improve my profession, write to the Lancet, supplement my income by literature, make friends and conciliate everyone I meet, wait ten years if need be, and then when my chance comes be prompt and decisive stepping into an honorary surgeonship.[1]

The irony of Conan Doyle's life is that the reverse happened: he did become a country (or at least a provincial) GP, and he turned out to be far more successful as a writer than as a doctor. Far from supplementing his medical income by literature, he eventually found that it was his writing that subsidised his sputtering medical practice. Like Percy Trevelyan, he discovered that starting up with neither capital to equip his surgery nor contacts to bring in paying patients was tough, and the first few years of his life in Portsmouth were spent in grinding poverty; for a while he did not even have a table to eat off, nor a bed to sleep in.[2] By working long hours and assiduous networking, Conan Doyle managed to earn £154 in his first year (1882) and £250 in his second, a sum that rose gradually to £300, where it stuck.[3] This was a reasonable living for the period, but not as good as the estimates given to a parliamentary inquiry in 1878, by which a doctor ought to be earning £300 within five years of starting practice and £500 within ten years, after which his income should increase steadily to £800 or £1000.[4] It was certainly a far cry from the two to five thousand pounds raked in by London specialists and prominent surgeons. The difficulty for graduates like Doyle was that although the market for medical services was growing as the Victorian middle class expanded and grew more affluent, it did not grow as fast as the supply of new doctors. For many years Parliament rebuffed requests to restrict the operations of irregular practitioners (those not licensed by the General Medical Council), preferring to allow a free market in which the consumer could choose the sort of medical care that he or she preferred. The outcome was that competition remained fierce and fees low. As a modern historian

[1] Martin Booth, *The Doctor and the Detective: A Biography of Sir Arthur Conan Doyle* (New York: St. Martin's Press, 2000), p. 69.

[2] *Memories and Adventures*; Arthur Conan Doyle, *The Stark Munro Letters* (London: Longmans, Green, 1895).

[3] *Memories and Adventures*, p. 70.

[4] Anne Digby, *Making a Medical Living: Doctors and Patients in the English Market for Medicine 1720-1911* (Cambridge University Press, 1994), p. 143.

of the medical profession comments: 'the newly qualified practitioner confronted a lay public whose recognition of the superior value of qualified practice was uncertain. They also faced competition from a range of unqualified practitioners (Quacks, herbalists, bonesetters, homeopaths, midwives, pox doctors etc), not to mention their fellow graduates and professionals.'[1] It was only in the early twentieth century that doctors secured legislation restricting the provision of medical services to members of their own ranks, a show of preference more reflective of the growing status and power of the medical elite than of any dramatic improvements in their curative capacities.[2]

Conan Doyle was also earning a little from fiction and journalism, and it was when travelling to Berlin in the hope of getting a saleable story about Robert Koch's announcement of a cure for tuberculosis in 1890 that he met a fellow medico who showed him a means of escape from the treadmill. Malcolm Morris, a specialist in dermatology (which at that time included syphilis), told him that the way to make money was to specialise, and suggested that he establish himself as an ophthalmologist. Conan Doyle duly went to Vienna to study eyes for a few months, then moved to London and nailed up his plate as an oculist. He attracted no clients, however, so he spent his empty hours writing Sherlock Holmes stories for the *Strand* magazine, the handsome payments for which met the rent on his consulting rooms. As he recalled in his memoirs, he sat there each day from ten to four

> with never a ring to disturb my serenity. Could better conditions for reflection and work be found? It was ideal, and so long as I was thoroughly unsuccessful in my professional venture there was every chance of improvement in my literary prospects. Therefore, when I returned to the lodgings at tea-time I bore my little sheaves with me, the first fruits of a considerable harvest.[3]

There is every reason to think that some of the stories later published in *Round the Red Lamp* were also written here.

---

[1] M. Jeanne Peterson, *The Medical Profession in Mid-Victorian London* (Berkeley: University of California Press, 1978), p. 9.

[2] Digby, *Making a Medical Living*; Tony Pensabene, *The Rise of the Medical Practitioner in Victoria*, Australian National University Health Research Project, Research Monograph, No. 2, 1980.

[3] *Memories and Adventures*, p. 95.

The other factor behind Conan Doyle's unromantic view of medical practitioners was the uncertain state of medical knowledge and the ineffectiveness of most available treatments. The main interest of the stories in *Round the Red Lamp* and in other medically focused writings is precisely the intimate glimpse they provide of grassroots medical practice at the moment when the old style Galenist-Hippocratic approaches were giving way to recognisably modern methods of disease control. As several recent histories of medicine have emphasised, it was only at the very end of the nineteenth century that medical advances (as opposed to improvements in urban sanitation and nutrition) began to raise life expectancy and increase the likelihood that a medical consultation would actually do some good.[1] The iconoclastic David Wootton has gone so far as to argue that until the early twentieth century most of the treatments prescribed by doctors (blood-letting, purges, doses of mercury for syphilis, and a bewildering array of herbal or chemical concoctions for other complaints) did more harm than good, and that it was the conservatism of medical culture itself (particularly the great man syndrome and the discipleship model of medical education) that blocked the adoption of new methods and generally stifled progress.[2] Conan Doyle himself seems to have been a pretty ordinary GP: he contributed nothing of clinical significance to medical journals, he failed to notice that his own wife was suffering from tuberculosis,[3] and he once mistook a gastric ulcer for indigestion:

> There was nothing to indicate anything more serious [than dyspepsia]. I therefore reassured her family, spoke lightly of the illness, and walked home to make up a bismuth mixture for her.... When I got home I found a messenger waiting to say that the lady was dead. This is the sort of thing which may happen to any man at any time.[4]

---

[1] James Le Fanu, *The Rise and Fall of Modern Medicine* (Boston: Little Brown, 1999); Robert Darby, *A Surgical Temptation: The Demonization of the Foreskin and the Rise of Circumcision in Britain* (University of Chicago Press, 2005), chap. 5, 'The Priests of the Body: Doctors and Disease in an Antisensual Age'.
[2] David Wootton, *Bad Medicine: Doctors Doing Harm Since Hippocrates* (New York: Oxford University Press, 2006).
[3] Booth, *The Doctor and the Detective*, p. 184.
[4] *Memories and Adventures*, p. 70.

Conan Doyle's point is that although incidents like this might harm a GP's reputation, there was nothing that he, or anybody else, could have done to treat the ulcer even if it had been possible to diagnose it correctly. After experiences such as these, it comes as less of a surprise to find him unusually aware of the limitations of his profession as a curative practice. In an address to medical students in 1910 he commented that when he graduated in 1881 medicine was like 'a blind man with a club, who swung it at random. Sometimes he hit the disease, and sometimes the patient. The club consisted ... of our very copious and hard worked pharmacopœia.'[1]

A glimpse into how the elaborate drug-diet regimes authorised by the Galenist-Hippocratic paradigm actually operated is offered by the treatment prescribed by Dr James Paterson in 1865. His testimony at Dr Edward Pritchard's trial also throws a disturbing light on the medical ethics and professional etiquette of the period. Paterson was called in by Pritchard to examine his ailing wife, and immediately concluded that she was a victim of antimony poisoning. Far from wondering about and addressing the cause of such an unusual condition, he gave the following directions for alleviating the symptoms:

> I prescribed for her small quantities, at short intervals, of champagne and brandy to recruit her strength; small pieces of ice to relieve the thirst and irritability of the stomach. If she tired of these, I said she should have recourse to granulated citrate of magnesia as a cooling, effervescing drink, and have a sinapism applied over the pit of the stomach. ... I also recommended small quantities, at frequent intervals, of easily digested, nutritious food, such as beef-tea, calf-foot jelly, chicken soup, arrowroot, and so on. I then wrote a prescription for twelve grains of calomel, twenty-four of blue or grey powder, twelve of powdered ipecacuanha, and six grains of aromatic powder, the whole to be carefully mixed, and divided into six equal parts—one powder to be taken every day. That prescription was with the view of allaying the biliary disturbance and soothing the mucous membrane of the alimentary canal.[2]

---

[1] Arthur Conan Doyle, 'The Romance of Medicine', St. Mary's Hospital Gazette, Vol. 16, 1910, reprinted in this edition, pp. 306-320.

[2] Testimony at trial of Dr Pritchard, in William Roughead (ed.), The Trial of Dr. Pritchard, (Sydney: Butterworth, n.d. [1906]), p. 142. A sinapism is a mustard plaster, which would do nothing but heat (and perhaps burn) the skin.

None of these nostrums would have done the slightest good, and several, such as calomel (mercury) and 'grey powder' (possibly zinc, or even arsenic), would probably have worsened the woman's condition. The only thing that could have saved Mrs Pritchard was removal from her husband's power.

A few days later Paterson found that Mrs Pritchard's condition had deteriorated markedly and that she seemed to be delirious. Again, he did not inquire as to the source of the antimony, but prescribed a sedative to help her sleep: 'thirty drops of a solution of morphia, [and] of ipecacuanha wine, five or ten drops of chlorodyne, and an ounce of cinnamon water ... to be repeated in four hours if the first draught did not give relief'.[1] It did give relief, and the next thing Dr Paterson learned is that the patient was dead. Asked at Dr Pritchard's trial why he had not taken action when he could see that the woman was being poisoned, he replied that it was 'because she was not my patient'. Pressed on the matter, he insisted that it 'was not my duty. I had no right to interfere in any family without being invited'. The court was incredulous at such a story, and the defence seized upon Paterson's refusal to intervene as evidence that he did not think that the antimony was being administered deliberately. In the course of questioning he revealed the rudimentary state of medical ethics at that time:

> Having been in a house where you thought there was poisoning going on, you did not consider it your duty to go back?—I had discharged my duty, so far as I thought incumbent upon me.
>
> By prescribing certain things, and not knowing whether the prescription was followed?—In any case where a consultation is held, the consulting physician has no right to go back to see the patient.
>
> Then it was the dignity of your profession that prevented you from going back?—It is the etiquette of our profession. [...] In any case where I had been called in for consultation, were I to go back, it would be a breach of the etiquette of my profession.[2]

Pritchard was found guilty of murdering both his wife and mother-in-law, and later confessed, but the fact that Paterson was neither charged nor disciplined over his failure to make any effort to save them sug-

---

[1] *Trial*, pp. 143-144.
[2] *Trial*, pp. 147-148.

gests that his conduct was not regarded as seriously out of line with prevailing standards of professional responsibility.

In his 1910 address, Conan Doyle went on to marvel at the wonderful progress of medicine over the previous thirty years and to affirm his conviction that the future promised even greater results:

> We fought a hidden enemy. It is true that the microbic origin of zymotic disease was taught thirty years ago, but we could hardly hope at that time that so many of these minute organisms could be actually separated, and that we should be able to cultivate these lowly vegetable growths with the same certainty as we grow watercress or sweet peas. This would indeed have seemed to us to be a most far-fetched chapter in the romance of medicine.[1]

Rather overlooking the fundamental discoveries of Louis Pasteur, Robert Koch and other European bacteriologists, the patriotic author praised the contributions of his fellow countrymen to the exposure of 'these forces of evil [and] their machinations', particularly singling out the work of Patrick Manson (filaria worm), Ronald Ross (malaria), David Bruce (Maltese fever), and Almroth Wright ('opsonin'). All these were indeed important advances, and even though there proved to be no such thing as opsonin, Wright's research did help lay the basis for a scientific understanding of antibodies and resistance. What is interesting, however, is that Conan Doyle's optimism did not last; when he composed his memoirs in the early 1920s he not only denied that he had ever been interested in medical progress, but even doubted whether there had been any progress worth noting: 'I had no great interest in the more recent developments of my own profession, and a very strong belief that much of the so-called progress was illusory.'[2]

There are, of course, many reasons why an Englishman born in 1859 might be less cheerful in 1924 than he had been in 1910: the war, the onset of old age, the coming of mass society, votes for women. It is still curious that Conan Doyle should conclude that progress was illusory at the very moment when medicine as a curative practice was, after 2000 years of stagnation and ineffectiveness, finally beginning

---

[1] 'Romance of Medicine', p. 315 in this edition. Zymotic meant diseases thought to arise from rotting organic matter.
[2] *Memories and Adventures*, p. 88.

to do some good. His attitude may be related to disappointment that neither the remarkable discoveries about germs that he had praised in 1910, nor the vastly improved knowledge about bodily processes arising from systematic studies of anatomy and physiology, had done much to relieve suffering, cure disease or prolong life. Even after it had been accepted that micro-organisms were the cause of most serious diseases, there was not much that could be done about them until the introduction of antibiotics and other 'miracle drugs' in the 1930s and 40s.[1] But Conan Doyle's change of heart may also be related to his increasingly otherworldly perspective as his interest in spiritualism and other forms of mysticism developed; emerging in the mid-1880s, these gathered strength steadily as the years passed, to the point where they came to determine his commitments and dominate his life after the First World War. In 1910 he had declared that one of the great benefits of a medical education was that it promoted 'a healthy scepticism ... the desire to prove every fact, and only to reason from such approved facts'.[2] At the same time, he had also warned that the great danger of a medical education was that it fostered 'undue materialism', and he criticised his own education for its failure to accommodate the discoveries of 'psychical research, scientific hypnotism, telepathy' and other agencies which 'emphasised the possibilities which lie outside the things we can see, handle, and explain'. Conan Doyle had rejected the Catholicism in which he had been reared, but he never abandoned the notion that an ordered universe implied some sort of divine lawmaker.[3] Although he professed an early interest in Darwinism, he thus followed Alfred Russell Wallace into spiritualism rather than Darwin and Huxley into atheism, and it was during his time at Portsmouth that he made first forays into the world of table-rapping and other supernatural phenomena, under the guidance of General Drayson.[4] The two sides of Conan Doyle's mind co-existed fairly happily for quite a while, and even co-operated productively: it was the cold, calculating Sherlock Holmes who particularly embodied the rational, materialis-

---

[1] Le Fanu, *Rise and Fall of Modern Medicine.*
[2] 'Romance of Medicine', p. 307.
[3] *Memories and Adventures*, p. 31.
[4] Daniel Stashower, *Teller of Tales: The Life of Arthur Conan Doyle* (New York: Henry Holt, 1999) has a detailed and sympathetic account of Conan Doyle's romance with spiritualism.

tic aspect. It is quite possible that his determination to kill his detective off in the early 1890s was related to the growing power of the other, the spiritual and irrational, side of his mind. A story such as 'A Physiologist's Wife' may be read as a comment on what Conan Doyle saw as the inadequacy of the Darwin-Huxley-Spencer materialism that he had embraced as a medical student, but was by then rejecting, and a fairly direct critique of the idea that man can live by intellect alone.[1]

Arthur Conan Doyle was most eager to be remembered as a prophet of spiritualism and as the author of well-researched historical romances, such as *The White Company* and his Napoleonic series. He was bitterly disappointed that the reading public far preferred his Sherlock Holmes stories, which he regarded as 'a lower stratum of literary achievement' and disparaged as lightweight pot-boilers.[2] In his reminiscences he makes no mention of *Round the Red Lamp* at all, and the only 'medical' stories that he refers to are 'A Physiologist's Wife' and one of the feeblest, 'A Straggler of '15'—a further indication of both his sentimentality and his desire to be known as an anti-materialist and a historical novelist, not as a writer of detective stories. Yet the fact remains that Conan Doyle would never have been asked to write stories about medical life, nor to have them collected in book form, had he not already become famous as the best-selling creator of Sherlock Holmes. With the possible exception of 'The Case of Lady Sannox', a truly chilling masterpiece, there is nothing in *Round the Red Lamp* that stands out as fiction, though 'Behind the Times' and a couple of others pass the test of good reportage. The interest of this collection and of Conan Doyle's other medical writings lies elsewhere, as a rare glimpse into the world of a provincial GP at the moment when old-style medicine was dying and the modern medical profession was emerging. As his obituary in the *Lancet* observed, both *Round the Red Lamp* and *The Stark Munro Letters* were of 'distinctly medical interest':

Professional developments, altering the conduct of medical practice,

---

[1] Anybody with more than a superficial acquaintance with the works of these thinkers knows that they were perfectly aware of the importance of the emotions in human and other animal life (Darwin wrote an entire book on the expression of the emotions), and that their own lives were as rich in emotional experience as they were productive of revolutionary advances in scientific understanding.

[2] *Memories and Adventures*, pp. 80-81, 99.

may have made these [stories] no longer typical, but they will repay reading for their observation of much that occurs now and much that lately formed routine.[1]

The *Lancet* was careful to point out, however, that it was as the creator of the world's greatest detective that Conan Doyle was likely to be best remembered.

There was much truth in this prediction, but Conan Doyle deserves to be associated with more than the world of 221B Baker Street. His tales of horror and the supernatural may seem tame by today's standards, but they were daring and innovative in their own time, and they set new directions in imaginative fiction. The realism of his medical stories may be unremarkable to us jaded post-modernists, but they shocked contemporaries, who found the topics and the treatment both offensive and disturbing. We must not forget that the late Victorian period was one of prudery and increasing censorship,[2] and that Conan Doyle was running a risk in writing, even as obliquely as he did, about tabooed subjects such as syphilis, genital mutilation and adultery. A year after *Round the Red Lamp*, Thomas Hardy's *Jude the Obscure* was published to such a chorus of abuse and condemnation that Hardy gave up writing novels and turned to poetry.

Conan Doyle's medical stories are also valuable for what they can teach us about the doctor-patient relationship and medical ethics in general. In their painstaking studies of his medical writings, Alvin Rodin and Jack Key have emphasised Conan Doyle's commitment to humanist values, and in particular his recognition of the obligation to treat patients as persons, not to dehumanise them as mere cases, like the surgeon Douglas Stone did with the veiled (and thus anonymous) woman he was called upon to treat. Conan Doyle was critical of doctors who were 'stuffed with accurate knowledge', yet who 'were so cold in their bearing, and so unsympathetic in their attitude, assuming

---

[1] 'Arthur Conan Doyle' (Obituary), *Lancet*, 12 July 1930, p. 90.

[2] Among many studies, see Peter Cominos, 'Late Victorian Respectability and the Social System', *International Review of Social History*, Vol. VIII, 1963, pp. 18-48, 216-250; Richard Davenport-Hines, *Sex, Death and Punishment: Attitudes to Sex and Sexuality in Britain Since the Renaissance* (London: Collins, 1990); Hera Cook, *The Long Sexual Revolution: English Women, Sex and Contraception 1800-1975* (Oxford University Press, 2004).

the role rather of a judge than a friend, that they left their half-frozen patients all the worse for their contact'.[1] His vision was of 'a noble, generous, kindly profession', in which the doctor went 'from house to house, and his step and his voice are loved and welcomed in each'.[2] As close as this picture may be to the ideal image that the medical profession has always sought to project, it was far cry from the realities of the period, when doctors were more inclined to be authoritarian, dogmatic and moralistic, and rather too fond of quoting proverbs about the need to be cruel in order to be kind.[3]

The principles of kindness and respect are no less relevant today than they were in the 1890s, and they have found an echo in much contemporary thinking about medical ethics, particularly as they relate to the rights of patients. In his recent study *Pilgrims in Medicine*, Thomas Faunce has sought to reconceptualise medical ethics as a system of doctor-patient regulation based on the fundamental premise that the role of the doctor—its basic telos, as he puts it—is 'the relief of individual patient suffering'. The wider aim is to formulate a system of medical ethics which integrates traditional principles stretching back to the Hippocratic Oath with modern ethical philosophy, law, and human rights, especially as codified in the various conventions and other instruments that have appeared since the Declaration of the Rights of Man (1789). Surveying the history of medical ethics, Faunce detects three persistent themes: first, that doctors must respect patients' autonomy and do them no harm; second, that all human beings have a right to physical integrity and must be informed of all material risks before any procedure; third, that all human beings are born equal in dignity. Although this approach is as radical as the style of the book is unconventional, Faunce's aim is to retain all that is positive in past schemes of doctor-patient regulation and unite them with modern conceptions of individual rights, particularly the rights to autonomy and inviolability of person. Despite criticism of legal positivism, he regards at least one tenet of medical law—that any touching without consent is likely to constitute battery—as fundamental to an ethical

---

[1] 'Romance of Medicine', p. 309.
[2] 'The Surgeon Talks'.
[3] For details of how these attitudes helped to promote widespread male genital mutilation in the late Victorian period, see my *Surgical Temptation*.

medical practice.[1] Judging from his attitude as expressed in his 1910 address to medical students, stories such as 'The Case of Lady Sannox', and his suggestion that mutilations might be 'worse than death'[2] Arthur Conan Doyle would probably agree.

ROBERT DARBY
Canberra

February 12, 2007

ABOUT THE EDITOR

ROBERT DARBY is an independent scholar with an interest in many aspects of medical and cultural history. He has published articles in a variety of journals, including *Social History of Medicine, Journal of the History of Sexuality, Journal of the History of Medicine, War in History,* and *Eighteenth Century Life.* He has previously edited a collection of stories by the Australian writer Marjorie Barnard, and he is the author of *A Surgical Temptation: The Demonization of the Foreskin and the Rise of Circumcision in Britain* (University of Chicago Press, 2005). He lives in Canberra, Australia.

---

[1] Thomas Alured Faunce, *Pilgrims in Medicine: An Allegory of Medical Humanities, Foundational Virtues, Ethical Principles, Law and Human Rights in Medical Personal and Professional Development* (Leiden: Martinus Nijhoff, 2005). See my review for H-Net, available at http://www.h-net.msu.edu/reviews/showrev. cgi?path=19181153409834.
[2] 'The Surgeon Talks'.

NOTE ON THE TEXTS

Round the Red Lamp: Being Facts and Fancies of Medical Life was first published in London in October 1894 by Methuen. An 1894 edition also appeared at New York, published by D. Appleton, and in 1895 Tauchnitz published a Continental edition of the book at Leipzig. The book went through numerous printings through at least the 1920s.

The text of the present edition follows the 1894 Methuen first edition verbatim, aside from a few obvious printer's errors which have been silently corrected. There are numerous differences among the London, New York, and Leipzig editions of 1894-95, mostly involving punctuation (single vs. double quotation marks, dashes vs. commas, 'Dr.' vs. 'Dr', etc.) In 1902, *Round the Red Lamp* appeared in the 'Author's Edition' of Conan Doyle's collected works. In the 'Author's Edition', Conan Doyle makes a number of substantive changes, sometimes deleting or extensively reworking entire paragraphs.

The texts of 'Crabbe's Practice', 'The Surgeon of Gaster Fell', 'The Retirement of Signor Lambert', and Doyle's nonfiction medical writings are all taken from their first appearances in various periodicals and are reproduced verbatim, which has resulted in some apparent inconsistencies, as some of these writings are punctuated differently from others. However, in keeping with Valancourt Books' editorial policy, these texts have been reproduced as they first appeared; no effort has been made to standardise or regularise spelling or punctuation.

Round the Red Lamp:

Being Facts and Fancies of Medical Life

THE PREFACE

*[Being an extract from a long and animated correspondence
with a friend in America.]*

I QUITE recognise the force of your objection that an invalid or a woman in weak health would get no good from stories which attempt to treat some features of medical life with a certain amount of realism. If you deal with this life at all, however, and if you are anxious to make your doctors something more than marionettes, it is quite essential that you should paint the darker side, since it is that which is principally presented to the surgeon or physician. He sees many beautiful things, it is true, fortitude and heroism, love and self-sacrifice; but they are all called forth (as our nobler qualities are always called forth) by bitter sorrow and trial. One cannot write of medical life and be merry over it.

Then why write of it, you may ask? If a subject is painful why treat it at all? I answer that it is the province of fiction to treat painful things as well as cheerful ones. The story which wiles away a weary hour fulfils an obviously good purpose, but not more so, I hold, than that which helps to emphasise the graver side of life. A tale which may startle the reader out of his usual grooves of thought, and shocks him into seriousness, plays the part of the alterative and tonic in medicine, bitter to the taste but bracing in the result. There are a few stories in this little collection which might have such an effect, and I have so far shared in your feeling that I have reserved them from serial publication. In book-form the reader can see that they are medical stories, and can, if he or she be so minded, avoid them.

Yours very truly,
A. CONAN DOYLE.

P. S.—You will see that nearly half of the contents have not appeared before.[1]

---

[1] The Appleton (New York) edition's postscript reads: 'P. S.—You ask about the Red Lamp. It is the usual sign of the general practitioner in England.'

ROUND THE RED LAMP

BEHIND THE TIMES

MY first interview with Dr James Winter was under dramatic circumstances. It occurred at two in the morning in the bedroom of an old country house. I kicked him twice on the white waistcoat and knocked off his gold spectacles, while he, with the aid of a female accomplice, stifled my angry cries in a flannel petticoat and thrust me into a warm bath. I am told that one of my parents, who happened to be present, remarked in a whisper that there was nothing the matter with my lungs. I cannot recall how Dr Winter looked at the time, for I had other things to think of, but his description of my own appearance is far from flattering. A fluffy head, a body like a trussed goose, very bandy legs, and feet with the soles turned inwards—those are the main items which he can remember.

From this time onwards the epochs of my life were the periodical assaults which Dr Winter made upon me. He vaccinated me, he cut me for an abscess, he blistered me for mumps. It was a world of peace and he the one dark cloud that threatened. But at last there came a time of real illness—a time when I lay for months together inside my wicker-work basket bed, and then it was that I learned that that hard face could relax, that those country-made, creaking boots could steal very gently to a bedside, and that that rough voice could thin into a whisper when it spoke to a sick child.

And now the child is himself a medical man, and yet Dr Winter is the same as ever. I can see no change since first I can remember him, save that perhaps the brindled hair is a trifle whiter, and the huge shoulders a little more bowed. He is a very tall man, though he loses a couple of inches from his stoop. That big back of his has curved itself over sick beds until it has set in that shape. His face is of a walnut brown, and tells of long winter drives over bleak country roads, with the wind and the rain in his teeth. It looks smooth at a little distance, but as you approach him you see that it is shot with innumerable fine wrinkles like a last year's apple. They are hardly to be seen when he is in repose; but when he laughs his face breaks like a starred glass, and you realise then that, though he looks old, he must be older than he looks.

How old that is I could never discover. I have often tried to find out, and have struck his stream as high up as George the Fourth and even of the Regency, but without ever getting quite to the source. His mind must have been open to impressions very early, but it must also have closed early, for the politics of the day have little interest for him, while he is fiercely excited about questions which are entirely prehistoric. He shakes his head when he speaks of the first Reform Bill and expresses grave doubts as to its wisdom, and I have heard him, when he was warmed by a glass of wine, say bitter things about Robert Peel and his abandoning of the Corn Laws.[1] The death of that statesman brought the history of England to a definite close, and Dr Winter refers to everything which had happened since then as to an insignificant anti-climax.

But it was only when I had myself become a medical man that I was able to appreciate how entirely he is a survival of a past generation. He had learned his medicine under that obsolete and forgotten system by which a youth was apprenticed to a surgeon, in the days when the study of anatomy was often approached through a violated grave. His views upon his own profession are even more reactionary than his politics. Fifty years have brought him little and deprived him of less. Vaccination was well within the teaching of his youth, though I think he has a secret preference for inoculation. Bleeding he would practise freely but for public opinion. Chloroform he regards as a dangerous innovation, and he always clicks with his tongue when it is mentioned. He has even been known to say vain things about Laennec, and to refer to the stethoscope as 'a newfangled French toy.' He carries one in his hat out of deference to the expectations of his patients; but he is very hard of hearing, so that it makes little difference whether he uses it or not.

He always reads, as a duty, his weekly medical paper, so that he has a general idea as to the advance of modern science. He always persists in looking upon it, however, as a huge and rather ludicrous experiment. The germ theory of disease set him chuckling for a long time, and his favourite joke in the sick-room was to say, 'Shut the door, or the germs will be getting in.'[2] As to the Darwinian theory, it struck him as being the crowning joke of the century. 'The children in the nursery and the ancestors in the stable,' he would cry, and laugh the tears out of his eyes.

He is so very much behind the day that occasionally, as things move round in their usual circle, he finds himself, to his bewilderment, in the front of the fashion. Dietetic treatment, for example, had been much in vogue in his youth, and he has more practical knowledge of it than anyone whom I have met. Massage, too, was familiar to him when it was new to our generation. He had been trained also at a time when instruments were in a rudimentary state, and when men learned to trust more to their own fingers. He has a model surgical hand, muscular in the palm, tapering in the fingers, 'with an eye at the end of each.' I shall not easily forget how Dr Patterson and I cut Sir John Sirwell, the County Member, and were unable to find the stone. It was a horrible moment. Both our careers were at stake. And then it was that Dr Winter, whom we had asked out of courtesy to be present, introduced into the wound a finger which seemed to our excited senses to be about nine inches long, and hooked out the stone at the end of it.

'It's always well to bring one in your waistcoat-pocket,' said he with a chuckle, 'but I suppose you youngsters are above all that.'

We made him president of our branch of the British Medical Association, but he resigned after the first meeting. 'The young men are too much for me,' he said. 'I don't understand what they are talking about.' Yet his patients do very well. He has the healing touch—that magnetic thing which defies explanation or analysis, but which is a very evident fact none the less. His mere presence leaves the patient with more hopefulness and vitality. The sight of disease affects him as dust does a careful housewife. It makes him angry and impatient. 'Tut, tut, this will never do!' he cries, as he takes over a new case. He would shoo death out of the room as though he were an intrusive hen. But when the intruder refuses to be dislodged, when the blood moves more slowly and the eyes grow dimmer, then it is that Dr Winter is of more avail than all the drugs in his surgery. Dying folk cling to his hand as if the presence of his bulk and vigour gives them more courage to face the change; and that kindly, wind-beaten face has been the last earthly impression which many a sufferer has carried into the unknown.

When Dr Patterson and I, both of us young, energetic, and up-to-date, settled in the district, we were most cordially received by the old doctor, who would have been only too happy to be relieved of some of his patients. The patients themselves, however, followed their own inclinations, which is a reprehensible way that patients have, so that we remained neglected with our modern instruments and our latest alkaloids, while he was serving out senna and calomel to all the countryside. We both of us loved the old fellow, but at the same time, in the privacy of our own intimate conversations, we could not help commenting upon this deplorable lack of judgment.

'It is all very well for the poorer people,' said Patterson, 'but after all the educated classes have a right to expect that their medical man will know the difference between a mitral murmur and a bronchitic rale. It's the judicial frame of mind, not the sympathetic, which is the essential one.'

I thoroughly agreed with Patterson in what he said. It happened, however, that very shortly afterwards the epidemic of influenza broke out, and we were all worked to death. One morning I met Patterson on my round, and found him looking rather pale and fagged out. He made the same remark about me. I was in fact feeling far from well, and I lay upon the sofa all afternoon with a splitting headache and pains in every joint. As evening closed in, I could no longer disguise the fact that the scourge was upon me, and I felt that I should have medical advice without delay. It was of Patterson naturally that I thought, but somehow the idea of him had suddenly become repugnant to me. I thought of his cold, critical attitude, of his endless questions, of his tests and his tappings. I wanted something more soothing—something more genial.

'Mrs Hudson,' said I to my housekeeper, 'would you kindly run along to old Dr Winter and tell him that I should be obliged to him if he would step round.'

She was back with an answer presently.

'Dr Winter will come round in an hour or so, sir, but he has just been called in to attend Dr Patterson.'

NOTES TO 'BEHIND THE TIMES'

1. The first Reform Act was passed in 1832 and enlarged the electorate by extending the franchise to middle class householders and some rural tenants. The Corn Laws, imposing a duty on imported grain, were introduced in 1815. They were repealed by Robert Peel's Tory administration in 1846-49 after a bitter struggle which set rural and agricultural interests against those of the commercial and industrial classes.

2. Conan Doyle recalled that when Robert Lister was introducing his system of antisepsis in the 1860s-70s, 'one sardonic professor of the old school used to say as he was operating, "Please shut the door or the germs will be getting in."'[1]

---

[1] See 'The Romance of Medicine', p. 314.

HIS FIRST OPERATION

IT was the first day of a winter session, and the third year's man was walking with the first year's man. Twelve o'clock was just booming out from the Tron Church.

'Let me see,' said the third year's man, 'you have never seen an operation?'

'Never.'

'Then this way, please. This is Rutherford's historic bar. A glass of sherry, please, for this gentleman. You are rather sensitive, are you not?'

'My nerves are not very strong, I am afraid.'

'Hum! Another glass of sherry for this gentleman. We are going to an operation now, you know.'

The novice squared his shoulders and made a gallant attempt to look unconcerned.

'Nothing very bad—eh?'

'Well, yes—pretty bad.'

'An—an amputation?'

'No, it's a bigger affair than that.'

'I think—I think they must be expecting me at home.'

'There's no sense in funking. If you don't go to-day you must to-morrow. Better get it over at once. Feel pretty fit?'

'Oh, yes, all right!'

The smile was not a success.

'One more glass of sherry, then. Now come on or we shall be late. I want you to be well in front.'

'Surely that is not necessary.'

'Oh, it is far better! What a drove of students! There are plenty of new men among them. You can tell them easily enough, can't you? If they were going down to be operated upon themselves they could not look whiter.'

'I don't think I should look as white.'

'Well, I was just the same myself. But the feeling soon wears off. You see a fellow with a face like plaster, and before the week is out he is eating his lunch in the dissecting rooms. I'll tell you all about the case when we get to the theatre.'

The students were pouring down the sloping street which led to the infirmary—each with his little sheaf of note-books in his hand. There were pale, frightened lads, fresh from the High Schools, and callous old chronics, whose generation had passed on and left them. They swept in an unbroken, tumultuous stream from the University gate to the hospital. The figures and gait of the men were young, but there was little youth in most of their faces. Some looked as if they ate too little—a few as if they drank too much. Tall and short, tweed coated and black, round-shouldered, bespectacled and slim, they crowded with clatter of feet and rattle of sticks through the hospital gate. Now and again they thickened into two lines as the carriage of a surgeon of the staff rolled over the cobblestones between.

'There's going to be a crowd at Archer's,' whispered the senior man with suppressed excitement. 'It is grand to see him at work. I've seen him jab all round the aorta until it made me jumpy to watch him. This way, and mind the whitewash.'

They passed under an archway and down a long, stone-flagged corridor with drab-coloured doors on either side, each marked with a number. Some of them were ajar, and the novice glanced into them with tingling nerves. He was reassured to catch a glimpse of cheery fires, lines of white-counterpaned beds and a profusion of coloured texts upon the wall. The corridor opened upon a small hall, with a fringe of poorly clad people seated all round upon benches. A young man with a pair of scissors stuck, like a flower, in his button-hole and a note-book in his hand, was passing from one to the other, whispering and writing.

'Anything good?' asked the third year's man.

'You should have been here yesterday,' said the out-patient clerk, glancing up. 'We had a regular field day. A popliteal aneurism, a Colles' fracture, a spina bifida, a tropical abscess, and an elephantiasis. How's that for a single haul?'

'I'm sorry I missed it. But they'll come again, I suppose. What's up with the old gentleman?'

A broken workman was sitting in the shadow, rocking himself slowly to and fro and groaning. A woman beside him was trying to console him, patting his shoulder with a hand which was spotted over with curious little white blisters.

'It's a fine carbuncle,' said the clerk, with the air of a connoisseur who describes his orchids to one who can appreciate them. 'It's on his back, and the passage is draughty, so we must not look at it, must we, daddy? Pemphigus,' he added carelessly, pointing to the woman's disfigured hands. 'Would you care to stop and take out a metacarpal?'

'No thank you, we are due at Archer's. Come on;' and they rejoined the throng which was hurrying to the theatre of the famous surgeon.

The tiers of horse-shoe benches, rising from the floor to the ceiling, were already packed, and the novice as he entered saw vague, curving lines of faces in front of him, and heard the deep buzz of a hundred voices, and sounds of laughter from somewhere up above him. His companion spied an opening on the second bench, and they both squeezed into it.

'This is grand,' the senior man whispered; 'you'll have a rare view of it all.'

Only a single row of heads intervened between them and the operating table. It was of unpainted deal, plain, strong and scrupulously clean. A sheet of brown waterproofing covered half of it, and beneath stood a large tin tray full of sawdust. On the further side, in front of the window, there was a board which was strewed with glittering instruments—forceps, tenacula, saws, canulas, and trocars. A line of knives, with long, thin, delicate blades, lay at one side. Two young men lounged in front of this; one threading needles, the other doing something to a brass coffee-pot-like thing which hissed out puffs of steam.

'That's Peterson,' whispered the senior. 'The big, bald man in the front row. He's the skin-grafting man, you know. And that's Anthony Browne, who took a larynx out successfully last winter. And there's Murphy, the pathologist, and Stoddart the eye man. You'll come to know them all soon.'

'Who are the two men at the table?'

'Nobody—dressers. One has charge of the instruments and the other of the puffing Billy. It's Lister's antiseptic spray, you know, and Archer's one of the carbolic-acid men.[1] Hayes is the leader of the cleanliness-and-cold-water school, and they all hate each other like poison.'

A flutter of interest passed through the closely-packed benches as a woman in petticoat and bodice was led in by two nurses. A red woollen shawl was draped over her head and round her neck. The face which looked out from it was that of a woman in the prime of her years, but drawn with suffering, and of a peculiar bees-wax tint. Her head drooped as she walked, and one of the nurses, with her arm round her waist, was whispering consolation in her ear. She gave a quick side glance at the instrument table as she passed, but the nurses turned her away from it.

'What ails her?' asked the novice.

'Cancer of the parotid. It's the devil of a case, extends right away back behind the carotids. There's hardly a man but Archer would dare to follow it. Ah, here he is himself.'

As he spoke, a small, brisk, iron-grey man came striding into the room, rubbing his hands together as he walked. He had a clean-shaven face, of the Naval officer type, with large, bright eyes, and a firm, straight mouth. Behind him came his big house surgeon, with his gleaming pince-nez and a trail of dressers, who grouped themselves into the corners of the room.

'Gentlemen,' cried the surgeon in a voice as hard and brisk as his manner. 'We have here an interesting case of tumour of the parotid, originally cartilaginous but now assuming malignant characteristics, and therefore requiring excision. On to the table, nurse! Thank you! Chloroform, clerk! Thank you! You can take the shawl off, nurse.'

The woman lay back upon the waterproofed pillow, and her murderous tumour lay revealed. In itself it was a pretty thing, ivory white with a mesh of blue veins, and curving gently from jaw to chest. But the lean, yellow face, and the stringy throat were in horrible contrast with the plumpness and sleekness of this monstrous growth. The surgeon placed a hand on each side of it and pressed it slowly backwards and forwards.

'Adherent at one place, gentlemen,' he cried. 'The growth involves the carotids and jugulars, and passes behind the ramus of the jaw, whither we must be prepared to follow it. It is impossible to say how deep our dissection may carry us. Carbolic tray, thank you! Dressings of carbolic gauze, if you please! Push the chloroform, Mr Johnson. Have the small saw ready in case it is necessary to remove the jaw.'

The patient was moaning gently under the towel which had been placed over her face. She tried to raise her arms and to draw up her knees, but two dressers restrained her. The heavy air was full of the penetrating smells of carbolic acid and of chloroform. A muffled cry came from under the towel, and then a snatch of a song, sung in a high, quavering, monotonous voice.

> 'He says, says he,
>   If you fly with me
>   You'll be mistress of the ice-cream van;
>   You'll be mistress of the—'

It mumbled off into a drone and stopped. The surgeon came across, still rubbing his hands, and spoke to an elderly man in front of the novice.

'Narrow squeak for the Government,' he said.

'Oh, ten is enough.'

'They won't have ten long. They'd do better to resign before they are driven to it.'

'Oh, I should fight it out.'

'What's the use. They can't get past the committee, even if they get a vote in the House. I was talking to—'

'Patient's ready, sir,' said the dresser.

'Talking to McDonald—but I'll tell you about it presently.' He walked back to the patient, who was breathing in long, heavy gasps. 'I propose,' said he, passing his hand over the tumour in an almost caressing fashion, 'to make a free incision over the posterior border, and to take another forward at right angles to the lower end of it. Might I trouble you for a medium knife, Mr Johnson.'

The novice, with eyes which were dilating with horror, saw the surgeon pick up the long, gleaming knife, dip it into a tin basin and balance it in his fingers as an artist might his brush. Then he saw him pinch up the skin above the tumour with his left hand. At the sight his nerves, which had already been tried once or twice that day, gave way utterly. His head swam round and he felt that in another instant he might faint. He dared not look at the patient. He dug his thumbs into his ears lest some scream should come to haunt him, and he fixed his eyes rigidly upon the wooden ledge in front of him. One glance, one cry, would, he knew, break down the shred of self-possession which he still retained. He tried to think of cricket, of green fields and rippling water, of his sisters at home—of anything rather than of what was going on so near him.

And yet, somehow, even with his ears stopped up, sounds seemed to penetrate to him and to carry their own tale. He heard, or thought that he heard, the long hissing of the carbolic engine. Then he was conscious of some movement among the dressers. Were there groans too breaking in upon him, and some other sound, some fluid sound, which was more dreadfully suggestive still? His mind would keep building up every step of the operation, and fancy made it more ghastly than fact could have been. His nerves tingled and quivered. Minute by minute the giddiness grew more marked, the numb, sickly feeling at his heart more distressing. And then suddenly, with a groan, his head pitching forward, and his brow cracking sharply upon the narrow, wooden shelf in front of him, he lay in a dead faint.

When he came to himself, he was lying in the empty theatre with his collar and shirt undone. The third year's man was dabbing a wet sponge over his face, and a couple of grinning dressers were looking on.

'All right,' cried the novice, sitting up and rubbing his eyes; 'I'm sorry to have made an ass of myself.'

'Well, so I should think,' said his companion. 'What on earth did you faint about?'

'I couldn't help it. It was that operation.'

'What operation?'

'Why, that cancer.'

There was a pause, and then the three students burst out laughing.

'Why, you juggins!' cried the senior man, 'there never was an operation at all! They found the patient didn't stand the chloroform well, and so the whole thing was off. Archer has been giving us one of his racy lectures, and you fainted just in the middle of his favourite story.'

NOTES TO 'HIS FIRST OPERATION'

First published in *Round the Red Lamp.*

1. Lister's antisepsis met opposition from those who thought that simple cleanliness was more effective against infection. The suggestion that 'antiseptic spray' and carbolic acid belonged to opposing factions is puzzling, since Lister's spray was carbolic acid.[1]

---

[1] For a thorough discussion of the carbolic versus cleanliness debate, see Christopher Lawrence and Richard Dixey, 'Practising on Principle: Joseph Lister and the Germ Theories of Disease', in Christopher Lawrence (ed.), *Medical Theory, Surgical Practice: Studies in the History of Medicine* (London: Routledge, 1992); Lindsay Granshaw, '"Upon this principle I have based a practice": The Development and Reception of Antisepsis in Britain, 1867-90', in John Pickard (ed.), *Medical Innovations in Historical Perspective* (New York: St. Martin's Press, 1992), pp. 17-46.

A STRAGGLER OF '15[1]

It was a dull October morning, and heavy, rolling fog-wreaths lay low over the wet grey roofs of the Woolwich houses. Down in the long, brick-lined streets all was sodden and greasy and cheerless. From the high buildings of the Arsenal came the whirr of many wheels, the thudding of weights, and the buzz and babel of human toil. Beyond, the dwellings of the working-men, smoke-stained and unlovely, radiated away in a lessening perspective of narrowing road and dwindling wall.

There were few folk in the streets, for the toilers had all been absorbed since break of day by the huge, smoke-spouting monster, which sucked in the manhood of the town, to belch it forth, weary and work-stained, every night. Stout women, with thick, red arms and dirty aprons, stood upon the whitened doorsteps, leaning upon their brooms, and shrieking their morning greetings across the road. One had gathered a small knot of cronies around her, and was talking energetically, with little shrill titters from her audience to punctuate her remarks.

'Old enough to know better!' she cried, in answer to an exclamation from one of the listeners. 'Why, 'ow old is he at all? Blessed if I could ever make out.'

'Well, it ain't so hard to reckon,' said a sharp-featured, pale-faced woman, with watery blue eyes. 'He's been at the battle o' Waterloo, and has the pension and medal to prove it.'

'That were a ter'ble long time agone,' remarked a third. 'It were afore I were born.'

'It were fifteen year after the beginnin' of the century,' cried a younger woman, who had stood leaning against the wall, with a smile of superior knowledge upon her face. 'My Bill was a-saying so last Sabbath, when I spoke to him o' old Daddy Brewster, here.'

'And suppose he spoke truth, Missus Simpson, 'ow long agone do that make it?'

'It's eighty-one now,' said the original speaker, checking off the years upon her coarse, red fingers, 'and that were fifteen. Ten and ten, and ten, and ten, and ten—why, it's only sixty and six year, so he ain't so old after all.'

'But he weren't a new-born babe at the battle, silly,' cried the young woman, with a chuckle. 'S'pose he were only twenty, then he couldn't be less than six-and-eighty now, at the lowest.'

'Ay, he's that—every day of it,' cried several.

'I've had 'bout enough of it,' remarked the large woman, gloomily. 'Unless his young niece, or grand-niece, or whatever she is, come to-day, I'm off; and he can find some one else to do his work. Your own 'ome first, says I.'

'Ain't he quiet, then, Missus Simpson?' asked the youngest of the group.

'Listen to him now,' she answered, with her hand half raised, and her head turned slantwise towards the open door. From the upper floor there came a shuffling, sliding sound, with a sharp tapping of a stick. 'There he go back and forrards, doing what he call his sentry-go. 'Arf the night through he's at that game, the silly old juggins. At six o'clock this very mornin' there he was beatin' with a stick at my door. "Turn out, guard!" he cried, and a lot more jargon that I could make nothing of. Then what with his coughin' and 'awkin' and spittin', there ain't no gettin' a wink o' sleep. Hark to him now!'

'Missus Simpson, Missus Simpson!' cried a cracked and querulous voice from above.

'That's him,' she cried, nodding her head with an air of triumph. 'He do go on somethin' scandalous. Yes, Mister Brewster, sir.'

'I want my morning ration, Missus Simpson.'

'It's just ready, Mister Brewster, sir.'

'Blessed if he ain't like a baby cryin' for its pap,' said the young woman.

'I feel as if I could shake his old bones up sometimes!' cried Mrs Simpson viciously. 'But who's for a 'arf of fourpenny?'

The whole company were about to shuffle off to the public-house, when a young girl stepped across the road and touched the housekeeper timidly upon the arm. 'I think that is No. 56 Arsenal View,' she said. 'Can you tell me if Mr Brewster lives here?'

The housekeeper looked critically at the newcomer. She was a girl of about twenty, broad-faced and comely, with a turned-up nose and large, honest, grey eyes. Her print dress, her straw hat, with its bunch of glaring poppies, and the bundle which she carried, had all a smack of the country.

'You're Norah Brewster, I s'pose,' said Mrs Simpson, eyeing her up and down with no friendly gaze.

'Yes; I've come to look after my grand-uncle Gregory.'

'And a good job too,' cried the housekeeper, with a toss of her head. 'It's about time that some of his own folk took a turn at it, for I've had enough of it. There you are, young woman! in you go, and make yourself at home. There's tea in the caddy, and bacon on the dresser, and the old man will be about you if you don't fetch him his breakfast. I'll send for my things in the evenin'.'

With a nod she strolled off with her attendant gossips in the direction of the public-house.

Thus left to her own devices, the country girl walked into the front room and took off her hat and jacket. It was a low-roofed apartment with a sputtering fire, upon which a small brass kettle was singing cheerily. A stained cloth lay over half the table, with an empty brown teapot, a loaf of bread, and some coarse crockery. Norah Brewster looked rapidly about her, and in an instant took over her new duties. Ere five minutes had passed the tea was made, two slices of bacon were frizzling on the pan, the table was re-arranged, the antimacassars straightened over the sombre brown furniture, and the whole room had taken a new air of comfort and neatness. This done she looked round curiously at the prints upon the walls. Over the fireplace, in a small, square case, a brown medal caught her eye, hanging from a strip of purple ribbon. Beneath was a slip of newspaper cutting. She stood on her tiptoes, with her fingers on the edge of the mantelpiece, and craned her neck up to see it, glancing down from time to time at the bacon which simmered and hissed beneath her. The cutting was yellow with age, and ran in this way:—

'On Tuesday an interesting ceremony was performed at the barracks of the third regiment of guards, when, in the presence of the Prince Regent, Lord Hill, Lord Saltoun, and an assemblage which comprised beauty as well as valour, a special medal was presented to Corporal Gregory Brewster, of Captain Haldane's flank company, in recognition of his gallantry in the recent great battle in the Lowlands.

It appears that on the ever-memorable 18th of June, four companies of the third guards and of the Coldstreams, under the command of Colonels Maitland and Byng, held the important farmhouse of Hougoumont at the right of the British position. At a critical point of the action these troops found themselves short of powder. Seeing that Generals Foy and Jerome Buonaparte were again massing their infantry for an attack on the position, Colonel Byng despatched Corporal Brewster to the rear to hasten up the reserve ammunition. Brewster came upon two powder tumbrils of the Nassau division, and succeeded, after menacing the drivers with his musket, in inducing them to convey their powder to Hougoumont. In his absence, however, the hedges surrounding the position had been set on fire by a howitzer battery of the French, and the passage of the carts full of powder became a most hazardous matter. The first tumbril exploded, blowing the driver to fragments. Daunted by the fate of his comrade, the second driver turned his horses, but Corporal Brewster, springing upon his seat, hurled the man down, and urging the powder cart through the flames, succeeded in forcing his way to his companions. To this gallant deed may be directly attributed the success of the British arms, for without powder it would have been impossible to have held Hougoumont, and the Duke of Wellington had repeatedly declared that had Hougoumont fallen, as well as La Haye Sainte, he would have found it impossible to have held his ground. Long may the heroic Brewster live to treasure the medal which he has so bravely won, and to look back with pride to the day when, in the presence of his comrades, he received this tribute to his valour from the august hands of the first gentleman of the realm.'

The reading of this old cutting increased in the girl's mind the veneration which she had always had for her warrior kinsman. From her infancy he had been her hero, and she remembered how her father used to speak of his courage and his strength, how he could strike down a bullock with a blow of his fist, and carry a fat sheep under either arm. True that she had never seen him, but a rude painting at home, which depicted a square-faced, clean-shaven, stalwart man with a great bearskin cap, rose ever before her memory when she thought of him.

She was still gazing at the brown medal and wondering what the *'dulce et decorum est'* might mean, which was inscribed upon the edge, when there came a sudden tapping and shuffling upon the stair, and there at the door was standing the very man who had been so often in her thoughts.

But could this indeed be he? Where was the martial air, the flashing eye, the warrior face which she had pictured? There, framed in the doorway, was a huge, twisted old man, gaunt and puckered, with twitching hands, and shuffling, purposeless feet. A cloud of fluffy white hair, a red-veined nose, two thick tufts of eyebrow and a pair of dimly-questioning, watery-blue eyes—these were what met her gaze. He leaned forward upon a stick, while his shoulders rose and fell with his crackling, rasping breathing.

'I want my morning rations,' he crooned, as he stumped forward to his chair. 'The cold nips me without 'em. See to my fingers!'

He held out his distorted hands, all blue at the tips, wrinkled and gnarled, with huge, projecting knuckles.

'It's nigh ready,' answered the girl, gazing at him with wonder in her eyes. 'Don't you know who I am, grand-uncle? I am Norah Brewster from Witham.'

'Rum is warm,' mumbled the old man, rocking to and fro in his chair, 'and schnapps is warm and there's 'eat in soup, but it's a dish o' tea for me. What did you say your name was?'

'Norah Brewster.'

'You can speak out, lass. Seems to me folk's voices isn't as loud as they used.'

'I'm Norah Brewster, uncle. I'm your grand-niece come down from Essex way to live with you.'

'You'll be brother Jarge's girl! Lor', to think o' little Jarge having a girl.'

He chuckled hoarsely to himself, and the long, stringy sinews of his throat jerked and quivered.

'I am the daughter of your brother George's son,' said she as she turned the bacon.

'Lor', but little Jarge was a rare un,' he continued. 'Eh, by Jimini, there was no chousing Jarge. He's got a bull pup o' mine that I gave him when I took the bounty. You've heard him speak of it, likely?'

'Why, grandpa George has been dead this twenty years,' said she, pouring out the tea.

'Well, it was a bootiful pup—ay, a well-bred un, by Jimini! I'm cold for lack of my rations. Rum is good, and so is schnapps, but I'd as lief have tea as either.'

He breathed heavily while he devoured his food.

'It's a middlin' goodish way you've come,' said he at last. 'Likely the stage left yesternight.'

'The what, uncle?'

'The coach that brought you.'

'Nay, I came by the mornin' train.'

'Lor', now, think o' that! You ain't afeard of those new-fangled things! To think of you comin' by railroad like that! What's the world a-comin' to!'

There was silence for some minutes while Norah sat stirring her tea and glancing sideways at the bluish lips and champing jaws of her companion.

'You must have seen a deal of life, uncle,' said she. 'It must seem a long, long time to you!'

'Not so very long, neither. I'm ninety come Candlemass; but it don't seem long since I took the bounty. And that battle, it might have been yesterday. I've got the smell of the burned powder in my nose yet. Eh, but I get a power o' good from my rations!'

He did indeed look less worn and colourless than when she first saw him. His face was flushed and his back more erect.

'Have you read that?' he asked, jerking his head towards the cutting.

'Yes, uncle, and I'm sure you must be proud of it.'

'Ah, it was a great day for me! A great day! The Regent was there, and a fine body of a man too! "The ridgment is proud of you," says he. "And I'm proud of the ridgment," say I. "A damned good answer, too!" says he to Lord Hill, and they both bust out a-laughing. But what be you a-peepin' out o' the window for?'

'Oh, uncle, here's a regiment of soldiers coming down the street, with the band playing in front of them.'

'A ridgment, eh? Where be my glasses? Lor' but I can hear the band, as plain as plain. Here's the pioneers an' the drum-major! What be their number, lass?'

His eyes were shining and his bony, yellow fingers, like the claws of some fierce old bird, dug into her shoulder.

'They don't seem to have no number, uncle. They've something wrote on their shoulders. Oxfordshire, I think it be.'

'Ah, yes,' he growled. 'I heard as they'd dropped the numbers and given them new-fangled names. There they go, by Jimini! They're young mostly, but they hain't forgot how to march. They have the swing—ay, I'll say that for them. They've got the swing.'

He gazed after them until the last files had turned the corner, and the measured tramp of their marching had died away in the distance.

He had just regained his chair when the door opened and a gentleman stepped in.

'Ah, Mr Brewster! Better to-day?' he asked.

'Come in, doctor! Yes, I'm better. But there's a deal o' bubbling in my chest. It's all them toobes. If I could but cut the phlegm I'd be right. Can't ye give me something to cut the phlegm?'

The doctor, a grave-faced, young man, put his fingers to the furrowed, blue-corded wrist.

'You must be careful,' he said. 'You must take no liberties.'

The thin tide of life seemed to thrill rather than to throb under his finger.

The old man chuckled.

'I've got brother Jarge's girl to look after me now. She'll see I don't break barracks or do what I hadn't ought to; why, darn my skin, I knew something was amiss!'

'With what?'

'Why, with them soldiers. You saw them pass, doctor—eh? They'd forgot their stocks. Not one on 'em had his stock on.' He croaked and chuckled for a long time over his discovery. 'It wouldn't ha' done for the Dook!' he muttered. 'No by Jimini! the Dook would ha' had a word there.'

The doctor smiled.

'Well, you are doing very well,' said he. 'I'll look in once a week or so and see how you are!' As Norah followed him to the door he beckoned her outside. 'He is very weak,' he whispered. 'If you find him failing you must send for me.'

'What ails him, doctor?'

'Ninety years ail him. His arteries are pipes of lime. His heart is shrunken and flabby. The man is worn out.'

Norah stood watching the brisk figure of the young doctor and pondering over these new responsibilities which had come upon her. When she turned, a tall, brown-faced artillery man, with the three gold chevrons of sergeant upon his arm, was standing, carbine in hand, at her elbow.

'Good morning, miss!' said he, raising one thick finger to his jaunty, yellow-banded cap. 'I b'lieve there's an old gentleman lives here of the name of Brewster, who was engaged in the battle o' Waterloo?'

'It's my grand-uncle, sir,' said Norah, casting down her eyes before the keen, critical gaze of the young soldier. 'He is in the front parlour.'

'Could I have a word with him, miss? I'll call again if it don't chance to be convenient.'

'I am sure that he would be very glad to see you, sir. He's in here, if you'll step in. Uncle, here's a gentleman who wants to speak with you.'

'Proud to see you, sir—proud and glad, sir!' cried the sergeant, taking three steps forward into the room, and grounding his carbine while he raised his hand, palm forwards, in a salute.

Norah stood by the door, with her mouth and eyes open, wondering whether her grand-uncle had ever, in his prime, looked like this magnificent creature; and whether he, in his turn, would ever come to resemble her grand-uncle.

The old man blinked up at his visitor, and shook his head slowly.

'Sit ye down, sergeant,' said he, pointing with his stick to a chair. 'You're full young for the stripes. Lordy, it's easier to get three now than one in my day. Gunners were old soldiers then, and the grey hairs came quicker than the three stripes.'

'I am eight years' service, sir,' cried the sergeant. 'Macdonald is my name—Sergeant Macdonald, of H. Battery, Southern Artillery Division. I have called as the spokesman of my mates at the gunners' barracks to say that we are proud to have you in the town, sir.'

Old Brewster chuckled and rubbed his bony hands.

'That were what the Regent said,' he cried. '"The ridgment is proud of ye," says he. "And I am proud of the ridgment," says I. "And a damned good answer too," says he, and he and Lord Hill bust out—a-laughin'.'

'The non-commissioned mess would be proud and honoured to see you, sir,' said Sergeant Macdonald. 'And if you could step as far you'll always find a pipe o' baccy and a glass of grog awaitin' you.'

The old man laughed until he coughed.

'Like to see me, would they? The dogs!' said he. 'Well, well, when the warm weather comes again I'll maybe drop in. Too grand for a canteen, eh? Got your mess just the same as the orficers. What's the world a-comin' to at all!'

'You was in the line, sir, was you not?' asked the sergeant, respectfully.

'The line?' cried the old man with shrill scorn. 'Never wore a shako in my life. I am a guardsman, I am. Served in the third guards—the same they call now the Scots Guards. Lordy, but they have all marched away, every man of them, from old Colonel Byng down to the drummer boys, and here am I a straggler—that's what I am, sergeant, a straggler! I'm here when I ought to be there. But it ain't my fault neither, for I'm ready to fall in when the word comes.'

'We've all got to muster there,' answered the sergeant. 'Won't you try my baccy, sir?' handing over a sealskin pouch.

Old Brewster drew a blackened clay pipe from his pocket, and began to stuff the tobacco into the bowl. In an instant it slipped through his fingers, and was broken to pieces on the floor. His lip quivered, his nose puckered up, and he began crying with the long, helpless sobs of a child.

'I've broke my pipe,' he cried.

'Don't, uncle, oh don't,' cried Norah, bending over him and patting his white head as one soothes a baby. 'It don't matter. We can easy get another.'

'Don't you fret yourself, sir,' said the sergeant. ''Ere's a wooden pipe with an amber mouth, if you'll do me the honour to accept it from me. I'd be real glad if you will take it.'

'Jimini!' cried he, his smiles breaking in an instant through his tears. 'It's a fine pipe. See to my new pipe, Norah. I lay that Jarge never had a pipe like that. You've got your firelock there, sergeant.'

'Yes, sir, I was on my way back from the butts when I looked in.'

'Let me have the feel of it. Lordy, but it seems like old times to have one's hand on a musket. What's the manual, sergeant, eh? Cock your firelock—look to your priming—present your firelock—eh, sergeant? Oh, Jimini, I've broke your musket in halves!'

'That's all right, sir,' cried the gunner, laughing, 'you pressed on the lever and opened the breech-piece. That's where we load 'em, you know.'

'Load 'em at the wrong end! Well, well, to think o' that. And no ramrod, neither! I've heered tell of it, but I never believed it afore. Ah, it won't come up to Brown Bess. When there's work to be done you mark my word and see if they don't come back to Brown Bess.'

'By the Lord, sir,' cried the sergeant, hotly, 'they need some change out in South Africa now. I see by this mornin's paper that the Government has knuckled under to these Boers. They're hot about it at the non-com. mess, I can tell you, sir.'

'Eh—eh,' croaked old Brewster. 'By Gosh! it wouldn't ha' done for the Dook; the Dook would ha' had a word to say over that!'

'Ah, that he would, sir!' cried the sergeant; 'and God send us another like him. But I've wearied you enough for one sitting. I'll look in again, and I'll bring a comrade or two with me if I may, for there isn't one but would be proud to have speech with you.'

So, with another salute to the veteran, and a gleam of white teeth at Norah, the big gunner withdrew, leaving a memory of blue cloth and of gold braid behind him. Many days had not passed, however, before he was back again, and during all the long winter he was a frequent visitor at Arsenal View. He brought others with him, and soon through all the lines, a pilgrimage to Daddy Brewster's came to be looked upon as the proper thing to do. Gunners and sappers, linesmen and dragoons, came bowing and bobbing into the little parlour, with clatter of side arms and clink of spurs, stretching their long legs across the patchwork rug, and hunting in the front of their tunics for the screw of tobacco, or paper of snuff, which they had brought as a sign of their esteem.

It was a deadly cold winter, with six weeks on end of snow on the ground, and Norah had a hard task to keep the life in that time-worn body. There were times when his mind would leave him, and when, save an animal outcry when the hour of his meals came round, no word would fall from him. As the warm weather came once more, however, and the green buds peeped forth again upon the trees, the blood thawed in his veins, and he would even drag himself as far as the door to bask in the life-giving sunshine.

'It do hearten me up so,' he said one morning, as he glowed in the hot May sun. 'It's a job to keep back the flies, though! They get owda-cious in this weather, and they do plague me cruel.'

'I'll keep them off you uncle,' said Norah.

'Eh, but it's fine! This sunshine makes me think o' the glory to come. You might read me a bit o' the Bible, lass. I find it wonderful soothing.'

'What part would you like, uncle?'

'Oh, them wars.'

'The wars?'

'Ay, keep to the wars! Give me the Old Testament for choice. There's more taste to it, to my mind! When parson comes he wants to get off to something else; but it's Joshua or nothing with me. Them Israelites was good soldiers—good growed soldiers, all of 'em.'

'But, uncle,' pleaded Norah, 'it's all peace in the next world.'

'No it ain't, gal.'

'Oh yes, uncle, surely!'

The old corporal knocked his stick irritably upon the ground.

'I tell ye it ain't, gal. I asked parson.'

'Well, what did he say?'

'He said there was to be a last fight. He even gave it a name, he did. The battle of Arm—Arm—'

'Armageddon.'

'Ay, that's the name parson said. I 'specs the third guards'll be there. And the Dook—the Dook'll have a word to say.'

An elderly, grey-whiskered gentleman had been walking down the street, glancing up at the numbers of the houses. Now, as his eyes fell upon the old man, he came straight for him.

'Hullo!' said he; 'perhaps you are Gregory Brewster?'

'My name, sir,' answered the veteran.

'You are the same Brewster, as I understand, who is on the roll of the Scots Guards as having been present at the battle of Waterloo?'

'I am that man, sir, though we called it the third guards in those days. It was a fine ridgment, and they only need me to make up a full muster.'

'Tut, tut! they'll have to wait years for that,' said the gentleman heartily. 'But I am the colonel of the Scots Guards, and I thought I would like to have a word with you.'

Old Gregory Brewster was up in an instant, with his hand to his rabbit-skin cap.

'God bless me!' he cried, 'to think of it; to think of it.'

'Hadn't the gentleman better come in?' suggested the practical Norah from behind the door.

'Surely, sir, surely; walk in, sir, if I may be so bold.'

In his excitement he had forgotten his stick, and as he led the way into the parlour his knees tottered, and he threw out his hands. In an instant the colonel had caught him on one side and Norah on the other.

'Easy and steady,' said the colonel, as he led him to his arm-chair.

'Thank ye, sir; I was near gone that time. But, Lordy! why, I can scarce believe it. To think of me, the corporal of the flank company, and you the colonel of the battalion. Jimini! How things come round, to be sure.'

'Why, we are very proud of you in London,' said the colonel. 'And so you are actually one of the men who held Hougoumont?' He looked at the bony, trembling hands with their huge, knotted knuckles, the stringy throat, and the heaving, rounded shoulders. Could this, indeed, be the last of that band of heroes? Then he glanced at the half-filled phials, the blue liniment bottles, the long-spouted kettle, and the sordid details of the sick-room. 'Better, surely, had he died under the blazing rafters of the Belgian farm-house,' thought the colonel.

'I hope that you are pretty comfortable and happy,' he remarked after a pause.

'Thank ye, sir. I have a good deal of trouble with my toobes—a deal of trouble. You wouldn't think the job it is to cut the phlegm. And I need my rations. I gets cold without 'em. And the flies! I ain't strong enough to fight against them.'

'How's the memory?' asked the colonel.

'Oh, there ain't nothing amiss there. Why, sir, I could give you the name of every man in Captain Haldane's flank company.'

'And the battle—you remember it?'

'Why, I sees it all afore me every time I shuts my eyes. Lordy, sir, you wouldn't hardly believe how clear it is to me. There's our line from the paregoric bottle[2] right along to the snuff box. D'ye see? Well, then, the pill-box is for Hougoumont on the right, where we was; and Norah's thimble for La Haye Sainte. There it is, all right, sir, and here were our guns, and here behind the reserves and the Belgians. Ach, them Belgians!' He spat furiously into the fire. 'Then here's the French where my pipe lies, and over here, where I put my baccy pouch, was the Proosians a-comin' up on our left flank. Jimini! but it was a glad sight to see the smoke of their guns.'

'And what was it that struck you most, now, in connection with the whole affair?' asked the colonel.

'I lost three half-crowns over it, I did,' crooned old Brewster. 'I shouldn't wonder if I was never to get that money now. I lent 'em to Jabez Smith, my rear rank man, in Brussels. "Only till pay-day, Grig," says he. By Gosh! he was stuck by a lancer at Quarter Brass, and me with not so much as a slip o' paper to prove the debt! Them three half-crowns is as good as lost to me.'

The colonel rose from his chair laughing.

'The officers of the Guards want you to buy yourself some little trifle which may add to your comfort,' he said. 'It is not from me, so you need not thank me.'

He took up the old man's tobacco pouch and slipped a crisp banknote inside it.

'Thank ye, kindly, sir. But there's one favour that I would like to ask you, colonel.'

'Yes, my man?'

'If I'm called, colonel, you won't grudge me a flag and a firing party?'

'All right, my man, I'll see to it,' said the colonel. 'Good-bye; I hope to have nothing but good news from you.'

'A kind gentleman, Norah,' croaked old Brewster, as they saw him walk past the window; 'but, Lordy, he ain't fit to hold the stirrup o' my Colonel Byng.'

It was on the very next day that the corporal took a sudden change for the worse. Even the golden sunlight streaming through the window seemed unable to warm that withered frame. The doctor came and shook his head in silence. All day the man lay with only his puffing blue lips and the twitching of his scraggy neck to show that he still held the breath of life. Norah and Sergeant Macdonald had sat by him in the afternoon, but he had shown no consciousness of their presence. He lay peacefully, his eyes half-closed, his hands under his cheek, as one who is very weary.

They had left him for an instant and were sitting in the front room where Norah was preparing the tea, when of a sudden they heard a shout that rang through the house. Loud and clear and swelling, it pealed in their ears, a voice full of strength and energy and fiery passion.

'The guards need powder,' it cried and yet again, 'the guards need powder.'

The sergeant sprang from his chair and rushed in, followed by the trembling Norah. There was the old man standing up, his blue eyes sparkling, his white hair bristling, his whole figure towering and expanding, with eagle head and glance of fire.

'The guards need powder,' he thundered once again, 'and by God they shall have it!'

He threw up his long arms and sank back with a groan into his chair. The sergeant stooped over him, and his face darkened.

'Oh, Archie, Archie,' sobbed the frightened girl, 'what do you think of him?'

The sergeant turned away.

'I think,' said he, 'that the third guards have a full muster now.'

NOTES TO 'A STRAGGLER OF '15'

First published in *Black and White*, 21 March 1891.

1. Conan Doyle thought very highly of this story, recalling in his
memoirs that it was 'a moving picture of an old soldier and his
ways. My own eyes were moist as I wrote it, and that is the sur-
est way to moisten those of others.' He later rewrote the piece as
a one-act play ('A Story of Waterloo') and sent it to Henry Irving,
'of whose genius I had been an admirer since those Edinburgh
days. ... To my great delight I found a note offering me £100 for the
copyright. It was a good bargain for him, for ... Corporal Gregory
Brewster became one of his stock parts, and it had the enormous advantage that the older he got the more naturally he played it. The
house laughed and sobbed, exactly as I had done when I wrote it.'[1]
   The story is really neither a fact nor a fancy of medical life, but
a reflection of Conan Doyle's interest in the Napoleonic era and evidence of his very Victorian fondness for a good tear-jerker. The acer-
bic George Bernard Shaw was less impressed, commenting in his review of the first performance of the play that Irving required no great
acting skill to play the part of a doddering old fool. He dismissed the
play as 'an organised and successful attack ... on our emotions' and an
'ingenious exploitation of the ready-made pathos of old age, the ignorant and maudlin sentiment attaching to the army and the "Dook",
and the vulgar conception of the Battle of Waterloo as a stand-up
fight between an Englishman and a Frenchman'.[2]

2. Paregoric is a camphorated tincture of opium, once used as a
remedy for diarrhœa.

---

[1] Arthur Conan Doyle, *Memories and Adventures* (1924; London: Greenhill, 1980),
p. 119.
[2] 'Mr. Irving Takes Paregoric', *Saturday Review*, 18 May 1895. Reprinted in *Our
Theatres in the Nineties*, 3 vols (London: Constable, 1932), Vol. I, pp. 113-120.

THE THIRD GENERATION

SCUDAMORE LANE, sloping down riverwards from just behind the Monument, lies at night in the shadow of two black and monstrous walls which loom high above the glimmer of the scattered gas-lamps. The foot-paths are narrow, and the causeway is paved with rounded cobblestones so that the endless drays roar along it like so many breaking waves. A few old-fashioned houses lie scattered among the business premises, and in one of these—half way down on the left-hand side— Dr Horace Selby conducts his large practice. It is a singular street for so big a man, but a specialist who has an European reputation can afford to live where he likes. In his particular branch, too, patients do not always regard seclusion to be a disadvantage.

It was only ten o'clock. The dull roar of the traffic which converged all day upon London Bridge had died away now to a mere confused murmur. It was raining heavily, and the gas shone dimly through the streaked and dripping glass, throwing little yellow circles upon the glistening cobblestones. The air was full of the sounds of rain, the thin swish of its fall, the heavier drip from the eaves, and the swirl and gurgle down the two steep gutters and through the sewer grating. There was only one figure in the whole length of Scudamore Lane. It was that of a man, and it stood outside the door of Dr Horace Selby.[1]

He had just rung and was waiting for an answer. The fanlight beat full upon the gleaming shoulders of his waterproof and upon his upturned features. It was a wan, sensitive, clear-cut face, with some subtle, nameless peculiarity in its expression—something of the startled horse in the white-rimmed eye, something, too, of the helpless child in the drawn cheek and the weakening of the lower lip. The man-servant knew the stranger as a patient at a bare glance at those frightened eyes. Such a look had been seen at that door before.

'Is the doctor in?'

The man hesitated.

'He has had a few friends to dinner, sir. He does not like to be disturbed outside his usual hours, sir.'

'Tell him that I *must* see him. Tell him that it is of the very first importance. Here is my card.' He fumbled with his trembling fingers in trying to draw one from the case. 'Sir Francis Norton is the name. Tell him that Sir Francis Norton of Deane Park must see him at once.'

'Yes, sir.' The butler closed his fingers upon the card and the half-sovereign which accompanied it. 'Better hang your coat up here in the hall. It is very wet. Now, if you will wait here in the consulting-room, I have no doubt that I shall be able to send the doctor in to you.'

It was a large and lofty room in which the young baronet found himself. The carpet was so soft and thick that his feet made no sound as he walked across it. The two gas-jets were turned only half way up, and the dim light with the faint aromatic smell which filled the air had a vaguely religious suggestion. He sat down in a shining leather arm-chair by the smouldering fire and looked gloomily about him. Two sides of the room were taken up with books, fat and sombre, with broad gold lettering upon their backs. Beside him was the high, old-fashioned mantelpiece of white marble, the top of it strewed with cotton wadding and bandages, graduated measures and little bottles. There was one with a broad neck, just above him, containing blue-stone, and another narrower one with what looked like the ruins of a broken pipe stem, and 'Caustic' outside upon a red label. Thermom-eters, hypodermic syringes, bistouries and spatulas were scattered thickly about, both on the mantelpiece and on the central table on either side of the sloping desk. On the same table to the right stood copies of the five books which Dr Horace Selby had written upon the subject with which his name is peculiarly associated, while on the left, on the top of a red medical directory, lay a huge glass model of a human eye, the size of a turnip, which opened down the centre to expose the lens and double chamber within.

Sir Francis Norton had never been remarkable for his powers of observation, and yet he found himself watching these trifles with the keenest attention. Even the corrosion of the cork of an acid bottle caught his eye and he wondered that the doctor did not use glass stop-pers. Tiny scratches where the light glinted off from the table, little stains upon the leather of the desk, chemical formulæ scribbled upon the labels of some of the phials—nothing was too slight to arrest his attention. And his sense of hearing was equally alert.[2] The heavy tick-ing of the solemn black clock above the fireplace struck quite painfully upon his ears. Yet, in spite of it, and in spite also of the thick, old-fashioned, wooden partition walls, he could hear the voices of men talking in the next room and could even catch scraps of their conversation. 'Second hand was bound to take it.' 'Why, you drew the last of them yourself!' 'How could I play the queen when I knew the ace was against me.' The phrases came in little spurts, falling back into the dull murmur of conversation. And then suddenly he heard the creaking of a door, and a step in the hall, and knew with a tingling mixture of impatience and horror that the crisis of his life was at hand.

Dr Horace Selby was a large, portly man, with an imposing presence. His nose and chin were bold and pronounced, yet his features were puffy—a combination which would blend more freely with the wig and cravat of the early Georges, than with the close-cropped hair and black frockcoat of the end of the 19th century. He was clean shaven, for his mouth was too good to cover, large, flexible and sensitive, with a kindly human softening at either corner, which, with his brown sympathetic eyes, had drawn out many a shame-struck sinner's secret. Two masterful little bushy side whiskers bristled out from under his ears, spindling away upwards to merge in the thick curves of his brindled hair. To his patients there was something reassuring in the mere bulk and dignity of the man. A high and easy bearing in medicine, as in war, bears with it a hint of victories in the past, and a promise of others to come. Dr Horace Selby's face was a consolation, and so, too, were the large, white, soothing hands, one of which he held out to his visitor.

'I am sorry to have kept you waiting. It is a conflict of duties, you perceive. A host to his guests and an adviser to his patient. But now I am entirely at your disposal, Sir Francis. But, dear me, you are very cold.'

'Yes, I am cold.'

'And you are trembling all over. Tut, tut, this will never do. This miserable night has chilled you. Perhaps some little stimulant—'

'No thank you. I would really rather not. And it is not the night which has chilled me. I am frightened, doctor.'

The doctor half turned in his chair and patted the arch of the young man's knee as he might the neck of a restless horse.

'What, then?' he asked, looking over his shoulder at the pale face with the startled eyes.

Twice the young man parted his lips. Then he stooped with a sudden gesture and turning up the right leg of his trousers he pulled down his sock and thrust forward his shin. The doctor made a clicking noise with his tongue as he glanced at it.

'Both legs?'

'No, only one.'

'Suddenly?'

'This morning.'

'Hum!' The doctor pouted his lips, and drew his finger and thumb down the line of his chin. 'Can you account for it?' he asked briskly.

'No.'

A trace of sternness came into the large, brown eyes.

'I need not point out to you that unless the most absolute frankness—'

The patient sprang from his chair.

'So help me God, doctor,' he cried, 'I have nothing in my life with which to reproach myself. Do you think that I would be such a fool as to come here and tell you lies. Once for all, I have nothing to regret.'

He was a pitiful, half-tragic and half-grotesque figure as he stood with one trouser leg rolled to his knee, and that ever-present horror still lurking in his eyes. A burst of merriment came from the card-players in the next room and the two looked at each other in silence.

'Sit down!' said the doctor abruptly. 'Your assurance is quite sufficient.' He stooped and ran his finger down the line of the young man's shin, raising it at one point. 'Hum! Serpiginous!' he murmured, shaking his head; 'any other symptoms?'

'My eyes have been a little weak.'

'Let me see your teeth!' He glanced at them, and again made the gentle clicking sound of sympathy and disapprobation.

'Now your eye!' He lit a lamp at the patient's elbow, and holding a small crystal lens to concentrate the light, he threw it obliquely upon the patient's eye. As he did so a glow of pleasure came over his large, expressive face, a flush of such enthusiasm as the botanist feels when he packs the rare plant into his tin knapsack, or the astronomer when the long-sought comet first swims into the field of his telescope.

'This is very typical—very typical indeed,' he murmured, turning to his desk and jotting down a few memoranda upon a sheet of paper. 'Curiously enough I am writing a monograph upon the subject. It is singular that you should have been able to furnish so well-marked a case.'

He had so forgotten the patient in his symptom that he had assumed an almost congratulatory air towards its possessor. He reverted to human sympathy again as his patient asked for particulars.

'My dear sir, there is no occasion for us to go into strictly professional details together,' said he soothingly. 'If, for example, I were to say that you have interstitial keratitis, how would you be the wiser? There are indications of a strumous diathesis. In broad terms I may say that you have a constitutional and hereditary taint.'[3]

The young baronet sank back in his chair and his chin fell forward upon his chest. The doctor sprang to a side table and poured out half a glass of liqueur brandy which he held to his patient's lips. A little fleck of colour came into his cheeks as he drank it down.

'Perhaps I spoke a little abruptly,' said the doctor. 'But you must have known the nature of your complaint, why otherwise should you have come to me?'

'God help me, I suspected it—but only to-day when my leg grew bad. My father had a leg like this.'

'It was from him, then?'

'No, from my grandfather. You have heard of Sir Rupert Norton, the great Corinthian.'

The doctor was a man of wide reading with a retentive memory. The name brought back to him instantly the remembrance of the sinister reputation of its owner—a notorious buck of the thirties, who had gambled and duelled and steeped himself in drink and debauchery until even the vile set with whom he consorted had shrunk away from him in horror, and left him to a sinister old age with the barmaid wife whom in some drunken frolic he had espoused. As he looked at the young man still leaning back in the leather chair, there seemed for the instant to flicker up behind him some vague presentiment of that foul old dandy with his dangling seals, many-wreathed scarf, and dark, satyric face. What was he now? An armful of bones in a mouldy box.

But his deeds—they were living and rotting the blood in the veins of an innocent man.

'I see that you have heard of him,' said the young baronet. 'He died horribly, I have been told, but not more horribly than he had lived. My father was his only son. He was a studious man, fond of books and canaries and the country. But his innocent life did not save him.'

'His symptoms were cutaneous, I understand.'

'He wore gloves in the house. That was the first thing I can remember. And then it was his throat, and then his legs. He used to ask me so often about my own health, and I thought him so fussy, for how could I tell what the meaning of it was. He was always watching me—always with a sidelong eye fixed upon me. Now at last I know what he was watching for.'[4]

'Had you brothers or sisters?'

'None, thank God!'

'Well, well, it is a sad case, and very typical of many which come in my way. You are no lonely sufferer, Sir Francis. There are many thousands who bear the same cross as you do.'

'But where is the justice of it, doctor?' cried the young man, springing from the chair and pacing up and down the consulting-room. 'If I were heir to my grandfather's sins as well as to their results I could understand it, but I am of my father's type; I love all that is gentle and beautiful, music and poetry and art. The coarse and animal is abhorrent to me. Ask any of my friends and they would tell you that. And now that this vile, loathsome thing—Ach, I am polluted to the marrow, soaked in abomination! And why? Haven't I a right to ask why? Did I do it? Was it my fault? Could I help being born? And look at me now, blighted and blasted, just as life was at its sweetest! Talk about the sins of the father! How about the sins of the Creator!'

He shook his two clinched hands in the air, the poor, impotent atom with his pin-point of brain caught in the whirl of the infinite.[5]

The doctor rose and placing his hands upon his shoulders he pressed him back into his chair again.

'There, there, my dear lad,' said he. 'You must not excite yourself! You are trembling all over. Your nerves cannot stand it. We must take these great questions upon trust. What are we after all? Half evolved creatures in a transition stage; nearer, perhaps, to the medusa on the one side than to perfected humanity on the other. With half a complete brain we can't expect to understand the whole of a complete fact, can we, now? It is all very dim and dark, no doubt, but I think that Pope's famous couplet sums up the whole matter, and from my heart, after fifty years of varied experience, I can say that—'

But the young baronet gave a cry of impatience and disgust.

'Words, words, words! You can sit comfortably there in your chair and say them—and think them too, no doubt. You've had your life. But I've never had mine. You've healthy blood in your veins. Mine is putrid. And yet I am as innocent as you. What would words do for you if you were in this chair and I in that. Ah, it's such a mockery and a make-belief! Don't think me rude though, doctor. I don't mean to be that. I only say that it is impossible for you or any other man to realise it. But I've a question to ask you, doctor. It's one on which my whole life must depend.'

He writhed his fingers together in an agony of apprehension.

'Speak out, my dear sir. I have every sympathy with you.'

'Do you think—do you think the poison has spent itself on me? Do you think if I had children that they would suffer?'

'I can only give one answer to that. "The third and fourth generation," says the trite old text. You may in time eliminate it from your system, but many years must pass before you can think of marriage.'

'I am to be married on Tuesday,' whispered the patient.

It was Dr Horace Selby's turn to be thrilled with horror. There were not many situations which would yield such a sensation to his well seasoned nerves. He sat in silence while the babble of the card-table broke in again upon them. 'We had a double ruff if you had returned a heart.' 'I was bound to clear the trumps.' They were hot and angry about it.

'How could you?' cried the doctor severely. 'It was criminal.'

'You forget that I have only learned how I stand to-day.' He put his two hands to his temples and pressed them convulsively. 'You are a man of the world, Dr Selby. You have seen or heard of such things before. Give me some advice. I'm in your hands. It is all very sudden and horrible, and I don't think I am strong enough to bear it.'

The doctor's heavy brows thickened into two straight lines and he bit his nails in perplexity.

'The marriage must not take place.'

'Then what am I to do?'

'At all costs it must not take place.'

'And I must give her up!'

'There can be no question about that?'

The young man took out a pocket-book and drew from it a small photograph, holding it out towards the doctor. The firm face softened as he looked at it.

'It is very hard on you, no doubt. I can appreciate it more now that I have seen that. But there is no alternative at all. You must give up all thought of it.'

'But this is madness, doctor—madness, I tell you. No, I won't raise my voice! I forgot myself! But realise it, man! I am to be married on Tuesday—this coming Tuesday, you know. And all the world knows it. How can I put such a public affront upon her? It would be monstrous.'

'None the less it must be done. My dear sir, there is no way out of it.'

'You would have me simply write brutally and break the engagement at the last moment without a reason? I tell you I couldn't do it.'

'I had a patient once who found himself in a somewhat similar situation some years ago,' said the doctor thoughtfully. 'His device was a singular one. He deliberately committed a penal offence and so compelled the young lady's people to withdraw their consent to the marriage.'

The young baronet shook his head.

'My personal honour is as yet unstained,' said he. 'I have little else left, but that at least I will preserve.'

'Well, well, it is a nice dilemma and the choice lies with you.'

'Have you no other suggestion?'

'You don't happen to have property in Australia?'

'None.'

'But you have capital?'

'Yes.'

'Then you could buy some—to-morrow morning, for example. A

thousand mining shares would do. Then you might write to say that urgent business affairs have compelled you to start at an hour's notice to inspect your property. That would give you six months at any rate.'

'Well, that would be possible—yes, certainly it would be possible. But think of her position—the house full of wedding presents—guests coming from a distance. It is awful. And you say there is no alternative.'

The doctor shrugged his shoulders.

'Well, then, I might write it now, and start to-morrow—eh? Perhaps you would let me use your desk. Thank you! I am so sorry to keep you from your guests so long. But I won't be a moment now.' He wrote an abrupt note of a few lines. Then, with a sudden impulse, he tore it to shreds and flung it into the fireplace. 'No, I can't sit down and tell her a lie, doctor,' said he rising. 'We must find some other way out of this. I will think it over, and let you know my decision. You must allow me to double your fee as I have taken such an unconscionable time. Now, good-bye, and thank you a thousand times for your sympathy and advice.'

'Why, dear me, you haven't even got your prescription yet. This is the mixture, and I should recommend one of these powders every morning and the chemist will put all directions upon the ointment box. You are placed in a cruel situation, but I trust that these may be but passing clouds. When may I hope to hear from you again?'

'To-morrow morning.'

'Very good. How the rain is splashing in the street. You have your waterproof there. You will need it. Good-bye, then, until to-morrow.'

He opened the door. A gust of cold, damp air swept into the hall. And yet the doctor stood for a minute or more watching the lonely figure which passed slowly through the yellow splotches of the gaslamps, and into the broad bars of darkness between. It was but his own shadow which trailed up the wall as he passed the lights, and yet it looked to the doctor's eye as though some huge and sombre figure walked by a mannikin's side, and led him silently up the lonely street.

Doctor Horace Selby heard again of his patient next morning and rather earlier than he had expected. A paragraph in the *Daily News* caused him to push away his breakfast untasted, and turned him sick and faint while he read it. 'A Deplorable Accident' it was headed, and it ran in this way:—

'A fatal accident of a peculiarly painful character is reported from King William Street. About eleven o'clock last night a young man was observed, while endeavouring to get out of the way of a hansom, to slip and fall under the wheels of a heavy two-horse dray. On being picked up, his injuries were found to be of a most shocking character, and he expired while being conveyed to the hospital. An examination of his pocket-book and card-case shows beyond any question that the deceased is none other than Sir Francis Norton of Deane Park, who has only within the last year come into the baronetcy. The accident is made the more deplorable as the deceased, who was only just of age, was on the eve of being married to a young lady belonging to one of the oldest families in the south. With his wealth and his talents the ball of fortune was at his feet, and his many friends will be deeply grieved to know that his promising career has been cut short in so sudden and tragic a fashion.'

NOTES TO 'THE THIRD GENERATION'

First published in *Round the Red Lamp*.

1. Horace Selby is reminiscent of Sir Alfred Cooper (d. 1908), who had a very successful practice treating venereal disease among London's rich and aristocratic families. He became honorary surgeon to fashionable military regiments and acquired a manner 'perfectly judged for the rich young blades who came to him with venereal infections'. The luxurious carriage in which he drove about became known as the clap trap.[1]

2. Norton's sharp eyes and acute hearing are inconsistent with having congenital syphilis, the usual symptoms of which included impaired vision and progressive hearing loss.

3. Symptoms of syphilis. The 'strumous diathesis' on the shin is now known as 'saber shins', an abnormality of the lower leg. The weakness of the eyes (suddenly making itself felt here!) and the distinctive teeth were two of the key symptoms identified by Jonathan Hutchinson (1828-1913), Victorian Britain's leading authority on the subject, as the signs of congenital syphilis. These were originally put forward in a paper given in 1858, 'On the Means of Recognising the Subjects of Inherited Syphilis in Adult Life', where he identified notched or peg-shaped incisors and a clouding of the corneas of the eyes as the tell-tale stigmata. He later added progressive deafness. These three signs—notched teeth, interstitial keratitis and hearing loss—were later known as Hutchinson's triad, and their formulation remains his most significant contribution to medical knowledge. The diagnosis was elaborated in many subsequent publications, including *A Clinical Memoir on Certain Diseases of the Eye and Ear Consequent Upon Syphilis* (1863) and *Syphilis* (1887), where he stated that 'interstitial keratitis ...

---

[1] Richard Davenport Hines, *Sex, Death and Punishment: Attitudes to Sex and Sexuality in Britain Since the Renaissance* (London: Collins, 1990), p. 160.

is always a consequence of syphilis and is in itself sufficient for the diagnosis'.[1]

4. Norton believes that he had inherited the disease from his rakish grandfather, a claim that goes to the heart of the nineteenth century's many uncertainties about congenital syphilis. Whether a father with syphilis and supposedly tainted sperm could communicate the disease to his unborn child at the moment of conception without infecting the mother was one of the most puzzling and disputed questions of syphilology. We know now that he cannot: congenital syphilis can be acquired only from the mother, either during gestation or at birth, meaning that the mother must herself have the disease. It was not, however, until the twentieth century, when serological testing became possible, that this point was established, and the dominant view in the late nineteenth century was that the father could and often did infect the child directly. The key figure in winning acceptance for this view was the French authority Paul Diday (1812-94), an English translation of whose influential text, *A Treatise on Syphilis in New-Born Children and Infants at the Breast*, was published in 1859. Diday specifically rejected the correct view of Philippe Ricord (1800-89), the leading venereologist of the early nineteenth century and famous for at last distinguishing syphilis from gonorrhœa, that it was 'not possible for a syphilitic father to communicate the disease to a child unless he has previously given a chancre to the mother'.[2] Unfortunately for medicine, though fortunately for the credibility of Conan Doyle's fiction, it was Diday's view that prevailed.

Diday's opinion was popularised in England by Jonathan Hutchinson, who asserted very definitely in his widely-read text *Syphilis* (1887) that direct inheritance of the disease from the father, independently of the mother, (called 'sperm inheritance') was common, and he chided those who doubted whether it was possible: 'The evidence on this point seems to me overwhelming', he wrote; it was well established 'that a child may at the time of conception take syphilis from its father

---

[1] Jonathan Hutchinson, *Syphilis* (London: Cassell, 1887) p. 75. See also John Thorne Crissey and Lawrence Charles Parish, *The Dermatology and Syphilology of the Nineteenth Century* (New York: Praeger Scientific, 1981), pp. 226-227.

[2] Paul Diday, *A Treatise on Syphilis in New-Born Children and Infants at the Breast*, trans. G. Whitley (London: New Sydenham Society, 1859), p. 15.

alone, from its mother, or from both simultaneously'.[1] Conan Doyle's picture of innocent wives and sons was thus in accord with the prevailing state of medical knowledge.

But whether syphilis could be transmitted to the third generation (inherited from a grandfather via the father), and whether Norton could show no signs of disease until adulthood, are separate and even more contentious questions. Jonathan Hutchinson denied that the first was possible: he rejected the proposition that syphilis could be transmitted beyond the second generation, and stated firmly that 'inherited syphilis cannot pass to the third generation'.[2] But others thought it could, including another distinguished French authority, Alfred Fournier (1832-1914), who believed that the disease 'in this [third] generation usually manifests itself by certain dystrophic stigmata, but that in 14 per cent. of 116 cases ... there were lesions of active syphilis in the third generation'. This was a summary of his opinion as given by an English expert, George Still, writing in a cooperative textbook in 1908; he reported further that Fournier had also found that 'only three fifths of the descendants of this generation survive to adult life'. If this was correct, there was a 60 per cent. chance that any children Francis Norton sired would at least survive as long as him. Still went on to say that although he had never 'come across a single instance of syphilis in the third generation', the possibility 'must remain at present *sub judice*'.[3]

On the final question of whether Norton could have reached adulthood without having shown any symptoms of disease, opinion is again divided. In today's world the vast majority of syphilitic babies are obviously sickly from birth, and nearly half die within a few weeks unless treated. Nineteenth century authorities repeatedly state that the appearance of symptoms may be delayed until 'later', but they are vague as to how much later that can be. Hutchinson devotes most of his efforts to describing the signs of syphilis in children, suggesting that he thought the disease usually manifested itself in childhood at the latest. Even in his original paper, dealing with its identification

---

[1] *Syphilis*, pp. 65, 67-68.

[2] *Syphilis* pp. 89-90.

[3] George Still, 'Congenital Syphilis' in D'Arcy Power and J. Keogh Murphy (eds), *A System of Syphilis*, 6 vols (London: Oxford University Press, 1908), Vol. I, pp. 288-289.

in adults, he had mentioned a distinctive physiognomy: 'A bad, pale earthy complexion, a thick pitted skin, a sunk and flattened nose, and scars of old fissures about the angles of the mouth.'[1] There is no suggestion of any such nastiness about the facial features of Conan Doyle's character.

We may therefore conclude that in making Francis Norton think he had inherited syphilis from his father, Conan Doyle was writing in accordance with the existing state of medical knowledge; that in making him think he had inherited it from his grandfather, he was contradicting England's leading authority on the subject, but that in such a controversial area he still had some licence for the scenario; but that in giving Norton no signs of syphilis until adulthood he was skating on very thin ice.

5. You might assume that Conan Doyle is in sympathy with Norton's railing against his grandfather and his miserable ultimate fate, but in the *Stark Munro Letters* the narrator takes a more Malthusian view:

> '[Nature] strengthens the race in two ways. The one is by improving those who are morally strong, which is done by increased knowledge and broadening religious views; the other ... is by the killing off ... of those who are morally weak. This is accomplished by drink and immorality. [...] I picture [these forces] as two great invisible hands hovering over the garden of life and plucking up the weeds. Looked at in one's own day one can only see that they produce degradation and misery. But at the end of a third generation from then, what has happened? The line of the drunkard and of the debauchee ... is either extinct or on the way towards it. Struma [i.e. syphilis], tubercle, nervous disease have all lent a hand towards the pruning off of that rotten branch, and the average of the race is thereby improved.'[2]

Syphilis haunted the late Victorian imagination with much the same intensity as AIDS haunts us today, and elicited many similarly irrational responses; but scared as the Victorians were by acquired syphilis, they were even more alarmed by the congenital variety, which

[1] Cited in Crissey and Parish, *Dermatology*, p. 226.
[2] Arthur Conan Doyle, *The Stark Munro Letters* (London: Longman, 1895), p. 100.

they saw as fostering degeneracy and threatening the very fibre of the race. It was closely linked with the fears of decadence, sexual excess, degeneration and atavism that were so prominent in the 1890s. As a purity campaigner such as Richard Armstrong intoned in 1885, syphilis was 'the sins of perished men—sins which themselves never perish till all their terrible effects are wrought out—that have laid on multitudes in this nineteenth century this heavy cross'.[1] Echoing Stark Munro, the physician Sir Victor Horsely lamented in 1904 that, owing to improved treatment, many syphilitics survived 'to produce stunted and diseased offspring'; to protect posterity, he thought such people should be sterilised.[2] The associated anxieties explains why public discussion of syphilis, such as in Ibsen's play *Ghosts* (first performed in London in 1891), provoked such hysterical reactions.[3]

---

[1] *Our Duty in the Matter of Purity*, cited in Joanne Townsend, *Private Diseases in Public Discourse: Venereal Disease in Victorian Society, Culture and Imagination*, Ph.D. thesis, University of Melbourne, 1999, p. 247.

[2] Davenport Hines, *Sex, Death and Punishment*, p. 162.

[3] For further information, see Judith Walkowitz, *City of Dreadful Delight: Narratives of Sexual Danger in Late Victorian London* (University of Chicago Press, 1992); Angus McLaren, *Prescription for Murder*, chap. 11, 'Degenerates'; J. Edward Chamberlin and Sander L. Gilman (eds), *Degeneration: The Dark Side of Progress* (New York: Columbia University Press, 1985); and Lesley Hall, 'Venereal Diseases and Society in Britain, From the Contagious Diseases Acts to the National Health Service', in Roger Davidson and Lesley Hall (eds), *Sex, Sin and Suffering: Venereal Disease and European Society Since 1870* (London: Routledge, 1999), pp. 120-136.

A FALSE START

'Is Doctor Horace Wilkinson at home?'

'I am he. Pray step in.'

The visitor looked somewhat astonished at having the door opened to him by the master of the house.

'I wanted to have a few words.'

The doctor, a pale, nervous young man, dressed in an ultra-professional, long black frockcoat, with a high white collar cutting off his dapper side-whiskers in the centre, rubbed his hands together and smiled. In the thick, burly man in front of him he scented a patient, and it would be his first. His scanty resources had begun to run somewhat low; and, although he had his first quarter's rent safely locked away in the right-hand drawer of his desk, it was becoming a question with him how he should meet the current expenses of his very simple house-keeping. He bowed, therefore, waved his visitor in, closed the hall door in a careless fashion, as though his own presence thereat had been a purely accidental circumstance, and finally led the burly stranger into his scantily-furnished front room, where he motioned him to a seat. Doctor Wilkinson planted himself behind his desk, and, placing his finger-tips together, he gazed with some apprehension at his companion. What was the matter with the man? He seemed very red in the face. Some of his old professors would have diagnosed his case by now, and would have electrified the patient by describing his own symptoms before he had said a word about them. Doctor Horace Wilkinson racked his brains for some clue, but Nature had fashioned him as a plodder—a very reliable plodder, and nothing more. He could think of nothing save that the visitor's watch-chain had a very brassy appearance, with a corollary to the effect that he would be lucky if he got half-a-crown out of him. Still, even half-a-crown was something in those early days of struggle.[1]

Whilst the doctor had been running his eyes over the stranger, the latter had been plunging his hands into pocket after pocket of his heavy coat. The heat of the weather, his dress, and this exercise of pocket-rummaging had all combined to still further redden his face, which had changed from brick to beet, with a gloss of moisture on his brow. This extreme ruddiness brought a clue at last to the observant doctor. Surely it was not to be attained without alcohol. In alcohol lay the secret of this man's trouble. Some little delicacy was needed, however, in showing him that he had read his case aright, that at a glance he had penetrated to the inmost sources of his ailments.[2]

'It's very hot,' observed the stranger, mopping his forehead.

'Yes. It is weather which tempts one to drink rather more beer than is good for one,' answered Doctor Horace Wilkinson looking very knowingly at his companion from over his finger-tips.

'Dear! dear! You shouldn't do that.'

'I! I never touch beer.'

'Neither do I. I've been an abstainer for twenty years.'

This was depressing. Doctor Wilkinson blushed until he was nearly as red as the other.

'May I ask what I can do for you?' he asked, picking up his stethoscope and tapping it gently against his thumb-nail.

'Yes, I was just going to tell you. I heard of your coming, but I couldn't get round before—'

He broke into a nervous little cough.

'Yes,' said the doctor encouragingly.

'I should have been here three weeks ago, but you know how these things get put off.'

He coughed again behind his large, red hand.

'I do not think that you need say anything more,' said the doctor, taking over the case with an easy air of command. 'Your cough is quite sufficient. It is entirely bronchial by the sound. No doubt the mischief is circumscribed at present, but there is always the danger that it may spread, so you have done wisely to come to me. A little judicious treatment will soon set you right. Your waistcoat, please, but not your shirt. Puff out your chest, and say ninety-nine in a deep voice.'

The red-faced man began to laugh.

'It's all right, doctor,' said he. 'That cough comes from chewing tobacco, and I know it's a very bad habit. Nine and ninepence is what I have to say to you, for I'm the officer of the Gas Company, and they have a claim against you for that on the meter.'

Doctor Horace Wilkinson collapsed into his chair.

'Then you're not a patient?' he gasped.

'Never needed a doctor in my life, sir.'

'Oh, that's all right.' The doctor concealed his disappointment under an affectation of facetiousness. 'You don't look as if you troubled them much. I don't know what we should do if everyone were as robust. I shall call at the Company's offices and pay this small amount.'

'If you could make it convenient, sir, now that I am here, it would save trouble—'

'Oh, certainly!'

These eternal little sordid money troubles were more trying to the doctor than plain living or scanty food. He took out his purse, and slid the contents on to the table. There were two half-crowns and some pennies. In his drawer he had ten golden sovereigns. But those were his rent. If he once broke in upon them he was lost. He would starve first.

'Dear me!' said he, with a smile, as at some strange, unheard-of incident. 'I have run short of small change. I am afraid I shall have to call upon the Company after all.'

'Very well, sir.'

The inspector rose, and with a practised glance around, which valued every article in the room, from the two-guinea carpet to the eight-shilling muslin curtains, he took his departure.

When he had gone, Doctor Wilkinson rearranged his room, as was his habit a dozen times in the day. He laid out his large *Quain's Dictionary of Medicine*[3] in the forefront of the table, so as to impress the casual patient that he had ever the best authorities at his elbow. Then he cleared all the little instruments out of his pocket-case—the scissors, the forceps, the bistouries, the lancets—and he laid them all out beside the stethoscope, to make as good a show as possible. His ledger, day-book and visiting-book were spread in front of him. There was no entry in any of them yet, but it would not look well to have the covers too glossy and new, so he rubbed them together, and daubed ink over them. Neither would it be well that any patient should observe that his name was the first in the book, so he filled up the first page of each with notes of imaginary visits paid to nameless patients during the last three weeks. Having done all this, he rested his head upon his hands and relapsed into the terrible occupation of waiting.

Terrible enough at any time to the young professional man, but most of all to one who knows that the weeks, and even the days, during which he can hold out are numbered. Economise as he would, the money would still slip away in the countless little claims which a man never understands until he lives under a rooftree of his own. Dr Wilkinson could not deny, as he sat at his desk and looked at the little heap of silver and coppers, that his chances of being a successful practitioner in Sutton were rapidly vanishing away.

And yet it was a bustling, prosperous town, with so much money in it that it seemed strange that a man with a trained brain and dexterous fingers should be starved out of it for want of employment. At his desk, Doctor Horace Wilkinson could see the never-ending double current of people which ebbed and flowed in front of his window. It was a busy street, and the air was for ever filled with the dull roar of life, the grinding of the wheels, and the patter of countless feet. Men, women and children, thousands and thousands of them, passed in the day, and yet each was hurrying on upon his own business, scarce glancing at the small brass plate, or wasting a thought upon the man who waited in the front room. And yet how many of them would obviously, glaringly have been the better for his professional assistance. Dyspeptic men, anæmic women, blotched faces, bilious complexions, they flowed past him, they needing him, he needing them, and yet the remorseless bar of professional etiquette kept them for ever apart. What could he do? Could he stand at his own front door, pluck the casual stranger by the sleeve, and whisper in his ear, 'Sir, you will forgive me for remarking that you are suffering from a severe attack of acne rosacea, which makes you a peculiarly unpleasant object. Allow me to suggest that a small prescription containing arsenic, which will not cost you more than you often spend upon a single meal, will be very much to your advantage.' Such an address would be a degradation to the high and lofty profession of medicine, and there are no such sticklers for the ethics of that profession as some to whom she has been but a bitter and a grudging mother.

Doctor Horace Wilkinson was still looking moodily out of the window, when there came a sharp clang at the bell. Often it had rung, and with every ring his hopes had sprung up, only to dwindle away again, and change to leaden disappointment, as he faced some beggar or touting tradesman. But the doctor's spirit was young and elastic, and again, in spite of all experience, it responded to that exhilarating summons. He sprang to his feet, cast his eyes over the table, thrust out his medical books a little more prominently, and hurried to the door. A groan escaped him as he entered the hall. He could see through the half-glazed upper panels that a gipsy van, hung round with wicker tables and chairs, had halted before his door, and that a couple of the vagrants, with a baby, were waiting outside. He had learned by experience that it was better not even to parley with such people.

'I have nothing for you,' said he, loosing the latch by an inch. 'Go away!' He closed the door, but the bell clanged once more. 'Get away! Get away,' he cried, impatiently, and walked back into his consulting-room. He had hardly seated himself when the bell went for the third time. In a towering passion he rushed back, flung open the door. 'What the—'

'If you please, sir, we need a doctor.'

In an instant he was rubbing his hands again, with his blandest professional smile. These were patients, then, whom he had tried to hunt from his doorstep—the very first patients, whom he had waited for so impatiently. They did not look very promising. The man, a tall, lank-haired gipsy, had gone back to the horse's head. There remained a small, hard-faced woman, with a great bruise all round her eye. She wore a yellow silk handkerchief round her head, and a baby, tucked in a red shawl, was pressed to her bosom.

'Pray step in, madam,' said Doctor Horace Wilkinson, with his very best sympathetic manner. In this case, at least, there could be no mistake as to diagnosis. 'If you will sit on this sofa, I shall very soon make you feel much more comfortable.'

He poured a little water from his carafe into a saucer, made a compress of lint, fastened it over the injured eye, and secured the whole with a spica bandage, *secundum artem*.

'Thank ye kindly, sir,' said the woman, when his work was finished; 'that's nice and warm, and may God bless your honour. But it wasn't about my eye at all that I came to see a doctor.'

'Not your eye?'

Doctor Horace Wilkinson was beginning to be a little doubtful as to the advantages of quick diagnosis. It is an excellent thing to be able to surprise a patient, but hitherto it was always the patient who had surprised him.

'The baby's got the measles.'

The mother parted the red shawl, and exhibited a little, dark, black-eyed gipsy baby, whose swarthy face was all flushed and mottled with a dark red rash. The child breathed with a rattling sound, and it looked up at the doctor with eyes which were heavy with want of sleep and crusted together at the lids.

'Hum! Yes. Measles, sure enough—and a smart attack.'

'I just wanted you to see him, sir, so that you could signify.'

'Could what?'

'Signify, if anything happened.'

'Oh, I see—certify.'

'And now that you've seen it, sir, I'll go on, for Reuben—that's my man—is in a hurry.'

'But don't you want any medicine?'

'Oh, now you've seen it, it's all right. I'll let you know if anything happens.'

'But you must have some medicine. The child is very ill.'

He descended into the little room which he had fitted as a surgery, and he made up a two-ounce bottle of cooling medicine. In such cities as Sutton there are few patients who can afford to pay a fee to both doctor and chemist, so that unless the physician is prepared to play the part of both he will have little chance of making a living at either.

'There is your medicine, madam. You will find the directions upon the bottle. Keep the child warm and give it a light diet.'

'Thank you kindly, sir.'

She shouldered her baby and marched for the door.

'Excuse me, madam,' said the doctor nervously. 'Don't you think it too small a matter to make a bill of? Perhaps it would be better if we had a settlement at once.'

The gipsy woman looked at him reproachfully out of her one uncovered eye.

'Are you going to charge me for that?' she asked. 'How much, then?'

'Well, say half-a-crown.'

He mentioned the sum in a half jesting way, as though it were too small to take serious notice of, but the gipsy woman raised quite a scream at the mention of it.

''Arf-a-crown! for that?'

'Well, my good woman, why not go to the poor doctor if you cannot afford a fee?'

She fumbled in her pocket, craning awkwardly to keep her grip upon the baby.

'Here's sevenpence,' she said at last, holding out a little pile of copper coins. 'I'll give you that and a wicker footstool.'

'But my fee is half-a-crown.'

The doctor's views of the glory of his profession cried out against this wretched haggling, and yet what was he to do?

'Where am I to get 'arf-a-crown? It is well for gentle-folk like you who sit in your grand houses, an' can eat an' drink what you like, an' charge 'arf-a-crown for just saying as much as "'Ow d'ye do." We can't pick up 'arf-crowns like that. What we gets we earns 'ard. This sevenpence is just all I've got. You told me to feed the child light. She must feed light, for what she's to have is more than I know.'

Whilst the woman had been speaking, Doctor Horace Wilkinson's eyes had wandered to the tiny heap of money upon the table which represented all that separated him from absolute starvation, and he chuckled to himself at the grim joke that he should appear to this poor woman to be a being living in the lap of luxury. Then he picked up the odd coppers, leaving only the two half-crowns upon the table.

'Here you are,' he said brusquely. 'Never mind the fee; and take these coppers. They may be of some use to you. Good-bye!'

He bowed her out, and closed the door behind her. After all, she was the thin edge of the wedge. These wandering people have great powers of recommendation. All large practices have been built up from such foundations. The hangers-on to the kitchen recommend to the kitchen, they to the drawing-room, and so it spreads. At least he could say now that he had had a patient.[4]

He went into the back room and lit the spirit kettle to boil the water for his tea, laughing the while at the recollection of his recent interview. If all patients were like this one it could easily be reckoned how many it would take to ruin him completely. Putting aside the dirt upon his carpet and the loss of time, there were twopence gone upon the bandage, fourpence or more upon the medicine, to say nothing of phial, cork, label and paper. Then he had given her fivepence, so that his first patient had absorbed altogether not less than one-sixth of his available capital. If five more were to come he would be a broken man. He sat down upon the portmanteau and shook with laughter at the thought, while he measured out his one spoonful and a half of tea at 1s. 8d. into the brown earthenware teapot. Suddenly, however, the laugh faded from his face, and he cocked his ear towards the door, standing listening with a slanting head and a sidelong eye. There had been a rasping of wheels against the curb, the sound of steps outside, and then a loud peal at the bell. With his teaspoon in his hand he peeped round the corner and saw with amazement that a carriage and pair were waiting outside, and that a powdered footman was standing at the door. The spoon tinkled down upon the floor, and he stood gazing in bewilderment. Then, pulling himself together, he threw open the door.

'Young man,' said the flunkey, 'tell your master, Doctor Wilkinson, that he is wanted just as quick as ever he can come to Lady Millbank, at The Towers. He is to come this very instant. We'd take him with us, but we have to go back to see if Doctor Mason is home yet. Just you stir your stumps and give him the message.'

The footman nodded and was off in an instant, while the coachman lashed his horses, and the carriage flew down the street.

Here was a new development! Doctor Horace Wilkinson stood at his door and tried to think it all out. Lady Millbank, of The Towers! People of wealth and position, no doubt. And a serious case, or why this haste and summoning of two doctors? But then, why in the name of all that is wonderful should he be sent for?

He was obscure, unknown, without influence. There must be some mistake. Yes, that must be the true explanation; or was it possible that someone was attempting a cruel hoax upon him. At any rate, it was too positive a message to be disregarded. He must set off at once and settle the matter one way or the other.

But he had one source of information. At the corner of the street was a small shop where one of the oldest inhabitants dispensed newspapers and gossip. He could get information there if anywhere. He put on his well-brushed top hat, secreted instruments and bandages in all his pockets, and without waiting for his tea, closed up his establishment and started off upon his adventure.

The stationer at the corner was a human directory to everyone and everything in Sutton, so that he soon had all the information which he wanted. Sir John Millbank was very well known in the town, it seemed. He was a merchant prince, an exporter of pens, three times mayor, and reported to be fully worth two millions sterling.

The Towers was his palatial seat, just outside the city. His wife had been an invalid for some years, and was growing worse. So far the whole thing seemed to be genuine enough. By some amazing chance these people really had sent for him.

And then another doubt assailed him, and he turned back into the shop.

'I am your neighbour, Dr Horace Wilkinson,' said he. 'Is there any other medical man of that name in the town?'

No, the stationer was quite positive that there was not.

That was final, then. A great good fortune had come in his way, and he must take prompt advantage of it. He called a cab, and drove furiously to The Towers, with his brain in a whirl, giddy with hope and delight at one moment, and sickened with fears and doubts at the next, lest the case should in some way be beyond his powers, or lest he should find at some critical moment that he was without the instrument or appliance which was needed. Every strange and *outré* case of which he had ever heard or read came back into his mind, and long before he reached The Towers he had worked himself into a positive conviction that he would be instantly required to do a trephining at the least.

The Towers was a very large house, standing back amid trees, at the head of a winding drive. As he drove up, the doctor sprang out, paid away half his worldly assets as a fare, and followed a stately footman who, having taken his name, led him through the oak-panelled, stained-glass hall, gorgeous with deers' heads and ancient armour, and ushered him into a large sitting-room beyond. A very irritable-looking, acid-faced man was seated in an arm-chair by the fireplace, while two young ladies in white were standing together in the bow window at the further end.

'Hullo! hullo! hullo! What's this—heh?' cried the irritable man. 'Are you Dr Wilkinson? Eh?'

'Yes, sir. I am Doctor Wilkinson.'

'Really, now. You seem very young—much younger than I expected. Well, well, well, Mason's old, and yet he don't seem to know much about it. I suppose we must try the other end now. You're the Wilkinson who wrote something about the lungs? Heh?'

Here was a light! The only two letters which the doctor had ever written to *The Lancet*—modest little letters thrust away in a back column among the wrangles about medical ethics, and the inquiries as to how much it took to keep a horse in the country—had been upon pulmonary disease. They had not been wasted, then. Some eye had picked them out and marked the name of the writer. Who could say that work was ever wasted, or that merit did not promptly meet with its reward?

'Yes, I have written on the subject.'

'Ha! Well, then, where's Mason?'

'I have not the pleasure of his acquaintance.'

'No? That's queer, too. He knows you, and thinks a lot of your opinion. You're a stranger in the town, are you not?'

'Yes. I have only been here a very short time.'

'That was what Mason said. He didn't give me the address. Said he would call on you and bring you, but when the wife got worse, of course I inquired for you and sent for you direct. I sent for Mason, too, but he was out. However, we can't wait for him, so just run away upstairs and do what you can.'

'Well, I am placed in a rather delicate position,' said Dr Horace Wilkinson, with some hesitation. 'I am here, as I understand, to meet my colleague, Dr Mason, in consultation. It would perhaps hardly be correct for me to see the patient in his absence. I think that I would rather wait.'

'Would you, by Jove! Do you think I'll let my wife get worse while the doctor is coolly kicking his heels in the room below? No, sir, I am a plain man, and I tell you that you will either go up or go out.'

The style of speech jarred upon the doctor's sense of the fitness of things, but still when a man's wife is ill much may be overlooked. He contented himself by bowing somewhat stiffly.

'I shall go up if you insist upon it,' said he.

'I do insist upon it. And another thing; I won't have her thumped about all over the chest, or any hocus-pocus of the sort. She has bronchitis and asthma, and that's all. If you can cure it, well and good. But it only weakens her to have you tapping and listening; and it does no good, either.'

Personal disrespect was a thing that the doctor could stand, but the profession was to him a holy thing, and a flippant word about it cut him to the quick.

'Thank you,' said he, picking up his hat, 'I have the honour to wish you a very good day. I do not care to undertake the responsibility of this case.'

'Hullo! what's the matter now?'

'It is not my habit to give opinions without examining my patient. I wonder that you should suggest such a course to a medical man. I wish you good day.'

But Sir John Millbank was a commercial man, and believed in the commercial principle that the more difficult a thing is to attain the more valuable it is. A doctor's opinion had been to him a mere matter of guineas. But here was a young man who seemed to care nothing either for his wealth or title. His respect for his judgment increased amazingly.

'Tut! tut!' said he, 'Mason is not so thin-skinned. There! there! Have your way! Do what you like and I won't say another word. I'll just run upstairs and tell Lady Millbank that you are coming.'

The door had hardly closed behind him when the two demure young ladies darted out of their corner, and fluttered with joy in front of the astonished doctor.

'Oh! well done, well done!' cried the taller, clapping her hands.

'Don't let him bully you, doctor,' said the other. 'Oh, it was so nice to hear you stand up to him. That's the way he does with poor Doctor Mason. Doctor Mason has never examined mamma yet. He always takes papa's word for everything. Hush, Maude, here he comes again.'

They subsided in an instant into their corner, as silent and demure as ever.

Doctor Horace Wilkinson followed Sir John up the broad, thick-carpeted staircase, and into the darkened sick room. In a quarter of an hour he had sounded and sifted the case to the uttermost, and descended with the husband once more to the drawing-room. In front of the fireplace were standing two gentlemen, the one a very typical, clean-shaven, general practitioner, the other a striking-looking man of middle age, with pale blue eyes and a long red beard.

'Hullo, Mason! You've come at last!'

'Yes, Sir John! And I have brought, as I promised, Doctor Wilkinson with me.'

'Doctor Wilkinson! Why, this is he.'

Doctor Mason stared in astonishment.

'I have never seen the gentleman before,' he cried.

'Nevertheless I am Doctor Wilkinson—Doctor Horace Wilkinson, of 114 Canal View.'

'Good gracious, Sir John!' cried Dr Mason. 'Did you think that in a case of such importance I should call in a junior local practitioner! This is Dr Adam Wilkinson, lecturer on pulmonary diseases at Regent's College, London, physician upon the staff of the St Swithin's Hospital, and author of a dozen works upon the subject. He happened to be in Sutton upon a visit, and I thought I would utilise his presence to have a first-rate opinion upon Lady Millbank.'

'Thank you,' said Sir John drily. 'But I fear my wife is rather tired now, for she has just been very thoroughly examined by this young gentleman. I think we will let it stop at that for the present, though, of course, as you have had the trouble of coming here, I should be glad to have a note of your fees.'

When Dr Mason had departed, looking very disgusted, and his friend the specialist very amused, Sir John listened to all the young physician had to say about the case.

'Now, I'll tell you what,' said he, when he had finished. 'I'm a man of my word, d'ye see? When I like a man I freeze to him. I'm a good friend and a bad enemy. I believe in you, and I don't believe in Mason. From now on you are my doctor, and that of my family. Come and see my wife every day. How does that suit your book?'

'I am extremely grateful to you for your kind intentions towards me, but I am afraid there is no possible way in which I can avail myself of them.'

'Heh! what d'ye mean?'

'I could not possibly take Dr Mason's place in the middle of a case like this. It would be a most unprofessional act.'[5]

'Oh, well, go your own way,' cried Sir John in despair. 'Never was such a man for making difficulties. You've had a fair offer and you've refused it, and now you can just go your own way.'

The millionaire stumped out of the room in a huff, and Dr Horace Wilkinson made his way homeward to his spirit lamp and his one-and-eightpenny tea, with his first guinea in his pocket, and with a feeling that he had upheld the best traditions of his profession.

And yet this false start of his was a true start also, for it soon came to Doctor Mason's ears that his junior had had it in his power to carry off his best patient and had forborne to do so. To the honour of the profession be it said that such forbearance is the rule rather than the exception, and yet in this case, with so very junior a practitioner and so very wealthy a patient, the temptation was greater than is usual. There was a grateful note, a visit, a friendship, and now the well-known firm of Mason & Wilkinson is doing the largest family practice in Sutton.

NOTES TO 'A FALSE START'

First published in *Gentlewoman*, Christmas 1891.

1. The description of Dr Wilkinson's practice closely matches that of Conan Doyle's own practice in his early days at Portsmouth, particularly the incident of the gas bill collector.

2. An allusion to Dr Joseph Bell, one of Conan Doyle's teachers at Edinburgh.

3. *Quain's Dictionary of Medicine*, originally compiled by Richard Quain of the Quain medical dynasty, was first published in 1816. It ran through many editions and was a standard reference text for most of the nineteenth century.

4. The incident of the gypsy is also reported in Conan Doyle's *Memories and Adventures* (pp. 67-68) and the *Stark Munro Letters* (pp. 266-67).

5. These sorts of niceties were what passed for medical ethics at this period. It was punctilious observance of professional etiquette that prevented Dr Paterson from saving Mrs Pritchard—see discussion in Introduction.

THE CURSE OF EVE

ROBERT JOHNSON was an essentially common-place man, with no feature to distinguish him from a million others. He was pale of face, ordinary in looks, neutral in opinions, thirty years of age, and a married man. By trade he was a gentleman's outfitter in the New North Road, and the competition of business squeezed out of him the little character that was left. In his hope of conciliating customers he had become cringing and pliable, until working ever in the same routine from day to day he seemed to have sunk into a soulless machine rather than a man. No great question had ever stirred him. At the end of this snug century, self-contained in his own narrow circle, it seemed impossible that any of the mighty, primitive passions of mankind could ever reach him. Yet birth, and lust, and illness, and death are changeless things, and when one of these harsh facts springs out upon a man at some sudden turn of the path of life, it dashes off for the moment his mask of civilisation and gives a glimpse of the stranger and stronger face below.

Johnson's wife was a quiet little woman, with brown hair and gentle ways. His affection for her was the one positive trait in his character. Together they would lay out the shop window every Monday morning, the spotless shirts in their green cardboard boxes below, the neckties above hung in rows over the brass rails, the cheap studs glistening from the white cards at either side, while in the background were the rows of cloth caps and the bank of boxes in which the more valuable hats were screened from the sunlight. She kept the books and sent out the bills. No one but she knew the joys and sorrows which crept into his small life. She had shared his exultation when the gentleman who was going to India had bought ten dozen shirts and an incredible number of collars, and she had been as stricken as he when, after the goods had gone, the bill was returned from the hotel address with the intimation that no such person had lodged there. For five years they had worked, building up the business, thrown together all the more closely because their marriage had been a childless one. Now, however, there were signs that a change was at hand, and that speedily. She was unable to come downstairs, and her mother, Mrs Peyton, came over from Camberwell to nurse her and to welcome her grandchild.

Little qualms of anxiety came over Johnson as his wife's time approached. However, after all, it was a natural process. Other men's wives went through it unharmed, and why should not his? He was himself one of a family of fourteen, and yet his mother was alive and hearty. It was quite the exception for anything to go wrong. And yet in spite of his reasonings the remembrance of his wife's condition was always like a sombre background to all his other thoughts.

Doctor Miles of Bridport Place, the best man in the neighbourhood, was retained five months in advance, and, as time stole on, many little packets of absurdly small white garments with frill work and ribbons began to arrive among the big consignments of male necessities. And then one evening, as Johnson was ticketing the scarfs in the shop, he heard a bustle upstairs, and Mrs Peyton came running down to say that Lucy was bad and that she thought the doctor ought to be there without delay.

It was not Robert Johnson's nature to hurry. He was prim and staid and liked to do things in an orderly fashion. It was a quarter of a mile from the corner of the New North Road where his shop stood to the doctor's house in Bridport Place. There were no cabs in sight so he set off upon foot, leaving the lad to mind the shop. At Bridport Place he was told that the doctor had just gone to Harman Street to attend a man in a fit. Johnson started off for Harman Street, losing a little of his primness as he became more anxious. Two full cabs but no empty ones passed him on the way. At Harman Street he learned that the doctor had gone on to a case of measles, fortunately he had left the address—69 Dunstan Road, at the other side of the Regent's Canal. Johnson's primness had vanished now as he thought of the women waiting at home, and he began to run as hard as he could down the Kingsland Road. Some way along he sprang into a cab which stood by the curb and drove to Dunstan Road. The doctor had just left, and Robert Johnson felt inclined to sit down upon the steps in despair.

Fortunately he had not sent the cab away, and he was soon back at Bridport Place. Doctor Miles had not returned yet, but they were expecting him every instant. Johnson waited drumming his fingers on his knees, in a high, dim lit room, the air of which was charged with a faint, sickly smell of ether. The furniture was massive, and the books in the shelves were sombre, and a squat black clock ticked mournfully on the mantelpiece. It told him that it was half-past seven, and that he had been gone an hour and a quarter. Whatever would the women think of him! Every time that a distant door slammed he sprang from his chair in a quiver of eagerness. His ears strained to catch the deep notes of the doctor's voice. And then, suddenly, with a gush of joy he heard a quick step outside, and the sharp click of the key in the lock. In an instant he was out in the hall, before the doctor's foot was over the threshold.

'If you please, doctor, I've come for you,' he cried; 'the wife was taken bad at six o'clock.'

He hardly knew what he expected the doctor to do. Something very energetic, certainly—to seize some drugs, perhaps, and rush excitedly with him through the gaslit streets. Instead of that Doctor Miles threw his umbrella into the rack, jerked off his hat with a somewhat peevish gesture, and pushed Johnson back into the room.

'Let's see! You *did* engage me, didn't you?' he asked in no very cordial voice.

'Oh, yes, doctor, last November. Johnson the outfitter, you know, in the New North Road.'

'Yes, yes. It's a bit overdue,' said the doctor, glancing at a list of names in a note-book with a very shiny cover. 'Well, how is she?'

'I don't—'

'Ah, of course, it's your first. You'll know more about it next time.'

'Mrs Peyton said it was time you were there, sir.'

'My dear sir, there can be no very pressing hurry in a first case. We shall have an all-night affair, I fancy. You can't get an engine to go without coals, Mr Johnson, and I have had nothing but a light lunch.'

'We could have something cooked for you—something hot and a cup of tea.'

'Thank you, but I fancy my dinner is actually on the table. I can do no good in the earlier stages. Go home and say that I am coming, and I will be round immediately afterwards.'

A sort of horror filled Robert Johnson as he gazed at this man who could think about his dinner at such a moment. He had not imagina-

tion enough to realise that the experience which seemed so appall-
ingly important to him, was the merest everyday matter of business
to the medical man who could not have lived for a year had he not,
amid the rush of work, remembered what was due to his own health.
To Johnson he seemed little better than a monster. His thoughts were
bitter as he sped back to his shop.

'You've taken your time,' said his mother-in-law reproachfully,
looking down the stairs as he entered.

'I couldn't help it!' he gasped. 'Is it over?'

'Over! She's got to be worse, poor dear, before she can be better.
Where's Doctor Miles?'

'He's coming after he's had dinner.'

The old woman was about to make some reply, when, from the
half-opened door behind, a high whinnying voice cried out for her.
She ran back and closed the door, while Johnson, sick at heart, turned
into the shop. There he sent the lad home and busied himself frantically in putting up shutters and turning out boxes. When all was
closed and finished he seated himself in the parlour behind the shop.
But he could not sit still. He rose incessantly to walk a few paces and
then fell back into a chair once more. Suddenly the clatter of china fell
upon his ear, and he saw the maid pass the door with a cup on a tray
and a smoking teapot.

'Who is that for, Jane?' he asked.

'For the mistress, Mr Johnson. She says she would fancy it.'

There was immeasurable consolation to him in that homely cup
of tea. It wasn't so very bad after all if his wife could think of such
things. So light-hearted was he that he asked for a cup also. He had
just finished it when the doctor arrived, with a small black leather bag
in his hand.

'Well, how is she?' he asked genially.

'Oh, she's very much better,' said Johnson, with enthusiasm.

'Dear me, that's bad!' said the doctor. 'Perhaps it will do if I look
in on my morning round?'

'No, no,' cried Johnson, clutching at his thick frieze overcoat. 'We
are so glad that you have come. And, doctor, please come down soon
and let me know what you think about it.'

The doctor passed upstairs, his firm, heavy steps resounding through the house. Johnson could hear his boots creaking as he walked about the floor above him, and the sound was a consolation to him. It was crisp and decided, the tread of a man who had plenty of self-confidence. Presently, still straining his ears to catch what was going on, he heard the scraping of a chair as it was drawn along the floor, and a moment later he heard the door fly open and someone come rushing downstairs. Johnson sprang up with his hair bristling, thinking that some dreadful thing had occurred, but it was only his mother-in-law, incoherent with excitement and searching for scissors and some tape. She vanished again and Jane passed up the stairs with a pile of newly-aired linen. Then, after an interval of silence, Johnson heard the heavy, creaking tread and the doctor came down into the parlour.

'That's better,' said he, pausing with his hand upon the door. 'You look pale, Mr Johnson.'

'Oh no, sir, not at all,' he answered deprecatingly, mopping his brow with his handkerchief.

'There is no immediate cause for alarm,' said Doctor Miles. 'The case is not all that we could wish it. Still we will hope for the best.'

'Is there danger, sir?' gasped Johnson.

'Well, there is always danger, of course. It is not altogether a favourable case, but still it might be much worse. I have given her a draught. I saw as I passed that they have been doing a little building opposite to you. It's an improving quarter. The rents go higher and higher. You have a lease of your own little place, eh?'

'Yes, sir, yes!' cried Johnson, whose ears were straining for every sound from above, and who felt none the less that it was very soothing that the doctor should be able to chat so easily at such a time. 'That's to say no, sir, I am a yearly tenant.'

'Ah, I should get a lease if I were you. There's Marshall, the watchmaker, down the street, I attended his wife twice and saw him through the typhoid when they took up the drains in Prince Street. I assure you his landlord sprung his rent nearly forty a year and he had to pay or clear out.'

'Did his wife get through it, doctor?'

'Oh yes, she did very well. Hullo! Hullo!' He slanted his ear to the ceiling with a questioning face, and then darted swiftly from the room.

It was March and the evenings were chill, so Jane had lit the fire, but the wind drove the smoke downwards and the air was full of its acrid taint. Johnson felt chilled to the bone, though rather by his apprehensions than by the weather. He crouched over the fire with his thin white hands held out to the blaze. At ten o'clock Jane brought in the joint of cold meat and laid his place for supper, but he could not bring himself to touch it. He drank a glass of the beer, however, and felt the better for it. The tension of his nerves seemed to have reacted upon his hearing, and he was able to follow the most trivial things in the room above. Once, when the beer was still heartening him, he nerved himself to creep on tiptoe up the stair and to listen to what was going on. The bedroom door was half an inch open, and through the slit he could catch a glimpse of the clean-shaven face of the doctor, looking wearier and more anxious than before. Then he rushed downstairs like a lunatic, and running to the door he tried to distract his thoughts by watching what was going on in the street. The shops were all shut, and some rollicking boon companions came shouting along from the public-house. He stayed at the door until the stragglers had thinned down, and then came back to his seat by the fire. In his dim brain he was asking himself questions which had never intruded themselves before. Where was the justice of it? What had his sweet, innocent little wife done that she should be used so? Why was nature so cruel? He was frightened at his own thoughts, and yet wondered that they had never occurred to him before.

As the early morning drew in, Johnson, sick at heart and shivering in every limb, sat with his great-coat huddled round him, staring at the grey ashes and waiting hopelessly for some relief. His face was white and clammy, and his nerves had been numbed into a half conscious state by the long monotony of misery. But suddenly all his feelings leapt into keen life again as he heard the bedroom door open and the doctor's steps upon the stair. Robert Johnson was precise and unemotional in everyday life, but he almost shrieked now as he rushed forward to know if it were over.

One glance at the stern, drawn face which met him showed that it was no pleasant news which had sent the doctor downstairs. His appearance had altered as much as Johnson's during the last few hours. His hair was on end, his face flushed, his forehead dotted with beads of perspiration. There was a peculiar fierceness in his eye, and about the lines of his mouth, a fighting look as befitted a man who for hours on end had been striving with the hungriest of foes for the most precious of prizes. But there was a sadness too, as though his grim opponent had been overmastering him. He sat down and leaned his head upon his hand like a man who is fagged out.

'I thought it my duty to see you, Mr Johnson, and to tell you that it is a very nasty case. Your wife's heart is not strong, and she has some symptoms which I do not like. What I wanted to say is that if you would like to have a second opinion I shall be very glad to meet anyone whom you might suggest.'

Johnson was so dazed by his want of sleep and the evil news that he could hardly grasp the doctor's meaning. The other, seeing him hesitate, thought that he was considering the expense.

'Smith or Hawley would come for two guineas,' said he. 'But I think Pritchard of the City Road is the best man.'

'Oh, yes, bring the best man,' cried Johnson.

'Pritchard would want three guineas. He is a senior man, you see.'

'I'd give him all I have if he would pull her through. Shall I run for him?'

'Yes. Go to my house first and ask for the green baize bag. The assistant will give it to you. Tell him I want the A.C.E. mixture. Her heart is too weak for chloroform. Then go for Pritchard and bring him back with you.'

It was heavenly for Johnson to have something to do and to feel that he was of some use to his wife. He ran swiftly to Bridport Place, his footfalls clattering through the silent streets, and the big dark policemen turning their yellow funnels of light on him as he passed. Two tugs at the night-bell brought down a sleepy, half-clad assistant, who handed him a stoppered glass bottle and a cloth bag which contained something which clinked when you moved it. Johnson thrust the bottle into his pocket, seized the green bag, and pressing his hat firmly down ran as hard as he could set foot to ground until he was in the City Road and saw the name of Pritchard engraved in white upon a red ground. He bounded in triumph up the three steps which led to the door, and as he did so there was a crash behind him. His precious bottle was in fragments upon the pavement.

For a moment he felt as if it were his wife's body that was lying there. But the run had freshened his wits and he saw that the mischief might be repaired. He pulled vigorously at the night-bell.

'Well, what's the matter?' asked a gruff voice at his elbow. He started back and looked up at the windows, but there was no sign of life. He was approaching the bell again with the intention of pulling it, when a perfect roar burst from the wall.

'I can't stand shivering here all night,' cried the voice. 'Say who you are and what you want or I shut the tube.'

Then for the first time Johnson saw that the end of a speaking-tube hung out of the wall just above the bell. He shouted up it,—

'I want you to come with me to meet Doctor Miles at a confinement at once.'

'How far?' shrieked the irascible voice.

'The New North Road, Hoxton.'

'My consultation fee is three guineas, payable at the time.'

'All right,' shouted Johnson. 'You are to bring a bottle of A.C.E. mixture with you.'

'All right! Wait a bit!'

Five minutes later an elderly, hard-faced man with grizzled hair flung open the door. As he emerged a voice from somewhere in the shadows cried,—

'Mind you take your cravat, John,' and he impatiently growled something over his shoulder in reply.

The consultant was a man who had been hardened by a life of ceaseless labour, and who had been driven, as so many others have been, by the needs of his own increasing family to set the commercial before the philanthropic side of his profession. Yet beneath his rough crust he was a man with a kindly heart.

'We don't want to break a record,' said he, pulling up and panting after attempting to keep up with Johnson for five minutes. 'I would go quicker if I could, my dear sir, and I quite sympathise with your anxiety, but really I can't manage it.'

So Johnson, on fire with impatience, had to slow down until they reached the New North Road, when he ran ahead and had the door open for the doctor when he came. He heard the two meet outside the bedroom, and caught scraps of their conversation. 'Sorry to knock you up—nasty case—decent people.' Then it sank into a mumble and the door closed behind them.

Johnson sat up in his chair now, listening keenly, for he knew that a crisis must be at hand. He heard the two doctors moving about, and was able to distinguish the step of Pritchard, which had a drag in it, from the clean, crisp sound of the other's footfall. There was silence for a few minutes and then a curious drunken, mumbling sing-song voice came quavering up, very unlike anything which he had heard hitherto. At the same time a sweetish, insidious scent, imperceptible perhaps to any nerves less strained than his, crept down the stairs and penetrated into the room. The voice dwindled into a mere drone and finally sank away into silence, and Johnson gave a long sigh of relief for he knew that the drug had done its work and that, come what might, there should be no more pain for the sufferer.

But soon the silence became even more trying to him than the cries had been. He had no clue now as to what was going on, and his mind swarmed with horrible possibilities. He rose and went to the bottom of the stairs again. He heard the clink of metal against metal, and the subdued murmur of the doctors' voices. Then he heard Mrs Peyton say something, in a tone as of fear or expostulation, and again the doctors murmured together. For twenty minutes he stood there leaning against the wall, listening to the occasional rumbles of talk without being able to catch a word of it. And then of a sudden there rose out of the silence the strangest little piping cry, and Mrs Peyton screamed out in her delight and the man ran into the parlour and flung himself down upon the horse-hair sofa, drumming his heels on it in his ecstasy.

But often the great cat Fate lets us go, only to clutch us again in a fiercer grip. As minute after minute passed and still no sound came from above save those thin, glutinous cries, Johnson cooled from his frenzy of joy, and lay breathless with his ears straining. They were moving slowly about. They were talking in subdued tones. Still minute after minute passing, and no word from the voice for which he listened. His nerves were dulled by his night of trouble, and he waited in limp wretchedness upon his sofa. There he still sat when the doctors came down to him—a bedraggled, miserable figure with his face grimy and his hair unkempt from his long vigil. He rose as they entered, bracing himself against the mantelpiece.

'Is she dead?' he asked.

'Doing well,' answered the doctor.

And at the words that little conventional spirit which had never known until that night the capacity for fierce agony which lay within it, learned for the second time that there were springs of joy also which it had never tapped before. His impulse was to fall upon his knees, but he was shy before the doctors.

'Can I go up?'

'In a few minutes.'

'I'm sure, doctor, I'm very—I'm very—' he grew inarticulate. 'Here are your three guineas, Doctor Pritchard. I wish they were three hundred.'

'So do I,' said the senior man, and they laughed as they shook hands.

Johnson opened the shop door for them and heard their talk as they stood for an instant outside.

'Looked nasty at one time.'

'Very glad to have your help.'

'Delighted, I'm sure. Won't you step round and have a cup of coffee?'

'No, thanks. I'm expecting another case.'

The firm step and the dragging one passed away to the right and the left. Johnson turned from the door still with that turmoil of joy in his heart. He seemed to be making a new start in life. He felt that he was a stronger and a deeper man. Perhaps all this suffering had an object then. It might prove to be a blessing both to his wife and to him. The very thought was one which he would have been incapable of conceiving twelve hours before. He was full of new emotions. If there had been a harrowing there had been a planting too.

'Can I come up?' he cried, and then, without waiting for an answer, he took the steps three at a time.

Mrs Peyton was standing by a soapy bath with a bundle in her hands. From under the curve of a brown shawl there looked out at him the strangest little red face with crumpled features, moist, loose lips, and eyelids which quivered like a rabbit's nostrils. The weak neck had let the head topple over, and it rested upon the shoulder.

'Kiss it, Robert!' cried the grandmother. 'Kiss your son!'

But he felt a resentment to the little, red, blinking creature. He could not forgive it yet for that long night of misery. He caught sight of a white face in the bed and he ran towards it with such love and pity as his speech could find no words for.

'Thank God it is over! Lucy, dear, it was dreadful!'

'But I'm so happy now. I never was so happy in my life.'

Her eyes were fixed upon the brown bundle.

'You mustn't talk,' said Mrs Peyton.

'But don't leave me,' whispered his wife.

So he sat in silence with his hand in hers. The lamp was burning dim and the first cold light of dawn was breaking through the window. The night had been long and dark but the day was the sweeter and the purer in consequence. London was waking up. The roar began to rise from the street. Lives had come and lives had gone, but the great machine was still working out its dim and tragic destiny.[1]

NOTES TO 'THE CURSE OF EVE'

First published in *Round the Red Lamp*.

1. Conan Doyle read an early version of this story, in which the woman dies, to a meeting of the Authors' Club, where it was not well received. Ralph Blumenfeld, a journalist on the *Daily Express*, recalled: 'Dr Conan Doyle rose to read from a new story which he had just completed. It was all about obstetrics and the terror of a household in which a woman was about to become a mother; all about the husband's agonies, the doctor's embarrassments and professional distress—I forget the details, but [remember] a long, gloomy, ghastly dissertation which ... made me feel unhappy and cold. Finally, the big man with the rough voice stopped talking and sat down abruptly. Walter Besant turned to me and said, "Have you ever heard worse?" I had not.'[1]

---

[1] Daniel Stashower, *Teller of Tales: The Life of Arthur Conan Doyle* (New York: Henry Holt, 1999), p. 134.

SWEETHEARTS[1]

IT is hard for the general practitioner who sits among his patients both morning and evening, and sees them in their homes between, to steal time for one little daily breath of cleanly air. To win it he must slip early from his bed and walk out between shuttered shops when it is chill but very clear, and all things are sharply outlined, as in a frost. It is an hour that has a charm of its own, when, but for a postman or a milkman, one has the pavement to oneself, and even the most common thing takes an ever-recurring freshness, as though causeway, and lamp, and signboard had all wakened to the new day. Then even an inland city may seem beautiful, and bear virtue in its smoke-tainted air.

But it was by the sea that I lived, in a town that was unlovely enough were it not for its glorious neighbour. And who cares for the town when one can sit on the bench at the headland, and look out over the huge blue bay, and the yellow scimitar that curves before it. I loved it when its great face was freckled with the fishing boats, and I loved it when the big ships went past, far out, a little hillock of white and no hull, with topsails curved like a bodice, so stately and demure. But most of all I loved it when no trace of man marred the majesty of Nature, and when the sun-bursts slanted down on it from between the drifting rain-clouds. Then I have seen the further edge draped in the gauze of the driving rain, with its thin grey shading under the slow clouds, while my headland was golden, and the sun gleamed upon the breakers and struck deep through the green waves beyond, showing up the purple patches where the beds of seaweed are lying. Such a morning as that, with the wind in his hair, and the spray on his lips, and the cry of the eddying gulls in his ear, may send a man back braced afresh to the reek of a sick-room, and the dead, drab weariness of practice.

It was on such another day that I first saw my old man. He came to my bench just as I was leaving it. My eye must have picked him out even in a crowded street, for he was a man of large frame and fine presence, with something of distinction in the set of his lip and the poise of his head. He limped up the winding path leaning heavily

---

upon his stick, as though those great shoulders had become too much at last for the failing limbs that bore them. As he approached, my eyes caught Nature's danger signal, that faint bluish tinge in nose and lip which tells of a labouring heart.

'The brae is a little trying, sir,' said I. 'Speaking as a physician, I should say that you would do well to rest here before you go further.'

He inclined his head in a stately, old-world fashion, and seated himself upon the bench. Seeing that he had no wish to speak I was silent also, but I could not help watching him out of the corners of my eyes, for he was such a wonderful survival of the early half of the century, with his low-crowned, curly-brimmed hat, his black satin tie which fastened with a buckle at the back, and, above all, his large, fleshy, clean-shaven face shot with its mesh of wrinkles. Those eyes, ere they had grown dim, had looked out from the box-seat of mail coaches, and had seen the knots of navvies as they toiled on the brown embankments. Those lips had smiled over the first numbers of 'Pickwick,' and had gossiped of the promising young man who wrote them. The face itself was a seventy-year almanack, and every seam an entry upon it where public as well as private sorrow left its trace. That pucker on the forehead stood for the Mutiny, perhaps; that line of care for the Crimean winter, it may be; and that last little sheaf of wrinkles, as my fancy hoped, for the death of Gordon. And so, as I dreamed in my foolish way, the old gentleman with the shining stock was gone, and it was seventy years of a great nation's life that took shape before me on the headland in the morning.

But he soon brought me back to earth again. As he recovered his breath he took a letter out of his pocket, and, putting on a pair of horn-rimmed eye-glasses, he read it through very carefully. Without any design of playing the spy I could not help observing that it was in a woman's hand. When he had finished it he read it again, and then sat with the corners of his mouth drawn down and his eyes staring vacantly out over the bay, the most forlorn-looking old gentleman that ever I have seen. All that is kindly within me was set stirring by that wistful face, but I knew that he was in no humour for talk, and so, at last, with my breakfast and my patients calling me, I left him on the bench and started for home.

I never gave him another thought until the next morning, when, at the same hour, he turned up upon the headland, and shared the bench which I had been accustomed to look upon as my own. He bowed again before sitting down, but was no more inclined than formerly to enter into conversation. There had been a change in him during the last twenty-four hours, and all for the worse. The face seemed more heavy and more wrinkled, while that ominous venous tinge was more pronounced as he panted up the hill. The clean lines of his cheek and chin were marred by a day's growth of grey stubble, and his large, shapely head had lost something of the brave carriage which had struck me when first I glanced at him. He had a letter there, the same, or another, but still in a woman's hand, and over this he was moping and mumbling in his senile fashion, with his brow puckered, and the corners of his mouth drawn down like those of a fretting child. So I left him, with a vague wonder as to who he might be, and why a single spring day should have wrought such a change upon him.

So interested was I that next morning I was on the look out for him. Sure enough, at the same hour, I saw him coming up the hill; but very slowly, with a bent back and a heavy head. It was shocking to me to see the change in him as he approached.

'I am afraid that our air does not agree with you, sir,' I ventured to remark.

But it was as though he had no heart for talk. He tried, as I thought, to make some fitting reply, but it slurred off into a mumble and silence. How bent and weak and old he seemed—ten years older at the least than when first I had seen him! It went to my heart to see this fine old fellow wasting away before my eyes. There was the eternal letter which he unfolded with his shaking fingers. Who was this woman whose words moved him so? Some daughter, perhaps, or grand-daughter, who should have been the light of his home instead of— I smiled to find how bitter I was growing, and how swiftly I was weaving a romance round an unshaven old man and his correspondence. Yet all day he lingered in my mind, and I had fitful glimpses of those two trembling, blue-veined, knuckly hands with the paper rustling between them.

I had hardly hoped to see him again. Another day's decline must, I thought, hold him to his room, if not to his bed. Great, then, was my surprise when, as I approached my bench, I saw that he was already there. But as I came up to him I could scarce be sure that it was indeed the same man. There were the curly-brimmed hat, and the shining stock, and the horn glasses, but where were the stoop and the grey-stubbled, pitiable face? He was clean-shaven and firm lipped, with a bright eye and a head that poised itself upon his great shoulders like an eagle on a rock. His back was as straight and square as a grena-dier's, and he switched at the pebbles with his stick in his exuberant vitality. In the button-hole of his well-brushed black coat there glinted a golden blossom, and the corner of a dainty red silk handkerchief lapped over from his breast pocket. He might have been the eldest son of the weary creature who had sat there the morning before.

'Good morning, sir, good morning!' he cried with a merry waggle of his cane.

'Good morning!' I answered; 'how beautiful the bay is looking.'

'Yes, sir, but you should have seen it just before the sun rose.'

'What, have you been here since then?'

'I was here when there was scarce light to see the path.'

'You are a very early riser.'

'On occasion, sir; on occasion!' He cocked his eye at me as if to gauge whether I were worthy of his confidence. 'The fact is, sir, that my wife is coming back to me to-day.'

I suppose that my face showed that I did not quite see the force of the explanation. My eyes, too, may have given him assurance of sympathy, for he moved quite close to me and began speaking in a low, confidential voice, as if the matter were of such weight that even the sea-gulls must be kept out of our councils.

'Are you a married man, sir?'

'No, I am not.'

'Ah, then you cannot quite understand it. My wife and I have been married for nearly fifty years, and we have never been parted, never at all, until now.'

'Was it for long?' I asked.

'Yes, sir. This is the fourth day. She had to go to Scotland. A mat-ter of duty, you understand, and the doctors would not let me go. Not that I would have allowed them to stop me, but she was on their side. Now, thank God! it is over, and she may be here at any moment.'

'Here!'

'Yes, here. This headland and bench were old friends of ours thirty years ago. The people with whom we stay are not, to tell the truth, very congenial, and we have little privacy among them. That is why we prefer to meet here. I could not be sure which train would bring her, but if she had come by the very earliest she would have found me waiting.'

'In that case—' said I, rising.

'No, sir, no,' he entreated, 'I beg that you will stay. It does not weary you, this domestic talk of mine?'

'On the contrary.'

'I have been so driven inwards during these few last days! Ah, what a nightmare it has been! Perhaps it may seem strange to you that an old fellow like me should feel like this.'

'It is charming.'

'No credit to me, sir! There's not a man on this planet but would feel the same if he had the good fortune to be married to such a woman. Perhaps, because you see me like this, and hear me speak of our long life together, you conceive that she is old, too.'

He laughed heartily, and his eyes twinkled at the humour of the idea.

'She's one of those women, you know, who have youth in their hearts, and so it can never be very far from their faces. To me she's just as she was when she first took my hand in hers in '45. A wee little bit stouter, perhaps, but then, if she had a fault as a girl, it was that she was a shade too slender. She was above me in station, you know—I a clerk, and she the daughter of my employer. Oh! it was quite a romance, I give you my word, and I won her; and, somehow, I have never got over the freshness and the wonder of it. To think that that sweet, lovely girl has walked by my side all through life, and that I have been able—'

He stopped suddenly, and I glanced round at him in surprise. He was shaking all over, in every fibre of his great body. His hands were clawing at the woodwork, and his feet shuffling on the gravel. I saw what it was. He was trying to rise, but was so excited that he could not. I half extended my hand, but a higher courtesy constrained me to draw it back again and turn my face to the sea. An instant afterwards he was up and hurrying down the path.

A woman was coming towards us. She was quite close before he had seen her—thirty yards at the utmost. I know not if she had ever been as he described her, or whether it was but some ideal which he carried in his brain. The person upon whom I looked was tall, it is true, but she was thick and shapeless, with a ruddy, full-blown face, and a skirt grotesquely gathered up. There was a green ribbon in her hat, which jarred upon my eyes, and her blouse-like bodice was full and clumsy. And this was the lovely girl, the ever youthful! My heart sank as I thought how little such a woman might appreciate him, how unworthy she might be of his love.

She came up the path in her solid way, while he staggered along to meet her. Then, as they came together, looking discreetly out of the furthest corner of my eye, I saw that he put out both his hands, while she, shrinking from a public caress, took one of them in hers and shook it. As she did so I saw her face, and I was easy in my mind for my old man. God grant that when this hand is shaking, and when this back is bowed, a woman's eyes may look so into mine.

A PHYSIOLOGIST'S WIFE

PROFESSOR AINSLIE GREY had not come down to breakfast at the usual hour. The presentation chiming-clock which stood between the terracotta busts of Claude Bernard and of John Hunter upon the dining-room mantelpiece had rung out the half-hour and the three-quarters. Now its golden hand was verging upon the nine, and yet there were no signs of the master of the house.[1]

It was an unprecedented occurrence. During the twelve years that she had kept house for him, his youngest sister had never known him a second behind his time. She sat now in front of the high silver coffee-pot, uncertain whether to order the gong to be resounded or to wait on in silence. Either course might be a mistake. Her brother was not a man who permitted mistakes.

Miss Ainslie Grey was rather above the middle height, thin, with peering, puckered eyes, and the rounded shoulders which mark the bookish woman. Her face was long and spare, flecked with colour above the cheek-bones, with a reasonable, thoughtful forehead, and a dash of absolute obstinacy in her thin lips and prominent chin. Snow-white cuffs and collar, with a plain dark dress, cut with almost quaker-like simplicity, bespoke the primness of her taste. An ebony cross hung over her flattened chest. She sat very upright in her chair, listening with raised eyebrows, and swinging her eye-glasses backwards and forwards with a nervous gesture which was peculiar to her.

Suddenly she gave a sharp, satisfied jerk of the head, and began to pour out the coffee. From outside there came the dull thudding sound of heavy feet upon thick carpet. The door swung open, and the Professor entered with a quick, nervous step. He nodded to his sister, and seating himself at the other side of the table, began to open the small pile of letters which lay beside his plate.

Professor Ainslie Grey was at that time forty-three years of age—nearly twelve years older than his sister. His career had been a brilliant one. At Edinburgh, at Cambridge, and at Vienna he had laid the foundations of his great reputation, both in physiology and in zoology.

His pamphlet, 'On the Mesoblastic Origin of Excitomotor Nerve Roots,' had won him his fellowship of the Royal Society; and his researches, 'Upon the Nature of Bathybius,[2] with some Remarks upon Lithococci,' had been translated into at least three European languages. He had been referred to by one of the greatest living authorities as being the very type and embodiment of all that was best in modern science. No wonder, then, that when the commercial city of Birchespool decided to create a medical school, they were only too glad to confer the chair of physiology upon Mr Ainslie Grey. They valued him the more from the conviction that their class was only one step in his upward journey, and that the first vacancy would remove him to some more illustrious seat of learning.

In person he was not unlike his sister. The same eyes, the same contour, the same intellectual forehead. His lips, however, were firmer, and his long, thin, lower jaw was sharper and more decided. He ran his finger and thumb down it from time to time, as he glanced over his letters.

'Those maids are very noisy,' he remarked, as a clack of tongues sounded in the distance.

'It is Sarah,' said his sister; 'I shall speak about it.'

She had handed over his coffee-cup, and was sipping at her own, glancing furtively through her narrowed lids at the austere face of her brother.

'The first great advance of the human race,' said the Professor, 'was when, by the development of their left frontal convolutions, they attained the power of speech. Their second advance was when they learned to control that power. Woman has not yet attained the second stage.'

He half closed his eyes as he spoke, and thrust his chin forward, but as he ceased he had a trick of suddenly opening both eyes very wide and staring sternly at his interlocutor.

'I am not garrulous, John,' said his sister.

'No, Ada; in many respects you approach the superior or male type.'

The Professor bowed over his egg with the manner of one who utters a courtly compliment; but the lady pouted, and gave an impatient little shrug of her shoulders.

'You were late this morning, John,' she remarked, after a pause.

'Yes, Ada; I slept badly. Some little cerebral congestion, no doubt due to over-stimulation of the centres of thought. I have been a little disturbed in my mind.'

His sister stared across at him in astonishment. The Professor's mental processes had hitherto been as regular as his habits. Twelve years' continual intercourse had taught her that he lived in a serene and rarefied atmosphere of scientific calm, high above the petty emotions which affect humbler minds.

'You are surprised, Ada,' he remarked. 'Well, I cannot wonder at it. I should have been surprised myself if I had been told that I was so sensitive to vascular influences. For, after all, all disturbances are vascular if you probe them deep enough. I am thinking of getting married.'

'Not Mrs O'James?' cried Ada Grey, laying down her egg-spoon.

'My dear, you have the feminine quality of receptivity very remarkably developed. Mrs O'James is the lady in question.'

'But you know so little of her. The Esdailes themselves know so little. She is really only an acquaintance, although she is staying at The Lindens. Would it not be wise to speak to Mrs Esdaile first, John?'

'I do not think, Ada, that Mrs Esdaile is at all likely to say anything which would materially affect my course of action. I have given the matter due consideration. The scientific mind is slow at arriving at conclusions, but having once formed them, it is not prone to change. Matrimony is the natural condition of the human race. I have, as you know, been so engaged in academical and other work, that I have had no time to devote to merely personal questions. It is different now, and I see no valid reason why I should forego this opportunity of seeking a suitable helpmate.'

'And you are engaged?'

'Hardly that, Ada. I ventured yesterday to indicate to the lady that I was prepared to submit to the common lot of humanity. I shall wait upon her after my morning lecture, and learn how far my proposals meet with her acquiescence. But you frown, Ada!'

His sister started, and made an effort to conceal her expression of annoyance. She even stammered out some few words of congratulation, but a vacant look had come into her brother's eyes, and he was evidently not listening to her.

'I am sure, John,' she said, 'that I wish you the happiness which you deserve. If I hesitated at all, it is because I know how much is at stake, and because the thing is so sudden, so unexpected.' Her thin white hand stole up to the black cross upon her bosom. 'These are moments when we need guidance, John. If I could persuade you to turn to spiritual—'

The Professor waved the suggestion away with a deprecating hand.

'It is useless to reopen that question,' he said. 'We cannot argue upon it. You assume more than I can grant. I am forced to dispute your premises. We have no common basis.'

His sister sighed.

'You have no faith,' she said.

'I have faith in those great evolutionary forces which are leading the human race to some unknown but elevated goal.'

'You believe in nothing.'

'On the contrary, my dear Ada, I believe in the differentiation of protoplasm.'

She shook her head sadly. It was the one subject upon which she ventured to dispute her brother's infallibility.

'This is rather beside the question,' remarked the Professor, folding up his napkin. 'If I am not mistaken, there is some possibility of another matrimonial event occurring in the family. Eh, Ada? What!'

His small eyes glittered with sly facetiousness as he shot a twinkle at his sister. She sat very stiff, and traced patterns upon the cloth with the sugar-tongs.

'Dr James M'Murdo O'Brien—' said the Professor, sonorously.

'Don't, John, don't!' cried Miss Ainslie Grey.

'Dr James M'Murdo O'Brien,' continued her brother inexorably, 'is a man who has already made his mark upon the science of the day. He is my first and my most distinguished pupil. I assure you, Ada, that his "Remarks upon the Bile-Pigments, with special reference to Uro-bilin," is likely to live as a classic. It is not too much to say that he has revolutionised our views about urobilin.'

He paused, but his sister sat silent, with bent head and flushed cheeks. The little ebony cross rose and fell with her hurried breathings.

'Dr James M'Murdo O'Brien has, as you know, the offer of the physiological chair at Melbourne. He has been in Australia five years, and has a brilliant future before him. To-day he leaves us for Edinburgh, and in two months' time, he goes out to take over his new duties. You know his feeling towards you. It rests with you as to whether he goes out alone. Speaking for myself, I cannot imagine any higher mission for a woman of culture than to go through life in the company of a man who is capable of such a research as that which Dr James M'Murdo O'Brien has brought to a successful conclusion.'

'He has not spoken to me,' murmured the lady.

'Ah, there are signs which are more subtle than speech,' said her brother, wagging his head. 'But you are pale. Your vasomotor system is excited. Your arterioles have contracted. Let me entreat you to compose yourself. I think I hear the carriage. I fancy that you may have a visitor this morning, Ada. You will excuse me now.'

With a quick glance at the clock he strode off into the hall, and within a few minutes he was rattling in his quiet, well-appointed brougham through the brick-lined streets of Birchespool.

His lecture over, Professor Ainslie Grey paid a visit to his laboratory, where he adjusted several scientific instruments, made a note as to the progress of three separate infusions of bacteria, cut half-a-dozen sections with a microtome, and finally resolved the difficulties of seven different gentlemen, who were pursuing researches in as many separate lines of inquiry. Having thus conscientiously and methodically completed the routine of his duties, he returned to his carriage and ordered the coachman to drive him to The Lindens. His face as he drove was cold and impassive, but he drew his fingers from time to time down his prominent chin with a jerky, twitchy movement.

The Lindens was an old-fashioned, ivy-clad house which had once been in the country, but was now caught in the long, red-brick feelers of the growing city. It still stood back from the road in the privacy of its own grounds. A winding path, lined with laurel bushes, led to the arched and porticoed entrance. To the right was a lawn, and at the far side, under the shadow of a hawthorn, a lady sat in a garden-chair with a book in her hands. At the click of the gate she started, and the Professor, catching sight of her, turned away from the door, and strode in her direction.

'What! won't you go in and see Mrs Esdaile?' she asked, sweeping out from under the shadow of the hawthorn.

She was a small woman, strongly feminine, from the rich coils of her light-coloured hair to the dainty garden slipper which peeped from under her cream-tinted dress. One tiny well-gloved hand was outstretched in greeting, while the other pressed a thick, green-covered volume against her side. Her decision and quick, tactful manner bespoke the mature woman of the world; but her upraised face had preserved a girlish and even infantile expression of innocence in its large, fearless, grey eyes, and sensitive, humorous mouth. Mrs O'James was a widow, and she was two-and-thirty years of age; but neither fact could have been deduced from her appearance.

'You will surely go in and see Mrs Esdaile,' she repeated, glancing up at him with eyes which had in them something between a challenge and a caress.

'I did not come to see Mrs Esdaile,' he answered, with no relaxation of his cold and grave manner; 'I came to see you.'

'I am sure I should be highly honoured,' she said, with just the slightest little touch of brogue in her accent. 'What are the students to do without their Professor?'

'I have already completed my academic duties. Take my arm, and we shall walk in the sunshine. Surely we cannot wonder that Eastern people should have made a deity of the sun. It is the great beneficent force of Nature—man's ally against cold, sterility, and all that is abhorrent to him. What were you reading?'

'Hale's *Matter and Life*.'

The Professor raised his thick eyebrows.

'Hale!' he said, and then again in a kind of whisper, 'Hale!'

'You differ from him?' she asked.

'It is not I who differ from him. I am only a monad—a thing of no moment. The whole tendency of the highest plane of modern thought differs from him. He defends the indefensible. He is an excellent observer, but a feeble reasoner. I should not recommend you to found your conclusions upon "Hale."'

'I must read *Nature's Chronicle* to counteract his pernicious influence,' said Mrs O'James, with a soft, cooing laugh.

Nature's Chronicle was one of the many books in which Professor

Ainslie Grey had enforced the negative doctrines of scientific agnosticism.

'It is a faulty work,' said he; 'I cannot recommend it. I would rather refer you to the standard writings of some of my older and more eloquent colleagues.'

There was a pause in their talk as they paced up and down on the green, velvet-like lawn in the genial sunshine.

'Have you thought at all,' he asked at last, 'of the matter upon which I spoke to you last night?'

She said nothing, but walked by his side with her eyes averted and her face aslant.

'I would not hurry you unduly,' he continued. 'I know that it is a matter which can scarcely be decided off-hand. In my own case, it cost me some thought before I ventured to make the suggestion. I am not an emotional man, but I am conscious in your presence of the great evolutionary instinct which makes either sex the complement of the other.'

'You believe in love, then?' she asked, with a twinkling, upward glance.

'I am forced to.'

'And yet you can deny the soul?'

'How far these questions are psychic and how far material is still *sub judice*,' said the Professor, with an air of toleration. 'Protoplasm may prove to be the physical basis of love as well as of life.'

'How inflexible you are!' she exclaimed; 'you would draw love down to the level of physics.'

'Or draw physics up to the level of love.'

'Come, that is much better,' she cried, with her sympathetic laugh. 'That is really very pretty, and puts science in quite a delightful light.'

Her eyes sparkled, and she tossed her chin with the pretty, wilful air of a woman who is mistress of the situation.

'I have reason to believe,' said the Professor, 'that my position here will prove to be only a stepping-stone to some wider scene of scientific activity. Yet, even here, my chair brings me in some fifteen hundred pounds a year, which is supplemented by a few hundreds from my books. I should therefore be in a position to provide you with those comforts to which you are accustomed. So much for my pecuniary position. As to my constitution, it has always been sound. I have never suffered from any illness in my life, save fleeting attacks of cephalalgia, the result of too prolonged a stimulation of the centres of cerebration. My father and mother had no sign of any morbid diathesis, but I will not conceal from you that my grandfather was afflicted with podagra.'

Mrs O'James looked startled.

'Is that very serious?' she asked.

'It is gout,' said the Professor.

'Oh, is that all? It sounded much worse than that.'

'It is a grave taint, but I trust that I shall not be a victim to atavism. I have laid these facts before you because they are factors which cannot be overlooked in forming your decision. May I ask now whether you see your way to accepting my proposal?'

He paused in his walk, and looked earnestly and expectantly down at her.

A struggle was evidently going on in her mind. Her eyes were cast down, her little slipper tapped the lawn, and her fingers played nervously with her chatelain. Suddenly, with a sharp, quick gesture which had in it something of *abandon* and recklessness, she held out her hand to her companion.

'I accept,' she said.

They were standing under the shadow of the hawthorn. He stooped gravely down, and kissed her glove-covered fingers.

'I trust that you may never have cause to regret your decision,' he said.

'I trust that *you* never may,' she cried, with a heaving breast.

There were tears in her eyes, and her lips twitched with some strong emotion.

'Come into the sunshine again,' said he. 'It is the great restorative. Your nerves are shaken. Some little congestion of the medulla and pons. It is always instructive to reduce psychic or emotional conditions to their physical equivalents. You feel that your anchor is still firm in a bottom of ascertained fact.'

'But it is so dreadfully unromantic,' said Mrs O'James, with her old twinkle.

'Romance is the offspring of imagination and of ignorance. Where science throws her calm, clear light there is happily no room for romance.'

'But is not love romance?' she asked.

'Not at all. Love has been taken away from the poets, and has been brought within the domain of true science. It may prove to be one of the great cosmic elementary forces. When the atom of hydrogen draws the atom of chlorine towards it to form the perfected molecule of hydrochloric acid, the force which it exerts may be intrinsically similar to that which draws me to you. Attraction and repulsion appear to be the primary forces. This is attraction.'

'And here is repulsion,' said Mrs O'James, as a stout, florid lady came sweeping across the lawn in their direction. 'So glad you have come out, Mrs Esdaile! Here is Professor Grey.'

'How do you do, Professor?' said the lady, with some little pomposity of manner. 'You were very wise to stay out here on so lovely a day. Is it not heavenly?'

'It is certainly very fine weather,' the Professor answered.

'Listen to the wind sighing in the trees!' cried Mrs Esdaile, holding up one finger. 'It is Nature's lullaby. Could you not imagine it, Professor Grey, to be the whisperings of angels?'

'The idea had not occurred to me, madam.'

'Ah, Professor, I have always the same complaint against you. A want of *rapport* with the deeper meanings of nature. Shall I say a want of imagination. You do not feel an emotional thrill at the singing of that thrush?'

'I confess that I am not conscious of one, Mrs Esdaile.'

'Or at the delicate tint of that background of leaves? See the rich greens!'

'Chlorophyll,' murmured the Professor.

'Science is so hopelessly prosaic. It dissects and labels, and loses sight of the great things in its attention to the little ones. You have a poor opinion of woman's intellect, Professor Grey. I think that I have heard you say so.'

'It is a question of avoirdupois,' said the Professor, closing his eyes and shrugging his shoulders. 'The female cerebrum averages two ounces less in weight than the male. No doubt there are exceptions. Nature is always elastic.'

'But the heaviest thing is not always the strongest,' said Mrs O'James, laughing. 'Isn't there a law of compensation in science? May we not hope to make up in quality for what we lack in quantity?'

'I think not,' remarked the Professor, gravely. 'But there is your luncheon-gong. No, thank you, Mrs Esdaile, I cannot stay. My carriage is waiting. Good-bye. Good-bye, Mrs O'James.'

He raised his hat and stalked slowly away among the laurel bushes.

'He has no taste,' said Mrs Esdaile—'no eye for beauty.'

'On the contrary,' Mrs O'James answered, with a saucy little jerk of the chin. 'He has just asked me to be his wife.'

As Professor Ainslie Grey ascended the steps of his house, the hall-door opened and a dapper gentleman stepped briskly out. He was somewhat sallow in the face, with dark, beady eyes, and a short, black beard with an aggressive bristle. Thought and work had left their traces upon his face, but he moved with the brisk activity of a man who had not yet bade good-bye to his youth.

'I'm in luck's way,' he cried. 'I wanted to see you.'

'Then come back into the library,' said the Professor; 'you must stay and have lunch with us.'

The two men entered the hall, and the Professor led the way into his private sanctum. He motioned his companion into an arm-chair.

'I trust that you have been successful, O'Brien,' said he. 'I should be loath to exercise any undue pressure upon my sister Ada; but I have given her to understand that there is no one whom I should prefer for a brother-in-law to my most brilliant scholar, the author of "Some Remarks upon the Bile-Pigments, with special reference to Urobilin."'

'You are very kind, Professor Grey—you have always been very kind,' said the other. 'I approached Miss Grey upon the subject; she did not say No.'

'She said Yes, then?'

'No; she proposed to leave the matter open until my return from Edinburgh. I go to-day, as you know, and I hope to commence my research to-morrow.'

'On the comparative anatomy of the vermiform appendix, by

James M'Murdo O'Brien,' said the Professor, sonorously. 'It is a glorious subject—a subject which lies at the very root of evolutionary philosophy.'

'Ah! she is the dearest girl,' cried O'Brien, with a sudden little spurt of Celtic enthusiasm—'she is the soul of truth and of honour.'

'The vermiform appendix—' began the Professor.

'She is an angel from heaven,' interrupted the other. 'I fear that it is my advocacy of scientific freedom in religious thought which stands in my way with her.'

'You must not truckle upon that point. You must be true to your convictions; let there be no compromise there.'

'My reason is true to agnosticism, and yet I am conscious of a void—a vacuum. I had feelings at the old church at home between the scent of the incense and the roll of the organ, such as I have never experienced in the laboratory or the lecture-room.'

'Sensuous—purely sensuous,' said the Professor, rubbing his chin. 'Vague hereditary tendencies stirred into life by the stimulation of the nasal and auditory nerves.'

'Maybe so, maybe so,' the younger man answered thoughtfully. 'But this was not what I wished to speak to you about. Before I enter your family, your sister and you have a claim to know all that I can tell you about my career. Of my worldly prospects I have already spoken to you. There is only one point which I have omitted to mention. I am a widower.'

The Professor raised his eyebrows.

'This is news indeed,' said he.

'I married shortly after my arrival in Australia. Miss Thurston was her name. I met her in society. It was a most unhappy match.'

Some painful emotion possessed him. His quick, expressive features quivered, and his white hands tightened upon the arms of the chair. The Professor turned away towards the window.

'You are the best judge,' he remarked; 'but I should not think that it was necessary to go into details.'

'You have a right to know everything—you and Miss Grey. It is not a matter on which I can well speak to her direct. Poor Jinny was the best of women, but she was open to flattery, and liable to be misled by designing persons. She was untrue to me, Grey. It is a hard thing to say of the dead, but she was untrue to me. She fled to Auckland with a man whom she had known before her marriage. The brig which carried them foundered, and not a soul was saved.'

'This is very painful, O'Brien,' said the Professor, with a deprecatory motion of his hand. 'I cannot see, however, how it affects your relation to my sister.'

'I have eased my conscience,' said O'Brien, rising from his chair; 'I have told you all that there is to tell. I should not like the story to reach you through any lips but my own.'

'You are right, O'Brien. Your action has been most honourable and considerate. But you are not to blame in the matter, save that perhaps you showed a little precipitancy in choosing a life-partner without due care and inquiry.'

O'Brien drew his hand across his eyes.

'Poor girl!' he cried. 'God help me, I love her still! But I must go.'

'You will lunch with us?'

'No, Professor; I have my packing still to do. I have already bade Miss Grey adieu. In two months I shall see you again.'

'You will probably find me a married man.'

'Married!'

'Yes, I have been thinking of it.'

'My dear Professor, let me congratulate you with all my heart. I had no idea. Who is the lady?'

'Mrs O'James is her name—a widow of the same nationality as yourself. But to return to matters of importance, I should be very happy to see the proofs of your paper upon the vermiform appendix. I may be able to furnish you with material for a footnote or two.'

'Your assistance will be invaluable to me,' said O'Brien, with enthusiasm, and the two men parted in the hall. The Professor walked back into the dining-room, where his sister was already seated at the luncheon-table.

'I shall be married at the registrar's,' he remarked; 'I should strongly recommend you to do the same.'

Professor Ainslie Grey was as good as his word. A fortnight's cessation of his classes gave him an opportunity which was too good to let pass. Mrs O'James was an orphan, without relations and almost without friends in the country. There was no obstacle in the way of a speedy wedding. They were married, accordingly, in the quietest manner possible, and went off to Cambridge together, where the Professor and his charming wife were present at several academic observances, and varied the routine of their honeymoon by incursions into biological laboratories and medical libraries. Scientific friends were loud in their congratulations, not only upon Mrs Grey's beauty, but upon the unusual quickness and intelligence which she displayed in discussing physiological questions. The Professor was himself astonished at the accuracy of her information. 'You have a remarkable range of knowledge for a woman, Jeannette,' he remarked upon more than one occasion. He was even prepared to admit that her cerebrum might be of the normal weight.

One foggy, drizzling morning they returned to Birchespool, for the next day would re-open the session, and Professor Ainslie Grey prided himself upon having never once in his life failed to appear in his lecture-room at the very stroke of the hour. Miss Ada Grey welcomed them with a constrained cordiality, and handed over the keys of office to the new mistress. Mrs Grey pressed her warmly to remain, but she explained that she had already accepted an invitation which would engage her for some months. The same evening she departed for the south of England.

A couple of days later the maid carried a card just after breakfast into the library where the Professor sat revising his morning lecture. It announced the re-arrival of Dr James M'Murdo O'Brien. Their meeting was effusively genial on the part of the younger man, and coldly precise on that of his former teacher.

'You see there have been changes,' said the Professor.

'So I heard. Miss Grey told me in her letters, and I read the notice in the *British Medical Journal*. So it's really married you are. How quickly and quietly you have managed it all!'

'I am constitutionally averse to anything in the nature of show or ceremony. My wife is a sensible woman—I may even go the length of saying that, for a woman, she is abnormally sensible. She quite agreed with me in the course which I have adopted.'

'And your research on Vallisneria?'

'This matrimonial incident has interrupted it, but I have resumed my classes, and we shall soon be quite in harness again.'

'I must see Miss Grey before I leave England. We have corresponded, and I think that all will be well. She must come out with me. I don't think I could go without her.'

The Professor shook his head.

'Your nature is not so weak as you pretend,' he said. 'Questions of this sort are, after all, quite subordinate to the great duties of life.'

O'Brien smiled.

'You would have me take out my Celtic soul and put in a Saxon one,' he said. 'Either my brain is too small or my heart is too big. But when may I call and pay my respects to Mrs Grey? Will she be at home this afternoon?'

'She is at home now. Come into the morning-room. She will be glad to make your acquaintance.'

They walked across the linoleum-paved hall. The Professor opened the door of the room, and walked in, followed by his friend. Mrs Grey was sitting in a basket-chair by the window, light and fairy-like in a loose-flowing, pink morning-gown. Seeing a visitor, she rose and swept towards them. The Professor heard a dull thud behind him. O'Brien had fallen back into a chair, with his hand pressed tight to his side.

'Jinny!' he gasped—'Jinny!'

Mrs Grey stopped dead in her advance, and stared at him with a face from which every expression had been struck out, save one of astonishment and horror. Then with a sharp intaking of the breath she reeled, and would have fallen had the Professor not thrown his long, nervous arm round her.

'Try this sofa,' said he.

She sank back among the cushions with the same white, cold, dead look upon her face. The Professor stood with his back to the empty fireplace and glanced from the one to the other.

'So, O'Brien,' he said at last, 'you have already made the acquaintance of my wife!'

'Your wife,' cried his friend hoarsely. 'She is no wife of yours. God help me, she is *my* wife.'

The Professor stood rigidly upon the hearth-rug. His long, thin fingers were intertwined, and his head sunk a little forward. His two companions had eyes only for each other.

'Jinny!' said he.

'James!'

'How could you leave me so, Jinny? How could you have the heart to do it? I thought you were dead. I mourned for your death—ay, and you have made me mourn for you living. You have withered my life.'

She made no answer, but lay back among her cushions with her eyes still fixed upon him.

'Why do you not speak?'

'Because you are right, James. I have treated you cruelly—shamefully. But it is not as bad as you think.'

'You fled with De Horta.'

'No, I did not. At the last moment my better nature prevailed. He went alone. But I was ashamed to come back after what I had written to you. I could not face you. I took passage alone to England under a new name, and here I have lived ever since. It seemed to me that I was beginning life again. I knew that you thought I was drowned. Who could have dreamed that fate would throw us together again! When the Professor asked me—'

She stopped and gave a gasp for breath.

'You are faint,' said the Professor,—'keep the head low; it aids the cerebral circulation.' He flattened down the cushion. 'I am sorry to leave you, O'Brien; but I have my class duties to look to. Possibly I may find you here when I return.'

With a grim and rigid face he strode out of the room. Not one of the three hundred students who listened to his lecture saw any change in his manner and appearance, or could have guessed that the austere gentleman in front of them had found out at last how hard it is to rise above one's humanity. The lecture over, he performed his routine duties in the laboratory, and then drove back to his own house. He did not enter by the front door, but passed through the garden to the folding glass casement which led out of the morning-room. As he approached he heard his wife's voice and O'Brien's in loud and animated talk. He paused among the rose-bushes, uncertain whether to interrupt them or no. Nothing was further from his nature than to play the eavesdropper; but as he stood, still hesitating, words fell upon his ear which struck him rigid and motionless.

'You are still my wife, Jinny,' said O'Brien; 'I forgive you from the bottom of my heart. I love you, and I have never ceased to love you, though you had forgotten me.'

'No, James, my heart was always in Melbourne. I have always been yours. I thought that it was better for you that I should seem to be dead.'

'You must choose between us now, Jinny. If you determine to remain here, I shall not open my lips. There shall be no scandal. If, on the other hand, you come with me, it's little I care about the world's opinion. Perhaps I am as much to blame as you. I thought too much of my work and too little of my wife.'

The Professor heard the cooing, caressing laugh which he knew so well.

'I shall go with you, James,' she said.

'And the Professor—?'

'The poor Professor! But he will not mind much, James; he has no heart.'

'We must tell him our resolution.'

'There is no need,' said Professor Ainslie Grey, stepping in through the open casement. 'I have overheard the latter part of your conversation. I hesitated to interrupt you before you came to a conclusion.'

O'Brien stretched out his hand and took that of the woman. They stood together with the sunshine on their faces. The Professor paused at the casement with his hands behind his back and his long black shadow fell between them.

'You have come to a wise decision,' said he. 'Go back to Australia together, and let what has passed be blotted out of your lives.'

'But you—you—' stammered O'Brien.

The Professor waved his hand.

'Never trouble about me,' he said.

The woman gave a gasping cry.

'What can I do or say?' she wailed. 'How could I have foreseen this? I thought my old life was dead. But it has come back again, with all its hopes and its desires. What can I say to you, Ainslie? I have brought shame and disgrace upon a worthy man. I have blasted your life. How you must hate and loathe me! I wish to God that I had never been born!'

'I neither hate nor loathe you, Jeannette,' said the Professor, quietly. 'You are wrong in regretting your birth, for you have a worthy mission before you in aiding the life-work of a man who has shown himself capable of the highest order of scientific research. I cannot with justice blame you personally for what has occurred. How far the individual monad is to be held responsible for hereditary and engrained tendencies, is a question upon which science has not yet said her last word.'

He stood with his fingers'-tips touching, and his body inclined as one who is gravely expounding a difficult and impersonal subject. O'Brien had stepped forward to say something, but the other's attitude and manner froze the words upon his lips. Condolence or sympathy would be an impertinence to one who could so easily merge his private griefs in broad questions of abstract philosophy.

'It is needless to prolong the situation,' the Professor continued, in the same measured tones. 'My brougham stands at the door. I beg that you will use it as your own. Perhaps it would be as well that you should leave the town without unnecessary delay. Your things, Jeannette, shall be forwarded.'

O'Brien hesitated with a hanging head.

'I hardly dare offer you my hand,' he said.

'On the contrary. I think that of the three of us you come best out of the affair. You have nothing to be ashamed of.'

'Your sister—'

'I shall see that the matter is put to her in its true light. Good-bye! Let me have a copy of your recent research. Good-bye, Jeannette!'

'Good-bye!'

Their hands met, and for one short moment their eyes also. It was only a glance, but for the first and last time the woman's intuition cast a light for itself into the dark places of a strong man's soul. She gave a little gasp, and her other hand rested for an instant, as white and as light as thistle-down, upon his shoulder.

'James, James!' she cried. 'Don't you see that he is stricken to the heart?'

He turned her quietly away from him.

'I am not an emotional man,' he said. 'I have my duties—my research on Vallisneria. The brougham is there. Your cloak is in the hall.

Tell John where you wish to be driven. He will bring you anything you need. Now go.'

His last two words were so sudden, so volcanic, in such contrast to his measured voice and mask-like face, that they swept the two away from him. He closed the door behind them and paced slowly up and down the room. Then he passed into the library and looked out over the wire blind. The carriage was rolling away. He caught a last glimpse of the woman who had been his wife. He saw the feminine droop of her head, and the curve of her beautiful throat.

Under some foolish, aimless impulse, he took a few quick steps towards the door. Then he turned, and, throwing himself into his study-chair he plunged back into his work.

There was little scandal about this singular domestic incident. The Professor had few personal friends, and seldom went into society. His marriage had been so quiet that most of his colleagues had never ceased to regard him as a bachelor. Mrs Esdaile and a few others might talk, but their field for gossip was limited, for they could only guess vaguely at the cause of this sudden separation.

The Professor was as punctual as ever at his classes, and as zealous in directing the laboratory work of those who studied under him. His own private researches were pushed on with feverish energy. It was no uncommon thing for his servants, when they came down of a morning, to hear the shrill scratchings of his tireless pen, or to meet him on the staircase as he ascended, grey and silent, to his room. In vain his friends assured him that such a life must undermine his health. He lengthened his hours until day and night were one long, ceaseless task.

Gradually under this discipline a change came over his appearance. His features, always inclined to gauntness, became even sharper and more pronounced. There were deep lines about his temples and across his brow. His cheek was sunken and his complexion bloodless. His knees gave under him when he walked; and once when passing out of his lecture-room he fell and had to be assisted to his carriage.

This was just before the end of the session; and soon after the holidays commenced, the professors who still remained in Birchespool were shocked to hear that their brother of the chair of physiology had sunk so low that no hopes could be entertained of his recovery. Two eminent physicians had consulted over his case without being able to give a name to the affection from which he suffered. A steadily decreasing vitality appeared to be the only symptom—a bodily weakness which left the mind unclouded. He was much interested himself in his own case, and made notes of his subjective sensations as an aid to diagnosis. Of his approaching end he spoke in his usual unemotional and somewhat pedantic fashion. 'It is the assertion,' he said, 'of the liberty of the individual cell as opposed to the cell-commune. It is the dissolution of a co-operative society. The process is one of great interest.'

And so one grey morning his co-operative society dissolved. Very quietly and softly he sank into his eternal sleep. His two physicians felt some slight embarrassment when called upon to fill in his certificate.

'It is difficult to give it a name,' said one.

'Very,' said the other.

'If he were not such an unemotional man, I should have said that he had died from some sudden nervous shock—from, in fact, what the vulgar would call a broken heart.'

'I don't think poor Grey was that sort of a man at all.'

'Let us call it cardiac, anyhow,' said the older physician.

So they did so.

NOTES TO 'A PHYSIOLOGIST'S WIFE'

First published in *Blackwood's Magazine*, September 1890.

1. Conan Doyle commented that this story was written under the influence of Henry James, but it seems more useful to see it as an expression of his rejection of the Darwin-Huxley-Spencer materialism that he had absorbed while a medical student. There is a suggestion that the professor may be a caricature of T. H. Huxley himself (and a very unfair one if it is, since he, along with Darwin, is known to have enjoyed a particularly happy and fulfilling marriage), but he really seems to have more in common with Sherlock Holmes. When he fails to notice the beauty of Miss Morstan, Watson exclaims: 'You really are an automaton—a calculating machine. There is something positively inhuman in you at times.' But Holmes replies with a smile:

> 'It is of the first importance not to allow your judgement to be biased by personal qualities. A client is to me a mere unit, a factor in a problem. The emotional qualities are antagonistic to clear reasoning. ... Love is an emotional thing, and whatever is emotional is opposed to that true, cold reason which I place above all things. I should never marry myself, lest I bias my judgement.' (*The Sign of Four*)

A better model for the heartless scientist would be the churchgoing paleontologist Richard Owen (1804-1892), whose 'lamentable coldness of heart' was probably a factor in his son's suicide. Even the genial Darwin, who strove to be friends with everybody, thought him a monster.[1]

2. Bathybius—A rather misleading reference to T. H. Huxley, who in 1868 had announced the discovery of a jelly-like substance in oceanic mud which he thought might be the 'primal slime' or protoplasm and the origin of life. He named it *Bathybius haeckelii* in honour of the German naturalist Ernst Haeckel, but seven years later it turned out

---

[1] See Bill Bryson, *A Short History of Nearly Everything* (London: Transworld, 2005), pp. 112-114.

to be nothing more than an inorganic precipitate formed when the mud was placed in alcohol.[1] The excitement of the find was well and truly over by the 1880s, suggesting that Conan Doyle was remembering the news from twenty or thirty years before the story was written (the period when he was interested in science), and thus that he had ceased to keep up to date with developments in biology. It is possible that the reference was prompted by a facetious article on the affair by the Duke of Argyll in *The Nineteenth Century* in 1887, to which Huxley replied that the clarification of 'Bathybius' was a good example of the self-correcting nature of scientific research.[2]

It may also be that Conan Doyle was offering a gesture of amends when he named the hero of a later fantasy adventure series Professor Challenger: *HMS Challenger* was the ship that carried the research party that demystified Bathybius in the course of its oceanographic survey in 1872-75.[3]

---

[1] For details, see Adrian Desmond, Huxley: *From Devil's Disciple to Evolution's High Priest* (Reading, Mass: Addison-Wesley, 1997), pp. 365 and 460.

[2] See Philip Rehbock, 'Huxley, Haeckel and the Oceanographers: The Case of *Bathybius haeckelii*', *Isis*, Vol. 66, 1975, pp. 504-533, and the essay by Stephen Jay Gould, 'Bathybius and Eozoon', in *The Panda's Thumb: More Reflections in Natural History* (Penguin 1980).

[3] For further details, see Samantha Weinberg, *A Fish Caught in Time: The Search for the Coelacanth* (London: Fourth Estate, 1999).

THE CASE OF LADY SANNOX

THE relations between Douglas Stone and the notorious Lady Sannox were very well known both among the fashionable circles of which she was a brilliant member, and the scientific bodies which numbered him among their most illustrious *confrères*. There was naturally, therefore, a very widespread interest when it was announced one morning that the lady had absolutely and for ever taken the veil, and that the world would see her no more. When, at the very tail of this rumour, there came the assurance that the celebrated operating surgeon, the man of steel nerves, had been found in the morning by his valet, seated on one side of his bed, smiling pleasantly upon the universe, with both legs jammed into one side of his breeches and his great brain about as valuable as a cap full of porridge, the matter was strong enough to give quite a little thrill of interest to folk who had never hoped that their jaded nerves were capable of such a sensation.

Douglas Stone in his prime was one of the most remarkable men in England. Indeed, he could hardly be said to have ever reached his prime, for he was but nine-and-thirty at the time of this little incident. Those who knew him best were aware that, famous as he was as a surgeon, he might have succeeded with even greater rapidity in any of a dozen lines of life. He could have cut his way to fame as a soldier, struggled to it as an explorer, bullied for it in the courts, or built it out of stone and iron as an engineer. He was born to be great, for he could plan what another man dare not do, and he could do what another man dare not plan. In surgery none could follow him. His nerve, his judgment, his intuition, were things apart. Again and again his knife cut away death, but grazed the very springs of life in doing it, until his assistants were as white as the patient. His energy, his audacity, his full-blooded self-confidence—does not the memory of them still linger to the south of Marylebone Road and the north of Oxford Street?

His vices were as magnificent as his virtues, and infinitely more picturesque. Large as was his income, and it was the third largest of all professional men in London, it was far beneath the luxury of his living. Deep in his complex nature lay a rich vein of sensualism, at the sport of which he placed all the prizes of his life. The eye, the ear, the touch, the palate, all were his masters. The bouquet of old vintages, the scent of rare exotics, the curves and tints of the daintiest potteries of Europe, it was to these that the quick-running stream of gold was transformed. And then there came his sudden mad passion for Lady Sannox, when a single interview with two challenging glances and a whispered word set him ablaze. She was the loveliest woman in London, and the only one to him. He was one of the handsomest men in London, but not the only one to her. She had a liking for new experiences, and was gracious to most men who wooed her. It may have been cause or it may have been effect that Lord Sannox looked fifty, though he was but six-and-thirty.

He was a quiet, silent, neutral-tinted man this lord, with thin lips and heavy eyelids, much given to gardening, and full of home-like habits. He had at one time been fond of acting, had even rented a theatre in London, and on its boards had first seen Miss Marion Dawson, to whom he had offered his hand, his title, and the third of a county. Since his marriage this early hobby had become distasteful to him. Even in private theatricals it was no longer possible to persuade him to exercise the talent which he had often shown that he possessed. He was happier with a spud and a watering-can among his orchids and chrysanthemums.

It was quite an interesting problem whether he was absolutely devoid of sense, or miserably wanting in spirit. Did he know his lady's ways and condone them, or was he a mere blind, doting fool? It was a point to be discussed over the teacups in snug little drawing-rooms, or with the aid of a cigar in the bow windows of clubs. Bitter and plain were the comments among men upon his conduct. There was but one who had a good word to say for him, and he was the most silent member in the smoking-room. He had seen him break in a horse at the University, and it seemed to have left an impression upon his mind.

But when Douglas Stone became the favourite all doubts as to Lord Sannox's knowledge or ignorance were set for ever at rest. There was no subterfuge about Stone. In his high-handed, impetuous fashion, he set all caution and discretion at defiance. The scandal became notorious. A learned body intimated that his name had been struck from the list of its vice-presidents. Two friends implored him to con-

sider his professional credit. He cursed them all three, and spent forty
guineas on a bangle to take with him to the lady. He was at her house
every evening, and she drove in his carriage in the afternoons. There
was not an attempt on either side to conceal their relations; but there
came at last a little incident to interrupt them.

It was a dismal winter's night, very cold and gusty, with the wind
whooping in the chimneys and blustering against the window-panes.
A thin spatter of rain tinkled on the glass with each fresh sough of the
gale, drowning for the instant the dull gurgle and drip from the eaves.
Douglas Stone had finished his dinner, and sat by his fire in the study,
a glass of rich port upon the malachite table at his elbow. As he raised
it to his lips, he held it up against the lamplight, and watched with the
eye of a connoisseur the tiny scales of beeswing which floated in its
rich ruby depths. The fire, as it spurted up, threw fitful lights upon
his bold, clear-cut face, with its widely-opened grey eyes, its thick and
yet firm lips, and the deep, square jaw, which had something Roman
in its strength and its animalism. He smiled from time to time as he
nestled back in his luxurious chair. Indeed, he had a right to feel well
pleased, for, against the advice of six colleagues, he had performed an
operation that day of which only two cases were on record, and the
result had been brilliant beyond all expectation. No other man in London would have had the daring to plan, or the skill to execute, such a
heroic measure.

But he had promised Lady Sannox to see her that evening and it
was already half-past eight. His hand was outstretched to the bell to
order the carriage when he heard the dull thud of the knocker. An
instant later there was the shuffling of feet in the hall, and the sharp
closing of a door.

'A patient to see you, sir, in the consulting-room,' said the butler.

'About himself?'

'No, sir; I think he wants you to go out.'

'It is too late,' cried Douglas Stone peevishly. 'I won't go.'

'This is his card, sir.'

The butler presented it upon the gold salver which had been given
to his master by the wife of a Prime Minister.

'"Hamil Ali, Smyrna." Hum! The fellow is a Turk, I suppose.'

'Yes, sir. He seems as if he came from abroad, sir. And he's in a terrible way.'

'Tut, tut! I have an engagement. I must go somewhere else. But I'll see him. Show him in here, Pim.'

A few moments later the butler swung open the door and ushered in a small and decrepit man, who walked with a bent back and with the forward push of the face and blink of the eyes which goes with extreme short sight. His face was swarthy, and his hair and beard of the deepest black. In one hand he held a turban of white muslin striped with red, in the other a small chamois leather bag.

'Good-evening,' said Douglas Stone, when the butler had closed the door. 'You speak English, I presume?'

'Yes, sir. I am from Asia Minor, but I speak English when I speak slow.'

'You wanted me to go out, I understand?'

'Yes, sir. I wanted very much that you should see my wife.'

'I could come in the morning, but I have an engagement which prevents me from seeing your wife to-night.'

The Turk's answer was a singular one. He pulled the string which closed the mouth of the chamois leather bag, and poured a flood of gold on to the table.

'There are one hundred pounds there,' said he, 'and I promise you that it will not take you an hour. I have a cab ready at the door.'

Douglas Stone glanced at his watch. An hour would not make it too late to visit Lady Sannox. He had been there later. And the fee was an extraordinarily high one. He had been pressed by his creditors lately, and he could not afford to let such a chance pass. He would go.

'What is the case?' he asked.

'Oh, it is so sad a one! So sad a one! You have not, perhaps, heard of the daggers of the Almohades?'

'Never.'

'Ah, they are Eastern daggers of a great age and of a singular shape, with the hilt like what you call a stirrup. I am a curiosity dealer, you understand, and that is why I have come to England from Smyrna, but next week I go back once more. Many things I brought with me, and I have a few things left, but among them, to my sorrow, is one of these daggers.'

'You will remember that I have an appointment, sir,' said the surgeon, with some irritation; 'pray confine yourself to the necessary details.'

'You will see that it is necessary. To-day my wife fell down in a faint in the room in which I keep my wares, and she cut her lower lip upon this cursed dagger of Almohades.'

'I see,' said Douglas Stone, rising. 'And you wish me to dress the wound?'

'No, no, it is worse than that.'

'What then?'

'These daggers are poisoned.'

'Poisoned!'

'Yes, and there is no man, East or West, who can tell now what is the poison or what the cure. But all that is known I know, for my father was in this trade before me, and we have had much to do with these poisoned weapons.'

'What are the symptoms?'

'Deep sleep, and death in thirty hours.'

'And you say there is no cure. Why then should you pay me this considerable fee?'

'No drug can cure, but the knife may.'

'And how?'

'The poison is slow of absorption. It remains for hours in the wound.'

'Washing, then, might cleanse it?'

'No more than in a snake-bite. It is too subtle and too deadly.'

'Excision of the wound, then?'

'That is it. If it be on the finger, take the finger off. So said my father always. But think of where this wound is, and that it is my wife. It is dreadful!'

But familiarity with such grim matters may take the finer edge from a man's sympathy. To Douglas Stone this was already an interesting case, and he brushed aside as irrelevant the feeble objections of the husband.

'It appears to be that or nothing,' said he brusquely. 'It is better to lose a lip than a life.'

'Ah, yes, I know that you are right. Well, well, it is kismet, and must be faced. I have the cab, and you will come with me and do this thing.'

Douglas Stone took his case of bistouries from a drawer, and placed it with a roll of bandage and a compress of lint in his pocket. He must waste no more time if he were to see Lady Sannox.

'I am ready,' said he, pulling on his overcoat. 'Will you take a glass of wine before you go out into this cold air?'

His visitor shrank away, with a protesting hand upraised.

'You forget that I am a Mussulman, and a true follower of the Prophet,' said he. 'But tell me what is the bottle of green glass which you have placed in your pocket?'

'It is chloroform.'

'Ah, that also is forbidden to us. It is a spirit, and we make no use of such things.'

'What! You would allow your wife to go through an operation without an anæsthetic?'

'Ah! she will feel nothing, poor soul. The deep sleep has already come on, which is the first working of the poison. And then I have given her of our Smyrna opium. Come, sir, for already an hour has passed.'

As they stepped out into the darkness, a sheet of rain was driven in upon their faces, and the hall lamp, which dangled from the arm of a marble Caryatid, went out with a fluff. Pim, the butler, pushed the heavy door to, straining hard with his shoulder against the wind, while the two men groped their way towards the yellow glare which showed where the cab was waiting. An instant later they were rattling upon their journey.

'Is it far?' asked Douglas Stone.

'Oh, no. We have a very little quiet place off the Euston Road.'

The surgeon pressed the spring of his repeater and listened to the little tings which told him the hour. It was a quarter past nine. He calculated the distances, and the short time which it would take him to perform so trivial an operation. He ought to reach Lady Sannox by ten o'clock. Through the fogged windows he saw the blurred gas lamps dancing past, with occasionally the broader glare of a shop front. The rain was pelting and rattling upon the leathern top of the carriage, and the wheels swashed as they rolled through puddle and mud. Opposite to him the white headgear of his companion gleamed faintly through the obscurity. The surgeon felt in his pockets and arranged his needles, his ligatures and his safety-pins, that no time might be wasted when they arrived. He chafed with impatience and drummed his foot upon the floor.

But the cab slowed down at last and pulled up. In an instant Douglas Stone was out, and the Smyrna merchant's toe was at his very heel.

'You can wait,' said he to the driver.

It was a mean-looking house in a narrow and sordid street. The surgeon, who knew his London well, cast a swift glance into the shadows, but there was nothing distinctive—no shop, no movement, nothing but a double line of dull, flat-faced houses, a double stretch of wet flagstones which gleamed in the lamplight, and a double rush of water in the gutters which swirled and gurgled towards the sewer gratings. The door which faced them was blotched and discoloured, and a faint light in the fan pane above it served to show the dust and the grime which covered it. Above, in one of the bedroom windows, there was a dull yellow glimmer. The merchant knocked loudly, and, as he turned his dark face towards the light, Douglas Stone could see that it was contracted with anxiety. A bolt was drawn, and an elderly woman with a taper stood in the doorway, shielding the thin flame with her gnarled hand.

'Is all well?' gasped the merchant.

'She is as you left her, sir.'

'She has not spoken?'

'No; she is in a deep sleep.'

The merchant closed the door, and Douglas Stone walked down the narrow passage, glancing about him in some surprise as he did so. There was no oilcloth, no mat, no hat-rack. Deep grey dust and heavy festoons of cobwebs met his eyes everywhere. Following the old woman up the winding stair, his firm footfall echoed harshly through the silent house. There was no carpet.

The bedroom was on the second landing. Douglas Stone followed the old nurse into it, with the merchant at his heels. Here, at least, there was furniture and to spare. The floor was littered and the corners piled with Turkish cabinets, inlaid tables, coats of chain mail, strange pipes, and grotesque weapons. A single small lamp stood upon a bracket on the wall. Douglas Stone took it down, and picking his way among the lumber, walked over to a couch in the corner, on which lay a woman dressed in the Turkish fashion, with yashmak and veil. The lower part of the face was exposed, and the surgeon saw a jagged cut which zigzagged along the border of the under lip.

'You will forgive the yashmak,' said the Turk. 'You know our views about woman in the East.'

But the surgeon was not thinking about the yashmak. This was no longer a woman to him. It was a case. He stooped and examined the wound carefully.

'There are no signs of irritation,' said he. 'We might delay the operation until local symptoms develop.'

The husband wrung his hands in incontrollable agitation.

'Oh! sir, sir,' he cried. 'Do not trifle. You do not know. It is deadly. I know, and I give you my assurance that an operation is absolutely necessary. Only the knife can save her.'

'And yet I am inclined to wait,' said Douglas Stone.

'That is enough!' the Turk cried, angrily. 'Every minute is of importance, and I cannot stand here and see my wife allowed to sink. It only remains for me to give you my thanks for having come, and to call in some other surgeon before it is too late.'

Douglas Stone hesitated. To refund that hundred pounds was no pleasant matter. But of course if he left the case he must return the money. And if the Turk were right and the woman died, his position before a coroner might be an embarrassing one.

'You have had personal experience of this poison?' he asked.

'I have.'

'And you assure me that an operation is needful.'

'I swear it by all that I hold sacred.'

'The disfigurement will be frightful.'

'I can understand that the mouth will not be a pretty one to kiss.'

Douglas Stone turned fiercely upon the man. The speech was a brutal one. But the Turk has his own fashion of talk and of thought, and there was no time for wrangling. Douglas Stone drew a bistoury from his case, opened it and felt the keen straight edge with his fore-finger. Then he held the lamp closer to the bed. Two dark eyes were gazing up at him through the slit in the yashmak. They were all iris, and the pupil was hardly to be seen.

'You have given her a very heavy dose of opium.'

'Yes, she has had a good dose.'

He glanced again at the dark eyes which looked straight at his own. They were dull and lustreless, but, even as he gazed, a little shift-ing sparkle came into them, and the lips quivered.

'She is not absolutely unconscious,' said he.

'Would it not be well to use the knife while it will be painless?'

The same thought had crossed the surgeon's mind. He grasped the wounded lip with his forceps, and with two swift cuts he took out a broad V-shaped piece. The woman sprang up on the couch with a dreadful gurgling scream. Her covering was torn from her face. It was a face that he knew. In spite of that protruding upper lip and that slobber of blood, it was a face that he knew. She kept on putting her hand up to the gap and screaming. Douglas Stone sat down at the foot of the couch with his knife and his forceps. The room was whirling round, and he had felt something go like a ripping seam behind his ear. A bystander would have said that his face was the more ghastly of the two. As in a dream, or as if he had been looking at something at the play, he was conscious that the Turk's hair and beard lay upon the table, and that Lord Sannox was leaning against the wall with his hand to his side, laughing silently. The screams had died away now, and the dreadful head had dropped back again upon the pillow, but Douglas Stone still sat motionless, and Lord Sannox still chuckled quietly to himself.

'It was really very necessary for Marion, this operation,' said he, 'not physically, but morally, you know, morally.'

Douglas Stone stooped forwards and began to play with the fringe of the coverlet. His knife tinkled down upon the ground, but he still held the forceps and something more.

'I had long intended to make a little example,' said Lord Sannox, suavely. 'Your note of Wednesday miscarried, and I have it here in my pocket-book. I took some pains in carrying out my idea. The wound, by the way, was from nothing more dangerous than my signet ring.'

He glanced keenly at his silent companion, and cocked the small revolver which he held in his coat pocket. But Douglas Stone was still picking at the coverlet.

'You see you have kept your appointment after all,' said Lord Sannox.

And at that Douglas Stone began to laugh. He laughed long and loudly. But Lord Sannox did not laugh now. Something like fear sharpened and hardened his features. He walked from the room, and he walked on tiptoe. The old woman was waiting outside.

'Attend to your mistress when she awakes,' said Lord Sannox.

Then he went down to the street. The cab was at the door, and the driver raised his hand to his hat.

'John,' said Lord Sannox, 'you will take the doctor home first. He will want leading downstairs, I think. Tell his butler that he has been taken ill at a case.'

'Very good, sir.'

'Then you can take Lady Sannox home.'

'And how about yourself, sir?'

'Oh, my address for the next few months will be Hotel di Roma, Venice. Just see that the letters are sent on. And tell Stevens to exhibit all the purple chrysanthemums next Monday, and to wire me the result.'

NOTES TO 'THE CASE OF LADY SANNOX'

BOTH this story and 'The Retirement of Signor Lambert' are remarkably daring and gruesome episodes which reflect the author's fascination with inflicted injury and possibly express his view that mutilations may be 'worse than death', as the speaker remarks in 'The Surgeon Talks', after recounting the incident in which an ear was amputated from the wrong person. Both stories are fairly transparent metaphors for genital mutilation, Lady Sannox suffering circumcision and Signor Lambert castration. His fate is just what you might expect an outraged and vindictive husband to want to do to his wife's paramour, but the fate of Lady Sannox is not interpreted so easily. You might, like Elaine Showalter, see the story, as a straightforward reference to female circumcision or clitoridectomy,[1] and this would be consistent with making the husband a mysterious figure from the East—not only allowing the woman to be veiled, thus concealing her identity and suppressing her individuality, but also alluding to the Middle Eastern practices of female genital mutilation that had recently been brought to the attention of the English public by travellers such as Richard Burton.

That is a possible interpretation, but as a doctor Conan Doyle would have known that female circumcision was not practised in England. Clitoridectomy had enjoyed a brief vogue in the early 1860s as a cure for various 'nervous complaints', but the procedure had been thoroughly discredited with the disgrace of its chief protagonist, Isaac Baker Brown, and his expulsion from the Obstetrical Society in 1867.[2] Circumcision of boys, however, was a different matter: by the early 1890s it was all the rage as the answer to the most feared diseases of the day, recommended by doctors as a sure-fire cure or preventive for all manner of medical and behavioural problems (from masturbation and bed wetting to epilepsy and hip-joint disease), and even touted as a life-long vaccination against syphilis and cancer. Leading members of the medical elite, such as Sir Jonathan Hutchinson, urged that the procedure be made compulsory for all boys, and predicted that

---

[1] Elaine Showalter, *Sexual Anarchy: Gender and Culture at the Fin de Siècle* (New York: Viking, 1990), p. 136.

[2] For a detailed account, see Robert Darby, *A Surgical Temptation*, chap. 7.

such a measure would bring the syphilis epidemic, then thought to be engulfing the nation, rapidly under control. To demonstrate Conan Doyle's relevance to the medical issues of today, I shall argue that the arguments used by the mysterious Turk to justify the excision of a woman's lip are remarkably similar to the arguments offered, then and now, for prophylactic circumcision of male infants and boys.

In the late Victorian period it was of course impossible to mention anything to do with the genitals outside specialist medical texts, but we need not be so crude as to see the story as the closest Conan Doyle could get to a description of female genital mutilation. Even so, it is a very explicit text: without her lip Lady Sannox will not be able to make love. In that Latin-literate age readers knew that the Latin for lips was *labia*, and some might well have known that the Renaissance anatomist Gabriele Falloppio used the word for the male foreskin as well as the external genitalia of the female. With most of the medical profession, teachers and purity campaigners zealously in favour, the 1890s were the decade during which the circumcision of boys really got going. As one enthusiast reported smugly in 1907, circumcision of infants was increasingly common in children's hospitals, though parents often had to be pressured or tricked into agreeing to it:

> Mothers often strongly object to have their baby boys circumcised, not only from dislike to subjecting them to a surgical operation … but also from a feeling of revulsion in subjecting them to a process which is regarded as a rite in other religious communities. My own experience in this matter has been that when the advantages of circumcision are explained to them, they yield.[1]

Whether Doyle's story was intended as a caustic comment on the increasingly common practice of circumcising young boys to discourage masturbation and guard against future disease, the parallels between Mr Stone's intervention and prophylactic male circumcision are disturbingly close. Is it likely that he would have been able to imagine a fictional doctor performing such an unspeakably cruel operation on a woman's lip unless he know that real doctors were actually carrying out similar procedures on the penises of little

---

[1] J. Bland-Sutton, 'Circumcision as a Rite and as a Surgical Operation', *British Medical Journal*, 15 June 1907, pp. 1408-1412.

boys? I shall briefly consider the issues of surrogate consent; the depersonalisation of the subject; the claimed medical benefit (the sacrifice is justified by the gains); and the claimed moral benefit.

Surrogate consent. The woman is lying unconscious, supposedly under the influence of the deadly poison, and incapable of giving consent to the proposed treatment. Although she is the patient, the subject of the procedure and the 'consumer' of the medical service, it is her husband who is the surgeon's client or customer: he has requested and paid for the operation and assures the surgeon that it is 'absolutely necessary' for the woman's good health. The surgeon accepts his client's assurances, but the woman's reaction on waking makes clear what her answer would have been had her own consent been sought. It is much the same with the circumcision of boys before they are capable of giving legal consent to the procedure. A guardian authorises the operation and a doctor carries it out, but the resentment of many boys later, when they learn what has been done to them, makes clear what their answer would have been had their own wishes been consulted.[1]

Attempting to explain why circumcision must be done to male babies and boys before legal consent is possible, Australia's leading intellectual champion of the procedure, Brian Morris, asserts that 'parental responsibility must override arguments based on the rights of the child' and that 'parents have the legal right to authorise surgical procedures in the best interests of their children'. When they are old enough to give legal consent males 'are reluctant to confront such issues' and are neither 'mature nor well-informed enough' to make the right decision for themselves. In other words, Morris concedes that if doctors waited until boys were old enough to make up their own mind, they would not consent to the operation—exactly the position of Lady Sannox.[2]

Depersonalisation of subject/patient. Those not socialised to see male circumcision as customary or beneficial cannot understand how anybody could cut into the vulnerable flesh of a baby or young boy and tear sensitive tissue from his most valued organ. As an Ameri-

---

[1] Tim Hammond, 'A Preliminary Poll of Men Circumcised in Infancy or Childhood', *BJU International*, Vol. 83, Supplement 1, Jan. 1999, pp. 85-92.

[2] Brian Morris, *In Favour of Circumcision* (Sydney: NSW University Press, 1999).

can mother writes, 'When I gazed upon my newborn son's beauti-
fully-formed body, I knew I could no more cut off a part of his penis
than I could a part of his ear or toe. In time, I would learn I was
not alone in my belief that little boys are perfect just the way they
are.'[1] The explanation for why some people can do it is not only their
conviction that greater benefits will follow or that tradition must be
respected, but the depersonalisation of the patient: in Conan Doyle's
story a yashmak (veil) covered most of the women's face, 'but the
surgeon was not thinking about the yashmak. This was no longer a
woman to him. It was a case.' And cases, after all, don't have current
feelings or subsequent histories.

Health benefits. The main justification for circumcision of male
minors has always been the claim that it will substantially improve
their health prospects, if not in infancy then in maturity, if not in
adulthood then in old age, if not in developed countries then in the
Third World. After many years of fruitless endeavour, evidence has
finally come to light that in Africa men who have unprotected intercourse with HIV positive partners are less likely, or will take longer, to
become infected if they have been circumcised. The protective effect
is estimated at 50 per cent., meaning that if it takes an uncircumcised
man eight sessions of unsafe sex to get infected, it will take a circumcised man twelve sessions. How this rather limited protection justifies
talk of a 'vaccine', or authorises circumcision of sexually inactive—
and thus not at risk—infants and boys, is by no means clear. In Conan
Doyle's story the Turk begs the surgeon to operate for the sake of the
woman's heath, and he finally agrees: 'It appears to be that or nothing.
It is better to lose a lip than a life.' It was acceptable to amputate the
lip of an unconscious woman, and thus one incapable of providing
consent, if there was reasonable certainty that she would otherwise
die. But if she were conscious and refused consent, or if the claim was
that the operation was necessary to save her was false, the amputation
would be nothing more than aggravated assault.

Closely related to health claims is the idea that the benefit gained
will outweigh the sacrifice of a sensitive and visually prominent part
of the body. The surgeon warns that 'The disfigurement will be fright-

---

[1] Laura Shanley, 'Rethinking Circumcision', *Pregnancy Today*, 22 August 2002,
seen at http://pregnancytoday.com/reference/articles/rethinkcirc.htm.

ful' and the Turk acknowledges that 'the mouth will not be a pretty one to kiss'; but what is that compared to the woman's life? It was a view held widely at that time. In an influential article published in the *Lancet* in 1900, E. Harding Freeland asserted that universal male circumcision would 'materially diminish' the incidence of syphilis and urged its universal application to male infants. He acknowledged that he was advocating 'the universal practice of an operation which has for its object the wholesale removal of a certain healthy structure as a preventive measure', and recognised that he therefore had to provide 'good evidence' that (1) the operation was free from risk; (2) the removal of the foreskin would inflict no physical disability on the individual; and (3) the benefits of the amputation were substantial and commensurate with the sacrifice. On the first point Freeland contented himself with the assertion that the risk of the operation was 'infinitesimal'. On the second he conceded that circumcision 'dull[ed] the sensibility' of the penis and thereby 'diminish[ed] sexual appetite and the pleasurable effects of coitus', but countered that this was no bar to procreation and thus not a serious deprivation. On the third point he cited some inconclusive statistics compiled in the early 1850s which purported to show a significantly lower rate of syphilis among Jewish (and thus circumcised) men in London, and his own experience as a ship's surgeon. And that was that.[1]

You might argue today that it is better to take away a boy's foreskin now than to see him contract AIDS at some unknown date in the future—and who would disagree? But the argument is valid only if circumcision were the only way to avoid AIDS and if it were pretty certain that he would get AIDS if he were not circumcised. In fact, the main risk factor for AIDS is not the foreskin, but unsafe sex; the best, cheapest and most certain way to avoid this easily avoidable disease is not to engage in unsafe sex practices and to avoid sex with partners likely to be HIV positive, such as prostitutes, casual sex workers and

---

[1] E. Harding Freeland, 'Circumcision as a Preventive of Syphilis and Other Disorders', *Lancet*, 29 December 1900, pp. 1869-1871.

the generally promiscuous.[1] There is plenty of time to get this message across to boys before they become sexually active.

Moral benefits. While the benefits of circumcision to physical health are dubious, inconsequential or superfluous, the claim that it offers moral benefits is on stronger ground: there is plenty of evidence that the amputation of the foreskin does damage the penis and nervous system in ways which make sex less enjoyable, and this was one of the main reasons why nineteenth century physicians were so strongly in favour of it. Discussing the necessity for circumcision in all cases of 'congenital phimosis', the influential surgeon John Erichsen considered the evils arising from even 'an abnormally long though not phimotic prepuce' to be so great that it was 'only humane and right from a moral point of view to practice early circumcision in all such cases'. He regarded phimosis as the wedge to encourage circumcision as widely as possible, as much for moral as health reasons:

> Every child who has a congenital phimosis ought to be circumcised; and even those who, without having phimosis, have an abnormally long and lax prepuce, would be improved greatly in health and morals by being subjected to the same operation. It would be well if the custom of eastern nations ... were introduced amongst us.[2]

An authority on 'male diseases' wrote similarly that while 'many cases of apparent phimosis in babies get well from the natural stretching of the prepuce by erections', he would 'strongly urge this little operation ... [in early infancy] on sanitary and moral grounds'.[3] In his influential pædiatrics textbook, L. Emmett Holt urged it in all cases 'because of

---

[1] As Philip Setel has shown in *A Plague of Paradoxes: AIDS, Culture and Demography in Northern Tanzania* (University of Chicago Press, 1999), there is a very high incidence of prostitution, of various kinds, throughout sub-Saharan Africa, and a very high incidence of HIV infection among the prostitutes. See also my review in *Archives of Sexual Behaviour*, Vol. 34, December 2005.

[2] John Erichsen, *The Science and Art of Surgery, Being a Treatise on Surgical Injuries, Diseases and Operations*, 7th ed., 2 vols. (London: Longmans Green, 1877), Vol. II, p. 931.

[3] Edred M. Corner, *Male Diseases in General Practice: An Introduction to Andrology* (London: Oxford University Press, 1910), p. 390.

the moral effect of the operation'.[1] When Peter Charles Remondino published his *History of Circumcision from the Earliest Times to the Present: Moral and Physical Reasons for its Performance* in 1891, moral concerns were uppermost: he vilified the foreskin at length as a 'moral outlaw' and claimed that the ancient origins of ritual circumcision lay in the desire of Judaic lawgivers to discourage the debaucheries practised among their idolatrous neighbours in the Middle East, and to deter boys from masturbation. Jonathan Hutchinson also urged the universal circumcision of boys as an incentive to chastity:

> The only function which the prepuce can be supposed to have is that of maintaining the penis in a condition susceptible of more acute sensation than would otherwise exist. It may be supposed to increase the pleasure of the act and the impulse to it. These are advantages, however, which in the present state of society can well be spared, and if in their loss some degree of increased sexual control should result, one should be thankful.[2]

Even if circumcision offered no worthwhile health benefits, its moral value alone made it worth doing. As Lord Sannox remarks to the surgeon when his wife has stopped screaming, 'It was really very necessary for Marion, this operation, not physically, you know, morally.'

That was the lesson in the eyes of the husband. The rest of us might wish that Sherlock Holmes had got involved in the case, for the whole sorry saga seems to bear out the truth of his observation that 'When a doctor does go wrong he is the first of criminals. He has nerve and he has knowledge.'

---

[1] L. Emmett Holt, *The Diseases of Infancy and Childhood* (London: Hirschfeld, 1897), p. 698.

[2] Jonathan Hutchinson, 'The Advantages of Circumcision', *Medical Review*, Vol. 3, 1900, p. 641-642.

A QUESTION OF DIPLOMACY

THE Foreign Minister was down with the gout. For a week he had been confined to the house, and he had missed two Cabinet Councils at a time when the pressure upon his department was severe. It is true that he had an excellent under-secretary and an admirable staff, but the Minister was a man of such ripe experience and of such proven sagacity that things halted in his absence. When his firm hand was at the wheel the great ship of State rode easily and smoothly upon her way; when it was removed she yawed and staggered until twelve British editors rose up in their omniscience and traced out twelve several courses, each of which was the sole and only path to safety. Then it was that the Opposition said vain things, and that the harassed Prime Minister prayed for his absent colleague.

The Foreign Minister sat in his dressing-room in the great house in Cavendish Square. It was May, and the square garden shot up like a veil of green in front of his window, but, in spite of the sunshine, a fire crackled and sputtered in the grate of the sick-room. In a deep-red plush arm-chair sat the great statesman, his head leaning back upon a silken pillow, one foot stretched forward and supported upon a padded rest. His deeply-lined, finely-chiselled face and slow-moving, heavily-pouched eyes were turned upwards towards the carved and painted ceiling, with that inscrutable expression which had been the despair and the admiration of his Continental colleagues upon the occasion of the famous Congress when he had made his first appearance in the arena of European diplomacy. Yet at the present moment his capacity for hiding his emotions had for the instant failed him, for about the lines of his strong, straight mouth and the puckers of his broad, overhanging forehead, there were sufficient indications of the restlessness and impatience which consumed him.

And indeed there was enough to make a man chafe, for he had much to think of, and yet was bereft of the power of thought. There was, for example, that question of the Dobrutscha and the navigation of the mouths of the Danube which was ripe for settlement. The Russian Chancellor had sent a masterly statement upon the subject, and it was the pet ambition of our Minister to answer it in a worthy fashion. Then there was the blockade of Crete, and the British fleet lying off Cape Matapan, waiting for instructions which might change the course of European history. And there were those three unfortunate Macedonian tourists, whose friends were momentarily expecting to receive their ears or their fingers in default of the exorbitant ransom which had been demanded. They must be plucked out of those mountains, by force or by diplomacy, or an outraged public would vent its wrath upon Downing Street. All these questions pressed for a solution, and yet here was the Foreign Minister of England, planted in an arm-chair, with his whole thoughts and attention riveted upon the ball of his right toe! It was humiliating—horribly humiliating! His reason revolted at it. He had been a respecter of himself, a respecter of his own will; but what sort of a machine was it which could be utterly thrown out of gear by a little piece of inflamed gristle? He groaned and writhed among his cushions.

But, after all, was it quite impossible that he should go down to the House? Perhaps the doctor was exaggerating the situation. There was a Cabinet Council that day. He glanced at his watch. It must be nearly over by now. But at least he might perhaps venture to drive down as far as Westminster. He pushed back the little round table with its bristle of medicine-bottles, and levering himself up with a hand upon either arm of the chair, he clutched a thick oak stick and hobbled slowly across the room. For a moment as he moved, his energy of mind and body seemed to return to him. The British fleet should sail from Matapan. Pressure should be brought to bear upon the Turks. The Greeks should be shown—Ow! In an instant the Mediterranean was blotted out, and nothing remained but that huge, undeniable, intrusive, red-hot toe. He staggered to the window and rested his left hand upon the ledge, while he propped himself upon his stick with his right. Outside lay the bright, cool, square garden, a few well-dressed passers-by, and a single, neatly-appointed carriage, which was driving away from his own door. His quick eye caught the coat-of-arms on the panel, and his lips set for a moment and his bushy eyebrows gathered ominously with a deep furrow between them. He hobbled back to his seat, and struck the gong which stood upon the table.

'Your mistress!' said he as the serving-man entered.

It was clear that it was impossible to think of going to the House.

The shooting up his leg warned him that his doctor had not overesti-
mated the situation. But he had a little mental worry now which had
for the moment eclipsed his physical ailments. He tapped the ground
impatiently with his stick until the door of the dressing-room swung
open, and a tall, elegant lady of rather more than middle age swept
into the chamber. Her hair was touched with grey, but her calm, sweet
face had all the freshness of youth, and her gown of green shot plush,
with a sparkle of gold passementerie at her bosom and shoulders,
showed off the lines of her fine figure to their best advantage.

'You sent for me, Charles?'

'Whose carriage was that which drove away just now?'

'Oh, you've been up!' she cried, shaking an admonitory forefinger. 'What an old dear it is! How can you be so rash? What am I to say
to Sir William when he comes? You know that he gives up his cases
when they are insubordinate.'

'In this instance the case may give him up,' said the Minister, peevishly; 'but I must beg, Clara, that you will answer my question.'

'Oh! the carriage! It must have been Lord Arthur Sibthorpe's.'

'I saw the three chevrons upon the panel,' muttered the invalid.

His lady had pulled herself a little straighter and opened her large
blue eyes.

'Then why ask?' she said. 'One might almost think, Charles, that
you were laying a trap! Did you expect that I should deceive you? You
have not had your lithia powder.'[1]

'For Heaven's sake, leave it alone! I asked because I was surprised
that Lord Arthur should call here. I should have fancied, Clara, that I
had made myself sufficiently clear on that point. Who received him?'

'I did. That is, I and Ida.'

'I will not have him brought into contact with Ida. I do not approve of it. The matter has gone too far already.'

Lady Clara seated herself on a velvet-topped footstool, and bent
her stately figure over the Minister's hand, which she patted softly between her own.

'Now you have said it, Charles,' said she. 'It has gone too far—I
give you my word, dear, that I never suspected it until it was past all
mending. I may be to blame—no doubt I am; but it was all so sudden.
The tail end of the season and a week at Lord Donnythorne's. That

was all. But oh! Charlie, she loves him so, and she is our only one! How can we make her miserable?'

'Tut, tut!' cried the Minister impatiently, slapping on the plush arm of his chair. 'This is too much. I tell you, Clara, I give you my word, that all my official duties, all the affairs of this great empire, do not give me the trouble that Ida does.'

'But she is our only one, Charles.'

'The more reason that she should not make a *mésalliance*.'

'*Mésalliance*, Charles! Lord Arthur Sibthorpe, son of the Duke of Tavistock, with a pedigree from the Heptarchy. Debrett takes them right back to Morcar, Earl of Northumberland.'

The Minister shrugged his shoulders.

'Lord Arthur is the fourth son of the poorest duke in England,' said he. 'He has neither prospects nor profession.'

'But, oh! Charlie, you could find him both.'

'I do not like him. I do not care for the connection.'

'But consider Ida! You know how frail her health is. Her whole soul is set upon him. You would not have the heart, Charles, to separate them?'

There was a tap at the door. Lady Clara swept towards it and threw it open.

'Yes, Thomas?'

'If you please, my lady, the Prime Minister is below.'

'Show him up, Thomas.'

'Now, Charlie, you must not excite yourself over public matters. Be very good and cool and reasonable, like a darling. I am sure that I may trust you.'

She threw her light shawl round the invalid's shoulders, and slipped away into the bedroom as the great man was ushered in at the door of the dressing-room.

'My dear Charles,' said he cordially, stepping into the room with all the boyish briskness for which he was famous, 'I trust that you find yourself a little better. Almost ready for harness, eh? We miss you sadly, both in the House and in the Council. Quite a storm brewing over this Grecian business. The *Times* took a nasty line this morning.'

'So I saw,' said the invalid, smiling up at his chief. 'Well, well, we must let them see that the country is not entirely ruled from Printing House Square yet. We must keep our own course without faltering.'

'Certainly, Charles, most undoubtedly,' assented the Prime Minister, with his hands in his pockets.

'It was so kind of you to call. I am all impatience to know what was done in the Council.'

'Pure formalities, nothing more. By the way, the Macedonian prisoners are all right.'

'Thank Goodness for that!'

'We adjourned all other business until we should have you with us next week. The question of a dissolution begins to press. The reports from the provinces are excellent.'

The Foreign Minister moved impatiently and groaned.

'We must really straighten up our foreign business a little,' said he. 'I must get Novikoff's Note answered. It is clever, but the fallacies are obvious. I wish, too, we could clear up the Afghan frontier. This illness is most exasperating. There is so much to be done, but my brain is clouded. Sometimes I think it is the gout, and sometimes I put it down to the colchicum.'[2]

'What will our medical autocrat say?' laughed the Prime Minister. 'You are so irreverent, Charles. With a bishop one may feel at one's ease. They are not beyond the reach of argument. But a doctor with his stethoscope and thermometer is a thing apart. Your reading does not impinge upon him. He is serenely above you. And then, of course, he takes you at a disadvantage. With health and strength one might cope with him. Have you read Hahnemann? What are your views upon Hahnemann?'[3]

The invalid knew his illustrious colleague too well to follow him down any of those by-paths of knowledge in which he delighted to wander. To his intensely shrewd and practical mind there was something repellent in the waste of energy involved in a discussion upon the Early Church or the twenty-seven principles of Mesmer.[4] It was his custom to slip past such conversational openings with a quick step and an averted face.

'I have hardly glanced at his writings,' said he. 'By the way, I suppose that there was no special departmental news?'

'Ah! I had almost forgotten. Yes, it was one of the things which

I had called to tell you. Sir Algernon Jones has resigned at Tangier. There is a vacancy there.'

'It had better be filled at once. The longer delay the more applicants.'

'Ah, patronage, patronage!' sighed the Prime Minister. 'Every vacancy makes one doubtful friend and a dozen very positive enemies. Who so bitter as the disappointed place-seeker? But you are right, Charles. Better fill it at once, especially as there is some little trouble in Morocco. I understand that the Duke of Tavistock would like the place for his fourth son, Lord Arthur Sibthorpe. We are under some obligation to the Duke.'

The Foreign Minister sat up eagerly.

'My dear friend,' he said, 'it is the very appointment which I should have suggested. Lord Arthur would be very much better in Tangier at present than in—in—'

'Cavendish Square?' hazarded his chief, with a little arch query of his eyebrows.

'Well, let us say London. He has manner and tact. He was at Constantinople in Norton's time.'

'Then he talks Arabic?'

'A smattering. But his French is good.'

'Speaking of Arabic, Charles, have you dipped into Averroes?'[5]

'No, I have not. But the appointment would be an excellent one in every way. Would you have the great goodness to arrange the matter in my absence?'

'Certainly, Charles, certainly. Is there anything else that I can do?'

'No. I hope to be in the House by Monday.'

'I trust so. We miss you at every turn. The *Times* will try to make mischief over that Grecian business. A leader-writer is a terribly irresponsible thing, Charles. There is no method by which he may be confuted, however preposterous his assertions. Good-bye! Read Porson![6] Goodbye!'

He shook the invalid's hand, gave a jaunty wave of his broadbrimmed hat, and darted out of the room with the same elasticity and energy with which he had entered it.

The footman had already opened the great folding door to usher the illustrious visitor to his carriage, when a lady stepped from the drawing-room and touched him on the sleeve. From behind the half-closed portiere of stamped velvet a little pale face peeped out, half-curious, half-frightened.

'May I have one word?'

'Surely, Lady Charles.'

'I hope it is not intrusive. I would not for the world overstep the limits——'

'My dear Lady Charles!' interrupted the Prime Minister, with a youthful bow and wave.

'Pray do not answer me if I go too far. But I know that Lord Arthur Sibthorpe has applied for Tangier. Would it be a liberty if I asked you what chance he has?'

'The post is filled up.'

'Oh!'

In the foreground and background there was a disappointed face.

'And Lord Arthur has it.'

The Prime Minister chuckled over his little piece of roguery.

'We have just decided it,' he continued. 'Lord Arthur must go in a week. I am delighted to perceive, Lady Charles, that the appointment has your approval. Tangier is a place of extraordinary interest. Catherine of Braganza and Colonel Kirke[7] will occur to your memory. Burton has written well upon Northern Africa. I dine at Windsor, so I am sure that you will excuse my leaving you. I trust that Lord Charles will be better. He can hardly fail to be so with such a nurse.'

He bowed, waved, and was off down the steps to his brougham. As he drove away, Lady Charles could see that he was already deeply absorbed in a paper-covered novel.

She pushed back the velvet curtains, and returned into the drawing-room. Her daughter stood in the sunlight by the window, tall, fragile, and exquisite, her features and outline not unlike her mother's, but frailer, softer, more delicate. The golden light struck one half of her high-bred, sensitive face, and glimmered upon her thickly-coiled flaxen hair, striking a pinkish tint from her closely-cut costume of fawn-coloured cloth with its dainty cinnamon ruchings. One little soft frill of chiffon nestled round her throat, from which the white, graceful neck and well-poised head shot up like a lily amid moss. Her thin white hands were pressed together, and her blue eyes turned beseech-ingly upon her mother.

'Silly girl! Silly girl!' said the matron, answering that imploring look. She put her hands upon her daughter's sloping shoulders and drew her towards her. 'It is a very nice place for a short time. It will be a stepping stone.'

'But oh! mamma, in a week! Poor Arthur!'

'He will be happy.'

'What! happy to part?'

'He need not part. You shall go with him.'

'Oh! mamma!'

'Yes, I say it.'

'Oh! mamma, in a week?'

'Yes indeed. A great deal may be done in a week. I shall order your *trousseau* to-day.'

'Oh! you dear, sweet angel! But I am so frightened! And papa? Oh! dear, I am so frightened!'

'Your papa is a diplomatist, dear.'

'Yes, ma.'

'But, between ourselves, he married a diplomatist too. If he can manage the British Empire, I think that I can manage him, Ida. How long have you been engaged, child?'

'Ten weeks, mamma.'

'Then it is quite time it came to a head. Lord Arthur cannot leave England without you. You must go to Tangier as the Minister's wife. Now, you will sit there on the settee, dear, and let me manage entirely. There is Sir William's carriage! I do think that I know how to manage Sir William. James, just ask the doctor to step in this way!'

A heavy, two-horsed carriage had drawn up at the door, and there came a single stately thud upon the knocker. An instant afterwards the drawing-room door flew open and the footman ushered in the famous physician. He was a small man, clean-shaven, with the old-fashioned black dress and white cravat with high-standing collar. He swung his golden *pince-nez* in his right hand as he walked, and bent forward with a peering, blinking expression, which was somehow suggestive of the dark and complex cases through which he had seen.

'Ah,' said he, as he entered. 'My young patient! I am glad of the opportunity.'

'Yes, I wish to speak to you about her, Sir William. Pray take this arm-chair.'

'Thank you, I will sit beside her,' said he, taking his place upon the settee. 'She is looking better, less anæmic unquestionably, and a fuller pulse. Quite a little tinge of colour, and yet not hectic.'

'I feel stronger, Sir William.'

'But she still has the pain in the side.'

'Ah, that pain!' He tapped lightly under the collar-bones, and then bent forward with his biaural stethoscope in either ear. 'Still a trace of dulness—still a slight crepitation,' he murmured.

'You spoke of a change, doctor.'

'Yes, certainly a judicious change might be advisable.'

'You said a dry climate. I wish to do to the letter what you recommend.'

'You have always been model patients.'

'We wish to be. You said a dry climate.'

'Did I? I rather forget the particulars of our conversation. But a dry climate is certainly indicated.'

'Which one?'

'Well, I think really that a patient should be allowed some latitude. I must not exact too rigid discipline. There is room for individual choice—the Engadine, Central Europe, Egypt, Algiers, which you like.'

'I hear that Tangier is also recommended.'

'Oh, yes, certainly; it is very dry.'

'You hear, Ida? Sir William says that you are to go to Tangier.'

'Or any—'

'No, no, Sir William! We feel safest when we are most obedient. You have said Tangier, and we shall certainly try Tangier.'

'Really, Lady Charles, your implicit faith is most flattering. It is not everyone who would sacrifice their own plans and inclinations so readily.'

'We know your skill and your experience, Sir William. Ida shall try Tangier. I am convinced that she will be benefited.'

'I have no doubt of it.'

'But you know Lord Charles. He is just a little inclined to decide medical matters as he would an affair of State. I hope that you will be firm with him.'

'As long as Lord Charles honours me so far as to ask my advice I am sure that he would not place me in the false position of having that advice disregarded.'

The medical baronet whirled round the cord of his *pince-nez* and pushed out a protesting hand.

'No, no, but you must be firm on the point of Tangier.'

'Having deliberately formed the opinion that Tangier is the best place for our young patient, I do not think that I shall readily change my conviction.'

'Of course not.'

'I shall speak to Lord Charles upon the subject now when I go upstairs.'

'Pray do.'

'And meanwhile she will continue her present course of treatment. I trust that the warm African air may send her back in a few months with all her energy restored.'

He bowed in the courteous, sweeping, old-world fashion which had done so much to build up his ten thousand a year, and, with the stealthy gait of a man whose life is spent in sick-rooms, he followed the footman upstairs.

As the red velvet curtains swept back into position, the Lady Ida threw her arms round her mother's neck and sank her face on to her bosom.

'Oh! mamma, you *are* a diplomatist!' she cried.

But her mother's expression was rather that of the general who looked upon the first smoke of the guns than of one who had won the victory.

'All will be right, dear,' said she, glancing down at the fluffy yellow curls and tiny ear. 'There is still much to be done, but I think we may venture to order the *trousseau*.'

'Oh! how brave you are!'

'Of course, it will in any case be a very quiet affair. Arthur must get the license. I do not approve of hole-and-corner marriages, but where the gentleman has to take up an official position some allowance must be made. We can have Lady Hilda Edgecombe, and the Trevors, and the Grevilles, and I am sure that the Prime Minister would run down if he could.'

'And papa?'

'Oh, yes; he will come too, if he is well enough. We must wait until Sir William goes, and, meanwhile, I shall write to Lord Arthur.'

Half an hour had passed, and quite a number of notes had been dashed off in the fine, bold, park-paling handwriting of Lady Charles, when the door clashed, and the wheels of the doctor's carriage were heard grating outside against the kerb. Lady Charles laid down her pen, kissed her daughter, and started off for the sick-room. The Foreign Minister was lying back in his chair, with a red silk handkerchief over his forehead, and his bulbous, cotton-wadded foot still protruding upon its rest.

'I think it is almost liniment time,' said the Lady, shaking a blue crinkled bottle. 'Shall I put on a little?'

'Oh! this pestilent toe!' groaned the sufferer. 'Sir William won't hear of my moving yet. I do think he is the most completely obstinate and pig-headed man that I have ever met. I tell him that he has mistaken his profession, and that I could find him a post at Constantinople. We need a mule out there.'

'Poor Sir William!' laughed Lady Charles. 'But how has he roused your wrath?'

'He is so persistent—so dogmatic.'

'Upon what point?'

'Well, he has been laying down the law about Ida. He has decreed, it seems, that she is to go to Tangier.'

'He said something to that effect before he went up to you.'

'Oh, he did, did he?'

The slow-moving, inscrutable eye came sliding round to her.

The Lady's face had assumed an expression of transparent obvious innocence, an intrusive candour which is never seen in nature save when a woman is bent upon deception.

'He examined her lungs, Charles. He did not say much, but his expression was very grave.'

'Not to say owlish,' interrupted the Minister.

'No, no, Charles; it is no laughing matter. He said that she must

have a change. I am sure that he thought more than he said. He spoke
of dulness and crepitation, and the effects of the African air. Then
the talk turned upon dry, bracing health resorts, and he agreed that
Tangier was the place. He said that even a few months there would
work a change.'

'And that was all?'

'Yes, that was all.'

Lord Charles shrugged his shoulders with the air of a man who is
but half convinced.

'But, of course,' said the Lady, serenely, 'if you think it better that
Ida should not go she shall not. The only thing is that if she should
get worse we might feel a little uncomfortable afterwards. In a weakness of that sort a very short time may make a difference. Sir William
evidently thought the matter critical. Still, there is no reason why he
should influence you. It is a little responsibility, however. If you take it
all upon yourself and free me from any of it, so that afterwards—'

'My dear Clara, how you do croak!'

'Oh! I don't wish to do that, Charles. But you remember what
happened to Lord Bellamy's child. She was just Ida's age. That was
another case in which Sir William's advice was disregarded.'

Lord Charles groaned impatiently.

'I have not disregarded it,' said he.

'No, no, of course not. I know your strong sense, and your good
heart too well, dear. You were very wisely looking at both sides of
the question. That is what we poor women cannot do. It is emotion
against reason, as I have often heard you say. We are swayed this way
and that, but you men are persistent, and so you gain your way with
us. But I am so pleased that you have decided for Tangier.'

'Have I?'

'Well, dear, you said that you would not disregard Sir William.'

'Well, Clara, admitting that Ida is to go to Tangier, you will allow
that it is impossible for me to escort her?'

'Utterly.'

'And for you?'

'While you are ill my place is by your side.'

'There is your sister?'

'She is going to Florida.'

'Lady Dumbarton, then?'

'She is nursing her father. It is out of the question.'

'Well, then, whom can we possibly ask? Especially just as the season is commencing. You see, Clara, the fates fight against Sir William.'

His wife rested her elbows against the back of the great red chair, and passed her fingers through the statesman's grizzled curls, stooping down as she did so until her lips were close to his ear.

'There is Lord Arthur Sibthorpe,' said she softly.

Lord Charles bounded in his chair, and muttered a word or two such as were more frequently heard from Cabinet Ministers in Lord Melbourne's time than now.

'Are you mad, Clara!' he cried. 'What can have put such a thought into your head?'

'The Prime Minister.'

'Who? The Prime Minister?'

'Yes, dear. Now do, do be good! Or perhaps I had better not speak to you about it any more.'

'Well, I really think that you have gone rather too far to retreat.'

'It was the Prime Minister, then, who told me that Lord Arthur was going to Tangier.'

'It is a fact, though it had escaped my memory for the instant.'

'And then came Sir William with his advice about Ida. Oh! Charlie, it is surely more than a coincidence!'

'I am convinced,' said Lord Charles, with his shrewd, questioning gaze, 'that it is very much more than a coincidence, Lady Charles. You are a very clever woman, my dear. A born manager and organiser.'

The lady brushed past the compliment.

'Think of our own young days, Charlie,' she whispered, with her fingers still toying with his hair. 'What were you then? A poor man, not even Ambassador at Tangier. But I loved you, and believed in you, and have I ever regretted it? Ida loves and believes in Lord Arthur, and why should she ever regret it either?'

Lord Charles was silent. His eyes were fixed upon the green branches which waved outside the window; but his mind had flashed back to a Devonshire country-house of thirty years ago, and to the one fateful evening when, between old yew hedges, he paced along beside a slender girl, and poured out to her his hopes, his fears, and his ambitions. He took the white, thin hand and pressed it to his lips.

'You have been a good wife to me, Clara,' said he.

She said nothing. She did not attempt to improve upon her advantage. A less consummate general might have tried to do so, and ruined all. She stood silent and submissive, noting the quick play of thought which peeped from his eyes and lip. There was a sparkle in the one and a twitch of amusement in the other, as he at last glanced up at her.

'Clara,' said he, 'deny it if you can! You have ordered the *trousseau*.'

She gave his ear a little pinch.

'Subject to your approval,' said she.

'You have written to the Archbishop.'

'It is not posted yet.'

'You have sent a note to Lord Arthur.'

'How could you tell that?'

'He is downstairs now.'

'No; but I think that is his brougham.'

'Lord Charles sank back with a look of half-comical despair.

'Who is to fight against such a woman?' he cried. 'Oh! if I could send you to Novikoff! He is too much for any of my men. But, Clara, I cannot have them up here.'

'Not for your blessing?'

'No, no!'

'It would make them so happy.'

'I cannot stand scenes.'

'Then I shall convey it to them.'

'And pray say no more about it—to-day, at any rate. I have been weak over the matter.'

'Oh! Charlie, you who are so strong!'

'You have outflanked me, Clara. It was very well done. I must congratulate you.'

'Well,' she murmured, as she kissed him, 'you know I have been studying a very clever diplomatist for thirty years.'

NOTES TO 'A QUESTION OF DIPLOMACY'

1. Lithium salts were sometimes used to treat gout—obviously the medical problem that afflicts the Foreign Minister. Gout arises from a disorder of uric acid metabolism, whereby crystals of monosodium urate are deposited on the cartilage of the joints, leading to inflammation and intense pain. The disease has been recognised since antiquity, when Greek and Roman writers noted that it affected only adult men (suggesting that a high level of testosterone had something to do with it) and tended to run in families. Gout is traditionally associated with red-faced gentlemen who drink too much port, but modern research has not confirmed the association between alcohol and the disease. Lead, however, is believed to be a predisposing or aggravating factor, and it may well be that the lead-lined pipes and lead stoppers used in wine bottles in the eighteenth century were part of the problem.[1]

2. Colchicine: an alkaloid derived from the bulb of the meadow crocus. This was known to be effective against gout in ancient times and is still the preferred treatment.

3. Samuel Hahnemann (1755-1843), founder of homeopathy, the major nineteenth century competitor for traditional Galenic medicine (bleeding, purging, heavy use of drugs). It was big in late Victorian times, when few major cities would have been without a homeopathic institute or hospital.[2]

4. Franz Anton Mesmer (1743-1815), founder of mesmerism, who developed the theory of animal magnetism and claimed that patients could be cured by touching each other while holding a rod connected to the lid of a tub filled with bottles of powdered brass and iron filings that gave the impression of a galvanic battery. Although discredited in

---

[1] See Roy Porter and G. S. Rousseau, *Gout: The Patrician's Malady* (Yale University Press, 2000).

[2] See T. M. Cook, *Samuel Hahnemann: The Founder of Homeopathy* (Wellingsborough: Thorsons, 1981).

France before the Revolution,[1] mesmerism won an immense following in mid-nineteenth century England.[2]

5. Averroes, European name for Ibn Rushd Abu'l Walid Muhammad (1126-98), Moorish physician and philosopher. He was for a time personal physician to the Caliph, but he fell out of favour in 1195, and his writings were burned as heretical.

6. Richard Porson (1759-1808), the classical scholar.

7. Catherine of Braganza, Portuguese wife of Charles II, brought Tangiers into English possession as part of her dowry. Percy Kirke (d. 1691) was colonel of the Tangiers or Queen's Regiment of Foot and governor of Tangiers during the 1680s.

---

[1] Stephen Jay Gould, 'The Chain of Reason and the Chain of Thumbs', in *Bully for Brontosaurus* (Penguin, 1992), 182-197.
[2] Alison Winter, *Mesmerised: Powers of Mind in Victorian Britain* (University of Chicago Press, 1997).

A MEDICAL DOCUMENT

MEDICAL men are, as a class, very much too busy to take stock of singular situations or dramatic events. Thus it happens that the ablest chronicler of their experiences in our literature was a lawyer. A life spent in watching over death-beds—or over birth-beds which are infinitely more trying—takes something from a man's sense of proportion, as constant strong waters might corrupt his palate. The overstimulated nerve ceases to respond. Ask the surgeon for his best experiences and he may reply that he has seen little that is remarkable, or break away into the technical. But catch him some night when the fire has spurted up and his pipe is reeking, with a few of his brother practitioners for company and an artful question or allusion to set him going. Then you will get some raw, green facts new plucked from the tree of life.

It is after one of the quarterly dinners of the Midland Branch of the British Medical Association. Twenty coffee cups, a dozen liqueur glasses, and a solid bank of blue smoke which swirls slowly along the high, gilded ceiling gives a hint of a successful gathering. But the members have shredded off to their homes. The line of heavy, bulge-pocketed overcoats and of stethoscope-bearing top hats is gone from the hotel corridor. Round the fire in the sitting-room three medicos are still lingering, however, all smoking and arguing, while a fourth, who is a mere layman and young at that, sits back at the table. Under cover of an open journal he is writing furiously with a stylographic pen, asking a question in an innocent voice from time to time and so flickering up the conversation whenever it shows a tendency to wane.

The three men are all of that staid middle age which begins early and lasts late in the profession. They are none of them famous, yet each is of good repute, and a fair type of his particular branch. The portly man with the authoritative manner and the white, vitriol splash upon his cheek is Charley Manson, chief of the Wormley Asylum, and author of the brilliant monograph—'Obscure Nervous Lesions in the Unmarried.'[1] He always wears his collar high like that, since the half-successful attempt of a student of Revelations to cut his throat with a splinter of glass. The second, with the ruddy face and the merry brown eyes, is a general practitioner, a man of vast experience, who, with his three assistants and his five horses, takes twenty-five hundred a year in half-crown visits and shilling consultations out of the poorest quarter of a great city. That cheery face of Theodore Foster is seen at the side of a hundred sick-beds a day, and if he has one-third more names on his visiting list than in his cash book he always promises himself that he will get level some day when a millionaire with a chronic complaint—the ideal combination—shall seek his services. The third, sitting on the right with his dress-shoes shining on the top of the fender, is Hargrave, the rising surgeon. His face has none of the broad humanity of Theodore Foster's, the eye is stern and critical, the mouth straight and severe, but there is strength and decision in every line of it, and it is nerve rather than sympathy which the patient demands when he is bad enough to come to Hargrave's door. He calls himself a jawman, 'a mere jawman,' as he modestly puts it, but in point of fact he is too young and too poor to confine himself to a specialty, and there is nothing surgical which Hargrave has not the skill and the audacity to do.

'Before, after, and during,' murmurs the general practitioner in answer to some interpolation of the outsider's. 'I assure you, Manson, one sees all sorts of evanescent forms of madness.'

'Ah, puerperal!' throws in the other, knocking the curved grey ash from his cigar. 'But you had some case in your mind, Foster.'

'Well, there was one only last week which was new to me. I had been engaged by some people of the name of Silcoe. When the trouble came round I went myself, for they would not hear of an assistant. The husband, who was a policeman, was sitting at the head of the bed on the further side. "This won't do," said I. "Oh yes, doctor, it must do," said she. "It's quite irregular, and he must go," said I. "It's that or nothing," said she. "I won't open my mouth or stir a finger the whole night," said he. So it ended by my allowing him to remain, and there he sat for eight hours on end. She was very good over the matter, but every now and again *he* would fetch a hollow groan, and I noticed that he held his right hand just under the sheet all the time, where I had no doubt that it was clasped by her left. When it was all happily over, I looked at him and his face was the colour of this cigar ash, and his head had dropped on to the edge of the pillow. Of course I thought he had fainted with emotion, and I was just telling myself what I thought of myself for having been such a fool as to let him stay there, when suddenly I saw that the sheet over his hand was all soaked with blood; I whisked it down, and there was the fellow's wrist half cut through. The woman had one bracelet of a policeman's handcuff over her left wrist and the other round his right one. When she had been in pain she had twisted with all her strength and the iron had fairly eaten into the bone of the man's arm. "Aye, doctor," said she, when she saw I had noticed it. "He's got to take his share as well as me. Turn and turn," said she.'

'Don't you find it a very wearing branch of the profession?' asks Foster after a pause.

'My dear fellow, it was the fear of it that drove me into lunacy work.'

'Aye, and it has driven men into asylums who never found their way on to the medical staff. I was a very shy fellow myself as a student, and I know what it means.'

'No joke that in general practice,' says the alienist.

'Well, you hear men talk about it as though it were, but I tell you it's much nearer tragedy. Take some poor, raw, young fellow who has just put up his plate in a strange town. He has found it a trial all his life, perhaps, to talk to a woman about lawn tennis and church services. When a young man *is* shy he is shyer than any girl. Then down comes an anxious mother and consults him upon the most intimate family matters. "I shall never go to that doctor again," says she afterwards. "His manner is so stiff and unsympathetic." Unsympathetic! Why, the poor lad was struck dumb and paralysed. I have known general practitioners who were so shy that they could not bring themselves to ask the way in the street. Fancy what sensitive men like that must endure before they get broken in to medical practice. And then they know that nothing is so catching as shyness, and that if they do not keep a face of stone, their patient will be covered with confusion. And so they keep their face of stone, and earn the reputation perhaps of having a heart to correspond. I suppose nothing would shake *your* nerve, Manson.'

'Well, when a man lives year in year out among a thousand lunatics, with a fair sprinkling of homicidals among them, one's nerves either get set or shattered. Mine are all right so far.'

'I was frightened once,' says the surgeon. 'It was when I was doing dispensary work. One night I had a call from some very poor people, and gathered from the few words they said that their child was ill. When I entered the room I saw a small cradle in the corner. Raising the lamp I walked over and putting back the curtains I looked down at the baby. I tell you it was sheer Providence that I didn't drop that lamp and set the whole place alight. The head on the pillow turned and I saw a face looking up at me which seemed to me to have more malignancy and wickedness than ever I had dreamed of in a nightmare. It was the flush of red over the cheek-bones, and the brooding eyes full of loathing of me, and of everything else, that impressed me. I'll never forget my start as, instead of the chubby face of an infant, my eyes fell upon this creature. I took the mother into the next room. "What is it?" I asked. "A girl of sixteen," said she, and then throwing up her arms, "Oh, pray God she may be taken!" The poor thing, though she spent her life in this little cradle, had great, long, thin limbs which she curled up under her. I lost sight of the case and don't know what became of it, but I'll never forget the look in her eyes.'[2]

'That's creepy,' says Doctor Foster. 'But I think one of my experiences would run it close. Shortly after I put up my plate I had a visit from a little hunch-backed woman, who wished me to come and attend to her sister in her trouble. When I reached the house, which was a very poor one, I found two other little hunched-backed women, exactly like the first, waiting for me in the sitting-room. Not one of them said a word, but my companion took the lamp and walked upstairs with her two sisters behind her, and me bringing up the rear. I can see those three queer shadows cast by the lamp upon the wall as clearly as I can see that tobacco pouch. In the room above was the fourth sister, a remarkably beautiful girl in evident need of my assistance. There was no wedding ring upon her finger. The three deformed sisters seated themselves round the room, like so many graven images, and all night not one of them opened her mouth. I'm not romancing, Hargrave; this is absolute fact. In the early morning a fearful thunderstorm broke out, one of the most violent I have ever known. The little garret burned blue with the lightning, and thunder roared and rattled as if it were on the very roof of the house. It wasn't much of a lamp I had, and it was a queer thing when a spurt of lightning came to see those three twisted figures sitting round the walls, or to have the voice of my patient drowned by the booming of the thunder. By Jove! I don't mind telling you that there was a time when I nearly bolted from the room. All came right in the end, but I never heard the true story of the unfortunate beauty and her three crippled sisters.'

'That's the worst of these medical stories,' sighs the outsider. 'They never seem to have an end.'

'When a man is up to his neck in practice, my boy, he has no time to gratify his private curiosity. Things shoot across him and he gets a glimpse of them, only to recall them, perhaps, at some quiet moment like this. But I've always felt, Manson, that your line had as much of the terrible in it as any other.'

'More,' groans the alienist. 'A disease of the body is bad enough, but this seems to be a disease of the soul. Is it not a shocking thing—a thing to drive a reasoning man into absolute Materialism—to think that you may have a fine, noble fellow with every divine instinct and that some little vascular change, the dropping, we will say, of a minute spicule of bone from the inner table of his skull on to the surface of his brain may have the effect of changing him to a filthy and pitiable creature with every low and debasing tendency? What a satire an asylum is upon the majesty of man, and no less upon the ethereal nature of the soul.'

'Faith and hope,' murmurs the general practitioner.

'I have no faith, not much hope, and all the charity I can afford,' says the surgeon. 'When theology squares itself with the facts of life I'll read it up.'

'You were talking about cases,' says the outsider, jerking the ink down into his stylographic pen.

'Well, take a common complaint which kills many thousands every year, like G.P. for instance.'

'What's G.P.?'

'General practitioner,' suggests the surgeon with a grin.

'The British public will have to know what G.P. is,' says the alienist gravely. 'It's increasing by leaps and bounds, and it has the distinction of being absolutely incurable. General paralysis is its full title, and I tell you it promises to be a perfect scourge. Here's a fairly typical case now which I saw last Monday week. A young farmer, a splendid fellow, surprised his fellows by taking a very rosy view of things at a time when the whole country-side was grumbling. He was going to give up wheat, give up arable land, too, if it didn't pay, plant two thousand acres of rhododendrons and get a monopoly of the supply for Covent Garden—there was no end to his schemes, all sane enough but just a bit inflated. I called at the farm, not to see him, but on an altogether different matter. Something about the man's way of talking struck me and I watched him narrowly. His lip had a trick of quivering, his words slurred themselves together, and so did his handwriting when he had occasion to draw up a small agreement. A closer inspection showed me that one of his pupils was ever so little larger than the other. As I left the house his wife came after me. "Isn't it splendid to see Job looking so well, doctor," said she; "he's that full of energy he can hardly keep himself quiet." I did not say anything, for I had not the heart, but I knew that the fellow was as much condemned to death as though he were lying in the cell at Newgate. It was a characteristic case of incipient G.P.'

'Good heavens!' cries the outsider. 'My own lips tremble. I often slur my words. I believe I've got it myself.'

Three little chuckles come from the front of the fire.

'There's the danger of a little medical knowledge to the layman.'

'A great authority has said that every first year's student is suffering in silent agony from four diseases,' remarks the surgeon. 'One is heart disease, of course; another is cancer of the parotid. I forget the two other.'

'Where does the parotid come in?'

'Oh, it's the last wisdom tooth coming through!'

'And what would be the end of that young farmer?' asks the outsider.

'Paresis of all the muscles, ending in fits, coma and death. It may be a few months, it may be a year or two. He was a very strong young man and would take some killing.'

'By the way,' says the alienist, 'did I ever tell you about the first certificate I ever signed? I stood as near ruin then as a man could go.'

'What was it, then?'

'I was in practice at the time. One morning a Mrs Cooper called upon me and informed me that her husband had shown signs of delusions lately. They took the form of imagining that he had been in the army and had distinguished himself very much. As a matter of fact he was a lawyer and had never been out of England. Mrs Cooper was of opinion that if I were to call it might alarm him, so it was agreed between us that she should send him up in the evening on some pretext to my consulting room, which would give me the opportunity of having a chat with him and, if I were convinced of his insanity, of signing his certificate. Another doctor had already signed, so that it only needed my concurrence to have him placed under treatment. Well, Mr Cooper arrived in the evening about half an hour before I had expected him, and consulted me as to some malarious symptoms from which he said that he suffered. According to his account he had just returned from the Abyssinian Campaign, and had been one of the first of the British forces to enter Magdala. No delusion could possibly be more marked, for he would talk of little else, so I filled in the papers without the slightest hesitation. When his wife arrived, after he had left, I put some questions to her to complete the form. "What is his age?" I asked. "Fifty," said she. "Fifty!" I cried. "Why, the man I examined could not have been more than thirty!" And so it came out that the real Mr Cooper had never called upon me at all, but that by one of those coincidences which take a man's breath away another Cooper, who really was a very distinguished young officer of artillery, had come in to consult me. My pen was wet to sign the paper when I discovered it,' says Dr Manson, mopping his forehead.

'We were talking about nerve just now,' observes the surgeon. 'Just after my qualifying I served in the Navy for a time, as I think you know. I was on the flag-ship on the West African Station, and I remember a singular example of nerve which came to my notice at that time. One of our small gunboats had gone up the Calabar river, and while there the surgeon died of coast fever. On the same day a man's leg was broken by a spar falling upon it, and it became quite obvious that it must be taken off above the knee if his life was to be saved. The young lieutenant who was in charge of the craft searched among the dead doctor's effects and laid his hands upon some chloroform, a hip-joint knife, and a volume of Grey's Anatomy. He had the man laid by the steward upon the cabin table, and with a picture of a cross section of the thigh in front of him he began to take off the limb. Every now and then, referring to the diagram, he would say: "Stand by with the lashings, steward. There's blood on the chart about here." Then he would jab with his knife until he cut the artery, and he and his assistant would tie it up before they went any further. In this way they gradually whittled the leg off, and upon my word they made a very excellent job of it. The man is hopping about the Portsmouth Hard at this day.

'It's no joke when the doctor of one of these isolated gunboats himself falls ill,' continues the surgeon after a pause. 'You might think it easy for him to prescribe for himself, but this fever knocks you down like a club, and you haven't strength left to brush a mosquito off your face. I had a touch of it at Lagos, and I know what I am telling you. But there was a chum of mine who really had a curious experience. The whole crew gave him up, and, as they had never had a funeral aboard the ship, they began rehearsing the forms so as to be ready. They thought that he was unconscious, but he swears he could hear every word that passed. "Corpse comin' up the 'atchway!" cried the cockney sergeant of Marines. "Present harms!" He was so amused, and so indignant too, that he just made up his mind that he wouldn't be carried through that hatchway, and he wasn't, either.'

'There's no need for fiction in medicine,' remarks Foster, 'for the facts will always beat anything you can fancy. But it has seemed to me sometimes that a curious paper might be read at some of these meetings about the uses of medicine in popular fiction.'

'How?'

'Well, of what the folk die of, and what diseases are made most use of in novels. Some are worn to pieces, and others, which are equally common in real life, are never mentioned. Typhoid is fairly frequent, but scarlet fever is unknown. Heart disease is common, but then heart disease, as we know it, is usually the sequel of some foregoing disease, of which we never hear anything in the romance. Then there is the mysterious malady called brain fever, which always attacks the heroine after a crisis, but which is unknown under that name to the text books. People when they are over-excited in novels fall down in a fit. In a fairly large experience I have never known anyone do so in real life. The small complaints simply don't exist. Nobody ever gets shingles or quinsy, or mumps in a novel. All the diseases, too, belong to the upper part of the body. The novelist never strikes below the belt.'[3]

'I'll tell you what, Foster,' says the alienist, 'there is a side of life which is too medical for the general public and too romantic for the professional journals, but which contains some of the richest human materials that a man could study. It's not a pleasant side, I am afraid, but if it is good enough for Providence to create, it is good enough for us to try and understand. It would deal with strange outbursts of savagery and vice in the lives of the best men, curious momentary weaknesses in the record of the sweetest women, known but to one or two, and inconceivable to the world around. It would deal, too, with the singular phenomena of waxing and of waning manhood, and would throw a light upon those actions which have cut short many an honoured career and sent a man to a prison when he should have been hurried to a consulting-room. Of all evils that may come upon the sons of men, God shield us principally from that one!'

'I had a case some little time ago which was out of the ordinary,' says the surgeon. 'There's a famous beauty in London society—I mention no names—who used to be remarkable a few seasons ago for the very low dresses which she would wear. She had the whitest of skins, and most beautiful of shoulders, so it was no wonder. Then gradually the frilling at her neck lapped upwards and upwards, until last year she astonished everyone by wearing quite a high collar at a time when it was completely out of fashion. Well, one day this very woman was shown into my consulting-room. When the footman was gone she suddenly tore off the upper part of her dress. "For God's sake do something for me!" she cried. Then I saw what the trouble was. A rodent ulcer was eating its way upwards, coiling on in its serpiginous fashion until the end of it was flush with her collar. The red streak of its trail was lost below the line of her bust. Year by year it had ascended and she had heightened her dress to hide it, until now it was about to invade her face. She had been too proud to confess her trouble, even to a medical man.'

'And did you stop it?'

'Well, with zinc chloride I did what I could. But it may break out again. She was one of those beautiful white-and-pink creatures who are rotten with struma. You may patch but you can't mend.'

'Dear! dear! dear!' cries the general practitioner, with that kindly softening of the eyes which had endeared him to so many thousands. 'I suppose we mustn't think ourselves wiser than Providence, but there are times when one feels that something is wrong in the scheme of things. I've seen some sad things in my life. Did I ever tell you that case where Nature divorced a most loving couple? He was a fine young fellow, an athlete and a gentleman, but he overdid athletics. You know how the force that controls us gives us a little tweak to remind us when we get off the beaten track. It may be a pinch on the great toe if we drink too much and work too little. Or it may be a tug on our nerves if we dissipate energy too much. With the athlete, of course, it's the heart or the lungs. He had bad phthisis and was sent to Davos. Well, as luck would have it, she developed rheumatic fever, which left her heart very much affected. Now, do you see the dreadful dilemma in which those poor people found themselves? When he came below 4000 feet or so, his symptoms became terrible. She could come up about 2500, and then her heart reached its limit. They had several interviews half way down the valley, which left them nearly dead, and at last, the doctors had to absolutely forbid it. And so for four years they lived within three miles of each other and never met. Every morning he would go to a place which overlooked the chalet in which she lived and would wave a great white cloth and she answer from below. They could see each other quite plainly with their field glasses, and they might have been in different planets for all their chance of meeting.'

'And one at last died,' says the outsider.

'No, sir. I'm sorry not to be able to clinch the story, but the man recovered and is now a successful stockbroker in Drapers Gardens. The woman, too, is the mother of a considerable family. But what are you doing there?'

'Only taking a note or two of your talk.'

The three medical men laugh as they walk towards their overcoats.

'Why, we've done nothing but talk shop,' says the general practitioner. 'What possible interest can the public take in that?'

NOTES TO 'A MEDICAL DOCUMENT'

First published in *Round the Red Lamp*.

1.   Probably a reference to masturbation or spermatorrhœa.[1]

2.   The incident of the deformed daughter is also reported in *Memories and Adventures* (pp. 69-71).

3.   The plot of 'The Naval Treaty', the second to last of the original (pre-Moriarty) Holmes stories (*Strand*, October 1893), relies on a prolonged bout of brain fever on the part of the official who apparently lost the document.

---

[1] See Robert Darby, 'Pathologising Male Sexuality: Lallemand, Spermatorrhoea and the Rise of Circumcision', *Journal of the History of Medicine and Allied Sciences*, Vol. 60, July 2005, pp. 283-319.

LOT NO. 249

Of the dealings of Edward Bellingham with William Monkhouse Lee, and of the cause of the great terror of Abercrombie Smith, it may be that no absolute and final judgment will ever be delivered. It is true that we have the full and clear narrative of Smith himself, and such corroboration as he could look for from Thomas Styles the servant, from the Reverend Plumptree Peterson, Fellow of Old's, and from such other people as chanced to gain some passing glance at this or that incident in a singular chain of events. Yet, in the main, the story must rest upon Smith alone, and the most will think that it is more likely that one brain, however outwardly sane, has some subtle warp in its texture, some strange flaw in its workings, than that the path of nature has been overstepped in open day in so famed a centre of learning and light as the University of Oxford. Yet when we think how narrow and how devious this path of Nature is, how dimly we can trace it, for all our lamps of science, and how from the darkness which girds it round great and terrible possibilities loom ever shadowly upwards, it is a bold and confident man who will put a limit to the strange by-paths into which the human spirit may wander.

In a certain wing of what we will call Old College in Oxford there is a corner turret of an exceeding great age. The heavy arch which spans the open door has bent downwards in the centre under the weight of its years, and the grey, lichen-blotched blocks of stone are bound and knitted together with withes and strands of ivy, as though the old mother had set herself to brace them up against wind and weather. From the door a stone stair curves upward spirally, passing two landings, and terminating in a third one, its steps all shapeless and hollowed by the tread of so many generations of the seekers after knowledge. Life has flowed like water down this winding stair, and, waterlike, has left these smooth-worn grooves behind it. From the long-gowned, pedantic scholars of Plantagenet days down to the young bloods of a later age, how full and strong had been that tide of young English life. And what was left now of all those hopes, those strivings, those fiery energies, save here and there in some old-world churchyard a few scratches upon a stone, and perchance a handful of dust in a mouldering coffin? Yet here were the silent stair and the grey old wall, with bend and saltire and many another heraldic device still to be read upon its surface, like grotesque shadows thrown back from the days that had passed.

In the month of May, in the year 1884, three young men occupied the sets of rooms which opened on to the separate landings of the old stair. Each set consisted simply of a sitting-room and of a bed-room, while the two corresponding rooms upon the ground-floor were used, the one as a coal-cellar, and the other as the living-room of the servant, or scout, Thomas Styles, whose duty it was to wait upon the three men above him. To right and to left was a line of lecture-rooms and of offices, so that the dwellers in the old turret enjoyed a certain seclusion, which made the chambers popular among the more studious undergraduates. Such were the three who occupied them now—Abercrombie Smith above, Edward Bellingham beneath him, and William Monkhouse Lee upon the lowest storey.

It was ten o'clock on a bright spring night, and Abercrombie Smith lay back in his arm-chair, his feet upon the fender, and his briar-root pipe between his lips. In a similar chair, and equally at his ease, there lounged on the other side of the fireplace his old school friend Jephro Hastie. Both men were in flannels, for they had spent their evening upon the river, but apart from their dress no one could look at their hard-cut, alert faces without seeing that they were open-air men—men whose minds and tastes turned naturally to all that was manly and robust. Hastie, indeed, was stroke of his college boat, and Smith was an even better oar, but a coming examination had already cast its shadow over him and held him to his work, save for the few hours a week which health demanded. A litter of medical books upon the table, with scattered bones, models and anatomical plates, pointed to the extent as well as the nature of his studies, while a couple of single-sticks and a set of boxing-gloves above the mantelpiece hinted at the means by which, with Hastie's help, he might take his exercise in its most compressed and least distant form. They knew each other very well—so well that they could sit now in that soothing silence which is the very highest development of companionship.

'Have some whisky,' said Abercrombie Smith at last between two cloudbursts. 'Scotch in the jug and Irish in the bottle.'

'No, thanks. I'm in for the skulls. I don't liquor when I'm training. How about you?'

'I'm reading hard. I think it best to leave it alone.'

Hastie nodded, and they relapsed into a contented silence.

'By the way, Smith,' asked Hastie, presently, 'have you made the acquaintance of either of the fellows on your stair yet?'

'Just a nod when we pass. Nothing more.'

'Hum! I should be inclined to let it stand at that. I know something of them both. Not much, but as much as I want. I don't think I should take them to my bosom if I were you. Not that there's much amiss with Monkhouse Lee.'

'Meaning the thin one?'

'Precisely. He is a gentlemanly little fellow. I don't think there is any vice in him. But then you can't know him without knowing Bellingham.'

'Meaning the fat one?'

'Yes, the fat one. And he's a man whom I, for one, would rather not know.'

Abercrombie Smith raised his eyebrows and glanced across at his companion.

'What's up, then?' he asked. 'Drink? Cards? Cad? You used not to be censorious.'

'Ah! you evidently don't know the man, or you wouldn't ask. There's something damnable about him—something reptilian. My gorge always rises at him. I should put him down as a man with secret vices—an evil liver. He's no fool, though. They say that he is one of the best men in his line that they have ever had in the college.'

'Medicine or classics?'

'Eastern languages. He's a demon at them. Chillingworth met him somewhere above the second cataract last long, and he told me that he just prattled to the Arabs as if he had been born and nursed and weaned among them. He talked Coptic to the Copts, and Hebrew to the Jews, and Arabic to the Bedouins, and they were all ready to kiss the hem of his frock-coat. There are some old hermit Johnnies up in those parts who sit on rocks and scowl and spit at the casual stranger. Well, when they saw this chap Bellingham, before he had said five words they just lay down on their bellies and wriggled. Chillingworth said that he never saw anything like it. Bellingham seemed to take it as his right, too, and strutted about among them and talked down to them like a Dutch uncle. Pretty good for an undergrad. of Old's, wasn't it?'

'Why do you say you can't know Lee without knowing Bellingham?'

'Because Bellingham is engaged to his sister Eveline. Such a bright little girl, Smith! I know the whole family well. It's disgusting to see that brute with her. A toad and a dove, that's what they always remind me of.'

Abercrombie Smith grinned and knocked his ashes out against the side of the grate.

'You show every card in your hand, old chap,' said he. 'What a prejudiced, green-eyed, evil-thinking old man it is! You have really nothing against the fellow except that.'

'Well, I've known her ever since she was as long as that cherry-wood pipe, and I don't like to see her taking risks. And it is a risk. He looks beastly. And he has a beastly temper, a venomous temper. You remember his row with Long Norton?'

'No; you always forget that I am a freshman.'

'Ah, it was last winter. Of course. Well, you know the towpath along by the river. There were several fellows going along it, Bellingham in front, when they came on an old market-woman coming the other way. It had been raining—you know what those fields are like when it has rained—and the path ran between the river and a great puddle that was nearly as broad. Well, what does this swine do but keep the path, and push the old girl into the mud, where she and her marketings came to terrible grief. It was a blackguard thing to do, and Long Norton, who is as gentle a fellow as ever stepped, told him what he thought of it. One word led to another, and it ended in Norton laying his stick across the fellow's shoulders. There was the deuce of a fuss about it, and it's a treat to see the way in which Bellingham looks at Norton when they meet now. By Jove, Smith, it's nearly eleven o'clock!'

'No hurry. Light your pipe again.'

'Not I. I'm supposed to be in training. Here I've been sitting gossiping when I ought to have been safely tucked up. I'll borrow your skull, if you can share it. Williams has had mine for a month. I'll take the little bones of your ear, too, if you are sure you won't need them. Thanks very much. Never mind a bag, I can carry them very well under my arm. Good-night, my son, and take my tip as to your neighbour.'

When Hastie, bearing his anatomical plunder, had clattered off down the winding stair, Abercrombie Smith hurled his pipe into the wastepaper basket, and drawing his chair nearer to the lamp, plunged into a formidable green-covered volume, adorned with great colored maps of that strange internal kingdom of which we are the hapless and helpless monarchs. Though a freshman at Oxford, the student was not so in medicine, for he had worked for four years at Glasgow and at Berlin, and this coming examination would place him finally as a member of his profession. With his firm mouth, broad forehead, and clear-cut, somewhat hard-featured face, he was a man who, if he had no brilliant talent, was yet so dogged, so patient, and so strong that he might in the end overtop a more showy genius. A man who can hold his own among Scotchmen and North Germans is not a man to be easily set back. Smith had left a name at Glasgow and at Berlin, and he was bent now upon doing as much at Oxford, if hard work and devotion could accomplish it.

He had sat reading for about an hour, and the hands of the noisy carriage clock upon the side table were rapidly closing together upon the twelve, when a sudden sound fell upon the student's ear—a sharp, rather shrill sound, like the hissing intake of a man's breath who gasps under some strong emotion. Smith laid down his book and slanted his ear to listen. There was no one on either side or above him, so that the interruption came certainly from the neighbour beneath—the same neighbour of whom Hastie had given so unsavoury an account. Smith knew him only as a flabby, pale-faced man of silent and studious habits, a man, whose lamp threw a golden bar from the old turret even after he had extinguished his own. This community in lateness had formed a certain silent bond between them. It was soothing to Smith when the hours stole on towards dawning to feel that there was another so close who set as small a value upon his sleep as he did. Even now, as his thoughts turned towards him, Smith's feelings were kindly. Hastie was a good fellow, but he was rough, strong-fibred, with no imagination or sympathy. He could not tolerate departures from what he looked upon as the model type of manliness. If a man could not be measured by a public-school standard, then he was beyond the pale with Hastie. Like so many who are themselves robust, he was apt to confuse the constitution with the character, to ascribe to want of principle what was really a want of circulation. Smith, with his stronger mind, knew his friend's habit, and made allowance for it now as his thoughts turned towards the man beneath him.

There was no return of the singular sound, and Smith was about to turn to his work once more, when suddenly there broke out in the silence of the night a hoarse cry, a positive scream—the call of a man who is moved and shaken beyond all control. Smith sprang out of his chair and dropped his book. He was a man of fairly firm fibre, but there was something in this sudden, uncontrollable shriek of horror which chilled his blood and pringled in his skin. Coming in such a place and at such an hour, it brought a thousand fantastic possibilities into his head. Should he rush down, or was it better to wait? He had all the national hatred of making a scene, and he knew so little of his neighbour that he would not lightly intrude upon his affairs. For a moment he stood in doubt and even as he balanced the matter there was a quick rattle of footsteps upon the stairs, and young Monkhouse Lee, half dressed and as white as ashes, burst into his room.

'Come down!' he gasped. 'Bellingham's ill.'

Abercrombie Smith followed him closely down stairs into the sitting-room which was beneath his own, and intent as he was upon the matter in hand, he could not but take an amazed glance around him as he crossed the threshold. It was such a chamber as he had never seen before—a museum rather than a study. Walls and ceiling were thickly covered with a thousand strange relics from Egypt and the East. Tall, angular figures bearing burdens or weapons stalked in an uncouth frieze round the apartments. Above were bull-headed, stork-headed, cat-headed, owl-headed statues, with viper-crowned, almond-eyed monarchs, and strange, beetle-like deities cut out of the blue Egyptian lapis lazuli. Horus and Isis and Osiris peeped down from every niche and shelf, while across the ceiling a true son of Old Nile, a great, hanging-jawed crocodile, was slung in a double noose.

In the centre of this singular chamber was a large, square table, littered with papers, bottles, and the dried leaves of some graceful, palm-like plant. These varied objects had all been heaped together in order to make room for a mummy case, which had been conveyed from the wall, as was evident from the gap there, and laid across the front of the table. The mummy itself, a horrid, black, withered thing, like a charred head on a gnarled bush, was lying half out of the case, with its clawlike hand and bony forearm resting upon the table. Propped up against the sarcophagus was an old yellow scroll of papyrus, and in front of it, in a wooden arm-chair, sat the owner of the room, his head thrown back, his widely-opened eyes directed in a horrified stare to the crocodile above him, and his blue, thick lips puffing loudly with every expiration.

'My God! he's dying!' cried Monkhouse Lee distractedly.

He was a slim, handsome young fellow, olive-skinned and dark-eyed, of a Spanish rather than of an English type, with a Celtic intensity of manner which contrasted with the Saxon phlegm of Abercombie Smith.

'Only a faint, I think,' said the medical student. 'Just give me a hand with him. You take his feet. Now on to the sofa. Can you kick all those little wooden devils off? What a litter it is! Now he will be all right if we undo his collar and give him some water. What has he been up to at all?'

'I don't know. I heard him cry out. I ran up. I know him pretty well, you know. It is very good of you to come down.'

'His heart is going like a pair of castanets,' said Smith, laying his hand on the breast of the unconscious man. 'He seems to me to be frightened all to pieces. Chuck the water over him! What a face he has got on him!'

It was indeed a strange and most repellent face, for colour and outline were equally unnatural. It was white, not with the ordinary pallor of fear but with an absolutely bloodless white, like the under side of a sole. He was very fat, but gave the impression of having at some time been considerably fatter, for his skin hung loosely in creases and folds, and was shot with a meshwork of wrinkles. Short, stubbly brown hair bristled up from his scalp, with a pair of thick, wrinkled ears protruding on either side. His light grey eyes were still open, the pupils dilated and the balls projecting in a fixed and horrid stare. It seemed to Smith as he looked down upon him that he had never seen nature's danger signals flying so plainly upon a man's countenance, and his thoughts turned more seriously to the warning which Hastie had given him an hour before.

'What the deuce can have frightened him so?' he asked.

'It's the mummy.'

'The mummy? How, then?'

'I don't know. It's beastly and morbid. I wish he would drop it. It's the second fright he has given me. It was the same last winter. I found him just like this, with that horrid thing in front of him.'

'What does he want with the mummy, then?'

'Oh, he's a crank, you know. It's his hobby. He knows more about these things than any man in England. But I wish he wouldn't! Ah, he's beginning to come to.'

A faint tinge of colour had begun to steal back into Bellingham's ghastly cheeks, and his eyelids shivered like a sail after a calm. He clasped and unclasped his hands, drew a long, thin breath between his teeth, and suddenly jerking up his head, threw a glance of recognition around him. As his eyes fell upon the mummy, he sprang off the sofa, seized the roll of papyrus, thrust it into a drawer, turned the key, and then staggered back on to the sofa.

'What's up?' he asked. 'What do you chaps want?'

'You've been shrieking out and making no end of a fuss,' said Monkhouse Lee. 'If our neighbour here from above hadn't come down, I'm sure I don't know what I should have done with you.'

'Ah, it's Abercrombie Smith,' said Bellingham, glancing up at him. 'How very good of you to come in! What a fool I am! Oh, my God, what a fool I am!'

He sunk his head on to his hands, and burst into peal after peal of hysterical laughter.

'Look here! Drop it!' cried Smith, shaking him roughly by the shoulder.

'Your nerves are all in a jangle. You must drop these little midnight games with mummies, or you'll be going off your chump. You're all on wires now.'

'I wonder,' said Bellingham, 'whether you would be as cool as I am if you had seen—'

'What then?'

'Oh, nothing. I meant that I wonder if you could sit up at night with a mummy without trying your nerves. I have no doubt that you are quite right. I dare say that I have been taking it out of myself too much lately. But I am all right now. Please don't go, though. Just wait for a few minutes until I am quite myself.'

'The room is very close,' remarked Lee, throwing open the window and letting in the cool night air.

'It's balsamic resin,' said Bellingham. He lifted up one of the dried palmate leaves from the table and frizzled it over the chimney of the lamp. It broke away into heavy smoke wreaths, and a pungent, biting odour filled the chamber. 'It's the sacred plant—the plant of the priests,' he remarked. 'Do you know anything of Eastern languages, Smith?'

'Nothing at all. Not a word.'

The answer seemed to lift a weight from the Egyptologist's mind.

'By the way,' he continued, 'how long was it from the time that you ran down, until I came to my senses?'

'Not long. Some four or five minutes.'

'I thought it could not be very long,' said he, drawing a long breath. 'But what a strange thing unconsciousness is! There is no measurement to it. I could not tell from my own sensations if it were seconds or weeks. Now that gentleman on the table was packed up in the days of the eleventh dynasty, some forty centuries ago, and yet if he could find his tongue, he would tell us that this lapse of time has been but a closing of the eyes and a reopening of them. He is a singularly fine mummy, Smith.'

Smith stepped over to the table and looked down with a professional eye at the black and twisted form in front of him. The features, though horribly discoloured, were perfect, and two little nut-like eyes still lurked in the depths of the black, hollow sockets. The blotched skin was drawn tightly from bone to bone, and a tangled wrap of black coarse hair fell over the ears. Two thin teeth, like those of a rat, overlay the shrivelled lower lip. In its crouching position, with bent joints and craned head, there was a suggestion of energy about the horrid thing which made Smith's gorge rise. The gaunt ribs, with their parchment-like covering, were exposed, and the sunken, leaden-hued abdomen, with the long slit where the embalmer had left his mark; but the lower limbs were wrapt round with coarse yellow bandages. A number of little clove-like pieces of myrrh and of cassia were sprinkled over the body, and lay scattered on the inside of the case.

'I don't know his name,' said Bellingham, passing his hand over the shrivelled head. 'You see the outer sarcophagus with the inscriptions is missing. Lot 249 is all the title he has now. You see it printed on his case. That was his number in the auction at which I picked him up.'

'He has been a very pretty sort of fellow in his day,' remarked Abercrombie Smith.

'He has been a giant. His mummy is six feet seven in length, and that would be a giant over there, for they were never a very robust race. Feel these great knotted bones, too. He would be a nasty fellow to tackle.'

'Perhaps these very hands helped to build the stones into the pyramids,' suggested Monkhouse Lee, looking down with disgust in his eyes at the crooked, unclean talons.

'No fear. This fellow has been pickled in natron, and looked after in the most approved style. They did not serve hodsmen in that fashion. Salt or bitumen was enough for them. It has been calculated that this sort of thing cost about seven hundred and thirty pounds in our money. Our friend was a noble at the least. What do you make of that small inscription near his feet, Smith?'

'I told you that I know no Eastern tongue.'

'Ah, so you did. It is the name of the embalmer, I take it. A very conscientious worker he must have been. I wonder how many modern works will survive four thousand years?'

He kept on speaking lightly and rapidly, but it was evident to Abercrombie Smith that he was still palpitating with fear. His hands shook, his lower lip trembled, and look where he would, his eye always came sliding round to his gruesome companion. Through all his fear, however, there was a suspicion of triumph in his tone and manner. His eye shone, and his footstep, as he paced the room, was brisk and jaunty. He gave the impression of a man who has gone through an ordeal, the marks of which he still bears upon him, but which has helped him to his end.

'You're not going yet?' he cried, as Smith rose from the sofa.

At the prospect of solitude, his fears seemed to crowd back upon him, and he stretched out a hand to detain him.

'Yes, I must go. I have my work to do. You are all right now. I think that with your nervous system you should take up some less morbid study.'

'Oh, I am not nervous as a rule; and I have unwrapped mummies before.'

'You fainted last time,' observed Monkhouse Lee.

'Ah, yes, so I did. Well, I must have a nerve tonic or a course of electricity. You are not going, Lee?'

'I'll do whatever you wish, Ned.'

'Then I'll come down with you and have a shake-down on your sofa. Good-night, Smith. I am so sorry to have disturbed you with my foolishness.'

They shook hands, and as the medical student stumbled up the spiral and irregular stair he heard a key turn in a door, and the steps of his two new acquaintances as they descended to the lower floor.

In this strange way began the acquaintance between Edward Bellingham and Abercrombie Smith, an acquaintance which the latter, at least, had no desire to push further. Bellingham, however, appeared to have taken a fancy to his rough-spoken neighbour, and made his advances in such a way that he could hardly be repulsed without absolute brutality. Twice he called to thank Smith for his assistance, and many times afterwards he looked in with books, papers and such other civilities as two bachelor neighbours can offer each other. He was, as Smith soon found, a man of wide reading, with catholic tastes and an extraordinary memory. His manner, too, was so pleasing and suave that one came, after a time, to overlook his repellent appearance. For a jaded and wearied man he was no unpleasant companion, and Smith found himself, after a time, looking forward to his visits, and even returning them.

Clever as he undoubtedly was, however, the medical student seemed to detect a dash of insanity in the man. He broke out at times

into a high, inflated style of talk which was in contrast with the simplicity of his life.

'It is a wonderful thing,' he cried, 'to feel that one can command
powers of good and of evil—a ministering angel or a demon of ven-
geance.' And again, of Monkhouse Lee, he said,—'Lee is a good fellow, an honest fellow, but he is without strength or ambition. He
would not make a fit partner for a man with a great enterprise. He
would not make a fit partner for me.'

At such hints and innuendoes stolid Smith, puffing solemnly at his
pipe, would simply raise his eyebrows and shake his head, with little
interjections of medical wisdom as to earlier hours and fresher air.

One habit Bellingham had developed of late which Smith knew to
be a frequent herald of a weakening mind. He appeared to be forever
talking to himself. At late hours of the night, when there could be no
visitor with him, Smith could still hear his voice beneath him in a low,
muffled monologue, sunk almost to a whisper, and yet very audible in
the silence. This solitary babbling annoyed and distracted the student,
so that he spoke more than once to his neighbour about it. Bellingham, however, flushed up at the charge, and denied curtly that he had
uttered a sound; indeed, he showed more annoyance over the matter
than the occasion seemed to demand.

Had Abercrombie Smith had any doubt as to his own ears he had
not to go far to find corroboration. Tom Styles, the little wrinkled
man-servant who had attended to the wants of the lodgers in the turret for a longer time than any man's memory could carry him, was
sorely put to it over the same matter.

'If you please, sir,' said he, as he tidied down the top chamber one
morning, 'do you think Mr Bellingham is all right, sir?'

'All right, Styles?'

'Yes sir. Right in his head, sir.'

'Why should he not be, then?'

'Well, I don't know, sir. His habits has changed of late. He's not
the same man he used to be, though I make free to say that he was
never quite one of my gentlemen, like Mr Hastie or yourself, sir. He's
took to talkin' to himself something awful. I wonder it don't disturb
you. I don't know what to make of him, sir.'

'I don't know what business it is of yours, Styles.'

'Well, I takes an interest, Mr Smith. It may be forward of me, but I can't help it. I feel sometimes as if I was mother and father to my young gentlemen. It all falls on me when things go wrong and the relations come. But Mr Bellingham, sir. I want to know what it is that walks about his room sometimes when he's out and when the door's locked on the outside.'

'Eh? you're talking nonsense, Styles.'

'Maybe so, sir; but I heard it more'n once with my own ears.'

'Rubbish, Styles.'

'Very good, sir. You'll ring the bell if you want me.'

Abercrombie Smith gave little heed to the gossip of the old man-servant, but a small incident occurred a few days later which left an unpleasant effect upon his mind, and brought the words of Styles forcibly to his memory.

Bellingham had come up to see him late one night, and was entertaining him with an interesting account of the rock tombs of Beni Hassan in Upper Egypt, when Smith, whose hearing was remarkably acute, distinctly heard the sound of a door opening on the landing below.

'There's some fellow gone in or out of your room,' he remarked.

Bellingham sprang up and stood helpless for a moment, with the expression of a man who is half incredulous and half afraid.

'I surely locked it. I am almost positive that I locked it,' he stammered. 'No one could have opened it.'

'Why, I hear someone coming up the steps now,' said Smith.

Bellingham rushed out through the door, slammed it loudly behind him, and hurried down the stairs. About half-way down Smith heard him stop, and thought he caught the sound of whispering. A moment later the door beneath him shut, a key creaked in a lock, and Bellingham, with beads of moisture upon his pale face, ascended the stairs once more, and re-entered the room.

'It's all right,' he said, throwing himself down in a chair. 'It was that fool of a dog. He had pushed the door open. I don't know how I came to forget to lock it.'

'I didn't know you kept a dog,' said Smith, looking very thoughtfully at the disturbed face of his companion.

'Yes, I haven't had him long. I must get rid of him. He's a great nuisance.'

'He must be, if you find it so hard to shut him up. I should have thought that shutting the door would have been enough, without locking it.'

'I want to prevent old Styles from letting him out. He's of some value, you know, and it would be awkward to lose him.'

'I am a bit of a dog-fancier myself,' said Smith, still gazing hard at his companion from the corner of his eyes. 'Perhaps you'll let me have a look at it.'

'Certainly. But I am afraid it cannot be to-night; I have an appointment. Is that clock right? Then I am a quarter of an hour late already. You'll excuse me, I am sure.'

He picked up his cap and hurried from the room. In spite of his appointment, Smith heard him re-enter his own chamber and lock his door upon the inside.

This interview left a disagreeable impression upon the medical student's mind. Bellingham had lied to him, and lied so clumsily that it looked as if he had desperate reasons for concealing the truth. Smith knew that his neighbour had no dog. He knew, also, that the step which he had heard upon the stairs was not the step of an animal. But if it were not, then what could it be? There was old Styles's statement about the something which used to pace the room at times when the owner was absent. Could it be a woman? Smith rather inclined to the view. If so, it would mean disgrace and expulsion to Bellingham if it were discovered by the authorities, so that his anxiety and falsehoods might be accounted for. And yet it was inconceivable that an undergraduate could keep a woman in his rooms without being instantly detected. Be the explanation what it might, there was something ugly about it, and Smith determined, as he turned to his books, to discourage all further attempts at intimacy on the part of his soft-spoken and ill-favoured neighbour.

But his work was destined to interruption that night. He had hardly caught up the broken threads when a firm, heavy footfall came three steps at a time from below, and Hastie, in blazer and flannels, burst into the room.

'Still at it!' said he, plumping down into his wonted arm-chair.

'What a chap you are to stew! I believe an earthquake might come and knock Oxford into a cocked hat, and you would sit perfectly placid with your books among the ruins. However, I won't bore you long. Three whiffs of baccy, and I am off.'

'What's the news, then?' asked Smith, cramming a plug of bird's-eye into his briar with his forefinger.

'Nothing very much. Wilson made 70 for the freshmen against the eleven. They say that they will play him instead of Buddicomb, for Buddicomb is clean off colour. He used to be able to bowl a little, but it's nothing but half-vollies and long hops now.'

'Medium right,' suggested Smith, with the intense gravity which comes upon a 'varsity man when he speaks of athletics.

'Inclining to fast, with a work from leg. Comes with the arm about three inches or so. He used to be nasty on a wet wicket. Oh, by-the-way, have you heard about Long Norton?'

'What's that?'

'He's been attacked.'

'Attacked?'

'Yes, just as he was turning out of the High Street, and within a hundred yards of the gate of Old's.'

'But who—'

'Ah, that's the rub! If you said "what," you would be more grammatical. Norton swears that it was not human, and, indeed, from the scratches on his throat, I should be inclined to agree with him.'

'What, then? Have we come down to spooks?'

Abercrombie Smith puffed his scientific contempt.

'Well, no; I don't think that is quite the idea, either. I am inclined to think that if any showman has lost a great ape lately, and the brute is in these parts, a jury would find a true bill against it. Norton passes that way every night, you know, about the same hour. There's a tree that hangs low over the path—the big elm from Rainy's garden. Norton thinks the thing dropped on him out of the tree. Anyhow, he was nearly strangled by two arms, which, he says, were as strong and as thin as steel bands. He saw nothing; only those beastly arms that tightened and tightened on him. He yelled his head nearly off, and a couple of chaps came running, and the thing went over the wall like a cat. He never got a fair sight of it the whole time. It gave Norton a shake up,

I can tell you. I tell him it has been as good as a change at the sea-side for him.'

'A garrotter, most likely,' said Smith.

'Very possibly. Norton says not; but we don't mind what he says. The garrotter had long nails, and was pretty smart at swinging himself over walls. By-the-way, your beautiful neighbour would be pleased if he heard about it. He had a grudge against Norton, and he's not a man, from what I know of him, to forget his little debts. But hallo, old chap, what have you got in your noddle?'

'Nothing,' Smith answered curtly.

He had started in his chair, and the look had flashed over his face which comes upon a man who is struck suddenly by some unpleasant idea.

'You looked as if something I had said had taken you on the raw. By-the-way, you have made the acquaintance of Master B. since I looked in last, have you not? Young Monkhouse Lee told me something to that effect.'

'Yes; I know him slightly. He has been up here once or twice.'

'Well, you're big enough and ugly enough to take care of yourself. He's not what I should call exactly a healthy sort of Johnny, though, no doubt, he's very clever, and all that. But you'll soon find out for yourself. Lee is all right; he's a very decent little fellow. Well, so long, old chap! I row Mullins for the Vice-Chancellor's pot on Wednesday week, so mind you come down, in case I don't see you before.'

Bovine Smith laid down his pipe and turned stolidly to his books once more. But with all the will in the world, he found it very hard to keep his mind upon his work. It would slip away to brood upon the man beneath him, and upon the little mystery which hung round his chambers. Then his thoughts turned to this singular attack of which Hastie had spoken, and to the grudge which Bellingham was said to owe the object of it. The two ideas would persist in rising together in his mind, as though there were some close and intimate connection between them. And yet the suspicion was so dim and vague that it could not be put down in words.

'Confound the chap!' cried Smith, as he shied his book on pathology across the room. 'He has spoiled my night's reading, and that's reason enough, if there were no other, why I should steer clear of him in the future.'

For ten days the medical student confined himself so closely to his studies that he neither saw nor heard anything of either of the men beneath him. At the hours when Bellingham had been accustomed to visit him, he took care to sport his oak,[1] and though he more than once heard a knocking at his outer door, he resolutely refused to answer it. One afternoon, however, he was descending the stairs when, just as he was passing it, Bellingham's door flew open, and young Monkhouse Lee came out with his eyes sparkling and a dark flush of anger upon his olive cheeks. Close at his heels followed Bellingham, his fat, unhealthy face all quivering with malignant passion.

'You fool!' he hissed. 'You'll be sorry.'

'Very likely,' cried the other. 'Mind what I say. It's off! I won't hear of it!'

'You've promised, anyhow.'

'Oh, I'll keep that! I won't speak. But I'd rather little Eva was in her grave. Once for all, it's off. She'll do what I say. We don't want to see you again.'

So much Smith could not avoid hearing, but he hurried on, for he had no wish to be involved in their dispute. There had been a serious breach between them, that was clear enough, and Lee was going to cause the engagement with his sister to be broken off. Smith thought of Hastie's comparison of the toad and the dove, and was glad to think that the matter was at an end. Bellingham's face when he was in a passion was not pleasant to look upon. He was not a man to whom an innocent girl could be trusted for life. As he walked, Smith wondered languidly what could have caused the quarrel, and what the promise might be which Bellingham had been so anxious that Monkhouse Lee should keep.

It was the day of the sculling match between Hastie and Mullins, and a stream of men were making their way down to the banks of the Isis. A May sun was shining brightly, and the yellow path was barred with the black shadows of the tall elm-trees. On either side the grey colleges lay back from the road, the hoary old mothers of minds looking out from their high, mullioned windows at the tide of young life which swept so merrily past them. Black-clad tutors, prim officials, pale reading men, brown-faced, straw-hatted young athletes in white sweaters or many-coloured blazers, all were hurrying towards the blue winding river which curves through the Oxford meadows.

Abercrombie Smith, with the intuition of an old oarsman, chose his position at the point where he knew that the struggle, if there were a struggle, would come. Far off he heard the hum which announced the start, the gathering roar of the approach, the thunder of running feet, and the shouts of the men in the boats beneath him. A spray of half-clad, deep-breathing runners shot past him, and craning over their shoulders, he saw Hastie pulling a steady thirty-six, while his opponent, with a jerky forty, was a good boat's length behind him. Smith gave a cheer for his friend, and pulling out his watch, was starting off again for his chambers, when he felt a touch upon his shoulder, and found that young Monkhouse Lee was beside him.

'I saw you there,' he said, in a timid, deprecating way. 'I wanted to speak to you, if you could spare me a half-hour. This cottage is mine. I share it with Harrington of King's. Come in and have a cup of tea.'

'I must be back presently,' said Smith. 'I am hard on the grind at present. But I'll come in for a few minutes with pleasure. I wouldn't have come out only Hastie is a friend of mine.'

'So he is of mine. Hasn't he a beautiful style? Mullins wasn't in it. But come into the cottage. It's a little den of a place, but it is pleasant to work in during the summer months.'

It was a small, square, white building, with green doors and shutters, and a rustic trellis-work porch, standing back some fifty yards from the river's bank. Inside, the main room was roughly fitted up as a study—deal table, unpainted shelves with books, and a few cheap oleographs upon the wall. A kettle sang upon a spirit-stove, and there were tea things upon a tray on the table.

'Try that chair and have a cigarette,' said Lee. 'Let me pour you out a cup of tea. It's so good of you to come in, for I know that your time is a good deal taken up. I wanted to say to you that, if I were you, I should change my rooms at once.'

'Eh?'

Smith sat staring with a lighted match in one hand and his unlit cigarette in the other.

'Yes; it must seem very extraordinary, and the worst of it is that

I cannot give my reasons, for I am under a solemn promise—a very solemn promise. But I may go so far as to say that I don't think Bellingham is a very safe man to live near. I intend to camp out here as much as I can for a time.'

'Not safe! What do you mean?'

'Ah, that's what I mustn't say. But do take my advice, and move your rooms. We had a grand row to-day. You must have heard us, for you came down the stairs.'

'I saw that you had fallen out.'

'He's a horrible chap, Smith. That is the only word for him. I have had doubts about him ever since that night when he fainted—you remember, when you came down. I taxed him to-day, and he told me things that made my hair rise, and wanted me to stand in with him. I'm not strait-laced, but I am a clergyman's son, you know, and I think there are some things which are quite beyond the pale. I only thank God that I found him out before it was too late, for he was to have married into my family.'

'This is all very fine, Lee,' said Abercrombie Smith curtly. 'But either you are saying a great deal too much or a great deal too little.'

'I give you a warning.'

'If there is real reason for warning, no promise can bind you. If I see a rascal about to blow a place up with dynamite no pledge will stand in my way of preventing him.'

'Ah, but I cannot prevent him, and I can do nothing but warn you.'

'Without saying what you warn me against.'

'Against Bellingham.'

'But that is childish. Why should I fear him, or any man?'

'I can't tell you. I can only entreat you to change your rooms. You are in danger where you are. I don't even say that Bellingham would wish to injure you. But it might happen, for he is a dangerous neighbour just now.'

'Perhaps I know more than you think,' said Smith, looking keenly at the young man's boyish, earnest face. 'Suppose I tell you that some one else shares Bellingham's rooms.'

Monkhouse Lee sprang from his chair in uncontrollable excitement.

'You know, then?' he gasped.

'A woman.'

Lee dropped back again with a groan.

'My lips are sealed,' he said. 'I must not speak.'

'Well, anyhow,' said Smith, rising, 'it is not likely that I should allow myself to be frightened out of rooms which suit me very nicely. It
would be a little too feeble for me to move out all my goods and chat-
tels because you say that Bellingham might in some unexplained way
do me an injury. I think that I'll just take my chance, and stay where I
am, and as I see that it's nearly five o'clock, I must ask you to excuse
me.'

He bade the young student adieu in a few curt words, and made
his way homeward through the sweet spring evening, feeling half-ruf-
fled, half-amused, as any other strong, unimaginative man might who
has been menaced by a vague and shadowy danger.

There was one little indulgence which Abercrombie Smith always
allowed himself, however closely his work might press upon him.
Twice a week, on the Tuesday and the Friday, it was his invariable custom to walk over to Farlingford, the residence of Doctor Plumptree
Peterson, situated about a mile and a half out of Oxford. Peterson had
been a close friend of Smith's elder brother Francis, and as he was a
bachelor, fairly well-to-do, with a good cellar and a better library, his
house was a pleasant goal for a man who was in need of a brisk walk.
Twice a week, then, the medical student would swing out there along
the dark country roads, and spend a pleasant hour in Peterson's comfortable study, discussing, over a glass of old port, the gossip of the
'varsity or the latest developments of medicine or of surgery.

On the day which followed his interview with Monkhouse Lee,
Smith shut up his books at a quarter past eight, the hour when he
usually started for his friend's house. As he was leaving his room, however, his eyes chanced to fall upon one of the books which Bellingham
had lent him, and his conscience pricked him for not having returned
it. However repellent the man might be, he should not be treated with
discourtesy. Taking the book, he walked downstairs and knocked at
his neighbour's door. There was no answer; but on turning the handle
he found that it was unlocked. Pleased at the thought of avoiding an

interview, he stepped inside, and placed the book with his card upon the table.

The lamp was turned half down, but Smith could see the details of the room plainly enough. It was all much as he had seen it before—the frieze, the animal-headed gods, the hanging crocodile, and the table littered over with papers and dried leaves. The mummy case stood upright against the wall, but the mummy itself was missing. There was no sign of any second occupant of the room, and he felt as he withdrew that he had probably done Bellingham an injustice. Had he a guilty secret to preserve, he would hardly leave his door open so that all the world might enter.

The spiral stair was as black as pitch, and Smith was slowly making his way down its irregular steps, when he was suddenly conscious that something had passed him in the darkness. There was a faint sound, a whiff of air, a light brushing past his elbow, but so slight that he could scarcely be certain of it. He stopped and listened, but the wind was rustling among the ivy outside, and he could hear nothing else.

'Is that you, Styles?' he shouted.

There was no answer, and all was still behind him. It must have been a sudden gust of air, for there were crannies and cracks in the old turret. And yet he could almost have sworn that he heard a footfall by his very side. He had emerged into the quadrangle, still turning the matter over in his head, when a man came running swiftly across the smooth-cropped lawn.

'Is that you, Smith?'

'Hullo, Hastie!'

'For God's sake come at once! Young Lee is drowned! Here's Harrington of King's with the news. The doctor is out. You'll do, but come along at once. There may be life in him.'

'Have you brandy?'

'No.'

'I'll bring some. There's a flask on my table.'

Smith bounded up the stairs, taking three at a time, seized the flask, and was rushing down with it, when, as he passed Bellingham's room, his eyes fell upon something which left him gasping and staring upon the landing.

The door, which he had closed behind him, was now open, and right in front of him, with the lamp-light shining upon it, was the mummy case. Three minutes ago it had been empty. He could swear to that. Now it framed the lank body of its horrible occupant, who stood, grim and stark, with his black shrivelled face towards the door. The form was lifeless and inert, but it seemed to Smith as he gazed that there still lingered a lurid spark of vitality, some faint sign of consciousness in the little eyes which lurked in the depths of the hollow sockets. So astounded and shaken was he that he had forgotten his errand, and was still staring at the lean, sunken figure when the voice of his friend below recalled him to himself.

'Come on, Smith!' he shouted. 'It's life and death, you know. Hurry up! Now, then,' he added, as the medical student reappeared, 'let us do a sprint. It is well under a mile, and we should do it in five minutes. A human life is better worth running for than a pot.'

Neck and neck they dashed through the darkness, and did not pull up until panting and spent, they had reached the little cottage by the river. Young Lee, limp and dripping like a broken water-plant, was stretched upon the sofa, the green scum of the river upon his black hair, and a fringe of white foam upon his leaden-hued lips. Beside him knelt his fellow-student Harrington, endeavouring to chafe some warmth back into his rigid limbs.

'I think there's life in him,' said Smith, with his hand to the lad's side. 'Put your watch glass to his lips. Yes, there's dimming on it. You take one arm, Hastie. Now work it as I do, and we'll soon pull him round.'

For ten minutes they worked in silence, inflating and depressing the chest of the unconscious man. At the end of that time a shiver ran through his body, his lips trembled, and he opened his eyes. The three students burst out into an irrepressible cheer.

'Wake up, old chap. You've frightened us quite enough.'

'Have some brandy. Take a sip from the flask.'

'He's all right now,' said his companion Harrington. 'Heavens, what a fright I got! I was reading here, and he had gone for a stroll as far as the river, when I heard a scream and a splash. Out I ran, and by the time that I could find him and fish him out, all life seemed to have gone. Then Simpson couldn't get a doctor, for he has a game-leg, and

I had to run, and I don't know what I'd have done without you fellows. That's right, old chap. Sit up.'

Monkhouse Lee had raised himself on his hands, and looked wildly about him.

'What's up?' he asked. 'I've been in the water. Ah, yes; I remember.'

A look of fear came into his eyes, and he sank his face into his hands.

'How did you fall in?'

'I didn't fall in.'

'How, then?'

'I was thrown in. I was standing by the bank, and something from behind picked me up like a feather and hurled me in. I heard nothing, and I saw nothing. But I know what it was, for all that.'

'And so do I,' whispered Smith.

Lee looked up with a quick glance of surprise.

'You've learned, then?' he said. 'You remember the advice I gave you?'

'Yes, and I begin to think that I shall take it.'

'I don't know what the deuce you fellows are talking about,' said Hastie, 'but I think, if I were you, Harrington, I should get Lee to bed at once. It will be time enough to discuss the why and the wherefore when he is a little stronger. I think, Smith, you and I can leave him alone now. I am walking back to college; if you are coming in that direction, we can have a chat.'

But it was little chat that they had upon their homeward path. Smith's mind was too full of the incidents of the evening, the absence of the mummy from his neighbour's rooms, the step that passed him on the stair, the reappearance—the extraordinary, inexplicable reappearance of the grisly thing—and then this attack upon Lee, corresponding so closely to the previous outrage upon another man against whom Bellingham bore a grudge. All this settled in his thoughts, together with the many little incidents which had previously turned him against his neighbour, and the singular circumstances under which he was first called in to him. What had been a dim suspicion, a vague, fantastic conjecture, had suddenly taken form, and stood out in his mind as a grim fact, a thing not to be denied. And yet, how monstrous it was! how unheard of! how entirely beyond all bounds of human experience. An impartial judge, or even the friend who walked by his side, would simply tell him that his eyes had deceived him, that the mummy had been there all the time, that young Lee had tumbled into the river as any other man tumbles into a river, and that a blue pill was the best thing for a disordered liver. He felt that he would have said as much if the positions had been reversed. And yet he could swear that Bellingham was a murderer at heart, and that he wielded a weapon such as no man had ever used in all the grim history of crime.

Hastie had branched off to his rooms with a few crisp and emphatic comments upon his friend's unsociability, and Abercrombie Smith crossed the quadrangle to his corner turret with a strong feeling of repulsion for his chambers and their associations. He would take Lee's advice, and move his quarters as soon as possible, for how could a man study when his ear was ever straining for every murmur or footstep in the room below? He observed, as he crossed over the lawn, that the light was still shining in Bellingham's window, and as he passed up the staircase the door opened, and the man himself looked out at him. With his fat, evil face he was like some bloated spider fresh from the weaving of his poisonous web.

'Good-evening,' said he. 'Won't you come in?'

'No,' cried Smith, fiercely.

'No? You are busy as ever? I wanted to ask you about Lee. I was sorry to hear that there was a rumour that something was amiss with him.'

His features were grave, but there was the gleam of a hidden laugh in his eyes as he spoke. Smith saw it, and he could have knocked him down for it.

'You'll be sorrier still to hear that Monkhouse Lee is doing very well, and is out of all danger,' he answered. 'Your hellish tricks have not come off this time. Oh, you needn't try to brazen it out. I know all about it.'

Bellingham took a step back from the angry student, and half-closed the door as if to protect himself.

'You are mad,' he said. 'What do you mean? Do you assert that I had anything to do with Lee's accident?'

'Yes,' thundered Smith. 'You and that bag of bones behind you; you worked it between you. I tell you what it is, Master B., they have given up burning folk like you, but we still keep a hangman, and, by George! if any man in this college meets his death while you are here, I'll have you up, and if you don't swing for it, it won't be my fault. You'll find that your filthy Egyptian tricks won't answer in England.'

'You're a raving lunatic,' said Bellingham.

'All right. You just remember what I say, for you'll find that I'll be better than my word.'

The door slammed, and Smith went fuming up to his chamber, where he locked the door upon the inside, and spent half the night in smoking his old briar and brooding over the strange events of the evening.

Next morning Abercrombie Smith heard nothing of his neighbour, but Harrington called upon him in the afternoon to say that Lee was almost himself again. All day Smith stuck fast to his work, but in the evening he determined to pay the visit to his friend Doctor Peterson upon which he had started upon the night before. A good walk and a friendly chat would be welcome to his jangled nerves.

Bellingham's door was shut as he passed, but glancing back when he was some distance from the turret, he saw his neighbour's head at the window outlined against the lamp-light, his face pressed apparently against the glass as he gazed out into the darkness. It was a blessing to be away from all contact with him, but if for a few hours, and Smith stepped out briskly, and breathed the soft spring air into his lungs. The half-moon lay in the west between two Gothic pinnacles, and threw upon the silvered street a dark tracery from the stone-work above. There was a brisk breeze, and light, fleecy clouds drifted swiftly across the sky. Old's was on the very border of the town, and in five minutes Smith found himself beyond the houses and between the hedges of a May-scented Oxfordshire lane.

It was a lonely and little frequented road which led to his friend's house. Early as it was, Smith did not meet a single soul upon his way. He walked briskly along until he came to the avenue gate, which opened into the long gravel drive leading up to Farlingford. In front of him he could see the cosy red light of the windows glimmering through the foliage. He stood with his hand upon the iron latch of the swinging gate, and he glanced back at the road along which he had come. Something was coming swiftly down it.

It moved in the shadow of the hedge, silently and furtively, a dark, crouching figure, dimly visible against the black background. Even as he gazed back at it, it had lessened its distance by twenty paces, and was fast closing upon him. Out of the darkness he had a glimpse of a scraggy neck, and of two eyes that will ever haunt him in his dreams. He turned, and with a cry of terror he ran for his life up the avenue. There were the red lights, the signals of safety, almost within a stone's throw of him. He was a famous runner, but never had he run as he ran that night.

The heavy gate had swung into place behind him, but he heard it dash open again before his pursuer. As he rushed madly and wildly through the night, he could hear a swift, dry patter behind him, and could see, as he threw back a glance, that this horror was bounding like a tiger at his heels, with blazing eyes and one stringy arm outthrown. Thank God, the door was ajar. He could see the thin bar of light which shot from the lamp in the hall. Nearer yet sounded the clatter from behind. He heard a hoarse gurgling at his very shoulder. With a shriek he flung himself against the door, slammed and bolted it behind him, and sank half-fainting on to the hall chair.

'My goodness, Smith, what's the matter?' asked Peterson, appearing at the door of his study.

'Give me some brandy!'

Peterson disappeared, and came rushing out again with a glass and a decanter.

'You need it,' he said, as his visitor drank off what he poured out for him. 'Why, man, you are as white as a cheese.'

Smith laid down his glass, rose up, and took a deep breath.

'I am my own man again now,' said he. 'I was never so unmanned before. But, with your leave, Peterson, I will sleep here to-night, for I don't think I could face that road again except by daylight. It's weak, I know, but I can't help it.'

Peterson looked at his visitor with a very questioning eye.

'Of course you shall sleep here if you wish. I'll tell Mrs Burney to make up the spare bed. Where are you off to now?'

'Come up with me to the window that overlooks the door. I want you to see what I have seen.'

They went up to the window of the upper hall whence they could look down upon the approach to the house. The drive and the fields on either side lay quiet and still, bathed in the peaceful moonlight.

'Well, really, Smith,' remarked Peterson, 'it is well that I know you to be an abstemious man. What in the world can have frightened you?'

'I'll tell you presently. But where can it have gone? Ah, now look, look! See the curve of the road just beyond your gate.'

'Yes, I see; you needn't pinch my arm off. I saw someone pass. I should say a man, rather thin, apparently, and tall, very tall. But what of him? And what of yourself? You are still shaking like an aspen leaf.'

'I have been within hand-grip of the devil, that's all. But come down to your study, and I shall tell you the whole story.'

He did so. Under the cheery lamplight, with a glass of wine on the table beside him, and the portly form and florid face of his friend in front, he narrated, in their order, all the events, great and small, which had formed so singular a chain, from the night on which he had found Bellingham fainting in front of the mummy case until his horrid experience of an hour ago.

'There now,' he said as he concluded, 'that's the whole black business. It is monstrous and incredible, but it is true.'

Doctor Plumptree Peterson sat for some time in silence with a very puzzled expression upon his face.

'I never heard of such a thing in my life, never!' he said at last. 'You have told me the facts. Now tell me your inferences.'

'You can draw your own.'

'But I should like to hear yours. You have thought over the matter, and I have not.'

'Well, it must be a little vague in detail, but the main points seem to me to be clear enough. This fellow Bellingham, in his Eastern studies, has got hold of some infernal secret by which a mummy—or possibly only this particular mummy—can be temporarily brought to life. He was trying this disgusting business on the night when he fainted. No doubt the sight of the creature moving had shaken his nerve, even though he had expected it. You remember that almost the first words he said were to call out upon himself as a fool. Well, he got more hardened afterwards, and carried the matter through without faint-

ing. The vitality which he could put into it was evidently only a passing thing, for I have seen it continually in its case as dead as this table.
He has some elaborate process, I fancy, by which he brings the thing
to pass. Having done it, he naturally bethought him that he might use
the creature as an agent. It has intelligence and it has strength. For
some purpose he took Lee into his confidence; but Lee, like a decent
Christian, would have nothing to do with such a business. Then they
had a row, and Lee vowed that he would tell his sister of Bellingham's
true character. Bellingham's game was to prevent him, and he nearly
managed it, by setting this creature of his on his track. He had already
tried its powers upon another man—Norton—towards whom he had
a grudge. It is the merest chance that he has not two murders upon
his soul. Then, when I taxed him with the matter, he had the strongest
reasons for wishing to get me out of the way before I could convey
my knowledge to anyone else. He got his chance when I went out,
for he knew my habits, and where I was bound for. I have had a narrow shave, Peterson, and it is mere luck you didn't find me on your
doorstep in the morning. I'm not a nervous man as a rule, and I never
thought to have the fear of death put upon me as it was to-night.'

'My dear boy, you take the matter too seriously,' said his companion. 'Your nerves are out of order with your work, and you make too
much of it. How could such a thing as this stride about the streets of
Oxford, even at night, without being seen?'

'It has been seen. There is quite a scare in the town about an escaped ape, as they imagine the creature to be. It is the talk of the
place.'

'Well, it's a striking chain of events. And yet, my dear fellow, you
must allow that each incident in itself is capable of a more natural
explanation.'

'What! even my adventure of to-night?'

'Certainly. You come out with your nerves all unstrung, and your
head full of this theory of yours. Some gaunt, half-famished tramp
steals after you, and seeing you run, is emboldened to pursue you.
Your fears and imagination do the rest.'

'It won't do, Peterson; it won't do.'

'And again, in the instance of your finding the mummy case empty, and then a few moments later with an occupant, you know that it

was lamplight, that the lamp was half turned down, and that you had no special reason to look hard at the case. It is quite possible that you may have overlooked the creature in the first instance.'

'No, no; it is out of the question.'

'And then Lee may have fallen into the river, and Norton been garrotted. It is certainly a formidable indictment that you have against Bellingham; but if you were to place it before a police magistrate, he would simply laugh in your face.'

'I know he would. That is why I mean to take the matter into my own hands.'

'Eh?'

'Yes; I feel that a public duty rests upon me, and, besides, I must do it for my own safety, unless I choose to allow myself to be hunted by this beast out of the college, and that would be a little too feeble. I have quite made up my mind what I shall do. And first of all, may I use your paper and pens for an hour?'

'Most certainly. You will find all that you want upon that side table.'

Abercrombie Smith sat down before a sheet of foolscap, and for an hour, and then for a second hour his pen travelled swiftly over it. Page after page was finished and tossed aside while his friend leaned back in his arm-chair, looking across at him with patient curiosity. At last, with an exclamation of satisfaction, Smith sprang to his feet, gathered his papers up into order, and laid the last one upon Peterson's desk.

'Kindly sign this as a witness,' he said.

'A witness? Of what?'

'Of my signature, and of the date. The date is the most important. Why, Peterson, my life might hang upon it.'

'My dear Smith, you are talking wildly. Let me beg you to go to bed.'

'On the contrary, I never spoke so deliberately in my life. And I will promise to go to bed the moment you have signed it.'

'But what is it?'

'It is a statement of all that I have been telling you to-night. I wish you to witness it.'

'Certainly,' said Peterson, signing his name under that of his companion. 'There you are! But what is the idea?'

'You will kindly retain it, and produce it in case I am arrested.'

'Arrested? For what?'

'For murder. It is quite on the cards. I wish to be ready for every event. There is only one course open to me, and I am determined to take it.'

'For Heaven's sake, don't do anything rash!'

'Believe me, it would be far more rash to adopt any other course. I hope that we won't need to bother you, but it will ease my mind to know that you have this statement of my motives. And now I am ready to take your advice and to go to roost, for I want to be at my best in the morning.'

Abercrombie Smith was not an entirely pleasant man to have as an enemy. Slow and easy-tempered, he was formidable when driven to action. He brought to every purpose in life the same deliberate resoluteness which had distinguished him as a scientific student. He had laid his studies aside for a day, but he intended that the day should not be wasted. Not a word did he say to his host as to his plans, but by nine o'clock he was well on his way to Oxford.

In the High Street he stopped at Clifford's, the gun-maker's, and bought a heavy revolver, with a box of central-fire cartridges. Six of them he slipped into the chambers, and half-cocking the weapon, placed it in the pocket of his coat. He then made his way to Hastie's rooms, where the big oarsman was lounging over his breakfast, with the *Sporting Times* propped up against the coffee-pot.

'Hullo! What's up?' he asked. 'Have some coffee?'

'No, thank you. I want you to come with me, Hastie, and do what I ask you.'

'Certainly, my boy.'

'And bring a heavy stick with you.'

'Hullo!' Hastie stared. 'Here's a hunting-crop that would fell an ox.'

'One other thing. You have a box of amputating knives. Give me the longest of them.'

'There you are. You seem to be fairly on the war trail. Anything else?'

'No; that will do.' Smith placed the knife inside his coat, and led

the way to the quadrangle. We are neither of us chickens, Hastie,' said
he. 'I think I can do this job alone, but I take you as a precaution. I am
going to have a little talk with Bellingham. If I have only him to deal
with, I won't, of course, need you. If I shout, however, up you come,
and lam out with your whip as hard as you can lick. Do you understand?'

'All right. I'll come if I hear you bellow.'

'Stay here, then. It may be a little time, but don't budge until I
come down.'

'I'm a fixture.'

Smith ascended the stairs, opened Bellingham's door and stepped
in. Bellingham was seated behind his table, writing. Beside him,
among his litter of strange possessions, towered the mummy case,
with its sale number 249 still stuck upon its front, and its hideous occupant stiff and stark within it. Smith looked very deliberately round
him, closed the door, locked it, took the key from the inside, and then
stepping across to the fireplace, struck a match and set the fire alight.
Bellingham sat staring, with amazement and rage upon his bloated
face.

'Well, really now, you make yourself at home,' he gasped.

Smith sat himself deliberately down, placing his watch upon the
table, drew out his pistol, cocked it, and laid it in his lap. Then he took
the long amputating knife from his bosom, and threw it down in front
of Bellingham.

'Now, then,' said he, 'just get to work and cut up that mummy.'

'Oh, is that it?' said Bellingham with a sneer.

'Yes, that is it. They tell me that the law can't touch you. But I
have a law that will set matters straight. If in five minutes you have not
set to work, I swear by the God who made me that I will put a bullet
through your brain!'

'You would murder me?'

Bellingham had half risen, and his face was the colour of putty.

'Yes.'

'And for what?'

'To stop your mischief. One minute has gone.'

'But what have I done?'

'I know and you know.'

'This is mere bullying.'

'Two minutes are gone.'

'But you must give reasons. You are a madman—a dangerous madman. Why should I destroy my own property? It is a valuable mummy.'

'You must cut it up, and you must burn it.'

'I will do no such thing.'

'Four minutes are gone.'

Smith took up the pistol and he looked towards Bellingham with an inexorable face. As the second-hand stole round, he raised his hand, and the finger twitched upon the trigger.

'There! there! I'll do it!' screamed Bellingham.

In frantic haste he caught up the knife and hacked at the figure of the mummy, ever glancing round to see the eye and the weapon of his terrible visitor bent upon him. The creature crackled and snapped under every stab of the keen blade. A thick yellow dust rose up from it. Spices and dried essences rained down upon the floor. Suddenly, with a rending crack, its backbone snapped asunder, and it fell, a brown heap of sprawling limbs, upon the floor.

'Now into the fire!' said Smith.

The flames leaped and roared as the dried and tinderlike *débris* was piled upon it. The little room was like the stoke-hole of a steamer and the sweat ran down the faces of the two men; but still the one stooped and worked, while the other sat watching him with a set face. A thick, fat smoke oozed out from the fire, and a heavy smell of burned rosin and singed hair filled the air. In a quarter of an hour a few charred and brittle sticks were all that was left of Lot No. 249.

'Perhaps that will satisfy you,' snarled Bellingham, with hate and fear in his little grey eyes as he glanced back at his tormentor.

'No; I must make a clean sweep of all your materials. We must have no more devil's tricks. In with all these leaves! They may have something to do with it.'

'And what now?' asked Bellingham, when the leaves also had been added to the blaze.

'Now the roll of papyrus which you had on the table that night. It is in that drawer, I think.'

'No, no,' shouted Bellingham. 'Don't burn that! Why, man, you don't know what you do. It is unique; it contains wisdom which is nowhere else to be found.'

'Out with it!'

'But look here, Smith, you can't really mean it. I'll share the knowledge with you. I'll teach you all that is in it. Or, stay, let me only copy it before you burn it!'

Smith stepped forward and turned the key in the drawer. Taking out the yellow, curled roll of paper, he threw it into the fire, and pressed it down with his heel. Bellingham screamed, and grabbed at it; but Smith pushed him back, and stood over it until it was reduced to a formless grey ash.

'Now, Master B.,' said he, 'I think I have pretty well drawn your teeth. You'll hear from me again, if you return to your old tricks. And now good-morning, for I must go back to my studies.'

And such is the narrative of Abercrombie Smith as to the singular events which occurred in Old College, Oxford, in the spring of '84. As Bellingham left the university immediately afterwards, and was last heard of in the Soudan, there is no one who can contradict his statement. But the wisdom of men is small, and the ways of nature are strange, and who shall put a bound to the dark things which may be found by those who seek for them?

NOTES TO 'LOT NO. 249'

First published in *Harper's Monthly Magazine*, September 1892.

1. Rooms in the Oxford colleges used to have two doors, the outer door made of solid oak. When this was shut ('sporting one's oak') it meant that the occupant was out or did not wish to be disturbed.

THE LOS AMIGOS FIASCO

I USED to be the leading practitioner of Los Amigos. Of course, everyone has heard of the great electrical generating gear there. The town is wide spread, and there are dozens of little townlets and villages all round, which receive their supply from the same centre, so that the works are on a very large scale. The Los Amigos folk say that they are the largest upon earth, but then we claim that for everything in Los Amigos except the gaol and the death-rate. Those are said to be the smallest.

Now, with so fine an electrical supply, it seemed to be a sinful waste of hemp that the Los Amigos criminals should perish in the old-fashioned manner. And then came the news of the electrocutions in the East, and how the results had not after all been so instantaneous as had been hoped. The Western Engineers raised their eyebrows when they read of the puny shocks by which these men had perished, and they vowed in Los Amigos that when an irreclaimable came their way he should be dealt handsomely by, and have the run of all the big dynamos. There should be no reserve, said the engineers, but he should have all that they had got. And what the result of that would be none could predict, save that it must be absolutely blasting and deadly. Never before had a man been so charged with electricity as they would charge him. He was to be smitten by the essence of ten thunderbolts. Some prophesied combustion, and some disintegration and disappearance. They were waiting eagerly to settle the question by actual demonstration, and it was just at that moment that Duncan Warner came that way.

Warner had been wanted by the law, and by nobody else, for many years. Desperado, murderer, train robber and road agent, he was a man beyond the pale of human pity. He had deserved a dozen deaths, and the Los Amigos folk grudged him so gaudy a one as that. He seemed to feel himself to be unworthy of it, for he made two frenzied attempts at escape. He was a powerful, muscular man, with a lion head, tangled black locks, and a sweeping beard which covered his broad chest. When he was tried, there was no finer head in all the crowded court. It's no new thing to find the best face looking from the dock. But his good looks could not balance his bad deeds. His advocate did all he knew, but the cards lay against him, and Duncan Warner was handed over to the mercy of the big Los Amigos dynamos.

I was there at the committee meeting when the matter was discussed. The town council had chosen four experts to look after the arrangements. Three of them were admirable. There was Joseph M'Connor, the very man who had designed the dynamos, and there was Joshua Westmacott, the chairman of the Los Amigos Electrical Supply Company, Limited. Then there was myself as the chief medical man, and lastly an old German of the name of Peter Stulpnagel. The Germans were a strong body at Los Amigos, and they all voted for their man. That was how he got on the committee. It was said that he had been a wonderful electrician at home, and he was eternally working with wires and insulators and Leyden jars; but, as he never seemed to get any further, or to have any results worth publishing, he came at last to be regarded as a harmless crank, who had made science his hobby. We three practical men smiled when we heard that he had been elected as our colleague, and at the meeting we fixed it all up very nicely among ourselves without much thought of the old fellow who sat with his ears scooped forward in his hands, for he was a trifle hard of hearing, taking no more part in the proceedings than the gentlemen of the press who scribbled their notes on the back benches.

We did not take long to settle it all. In New York a strength of some two thousand volts had been used, and death had not been instantaneous. Evidently their shock had been too weak. Los Amigos should not fall into that error. The charge should be six times greater, and therefore, of course, it would be six times more effective. Nothing could possibly be more logical. The whole concentrated force of the great dynamos should be employed on Duncan Warner.

So we three settled it, and had already risen to break up the meeting, when our silent companion opened his mouth for the first time.

'Gentlemen,' said he, 'you appear to me to show an extraordinary ignorance upon the subject of electricity. You have not mastered the first principles of its actions upon a human being.'

The committee was about to break into an angry reply to this brusque comment, but the chairman of the Electrical Company tapped his forehead to claim its indulgence for the crankiness of the speaker.

'Pray tell us, sir,' said he, with an ironical smile, 'what is there in our conclusions with which you find fault?'

'With your assumption that a large dose of electricity will merely increase the effect of a small dose. Do you not think it possible that it might have an entirely different result? Do you know anything, by actual experiment, of the effect of such powerful shocks?'

'We know it by analogy,' said the chairman, pompously. 'All drugs increase their effect when they increase their dose; for example—for example—'

'Whisky,' said Joseph M'Connor.

'Quite so. Whisky. You see it there.'

Peter Stulpnagel smiled and shook his head.

'Your argument is not very good,' said he. 'When I used to take whisky, I used to find that one glass would excite me, but that six would send me to sleep, which is just the opposite. Now, suppose that electricity were to act in just the opposite way also, what then?'

We three practical men burst out laughing. We had known that our colleague was queer, but we never had thought that he would be as queer as this.

'What then?' repeated Peter Stulpnagel.

'We'll take our chances,' said the chairman.

'Pray consider,' said Peter, 'that workmen who have touched the wires, and who have received shocks of only a few hundred volts, have died instantly. The fact is well known. And yet when a much greater force was used upon a criminal at New York, the man struggled for some little time. Do you not clearly see that the smaller dose is the more deadly?'

'I think, gentlemen, that this discussion has been carried on quite long enough,' said the chairman, rising again. 'The point, I take it, has already been decided by the majority of the committee, and Duncan Warner shall be electrocuted on Tuesday by the full strength of the Los Amigos dynamos. Is it not so?'

'I agree,' said Joseph M'Connor.

'I agree,' said I.

'And I protest,' said Peter Stulpnagel.

'Then the motion is carried, and your protest will be duly entered in the minutes,' said the chairman, and so the sitting was dissolved.

The attendance at the electrocution was a very small one. We four members of the committee were, of course, present with the executioner, who was to act under their orders. The others were the United States Marshal, the governor of the gaol, the chaplain, and three members of the press. The room was a small brick chamber, forming an out-house to the Central Electrical station. It had been used as a laundry, and had an oven and copper at one side, but no other furniture save a single chair for the condemned man. A metal plate for his feet was placed in front of it, to which ran a thick, insulated wire. Above, another wire depended from the ceiling, which could be connected with a small metallic rod projecting from a cap which was to be placed upon his head. When this connection was established Duncan Warner's hour was come.

There was a solemn hush as we waited for the coming of the prisoner. The practical engineers looked a little pale, and fidgeted nervously with the wires. Even the hardened Marshal was ill at ease, for a mere hanging was one thing, and this blasting of flesh and blood a very different one. As to the pressmen, their faces were whiter than the sheets which lay before them. The only man who appeared to feel none of the influence of these preparations was the little German crank, who strolled from one to the other with a smile on his lips and mischief in his eyes. More than once he even went so far as to burst into a shout of laughter, until the chaplain sternly rebuked him for his ill-timed levity.

'How can you so far forget yourself, Mr Stulpnagel,' said he, 'as to jest in the presence of death?'

But the German was quite unabashed.

'If I were in the presence of death I should not jest,' said he, 'but since I am not I may do what I choose.'

This flippant reply was about to draw another and a sterner reproof from the chaplain, when the door was swung open and two warders entered leading Duncan Warner between them. He glanced round him with a set face, stepped resolutely forward, and seated himself upon the chair.

'Touch her off!' said he.

It was barbarous to keep him in suspense. The chaplain murmured a few words in his ear, the attendant placed the cap upon his head, and then, while we all held our breath, the wire and the metal were brought in contact.

'Great Scott!' shouted Duncan Warner.

He had bounded in his chair as the frightful shock crashed through his system. But he was not dead. On the contrary, his eyes gleamed far more brightly than they had done before. There was only one change, but it was a singular one. The black had passed from his hair and beard as the shadow passes from a landscape. They were both as white as snow. And yet there was no other sign of decay. His skin was smooth and plump and lustrous as a child's.

The Marshal looked at the committee with a reproachful eye.

'There seems to be some hitch here, gentlemen,' said he.

We three practical men looked at each other.

Peter Stulpnagel smiled pensively.

'I think that another one should do it,' said I.

Again the connection was made, and again Duncan Warner sprang in his chair and shouted, but, indeed, were it not that he still remained in the chair none of us would have recognised him. His hair and his beard had shredded off in an instant, and the room looked like a barber's shop on a Saturday night. There he sat, his eyes still shining, his skin radiant with the glow of perfect health, but with a scalp as bald as a Dutch cheese, and a chin without so much as a trace of down. He began to revolve one of his arms, slowly and doubtfully at first, but with more confidence as he went on.

'That jint,' said he, 'has puzzled half the doctors on the Pacific Slope. It's as good as new, and as limber as a hickory twig.'

'You are feeling pretty well?' asked the old German.

'Never better in my life,' said Duncan Warner cheerily.

The situation was a painful one. The Marshal glared at the committee. Peter Stulpnagel grinned and rubbed his hands. The engineers scratched their heads. The bald-headed prisoner revolved his arm and looked pleased.

'I think that one more shock—' began the chairman.

'No, sir,' said the Marshal; 'we've had foolery enough for one morning. We are here for an execution, and a execution we'll have.'

'What do you propose?'

'There's a hook handy upon the ceiling. Fetch in a rope, and we'll soon set this matter straight.'

There was another awkward delay while the warders departed for the cord. Peter Stulpnagel bent over Duncan Warner, and whispered something in his ear. The desperado started in surprise.

'You don't say?' he asked.

The German nodded.

'What! No ways?'

Peter shook his head, and the two began to laugh as though they shared some huge joke between them.

The rope was brought, and the Marshal himself slipped the noose over the criminal's neck. Then the two warders, the assistant and he swung their victim into the air. For half an hour he hung—a dreadful sight—from the ceiling. Then in solemn silence they lowered him down, and one of the warders went out to order the shell to be brought round. But as he touched ground again what was our amazement when Duncan Warner put his hands up to his neck, loosened the noose, and took a long, deep breath.

'Paul Jefferson's sale is goin' well,' he remarked, 'I could see the crowd from up yonder,' and he nodded at the hook in the ceiling.

'Up with him again!' shouted the Marshal, 'we'll get the life out of him somehow.'

In an instant the victim was up at the hook once more.

They kept him there for an hour, but when he came down he was perfectly garrulous.

'Old man Plunket goes too much to the Arcady Saloon,' said he. 'Three times he's been there in an hour; and him with a family. Old man Plunket would do well to swear off.'

It was monstrous and incredible, but there it was. There was no getting round it. The man was there talking when he ought to have been dead. We all sat staring in amazement, but United States Marshal Carpenter was not a man to be euchred so easily. He motioned the others to one side, so that the prisoner was left standing alone.

'Duncan Warner,' said he, slowly, 'you are here to play your part, and I am here to play mine. Your game is to live if you can, and my game is to carry out the sentence of the law. You've beat us on electricity. I'll give you one there. And you've beat us on hanging, for you seem to thrive on it. But it's my turn to beat you now, for my duty has to be done.'

He pulled a six-shooter from his coat as he spoke, and fired all the shots through the body of the prisoner. The room was so filled with smoke that we could see nothing, but when it cleared the prisoner was still standing there, looking down in disgust at the front of his coat.

'Coats must be cheap where you come from,' said he. 'Thirty dollars it cost me, and look at it now. The six holes in front are bad enough, but four of the balls have passed out, and a pretty state the back must be in.'

The Marshal's revolver fell from his hand, and he dropped his arms to his sides, a beaten man.

'Maybe some of you gentlemen can tell me what this means,' said he, looking helplessly at the committee.

Peter Stulpnagel took a step forward.

'I'll tell you all about it,' said he.

'You seem to be the only person who knows anything.'

'I *am* the only person who knows anything. I should have warned these gentlemen; but, as they would not listen to me, I have allowed them to learn by experience. What you have done with your electricity is that you have increased this man's vitality until he can defy death for centuries.'

'Centuries!'

'Yes, it will take the wear of hundreds of years to exhaust the enormous nervous energy with which you have drenched him. Electricity is life, and you have charged him with it to the utmost. Perhaps in fifty years you might execute him, but I am not sanguine about it.'

'Great Scott! What shall I do with him?' cried the unhappy Marshal.

Peter Stulpnagel shrugged his shoulders.

'It seems to me that it does not much matter what you do with him now,' said he.

'Maybe we could drain the electricity out of him again. Suppose we hang him up by the heels?'

'No, no, it's out of the question.'

'Well, well, he shall do no more mischief in Los Amigos, anyhow,' said the Marshal, with decision. 'He shall go into the new gaol. The prison will wear him out.'

'On the contrary,' said Peter Stulpnagel, 'I think that it is much more probable that he will wear out the prison.'

It was rather a fiasco, and for years we didn't talk more about it than we could help, but it's no secret now, and I thought you might like to jot down the facts in your case-book.

NOTES TO 'THE LOS AMIGOS FIASCO'

First published in the *Idler*, December 1892.

1. Los Amigos may refer to Los Angeles, though Rodin and Key point out that the first recorded use of electricity for the purpose of execution was at Auburn State Prison, New York, on 6 August 1890.[1]

The idea that electricity was in some way the spark or source of life goes back at least to Luigi Galvani and his famous demonstration in the 1780s that the legs of a dead frog could be made to twitch by the application of an electric current. The immense possibilities opened up by this observation rather dazzled nineteenth century intellectuals: long before it was harnessed as a source of light and power, electricity was regarded by vitalists as the life force and essence of the soul; hailed by mesmerists as the explanation for the 'magnetic attraction' which allowed telepathic communication; applied by doctors to a bewildering array of medical conditions, from spermatorrhœa and impotence to indigestion and headaches; and sometimes cited by spiritualists as proof that messages could be sent across the ether.[2] Conan Doyle was probably familiar with all these currents of thought, though here and in 'Crabbe's Practice' (where another 'corpse' is bought back to life by the application of an electric shock) he is probably just having a joke at the expense of the idea.

Contrary to popular belief (including Rodin and Key), electricity was not the means by which Dr Frankenstein brought his monster to life. As John Sutherland has pointed out,[3] despite the iconic image of flashing electrodes promoted by innumerable stage and cinema adaptations, the original novel does not reveal the process by which

---

[1] *Conan Doyle's Tales of Medical Humanism and Values*, p. 270.

[2] For an intriguing account, showing that while people were frightened to introduce electricity as a source of light or power in their homes, they had little or no reluctance in accepting the various electric 'therapeutic' devices prescribed by doctors, see Linda Simon, *Dark Light: Electricity and Anxiety from the Telegraph to the X-Ray* (New York: Harcourt, 2004).

[3] John Sutherland, 'How Does Victor Make His Monsters?', in *Is Heathcliff a Murderer? Puzzles in Nineteenth Century Fiction* (Oxford University Press, 1996), pp. 24-34.

the monsters were created and vivified. The only hint that electricity might have had something to do with it appears in Mary Shelley's introduction to the 1831 edition:

> Many and long were the conversations between Lord Byron and Shelley, to which I was a devout but nearly silent listener. During one of these, various philosophical doctrines were discussed, and among others the nature and principle of life, and whether there was any probability of its ever being discovered and communicated. They talked of the experiments of Dr Darwin ... who preserved a piece of vermicelli in a glass case, till by some extraordinary means it began to move with voluntary motion. Not thus, after all, would life be given. Perhaps a corpse would be re-animated; galvanism had given token of such things: perhaps the component parts of a creature might be manufactured, brought together, and endued with vital warmth.[1]

When Conan Doyle wanted to bring a genuine corpse to life, or keep a human body alive beyond its natural span (as in 'Lot No. 249' or 'The Ring of Thoth'), he was more likely to rely on magical Egyptian mysteries than modern technology.

---

[1] Mary Shelley, Author's Introduction (1831), in *Frankenstein, or, The Modern Prometheus*, ed. Maurice Hindle (Penguin Classics, 2003), p. 8. It does seem odd that the reputed author should be speculating so uncertainly about what is presumably her own book.

THE DOCTORS OF HOYLAND

DOCTOR JAMES RIPLEY was always looked upon as an exceedingly lucky dog by all of the profession who knew him. His father had preceded him in a practice in the village of Hoyland, in the north of Hampshire, and all was ready for him on the very first day that the law allowed him to put his name at the foot of a prescription. In a few years the old gentleman retired, and settled on the South Coast, leaving his son in undisputed possession of the whole country side. Save for Doctor Horton, near Basingstoke, the young surgeon had a clear run of six miles in every direction, and took his fifteen hundred pounds a year, though, as is usual in country practices, the stable swallowed up most of what the consulting-room earned.

Doctor James Ripley was two-and-thirty years of age, reserved, learned, unmarried, with set, rather stern features, and a thinning of the dark hair upon the top of his head, which was worth quite a hundred a year to him. He was particularly happy in his management of ladies. He had caught the tone of bland sternness and decisive suavity which dominates without offending. Ladies, however, were not equally happy in their management of him. Professionally, he was always at their service. Socially, he was a drop of quicksilver. In vain the country mammas spread out their simple lures in front of him. Dances and picnics were not to his taste, and he preferred during his scanty leisure to shut himself up in his study, and to bury himself in Virchow's Archives and the professional journals.

Study was a passion with him, and he would have none of the rust which often gathers round a country practitioner. It was his ambition to keep his knowledge as fresh and bright as at the moment when he had stepped out of the examination hall. He prided himself on being able at a moment's notice to rattle off the seven ramifications of some obscure artery, or to give the exact percentage of any physiological compound. After a long day's work he would sit up half the night performing iridectomies and extractions upon the sheep's eyes sent in by the village butcher, to the horror of his housekeeper, who had to remove the *débris* next morning. His love for his work was the one fanaticism which found a place in his dry, precise nature.

It was the more to his credit that he should keep up to date in his knowledge, since he had no competition to force him to exertion. In the seven years during which he had practised in Hoyland three rivals had pitted themselves against him, two in the village itself and one in the neighbouring hamlet of Lower Hoyland. Of these one had sickened and wasted, being, as it was said, himself the only patient whom he had treated during his eighteen months of ruralising. A second had bought a fourth share of a Basingstoke practice, and had departed honourably, while a third had vanished one September night, leaving a gutted house and an unpaid drug bill behind him. Since then the district had become a monopoly, and no one had dared to measure himself against the established fame of the Hoyland doctor.

It was, then, with a feeling of some surprise and considerable curiosity that on driving through Lower Hoyland one morning he perceived that the new house at the end of the village was occupied, and that a virgin brass plate glistened upon the swinging gate which faced the high road. He pulled up his fifty guinea chestnut mare and took a good look at it. 'Verrinder Smith, M.D.,' was printed across it in very neat, small lettering. The last man had had letters half a foot long, with a lamp like a fire-station. Doctor James Ripley noted the difference, and deduced from it that the new-comer might possibly prove a more formidable opponent. He was convinced of it that evening when he came to consult the current medical directory. By it he learned that Doctor Verrinder Smith was the holder of superb degrees, that he had studied with distinction at Edinburgh, Paris, Berlin, and Vienna, and finally that he had been awarded a gold medal and the Lee Hopkins scholarship for original research, in recognition of an exhaustive inquiry into the functions of the anterior spinal nerve roots. Doctor Ripley passed his fingers through his thin hair in bewilderment as he read his rival's record. What on earth could so brilliant a man mean by putting up his plate in a little Hampshire hamlet.

But Doctor Ripley furnished himself with an explanation to the riddle. No doubt Dr Verrinder Smith had simply come down there in order to pursue some scientific research in peace and quiet. The plate was up as an address rather than as an invitation to patients. Of course, that must be the true explanation. In that case the presence of this brilliant neighbour would be a splendid thing for his own studies.

He had often longed for some kindred mind, some steel on which he might strike his flint. Chance had brought it to him, and he rejoiced exceedingly.

And this joy it was which led him to take a step which was quite at variance with his usual habits. It is the custom for a new-comer among medical men to call first upon the older, and the etiquette upon the subject is strict. Doctor Ripley was pedantically exact on such points, and yet he deliberately drove over next day and called upon Doctor Verrinder Smith. Such a waiving of ceremony was, he felt, a gracious act upon his part, and a fit prelude to the intimate relations which he hoped to establish with his neighbour.

The house was neat and well appointed, and Doctor Ripley was shown by a smart maid into a dapper little consulting room. As he passed in he noticed two or three parasols and a lady's sun bonnet hanging in the hall. It was a pity that his colleague should be a married man. It would put them upon a different footing, and interfere with those long evenings of high scientific talk which he had pictured to himself. On the other hand, there was much in the consulting room to please him. Elaborate instruments, seen more often in hospitals than in the houses of private practitioners, were scattered about. A sphygmograph stood upon the table and a gasometer-like engine, which was new to Dr Ripley, in the corner. A book-case full of ponderous volumes in French and German, paper-covered for the most part, and varying in tint from the shell to the yoke of a duck's egg, caught his wandering eyes, and he was deeply absorbed in their titles when the door opened suddenly behind him. Turning round, he found himself facing a little woman, whose plain, palish face was remarkable only for a pair of shrewd, humorous eyes of a blue which had two shades too much green in it. She held a *pince-nez* in her left hand, and the doctor's card in her right.

'How do you do, Doctor Ripley?' said she.

'How do you do, madam?' returned the visitor. 'Your husband is perhaps out?'

'I am not married,' said she simply.

'Oh, I beg your pardon! I meant the doctor—Dr Verrinder Smith.'

'I am Doctor Verrinder Smith.'

Doctor Ripley was so surprised that he dropped his hat and forgot to pick it up again.

'What!' he grasped, 'the Lee Hopkins prizeman! You!'

He had never seen a woman doctor before, and his whole conservative soul rose up in revolt at the idea. He could not recall any Biblical injunction that the man should remain ever the doctor and the woman the nurse, and yet he felt as if a blasphemy had been committed. His face betrayed his feelings only too clearly.

'I am sorry to disappoint you,' said the lady drily.

'You certainly have surprised me,' he answered, picking up his hat.

'You are not among our champions, then?'

'I cannot say that the movement has my approval.'

'And why?'

'I should much prefer not to discuss it.'

'But I am sure you will answer a lady's question.'

'Ladies are in danger of losing their privileges when they usurp the place of the other sex. They cannot claim both.'

'Why should a woman not earn her bread by her brains?'

Doctor Ripley felt irritated by the quiet manner in which the lady cross-questioned him.

'I should much prefer not to be led into a discussion, Miss Smith.'

'Doctor Smith,' she interrupted.

'Well, Doctor Smith! But if you insist upon an answer, I must say that I do not think medicine a suitable profession for women and that I have a personal objection to masculine ladies.'

It was an exceedingly rude speech, and he was ashamed of it the instant after he had made it. The lady, however, simply raised her eyebrows and smiled.

'It seems to me that you are begging the question,' said she. 'Of course, if it makes women masculine that *would* be a considerable deterioration.'

It was a neat little counter, and Doctor Ripley, like a pinked fencer, bowed his acknowledgment.

'I must go,' said he.

'I am sorry that we cannot come to some more friendly conclusion since we are to be neighbours,' she remarked.

He bowed again, and took a step towards the door.

'It was a singular coincidence,' she continued, 'that at the instant that you called I was reading your paper on "Locomotor Ataxia," in the *Lancet*.'

'Indeed,' said he drily.

'I thought it was a very able monograph.'

'You are very good.'

'But the views which you attribute to Professor Pitres, of Bordeaux, have been repudiated by him.'

'I have his pamphlet of 1890,' said Doctor Ripley angrily.

'Here is his pamphlet of 1891.' She picked it from among a litter of periodicals. 'If you have time to glance your eye down this passage—'

Doctor Ripley took it from her and shot rapidly through the paragraph which she indicated. There was no denying that it completely knocked the bottom out of his own article. He threw it down, and with another frigid bow he made for the door. As he took the reins from the groom he glanced round and saw that the lady was standing at her window, and it seemed to him that she was laughing heartily.

All day the memory of this interview haunted him. He felt that he had come very badly out of it. She had showed herself to be his superior on his own pet subject. She had been courteous while he had been rude, self-possessed when he had been angry. And then, above all, there was her presence, her monstrous intrusion to rankle in his mind. A woman doctor had been an abstract thing before, repugnant but distant. Now she was there in actual practice, with a brass plate up just like his own, competing for the same patients. Not that he feared competition, but he objected to this lowering of his ideal of womanhood. She could not be more than thirty, and had a bright, mobile face, too. He thought of her humorous eyes, and of her strong, well-turned chin. It revolted him the more to recall the details of her education. A man, of course, could come through such an ordeal with all his purity, but it was nothing short of shameless in a woman.

But it was not long before he learned that even her competition was a thing to be feared. The novelty of her presence had brought a

few curious invalids into her consulting rooms, and, once there, they
had been so impressed by the firmness of her manner and by the singular, new-fashioned instruments with which she tapped, and peered,
and sounded, that it formed the core of their conversation for weeks
afterwards. And soon there were tangible proofs of her powers upon
the country side. Farmer Eyton, whose callous ulcer had been quietly
spreading over his shin for years back under a gentle *régime* of zinc
ointment, was painted round with blistering fluid, and found, after
three blasphemous nights, that his sore was stimulated into healing.
Mrs Crowder, who had always regarded the birthmark upon her second daughter Eliza as a sign of the indignation of the Creator at a
third helping of raspberry tart which she had partaken of during a
critical period, learned that, with the help of two galvanic needles, the
mischief was not irreparable. In a month Doctor Verrinder Smith was
known, and in two she was famous.

Occasionally, Doctor Ripley met her as he drove upon his rounds.
She had started a high dog-cart, taking the reins herself, with a little
tiger behind. When they met he invariably raised his hat with punctilious politeness, but the grim severity of his face showed how formal
was the courtesy. In fact, his dislike was rapidly deepening into absolute detestation. 'The unsexed woman,' was the description of her
which he permitted himself to give to those of his patients who still
remained staunch. But, indeed, they were a rapidly-decreasing body,
and every day his pride was galled by the news of some fresh defec-
tion. The lady had somehow impressed the country folk with almost
superstitious belief in her power, and from far and near they flocked
to her consulting room.

But what galled him most of all was, when she did something
which he had pronounced to be impracticable. For all his knowledge
he lacked nerve as an operator, and usually sent his worst cases up to
London. The lady, however, had no weakness of the sort, and took
everything that came in her way. It was agony to him to hear that she
was about to straighten little Alec Turner's club foot, and right at the
fringe of the rumour came a note from his mother, the rector's wife,
asking him if he would be so good as to act as chloroformist. It would
be inhumanity to refuse, as there was no other who could take the
place, but it was gall and wormwood to his sensitive nature. Yet, in

spite of his vexation, he could not but admire the dexterity with which the thing was done. She handled the little wax-like foot so gently, and held the tiny tenotomy knife as an artist holds his pencil. One straight insertion, one snick of a tendon, and it was all over without a stain upon the white towel which lay beneath. He had never seen anything more masterly, and he had the honesty to say so, though her skill increased his dislike of her. The operation spread her fame still further at his expense, and self-preservation was added to his other grounds for detesting her. And this very detestation it was which brought matters to a curious climax.

One winter's night, just as he was rising from his lonely dinner, a groom came riding down from Squire Faircastle's, the richest man in the district, to say that his daughter had scalded her hand, and that medical help was needed on the instant. The coachman had ridden for the lady doctor, for it mattered nothing to the Squire who came as long as it were speedily. Doctor Ripley rushed from his surgery with the determination that she should not effect an entrance into this stronghold of his if hard driving on his part could prevent it. He did not even wait to light his lamps, but sprang into his gig and flew off as fast as hoof could rattle. He lived rather nearer to the Squire's than she did, and was convinced that he could get there well before her.

And so he would but for that whimsical element of chance, which will for ever muddle up the affairs of this world and dumbfound the prophets. Whether it came from the want of his lights, or from his mind being full of the thoughts of his rival, he allowed too little by half a foot in taking the sharp turn upon the Basingstoke road. The empty trap and the frightened horse clattered away into the darkness, while the Squire's groom crawled out of the ditch into which he had been shot. He struck a match, looked down at his groaning companion, and then, after the fashion of rough, strong men when they see what they have not seen before, he was very sick.

The doctor raised himself a little on his elbow in the glint of the match. He caught a glimpse of something white and sharp bristling through his trouser leg half way down the shin.

'Compound!' he groaned. 'A three months' job,' and fainted.

When he came to himself the groom was gone, for he had scudded off to the Squire's house for help, but a small page was holding a gig-lamp in front of his injured leg, and a woman, with an open case of polished instruments gleaming in the yellow light, was deftly slitting up his trouser with a crooked pair of scissors.

'It's all right, doctor,' said she soothingly. 'I am so sorry about it. You can have Doctor Horton to-morrow, but I am sure you will allow me to help you to-night. I could hardly believe my eyes when I saw you by the roadside.'

'The groom has gone for help,' groaned the sufferer.

'When it comes we can move you into the gig. A little more light, John! So! Ah, dear, dear, we shall have laceration unless we reduce this before we move you. Allow me to give you a whiff of chloroform, and I have no doubt that I can secure it sufficiently to—'

Doctor Ripley never heard the end of that sentence. He tried to raise a hand and to murmur something in protest, but a sweet smell was in his nostrils, and a sense of rich peace and lethargy stole over his jangled nerves. Down he sank, through clear, cool water, ever down and down into the green shadows beneath, gently, without effort, while the pleasant chiming of a great belfry rose and fell in his ears. Then he rose again, up and up, and ever up, with a terrible tightness about his temples, until at last he shot out of those green shadows and was in the light once more. Two bright, shining, golden spots gleamed before his dazed eyes. He blinked and blinked before he could give a name to them. They were only the two brass balls at the end posts of his bed, and he was lying in his own little room, with a head like a cannon ball, and a leg like an iron bar. Turning his eyes, he saw the calm face of Doctor Verrinder Smith looking down at him.

'Ah, at last!' said she. 'I kept you under all the way home, for I knew how painful the jolting would be. It is in good position now with a strong side splint. I have ordered a morphia draught for you. Shall I tell your groom to ride for Doctor Horton in the morning?'

'I should prefer that you should continue the case,' said Doctor Ripley feebly, and then, with a half hysterical laugh,—'You have all the rest of the parish as patients, you know, so you may as well make the thing complete by having me also.'

It was not a very gracious speech, but it was a look of pity and not of anger which shone in her eyes as she turned away from his bedside.

Doctor Ripley had a brother, William, who was assistant surgeon at a London hospital, and who was down in Hampshire within a few hours of his hearing of the accident. He raised his brows when he heard the details.

'What! You are pestered with one of those!' he cried.

'I don't know what I should have done without her.'

'I've no doubt she's an excellent nurse.'

'She knows her work as well as you or I.'

'Speak for yourself, James,' said the London man with a sniff. 'But apart from that, you know that the principle of the thing is all wrong.'

'You think there is nothing to be said on the other side?'

'Good heavens! do you?'

'Well, I don't know. It struck me during the night that we may have been a little narrow in our views.'

'Nonsense, James. It's all very fine for women to win prizes in the lecture room, but you know as well as I do that they are no use in an emergency. Now I warrant that this woman was all nerves when she was setting your leg. That reminds me that I had better just take a look at it and see that it is all right.'

'I would rather that you did not undo it,' said the patient. 'I have her assurance that it is all right.'

Brother William was deeply shocked.

'Of course, if a woman's assurance is of more value than the opinion of the assistant surgeon of a London hospital, there is nothing more to be said,' he remarked.

'I should prefer that you did not touch it,' said the patient firmly, and Doctor William went back to London that evening in a huff.

The lady, who had heard of his coming, was much surprised on learning his departure.

'We had a difference upon a point of professional etiquette,' said Doctor James, and it was all the explanation he would vouchsafe.

For two long months Doctor Ripley was brought in contact with his rival every day, and he learned many things which he had not known before. She was a charming companion, as well as a most assiduous doctor. Her short presence during the long, weary day was like a flower in a sand waste. What interested him was precisely what interested her, and she could meet him at every point upon equal terms. And yet under all her learning and her firmness ran a sweet, womanly nature, peeping out in her talk, shining in her greenish eyes, showing itself in a thousand subtle ways which the dullest of men could read. And he, though a bit of a prig and a pedant, was by no means dull, and had honesty enough to confess when he was in the wrong.

'I don't know how to apologise to you,' he said in his shame-faced fashion one day, when he had progressed so far as to be able to sit in an arm-chair with his leg upon another one; 'I feel that I have been quite in the wrong.'

'Why, then?'

'Over this woman question. I used to think that a woman must inevitably lose something of her charm if she took up such studies.'

'Oh, you don't think they are necessarily unsexed, then?' she cried, with a mischievous smile.

'Please don't recall my idiotic expression.'

'I feel so pleased that I should have helped in changing your views. I think that it is the most sincere compliment that I have ever had paid me.'

'At any rate, it is the truth,' said he, and was happy all night at the remembrance of the flush of pleasure which made her pale face look quite comely for the instant.

For, indeed, he was already far past the stage when he would acknowledge her as the equal of any other woman. Already he could not disguise from himself that she had become the one woman. Her dainty skill, her gentle touch, her sweet presence, the community of their tastes, had all united to hopelessly upset his previous opinions. It was a dark day for him now when his convalescence allowed her to miss a visit, and darker still that other one which he saw approaching when all occasion for her visits would be at an end. It came round at last, however, and he felt that his whole life's fortune would hang upon the issue of that final interview. He was a direct man by nature, so he laid his hand upon hers as it felt for his pulse, and he asked her if she would be his wife.

'What, and unite the practices?' said she.

He started in pain and anger.

'Surely you do not attribute any such base motive to me!' he cried. 'I love you as unselfishly as ever a woman was loved.'

'No, I was wrong. It was a foolish speech,' said she, moving her chair a little back, and tapping her stethoscope upon her knee. 'Forget that I ever said it. I am so sorry to cause you any disappointment, and I appreciate most highly the honour which you do me, but what you ask is quite impossible.'

With another woman he might have urged the point, but his instincts told him that it was quite useless with this one. Her tone of voice was conclusive. He said nothing, but leaned back in his chair a stricken man.

'I am so sorry,' she said again. 'If I had known what was passing in your mind I should have told you earlier that I intended to devote my life entirely to science. There are many women with a capacity for marriage, but few with a taste for biology. I will remain true to my own line, then. I came down here while waiting for an opening in the Paris Physiological Laboratory. I have just heard that there is a vacancy for me there, and so you will be troubled no more by my intrusion upon your practice. I have done you an injustice just as you did me one. I thought you narrow and pedantic, with no good quality. I have learned during your illness to appreciate you better, and the recollection of our friendship will always be a very pleasant one to me.'

And so it came about that in a very few weeks there was only one doctor in Hoyland. But folks noticed that the one had aged many years in a few months, that a weary sadness lurked always in the depths of his blue eyes, and that he was less concerned than ever with the eligible young ladies whom chance, or their careful country mammas, placed in his way.

NOTES TO 'THE DOCTORS OF HOYLAND'

First published in the *Idler*, April 1894.

1. The number of women doctors was increasing steadily in the late nineteenth century: 8 in 1871, 25 in 1881, 101 in 1891 and 212 in 1901.[1] It is interesting that while Conan Doyle, judging by this story, welcomed women into the medical profession, he was not in favour of giving them the vote.

---

[1] F. B. Smith, *The People's Health 1830-1910* (Canberra: ANU Press, 1979), p. 382.

THE SURGEON TALKS

'MEN die of the diseases which they have studied most,' remarked the surgeon, snipping off the end of a cigar with all his professional neatness and finish. 'It's as if the morbid condition was an evil creature which, when it found itself closely hunted, flew at the throat of its pursuer. If you worry the microbes too much they may worry you. I've seen cases of it, and not necessarily in microbic diseases either. There was, of course, the well-known instance of Liston and the aneurism; and a dozen others that I could mention. You couldn't have a clearer case than that of poor old Walker of St Christopher's. Not heard of it? Well, of course, it was a little before your time, but I wonder that it should have been forgotten. You youngsters are so busy in keeping up to the day that you lose a good deal that is interesting of yesterday.

'Walker was one of the best men in Europe on nervous disease. You must have read his little book on sclerosis of the posterior columns. It's as interesting as a novel, and epoch-making in its way. He worked like a horse, did Walker—huge consulting practice—hours a day in the clinical wards—constant original investigations. And then he enjoyed himself also. *"De mortuis,"* of course, but still it's an open secret among all who knew him. If he died at forty-five, he crammed eighty years into it. The marvel was that he could have held on so long at the pace at which he was going. But he took it beautifully when it came.

'I was his clinical assistant at the time. Walker was lecturing on locomotor ataxia to a wardful of youngsters. He was explaining that one of the early signs of the complaint was that the patient could not put his heels together with his eyes shut without staggering. As he spoke, he suited the action to the word. I don't suppose the boys noticed anything. I did, and so did he, though he finished his lecture without a sign.

'When it was over he came into my room and lit a cigarette.

'"Just run over my reflexes, Smith," said he.

'There was hardly a trace of them left. I tapped away at his knee-tendon and might as well have tried to get a jerk out of that sofa-cushion. He stood with his eyes shut again, and he swayed like a bush in the wind.

'"So," said he, "it was not intercostal neuralgia after all."[1]

'Then I knew that he had had the lightning pains, and that the case was complete. There was nothing to say, so I sat looking at him while he puffed and puffed at his cigarette. Here he was, a man in the prime of life, one of the handsomest men in London, with money, fame, social success, everything at his feet, and now, without a moment's warning, he was told that inevitable death lay before him, a death accompanied by more refined and lingering tortures than if he were bound upon a Red Indian stake. He sat in the middle of the blue cigarette cloud with his eyes cast down, and the slightest little tightening of his lips. Then he rose with a motion of his arms, as one who throws off old thoughts and enters upon a new course.

'"Better put this thing straight at once," said he. "I must make some fresh arrangements. May I use your paper and envelopes?"

'He settled himself at my desk and he wrote half a dozen letters. It is not a breach of confidence to say that they were not addressed to his professional brothers. Walker was a single man, which means that he was not restricted to a single woman.[2] When he had finished, he walked out of that little room of mine, leaving every hope and ambition of his life behind him. And he might have had another year of ignorance and peace if it had not been for the chance illustration in his lecture.

'It took five years to kill him, and he stood it well. If he had ever been a little irregular he atoned for it in that long martyrdom. He kept an admirable record of his own symptoms, and worked out the eye changes more fully than has ever been done. When the ptosis got very bad he would hold his eyelid up with one hand while he wrote. Then, when he could not co-ordinate his muscles to write, he dictated to his nurse. So died, in the odour of science, James Walker, æt. 45.

'Poor old Walker was very fond of experimental surgery, and he broke ground in several directions. Between ourselves, there may have been some more ground-breaking afterwards, but he did his best for his cases. You know M'Namara, don't you? He always wears his hair long. He lets it be understood that it comes from his artistic strain, but it is really to conceal the loss of one of his ears. Walker cut the other one off, but you must not tell Mac I said so.

'It was like this. Walker had a fad about the portio dura—the motor to the face, you know—and he thought paralysis of it came from a disturbance of the blood supply. Something else which counterbalanced that disturbance might, he thought, set it right again. We had a very obstinate case of Bell's paralysis in the wards, and had tried it with every conceivable thing, blistering, tonics, nerve-stretching, galvanism, needles, but all without result. Walker got it into his head that removal of the ear would increase the blood supply to the part, and he very soon gained the consent of the patient to the operation.

'Well, we did it at night. Walker, of course, felt that it was something of an experiment, and did not wish too much talk about it unless it proved successful. There were half-a-dozen of us there, M'Namara and I among the rest. The room was a small one, and in the centre was the narrow table, with a mackintosh over the pillow, and a blanket which extended almost to the floor on either side. Two candles, on a side-table near the pillow, supplied all the light. In came the patient, with one side of his face as smooth as a baby's, and the other all in a quiver with fright. He lay down, and the chloroform towel was placed over his face, while Walker threaded his needles in the candle light. The chloroformist stood at the head of the table, and M'Namara was stationed at the side to control the patient. The rest of us stood by to assist.

'Well, the man was about half over when he fell into one of those convulsive flurries which come with the semi-unconscious stage. He kicked and plunged and struck out with both hands. Over with a crash went the little table which held the candles, and in an instant we were left in total darkness. You can think what a rush and a scurry there was, one to pick up the table, one to find the matches, and some to restrain the patient who was still dashing himself about. He was held down by two dressers, the chloroform was pushed, and by the time the candles were relit, his incoherent, half-smothered shoutings had changed to a stertorous snore. His head was turned on the pillow and the towel was still kept over his face while the operation was carried through. Then the towel was withdrawn, and you can conceive our amazement when we looked upon the face of M'Namara.

'How did it happen? Why, simply enough. As the candles went over, the chloroformist had stopped for an instant and had tried to catch them. The patient, just as the light went out, had rolled off and under the table. Poor M'Namara, clinging frantically to him, had been dragged across it, and the chloroformist, feeling him there, had naturally clapped the towel across his mouth and nose. The others had secured him, and the more he roared and kicked the more they drenched him with chloroform. Walker was very nice about it, and made the most handsome apologies. He offered to do a plastic on the spot, and make as good an ear as he could, but M'Namara had had enough of it. As to the patient, we found him sleeping placidly under the table, with the ends of the blanket screening him on both sides. Walker sent M'Namara round his ear next day in a jar of methylated spirit, but Mac's wife was very angry about it, and it led to a good deal of ill-feeling.

'Some people say that the more one has to do with human nature, and the closer one is brought in contact with it, the less one thinks of it. I don't believe that those who know most would uphold that view. My own experience is dead against it. I was brought up in the miserable-mortal-clay school of theology, and yet here I am, after thirty years of intimate acquaintance with humanity, filled with respect for it. The evil lies commonly upon the surface. The deeper strata are good. A hundred times I have seen folk condemned to death as suddenly as poor Walker was. Sometimes it was to blindness or to mutilations which are worse than death. Men and women, they almost all took it beautifully, and some with such lovely unselfishness, and with such complete absorption in the thought of how their fate would affect others, that the man about town, or the frivolously-dressed woman has seemed to change into an angel before my eyes. I have seen death-beds, too, of all ages and of all creeds and want of creeds. I never saw any of them shrink, save only one poor, imaginative young fellow, who had spent his blameless life in the strictest of sects. Of course, an exhausted frame is incapable of fear, as anyone can vouch who is told, in the midst of his sea-sickness, that the ship is going to the bottom. That is why I rate courage in the face of mutilation to be higher than courage when a wasting illness is fining away into death.

'Now, I'll take a case which I had in my own practice last

Wednesday. A lady came, in to consult me—the wife of a well-known sporting baronet. The husband had come with her, but remained, at her request, in the waiting-room. I need not go into details, but it proved to be a peculiarly malignant case of cancer. "I knew it," said she. "How long have I to live?" "I fear that it may exhaust your strength in a few months," I answered. "Poor old Jack!" said she. "I'll tell him that it is not dangerous." "Why should you deceive him?" I asked. "Well, he's very uneasy about it, and he is quaking now in the waiting-room. He has two old friends to dinner to-night, and I haven't the heart to spoil his evening. To-morrow will be time enough for him to learn the truth." Out she walked, the brave little woman, and a moment later her husband, with his big, red face shining with joy came plunging into my room to shake me by the hand. No, I respected her wish and I did not undeceive him. I dare bet that evening was one of the brightest, and the next morning the darkest, of his life.

'It's wonderful how bravely and cheerily a woman can face a crushing blow. It is different with men. A man can stand it without complaining, but it knocks him dazed and silly all the same. But the woman does not lose her wits any more than she does her courage. Now, I had a case only a few weeks ago which would show you what I mean. A gentleman consulted me about his wife, a very beautiful woman. She had a small tubercular nodule upon her upper arm, according to him. He was sure that it was of no importance, but he wanted to know whether Devonshire or the Riviera would be the better for her. I examined her and found a frightful sarcoma of the bone, hardly showing upon the surface, but involving the shoulder-blade and clavicle as well as the humerus. A more malignant case I have never seen. I sent her out of the room and I told him the truth. What did he do? Why, he walked slowly round that room with his hands behind his back, looking with the greatest interest at the pictures. I can see him now, putting up his gold *pince-nez* and staring at them with perfectly vacant eyes, which told me that he saw neither them nor the wall behind them. "Amputation of the arm?" he asked at last. "And of the collar-bone and shoulder-blade," said I. "Quite so. The collar-bone and shoulder-blade," he repeated, still staring about him with those lifeless eyes. It settled him. I don't believe he'll ever be the same man again. But the woman took it as bravely and brightly as could be, and she has done very well since. The mischief was so great that the arm snapped as we drew it from the night-dress. No, I don't think that there will be any return, and I have every hope of her recovery.

'The first patient is a thing which one remembers all one's life. Mine was commonplace, and the details are of no interest. I had a curious visitor, however, during the first few months after my plate went up. It was an elderly woman, richly dressed, with a wicker-work picnic basket in her hand. This she opened with the tears streaming down her face, and out there waddled the fattest, ugliest, and mangiest little pug dog that I have ever seen. "I wish you to put him painlessly out of the world, doctor," she cried. "Quick, quick, or my resolution may give way." She flung herself down, with hysterical sobs, upon the sofa. The less experienced a doctor is, the higher are his notions of professional dignity, as I need not remind you, my young friend, so I was about to refuse the commission with indignation, when I bethought me that, quite apart from medicine, we were gentleman and lady, and that she had asked me to do something for her which was evidently of the greatest possible importance in her eyes. I led off the poor little doggie, therefore, and with the help of a saucerful of milk and a few drops of prussic acid his exit was as speedy and painless as could be desired. "Is it over?" she cried as I entered. It was really tragic to see how all the love which should have gone to husband and children had, in default of them, been centred upon this uncouth little animal. She left, quite broken down, in her carriage, and it was only after her departure that I saw an envelope sealed with a large red seal, and lying upon the blotting pad of my desk. Outside, in pencil, was written:—"I have no doubt that you would willingly have done this without a fee, but I insist upon your acceptance of the enclosed." I opened it with some vague notions of an eccentric millionaire and a fifty pound note, but all I found was a postal order for four and sixpence. The whole incident struck me as so whimsical that I laughed until I was tired. You'll find there's so much tragedy in a doctor's life, my boy, that he would not be able to stand it if it were not for the strain of comedy which comes every now and then to leaven it.

'And a doctor has very much to be thankful for also. Don't you ever forget it. It is such a pleasure to do a little good that a man should pay for the privilege instead of being paid for it. Still, of course, he has his home to keep up and his wife and children to support. But his patients are his friends—or they should be so. He goes from house to house, and his step and his voice are loved and welcomed in each. What could a man ask for more than that? And besides, he is forced to be a good man. It is impossible for him to be anything else. How can a man spend his whole life in seeing suffering bravely borne and yet remain a hard or a vicious man? It is a noble, generous, kindly profession, and you youngsters have got to see that it remains so.'

NOTES TO 'THE SURGEON TALKS'

First published in *Round the Red Lamp*.

1. Sclerosis, locomotor ataxia (the tendency to fall over and generally lose coordination in the limbs), loss of reflexes and shooting pains are all symptoms of syphilis. In the 1870s the German neurologist Wilhelm Erb (1840-1921) had established that the absence of the knee jerk reflex was a sign of locomotor ataxia and thus syphilis. The implication is thus that Walker died of syphilis.

2. The letters were to his various mistresses and possibly prostitutes.

Other Medical Tales

CRABBE'S PRACTICE[1]

By A. Conan Doyle, m.b., c.m.,

Author of "An Exciting Christmas Eve," etc.

John Waterhouse Crabbe was a man of ready resource and great originality of mind. When I first met him he was a medical student at Edinburgh University, and had distinguished himself in the classes. The circumstances of this first meeting were so characteristic that I shall preface my story by narrating them.

It occurred somewhere in the early part of the year 1877, when the Bulgarian atrocities[2] were engaging the public attention, and indignation meetings were being held throughout the country. One of these was arranged to come off in the music-hall at Edinburgh, and as Scotch feeling ran very high upon the subject, the great building was densely crammed by an enormous crowd. Curiosity had led me to be present, but I had taken the precaution to come late so as to obtain a place in the doorway and be able to beat a retreat whenever I wished.

From this coign of vantage I could hear the speeches of the successive orators, and could look with pity upon the crowded thousands densely packed in the main body of the building. The meeting had been an enthusiastic one. Every point which told against the Government of the day had been applauded to the echo, and not one dissentient murmur had been heard until the most important part of the proceedings had been reached, when the chairman had to submit the first resolution to his audience. Then in the midst of the hush with which every one listened to his words a stentorian voice in the centre of the hall suddenly roared out,

"What did Gladstone do in the year '66?"

From every part of the great meeting there came angry cries of "Silence! Order! Turn him out!" but in spite of these hostile demonstrations the inquisitive gentleman was still heard to be loudly demanding an answer to his question. At last matters reached a climax. There was an eddy in the great crowd, a confused struggle, and then a current which set in towards the door, on which the noisy politician was borne violently forward and ejected from the room, still bellow-

ing his thirst for knowledge as to the movements of the great Liberal
statesman in the year named.

Some little time afterwards, becoming tired of the proceedings,
I left for home. When I descended into the street the very first thing
I saw was the gentleman whom I had seen borne past me, standing
with his back against a lamp-post, puffing away very contentedly at a
cigar.

"Excuse the liberty I take," I said, going up to him, "but would
you mind telling me what it was that Gladstone *did* do in the year
'66?"

He looked at me for a moment with a most comical expression
on his face, and then putting his arm through mine turned down the
street with me.

"You're a medical, like myself," he remarked; "I know you by
sight. To tell you the truth I have not the least idea what Gladstone
did, nor do I care. I wanted to get out into the fresh air, and as it
seemed impossible to do it by fair means, I had to get them to put me
out, which they very promptly did."

We walked home together, and that evening began a friendship
which lasted for several years. Crabbe, however, shortly afterwards
took his degree, and having married a dear little wife started a practice in a large English watering-place, which we shall call Bridport.
He sunk out of my sight for some time, though I had every reason to
believe that he was doing well.

One day, nearly two years after I had heard from him last, I received a telegram in which he begged me to run to Bridport, as he
wished to consult me on a matter of importance. I was very busy myself at the time, but I determined to make an effort and get a couple
of days clear. When I arrived there I was met at the station by Crabbe
himself, his hat upon the back of his head, his frock coat flying in the
wind, and in every way the same eccentric, careless fellow that he
had been in his student days. He shook me heartily by the hand, and
seemed as glad to see me as I was to see him.

"My wife will be delighted that you have come," he said—or rather roared, for his voice was a most powerful one. "We have a great
deal to talk to you about. Come along up to my house."

The house in question proved to be a large substantial building in
a fashionable neighbourhood. I was surprised at such magnificence,

knowing as I did that Crabbe's means were limited, and still more astonished was I when I saw the sumptuous hall and splendid consulting-room which he had had fitted up for his patients.

"You have a delightful place," I remarked to his wife after supper.

"Yes," she replied, somewhat dubiously, as it seemed to me.

"There's only one thing we want," Crabbe said.

"What is that?" I asked, imagining that he meant a conservatory or some other additional piece of luxury.

"A patient," he remarked, solemnly. "Oh, don't suppose I'm joking. I'm thoroughly in earnest, I assure you. Not a patient has crossed the threshold for more weeks than I can count."

"But the furniture—the consulting-room?" I stammered.

"Yes, there they are," Crabbe said, with a somewhat bitter laugh. "They look very nice, and we have spent our capital on them, but as a speculation they are a decided failure. My earnings in two years would not pay for the carpet in the front room, and now our money is coming to an end. That is what we want your advice about, for we both respect your opinion."

"A very pretty problem too," I thought to myself, disconsolately.

"You see, Hudson," Crabbe remarked, "the fact is that my father used eight or nine years ago to do a great practice in this town. It seemed to me that I had only to come down here and set up in the same style in which he used to live, and I should have all his old patients rallying round me. I accordingly came down and set up, but there has been no appreciable rally as yet. I can go out for a walk without any very great dread of missing anything important by my absence."

"Perhaps they may come yet," I hazarded.

"When they do they'll find me gone," Crabbe replied. "You can't go on living for ever on a small capital while nothing is coming in. It does rile me," he continued, giving the fire a lunge, "to see the people flocking into Maxwell's across the road there. He was ploughed twice for his final, to my certain knowledge, and was reckoned the stupidest man of his year, and yet he does all the practice about here. Why, only yesterday I saw my milkman strain his ankle when coming down my garden steps, and you'll hardly believe me when I tell you that he actually limped across the road in order to consult Maxwell as to his injuries."

"That was very hard," I said.

"Oh, we have got pretty well used to hard things," Crabbe remarked. "The only really good patient that I have had went away without paying his bill, and I have never heard of him since. However, the question is, Hudson, what should our next move be? I want your unbiased opinion on the matter."

"Leave it open until to-morrow," I said, "so as to give me time. In the meanwhile, let us drop the subject altogether." So we began talking about old times and college reminiscences until the fire was low and the night far advanced.

On the next day Crabbe and I sat in the bow-window of his drawing-room watching the people passing, and discussing the question which we had left the night before.

"Do you think?" I asked him, "that there is any chance of your succeeding here?"

"I am bound to succeed," he said, "if I could only hold on until people become aware of my existence, and realise that I am my father's son."

"But surely they can read your plate!" I said.

"Not they," he answered. "Look at all these people passing. How many of them glance at it; and of those that do, how many give the matter a second thought, or connect me with the Doctor Crabbe of ten years ago? If I had some means of letting them know how matters stand I would soon have a practice. Unfortunately we are not allowed to advertise, and I see no other way of letting them know."

"Why don't you have an accident in front of your door?" I said, laughingly, the joke provoked by Crabbe's preternaturally solemn face. "That would get into the papers, and draw attention to you."

"My dear fellow," Crabbe remonstrated, "do be practical. There are a good many philanthropists in the world, but no one quite so kind as to break his limbs to order in front of my house to get me a practice."

"Wait a bit," I said, warming up to the subject. "Supposing that the street was crowded, just in the busiest part of the day—"

"Quite so," said Crabbe, impatiently.

"And suppose just at that time a fashionably-dressed young man was to fall down before your gate. And suppose the said young man to be carried in here, and you to treat him with such skill that he walked out again as well as ever in a few minutes, and suppose all this to get into the papers, don't you think it would attract the attention of the citizens of Bridport to the fact of your existence?"

"It would be the making of me," Crabbe said, emphatically.

"Then I'm the fashionably-dressed young man!" I cried, entering into the spirit of the thing. "So mind that you are on the alert, and don't let them carry me over to Maxwell's."

"But, my dear fellow," said Crabbe, "I had no idea you were an epileptic."

"Neither I am," I answered; "but I intend to become one."

"It's awfully good of you!" Crabbe exclaimed, taking the matter gravely. "Do you mean to say that you will really have an attack?"

"Fifty if you like," I answered, cheerfully. "By the way, would you like an epileptic or an apoplectic one, or would you prefer something more ornate—a sudden attack of multiple sclerosis or locomotor ataxia? You may command me in anything."

"You've hit on an excellent idea," my friend said, thoughtfully; "but don't you think it might be improved upon? We can only do it once, for it wouldn't do to have the same young man continually turning up and having fits in front of my gate. Don't you think an accident might be more effective?"

"Quite so," I answered. "But I draw the line at falling out of windows or being run over by waggons in your service."

"Have you seen those two letters lately in the medical papers," Crabbe asked, "in which a man claims to have caused the heart to beat after it had stopped by running a fine needle into it, and so stimulating it?"

"Yes."

"Well, there you are!" cried Crabbe, triumphantly. "If I ran a needle into you, and so restored life, that would be something worth talking about."

"Something worth shouting about, from my point of view!" I remarked.

"Can you swim?"

"Like a duck!" I answered.

"Then we'll do it!" Crabbe said, resolutely. "Come along out for a walk, and I'll explain as we go;" and, taking our hats, we set off in the direction of the docks.

As we went Crabbe explained to me his idea. It was that I should take a wherry next morning, and while rowing in the harbour should manage to fall overboard. I was to remain under water as long as possible, and when I was eventually fished in by the boatman I was to give no sign. Crabbe was to be on the bank, as though by accident, and was immediately to apply every known restorative, but without avail. A survey of the spot showed that we could rely upon unlimited stimulants, and also that a convenient chemist in the vicinity kept a galvanic battery, with which Crabbe might endeavour to bring some spark of life into me. Eventually, when all other means had failed, he was to pretend to plunge a needle in between my ribs, on which I was at once to sit up and begin conversing as though quite recovered.

This was the plan which Crabbe sketched out, and to which I, in the innate fun of a nature bubbling over with thoughtless mischief, though really meaning no wrong, immediately gave my cordial assent.

We went over the scene of operations together, and arranged every preliminary of what I then thought a capital joke.

"Remember," said Crabbe, as I left him that night, "it is my last chance in Bridport. If we fail, there is nothing for it but bankruptcy."

"All right," I answered, cheerfully. "Be steady with that needle."

"No fear! Ten o'clock to-morrow."

"Ten o'clock," I repeated, and with a hearty shake of the hands I parted from him, and sought a bed at the hotel.

We had agreed that this was the best course, in order that there might be no suspicion of collusion between us.

On the eventful morning I was up betimes, and, having taken a couple of strong cups of coffee to fortify me against the troubles in store, I set off for the docks. It was market day, and the town was particularly full of people, more especially near the scene of our operations. As I came along the Apostles' Wharf, and so to the lower dock, I saw a man attired in a dark coat and professional hat standing listlessly upon the swinging bridge and looking down upon the water beneath. It was Crabbe, but I gave him no sign of recognition. Close to the bridge were some steps, where the wherrymen plied their trade. There was a chorus of shouts of "A boat this morning, your honour?" as I approached them.

"That seems a smart craft of yours," I remarked to one of them.

"She is that, sir. Won't your honour come out in her and have a row round the shipping?"

"I don't mind if I do have a short spin," I said, and stepping into her we shot out into the harbour. The stagnant brown water looked particularly uninviting, but it was too late to retreat.

"Turn round," I said, "and row up under the bridge."

We were just under the spot where Crabbe was standing, and about fifty yards from the shore, when I rose in the boat and said,

"Here, change places with me and let me manage the sculls."

"All right, sir," said the boatman, and then, "Hullo! Look out, sir, look out, you'll be over as sure as fate!"

His warning came too late, however, for in changing places I had tripped over a thwart, given a stagger, and fallen headlong into the water.

I have seldom felt a more unpleasant sensation than when the thick turbid stream closed over my head. I was an excellent swimmer, however, and knew that even with my clothes on I was as safe in the water as upon dry land. I kept down accordingly as long as I could. When I rose to the surface I heard the boatman shouting frantically for assistance, and he made a plunge at me with his boathook, which I managed to avoid by sinking again.

Three times I rose and three times I went down, and when at last I suffered myself to be hauled aboard the boat and so conveyed to *terra firma*, I flatter myself that I looked blue enough and cold enough to make a most creditable "subject."

A sympathising crowd gathered round me in a moment as I was laid motionless and dripping upon the hard round stones of the quay.

"Run for a doctor," roared one.

"He's dead, poor fellow!" cried another.

"Run for Mr. McCluskey the chemist." "Get some brandy!" "Turn him upside down!" "Shake him!" "Roll him!" "Put him on a mustard plaster!"

These and a few other remedies were suggested, and no doubt would have been put into practice had it not been for the arrival of my accomplice.

"Excuse me, my good people," I heard him say, as he approached, "I am a medical man. Can my services be of any avail?"

"Clear the way for the doctor," shouted a chorus of gruff voices.

"Dear me! Dear me!" ejaculated Crabbe. "This is very sad. Stand back, my friends, and give him air. All that medicine can do shall be done. Poor young man!"

"Please, doctor," remarked an inquisitive bystander, who had thrust his hand inside my shirt, "His heart is a-beating like anything."

"The last convulsive flutter, perhaps," Crabbe said, solemnly, pushing the man aside; "but we are bound not to throw away a chance. Get some brandy. Inspector," to a policeman who had appeared on the scene, "I am Dr. Crabbe, the son of Dr. Crabbe who used to practise in Melville Terrace."

"It's the son of old Dr. Crabbe," chorused the crowd. "Run for the brandy. He'll pull him through."

The brandy was duly brought and held to my lips, with the effect of a perceptible diminution in the contents of the glass, for I was beginning to feel cold, and to repent of our wild, thoughtless escapade.

"He's a-drinkin' it!" exclaimed the meddlesome individual who had previously spoken.

"That's no sign he's alive," Crabbe answered, with the greatest serenity. "It may be a post-mortem phenomenon, depending upon contraction of the œsophageal muscles."

I was so much amused by this barefaced statement that I could not prevent an internal gurgle of merriment from escaping from me.

"There's the death rattle!" someone exclaimed, and then Crabbe, seizing me, began hauling my arms furiously about.

"Marshall Hall's method of artificial respiration," he panted for the benefit of the crowd. Then, as that had no effect, he proceeded to roll me backwards and forwards upon the stones, after the fashion recommended by Sylvestre. To this day I have an uneasy feeling about the spine when I think of it.

"It is all in vain!" Crabbe exclaimed after he had bumped and bruised me for ten minutes without eliciting the slightest sign of animation, "but the resources of science are not yet exhausted. Who has got a galvanic battery?"

"You'll get one up at Mr. McCluskey's the chemist," some one answered.

"Run for it, then. In the meantime, let us carry this unfortunate young man up to the inn, where we can lay him upon a bed."

I was hoisted upon a shutter, and carried up to the Mariner's

Arms, escorted, as it seemed to me, by an appreciable percentage of the population of Bridport. As far as I could see through my half-closed lids the great crowd extended, all craning their necks to get a glimpse at me. Crabbe followed the shutter with a most funereal expression upon his face, shaking his head dolorously. Behind him came about a dozen prominent citizens of the town, all deeply interested in the proceedings.

I was carried up the stairs of the Mariner's Arms and laid upon a bed, where I was muffled up in thick blankets. The twelve prominent citizens stationed themselves in the room and upon the stairs, while the general public filled the passage and extended right down to the water's edge.

"We have now tried the effect of artificial respiration," said my friend, as though he were lecturing to a class; "we have also used stimulants and friction. We shall next endeavour to stimulate the heart's action by the use of electricity. If that fails we have still one resource left which we can fall back upon."

There were murmurs of applause from the audience at this display of erudition upon the part of the doctor, and a hush of suspense ensued as a shining mahogany case was handed upstairs, which contained the galvanic battery.

"Oh, look!" said the landlady of the Mariner's Arms, who had been most assiduous in piling blankets upon me. "Hain't he got a colour! Wouldn't you say there weren't nothing the matter with him!"

"Yes, such cases may be deceptive," Crabbe answered demurely. "Now, gentlemen," he continued, addressing the prominent citizens who blocked up the door of the room, "I am about to apply the negative pole of this battery over this young man's phrenhic nerve, while I place the other in the region of his heart. This treatment is sometimes attended with surprising results."

It certainly was upon that occasion. Whether Crabbe did it accidentally, or whether a mischievous impulse suddenly overcame him, I have never been able to determine, but certain it is that next moment he sent a tremendous electric shock crashing and jarring through my system. The effect upon me was extraordinary. I shot out of bed, my hair bristling with indignation and electricity.

"You stupid ass!" I roared, seizing Crabbe by the throat. "Isn't it enough to bang me and thump me on the stones, without turning me into a lightning-conductor! Take this thing away!" with which I kicked viciously at the mahogany box.

It chanced, however, that some well-meaning individual had removed my boots while I lay upon the bed, so that my kick, though it had no perceptible effect upon the box, had a very considerable one upon me. Consequently I danced furiously round the room, holding my injured toe in my hand, and roaring lustily, forgetful of all my former injuries. I was thus punished smartly after all for my share in the adventure.

My sudden resurrection had a wonderful effect upon the crowd. The landlady fainted, two of the prominent citizens lost their equilibrium, and, rolling down upon the others, the whole twelve, like a pack of cards, went clattering down the stairs. The housemaid, who had been dandling the baby out of the window and conversing with a friend below, was so startled that she nearly dropped the infant upon the head of her acquaintance. In the meanwhile the crowd outside, having a vague idea that something wonderful had happened, and that I was coming round, set up an enthusiastic whooping and cheering.

Crabbe was quite equal to the occasion. "Don't be a fool, Bob!" he whispered in my ear as he supported me back to the bed. "This is a most gratifying result," he continued, addressing his considerably diminished audience—"an extraordinary case! Our young friend will recover, but"—here he tapped his forehead ominously—"these wild words and actions of his show temporary mischief here. I shall accompany him to his hotel and see that he is cared for. Remember, gentlemen, in case there should be any inquiries about this matter, that my name is Crabbe, the son of the late Dr. Crabbe, of Melville Terrace."

A cab was quickly obtained, and Crabbe and I drove off together, amid tremendous cheering from the crowd.

I left early by the next morning's train, but received a letter in a few days from Crabbe, in which he gave me the news. "You will be surprised to hear," he said, "that I have seen more patients during the last week than during the preceding two years! There is no chance of any one not knowing of my existence now. I enclose cuttings from the 'Bridport Gazette' and the 'Bridport Evening News,' together with a leader on the 'Extraordinary Rescue' in the 'Dumpshire Chronicle.' The practice promises to be a great success."

It has really become so, and Crabbe, it is only fair to say, richly deserves it as a clever as well as hardworking practitioner. He always stood high in the classes at college, and he now occupies an equally enviable place in the esteem of his fellow-townsmen. If he has any regret, it is because that what now in his calmer moments he feels to have been an unjustifiable ruse should have had anything to do with first making his merits known to a public with whom "fashion" was allowed to overshadow merit.

NOTES TO 'CRABBE'S PRACTICE'

First published in the *Boy's Own Annual*, Christmas 1884.

1. The story is based on the extraordinary medical practice of the erratic George Turnavine Budd, a fellow graduate from Edinburgh, who invited Conan Doyle to become his partner in Plymouth. Budd made a lot of money for a while by treating patients for free but charging them for the various (useless) drugs he prescribed, made up on the premises by his wife. The idea was that his partner would handle any surgical cases, but the arrangement broke down after only six months, at which point Conan Doyle moved to Portsmouth and set up his own practice. Despite his Edinburgh education, Budd was a quackish medical salesman, more like an old-style showman than an instance of the new breed of sober professional emerging in the wake of the Medical Act of 1858. Budd's style of operation is described in greater detail in *The Stark Munro Letters* (1895).

2. The Bulgarian atrocities occurred in 1876. At that time the Ottoman Empire covered much of southeastern Europe, but it was increasingly challenged by nationalist uprisings, supported by Russia, which sought liberation from its rule. Rebellions in 1875-76 were suppressed by Ottoman forces, often with great brutality, and there were several large-scale massacres of Christians and other non-Muslims, burning of churches, destruction of villages, etc. In Britain the ruling Conservative Party under Benjamin Disraeli was anxious to block Russian influence in the Balkans and therefore supported the Turks while downplaying their violence. This policy outraged liberal opinion, especially the Liberal Party leader, William Gladstone, who attacked the cynicism of the government's position in many speeches; in a lengthy pamphlet, *The Bulgarian Horrors*, he urged action to curb the Turks and to support Britain's fellow Christians. The issue aroused as fiercely partisan passions as similar conflicts in the Balkans, the Middle East and Africa in our own day, but in the 1870s educated middle class opinion tended to sympathise with the Christians as victims of a cruel and backward oriental despotism. The emotional intensity depicted in Conan Doyle's story is just what would be expected at a meeting of university students on this issue.[1]

---

[1] For details, see R. W. Seton-Watson, *Disraeli, Gladstone and the Eastern Question* (1935; London: Frank Cass, 1962), esp. chap. III.

THE SURGEON OF GASTER FELL

CHAPTER I.—HOW THE WOMAN CAME TO KIRKBY-MALHOUSE.

BLEAK and windswept is the little Yorkshire town of Kirkby-Malhouse, and harsh and forbidding are the fells upon which it stands. It stretches in a single line of gray stone, slate-roofed houses, dotted down the furze-clad slope of the long rolling moor. To north and to south stretch the swelling curves of the Yorkshire uplands, peeping over each other's backs to the skyland, with a tinge of yellow in the foreground, which shades away to olive in the distance, save where the long gray scars of rock protrude through the scanty and barren soil. From the little knoll above the church one may see to the westward a fringe of gold upon an arc of silver, where the great Morecambe sands are washed by the Irish Sea. To the east, Ingleborough looms purple in the distance; while Pennigent shoots up the tapering peak, whose great shadow, like Nature's own sun-dial, sweeps slowly round over a vast expanse of savage and sterile country.

In this lonely and secluded village, I, James Upperton, found myself in the summer of '85. Little as the wild hamlet had to offer, it contained that for which I yearned above all things—seclusion and freedom from all which might distract my mind from the high and weighty subjects which engaged it. I was weary of the long turmoil and profitless strivings of life. From early youth my days had been spent in wild adventure and strange experiences, until, at the age of thirty-nine, there were very few lands upon which I had not set foot, and scarcely any joy or sorrow of which I had not tasted. Among the first of Europeans, I had penetrated to the desolate shores of Lake Tanganyika; and I had twice made my way to those unvisited and impenetrable jungles which skirt the great tableland of the Roraima. As a soldier of fortune, I had served under many flags. I was with Jackson in the Shenandoah Valley; and I fought with Chanzy in the army of the Loire. It may well seem strange that, after a life so exciting, I could give myself up to the dull routine and trivial interests of the West Riding hamlet.

And yet there are excitements of the mind to which mere bodily peril or the exaltation of travel is mean and commonplace. For years I had devoted myself to the study of the mystic and hermetic philosophies, Egyptian, Indian, Grecian, and medieval, until out of the vast chaos there had dimly dawned upon me a huge symmetrical design; and I seemed to grasp the key of that symbolism which was used by those learned men to screen their precious knowledge from the vulgar and the wicked. Gnostics and Neo-platonists, Chaldeans, Rosicrucians, and Indian Mystics, I saw and understood in which each played a part. To me the jargon of Paracelsus, the mysteries of the alchemists, and the visions of Swedenborg were all pregnant with meaning. I had deciphered the mysterious inscriptions of El Biram; and I knew the import of those strange characters which have been engraved by an unknown race upon the cliffs of Southern Turkestan. Immersed in these great and engrossing studies, I asked nothing from life save a garret for myself and for my books, where I might pursue my studies without interference or interruption.

But even in the little moorside village I found that it was impossible to shake off the censorship of one's fellow-mortals. When I went forth, the rustics would eye me askance, and mothers would whip up their children as I passed down the village street. At night, I have glanced out through my diamond-paned lattice to find that a group of foolish staring peasants had been craning their necks in an ecstacy of fear and curiosity to watch me at my solitary task. My landlady, too, became garrulous with a clatter of questions under every small pretext, and a hundred small ruses and wiles by which to tempt me to speak to her of myself and of my plans. All this was ill to bear; but when at last I heard that I was no longer to be the sole lodger, and that a lady, a stranger, had engaged the other room, I felt that indeed it was time for one who sought the quiet and the peace of study to seek some more tranquil surrounding.

In my frequent walks I had learnt to know well the wild and desolate region where Yorkshire borders on both Lancashire and Westmorland. From Kirkby-Malhouse I had frequently made my way to this lonesome wilderness, and had traversed it from end to end. In the gloomy majesty of its scenery, and the appalling stillness and loneliness of its rock-strewn melancholy solitudes, it seemed to offer me a secure asylum from espionage and criticism. As it chanced, I had in my rambles come upon an isolated dwelling in the very heart of these lonely moors, which I at once determined should be my own. It was a two-roomed cottage, which had once belonged to some shepherd, but had long been deserted, and was crumbling rapidly to ruin. In the winter floods, the Gaster Beck, which runs down Gaster Fell, where the little sheiling stood, had overswept its bank and torn away a portion of the wall. The roof, too, was in ill case, and the scattered slates lay thick against the grass. Yet the main shell of the house stood firm and true; and it was no great task for me to have all that was amiss set right. Though not rich, I could yet afford to carry out so modest a whim in a lordly way. There came slaters and masons from Kirkby-Malhouse, and soon the lonely cottage upon Gaster Fell was as strong and weather-tight as ever.

The two rooms I laid out in a widely different manner—my own tastes are of a Spartan turn, and the outer chamber was so planned as to accord with them. An oil-stove by Rippingille of Birmingham furnished me with the means of cooking; while two great bags, the one of flour, and the other of potatoes, made me independent of all supplies from without. In diet I had long been a Pythagorean, so that the scraggy long-limbed sheep which browsed upon the wiry grass by the Gaster Beck had little to fear from their new companion. A nine-gallon cask of oil served me as a sideboard; while a square table, a deal chair, and a truckle-bed completed the list of my domestic fittings. At the head of my couch hung two unpainted shelves—the lower for my dishes and cooking utensils, the upper for the few portraits which took me back to the little that was pleasant in the long wearisome toiling for wealth and for pleasure which had marked the life I had left behind.

If this dwelling-room of mine were plain even to squalor, its poverty was more than atoned for by the luxury of the chamber which was destined to serve me as my study. I had ever held that it was best for the mind to be surrounded by such objects as would be in harmony with the studies which occupied it, and that the loftiest and most ethereal conditions of thought are only possible amid surroundings which please the eye and gratify the senses. The room which I had set apart for my mystic studies was set forth in a style as gloomy and majestic as the thoughts and aspirations with which it was to harmonise. Both walls and ceilings were covered with a paper of the richest and glossiest black, on which was traced a lurid and arabesque pattern of dead gold. A black velvet curtain covered the single diamond-paned window; while a thick yielding carpet of the same material prevented the sound of my own footfall, as I paced backwards and forwards, from breaking the current of my thoughts. Along the cornice ran gold rods, from which depended six pictures, all of the sombre and imaginative caste, which chimed best with my fancy. Two, as I remember, were from the brush of Fuseli; one from Noel Paton; one from Gustave Doré; two from Martin; with a little water-colour by the incomparable Blake. From the centre of the ceiling hung a single gold thread, so thin as to be scarce visible, but of great toughness. From this swung a dove of the same metal, with wings outstretched. The bird was hollow, and contained perfumed oil; while a sylph-like figure, curiously fashioned from pink crystal, hovered over the lamp, and imparted a rich and soft glow to its light. A brazen fireplace backed with malachite, two tiger skins upon the carpet, a buhl table, and two reclining chairs in amber plush and ebony, completed the furniture of my bijou study, save only that under the window stretched the long bookshelves, which contained the choicest works of those who have busied themselves with the mystery of life.

Boehme, Swedenborg, Damton, Berto, Lacci, Sinnett, Hardinge, Britten, Dunlop, Amberley, Winwood Read, Des Mousseux, Alan Kardec, Lepsius, Sepher, Toldo, and the Abbé Dubois—these were some of those who stood marshalled between my oaken shelves. When the lamp was lit of a night and the lurid flickering light played over the sombre and bizarre surroundings, the effect was all that I could wish. Nor was it lessened by the howling of the wind as it swept over the melancholy waste around me. Here at last, I thought, is a back-eddy in life's hurried stream, where I may lie in peace, forgetting and forgotten.

And yet it was destined that ere ever I reached this quiet harbour I should learn that I was still one of humankind, and that it is an ill thing to strive to break the bond which binds us to our fellows. It was but two nights before the date I had fixed upon for my change of dwelling, when I was conscious of a bustle in the house beneath, with the bearing of heavy burdens up the creaking stair, and the harsh voice of my landlady, loud in welcome and protestations of joy. From time to time, amid her whirl of words, I could hear a gentle and softly modulated voice, which struck pleasantly upon my ear after the long weeks during which I had listened only to the rude dialect of the dalesmen.

For an hour I could hear the dialogue beneath—the high voice and the low, with clatter of cup and clink of spoon, until, at last, a light quick step passed my study door, and I knew that my new fellow-lodger had sought her room. Already my fears had been fulfilled, and my studies the worse for her coming. I vowed in my mind that the second sunset should find me installed, safe from all such petty influences, in my sanctuary at Gaster Fell.

On the morning after this incident I was up betimes, as is my wont; but I was surprised, on my glancing from my window to see that our new inmate was earlier still. She was walking down the narrow pathway which zigzags over the fell—a tall woman, slender, her head sunk upon her breast, her arms filled with a bristle of wildflowers, which she had gathered in her morning rambles. The white and pink of her dress, and the touch of deep-red ribbon in her broad drooping hat, formed a pleasant dash of colour against the dun-tinted landscape. She was some distance off when I first set eyes upon her, yet I knew that this wandering woman could be none other than our arrival of last night, for there was a grace and refinement in her bearing which marked her from the dwellers of the fells. Even as I watched, she passed swiftly and lightly down the pathway, and turning through the wicket gate, at the farther end of our cottage garden, she seated herself upon the green bank which faced my window, and strewing her flowers in front of her, set herself to arrange them.

As she sat there, with the rising sun at her back, and the glow of morning spreading like an auriole round her stately and well-poised head, I could see that she was a woman of extraordinary personal beauty. Her face was Spanish rather than English in its type—oval, olive, with black sparkling eyes, and a sweetly sensitive mouth. From under the broad straw hat, two thick coils of blue-black hair curved down on either side of her graceful queenly neck. I was surprised, as I watched her, to see that her shoes and skirt bore witness to a journey rather than to a mere morning ramble. Her light dress was stained, wet and bedraggled; while her boots were thick with the yellow soil of the fells. Her face, too, wore a weary expression, and her young beauty seemed to be clouded over by the shadow of inward trouble. Even as I watched her, she burst suddenly into wild weeping, and throwing down her bundle of flowers, ran swiftly into the house.

Distrait as I was, and weary of the ways of the world, I was conscious of a sudden pang of sympathy and grief as I looked upon the spasm of despair which seemed to convulse this strange and beautiful woman. I bent to my books, and yet my thoughts would ever turn to her proud clear-cut face, her weather-stained dress, her drooping head, and the sorrow which lay in each line and feature of her pensive face. Again and again I found myself standing at my casement, and glancing out to see if there were signs of her return. There on the green bank was the litter of golden gorse and purple marshmallow where she had left them; but through the whole morning I neither saw nor heard anything from her who had so suddenly aroused my curiosity and stirred my long-slumbering emotions.

Mrs Adams, my landlady, was wont to carry up my frugal breakfast; yet it was very rarely that I allowed her to break the current of my thoughts, or to draw my mind by her idle chatter from weightier things. This morning, however, for once she found me in a listening mood, and with little prompting, proceeded to pour into my ears all that she know of our beautiful visitor.

'Miss Eva Cameron be her name, sir,' she said; 'but who she be, or where she come fra, I know little more than yoursel'. Maybe it was the same reason that brought her to Kirkby-Malhouse as fetched you there yoursel', sir.'

'Possibly,' said I, ignoring the covert question; 'but I should hardly have thought that Kirkby-Malhouse was a place which offered any great attraction to a young lady.'

'It's a gay place when the fair is on,' said Mrs Adams; 'yet maybe it's just health and rest as the young lady is seeking.'

'Very likely,' said I, stirring my coffee; 'and no doubt some friend of yours has advised her to seek it in your very comfortable apartments.'

'Heh, sir!' she cried, 'there's the wonder of it. The leddy has just come fra France; and how her folk came to learn of me is just a wonder. A week ago, up comes a man to my door—a fine man, sir and a gentleman, as one could see with half an eye. "You are Mrs Adams," says he. "I engage your rooms for Miss Cameron," says he. "She will be here in a week," says he; and then off without a word of terms. Last night there comes the young leddy hersel'—soft-spoken and downcast, with a touch of the French in her speech.—But my sakes, sir! I must away and mak' her some tea, for she'll feel lonesome-like, poor lamb, when she wakes under a strange roof.'

CHAPTER II.—HOW I WENT FORTH TO GASTER FELL.

I WAS still engaged upon my breakfast, when I heard the clatter of dishes, and the landlady's footfall as she passed towards her new lodger's room. An instant afterwards she had rushed down the passage and burst in upon me with uplifted hands and startled eyes. 'Lord 'a mercy, sir!' she cried, 'and asking your pardon for troubling you, but I'm feard o' the young leddy, sir; she is not in her room.'

'Why, there she is,' said I, standing up and glancing through the casement. 'She has gone back for the flowers she left upon the bank.'

'Oh, sir, see to her boots and her dress!' cried the landlady wildly. 'I wish her mother was here, sir—I do. Where she has been is more than I ken; but her bed has not been lain on this night.'

'She has felt restless, doubtless, and had gone for a walk, though the hour was certainly a strange one.'

Mrs Adams pursed her lip and shook her head. But even as she stood at the casement, the girl beneath looked smilingly up at her, and beckoned to her with a merry gesture to open the window.

'Have you my tea there?' she asked, in a rich clear voice, with a touch of the mincing French accent.

'It is in your room, miss.'

'Look at my boots, Mrs Adams!' she cried, thrusting them out from under her skirt. 'These fells of yours are dreadful places—effroyable—one inch, two inch; never have I seen such mud!—My dress, too—voilà!'

'Eh, miss, but you are in a pickle,' cried the landlady, as she gazed down at the bedraggled gown. 'But you must be main-weary and heavy for sleep.'

'No, no,' she answered, laughing. 'I care not for sleep. What is sleep? It is a little death—voilà tout. But for me to walk, to run, to breathe the air—that is to live. I was not tired, and so all night I have explored these fells of Yorkshire.'

'Lord 'a mercy, miss, and where did you go?' asked Mrs Adams.

She waved her hand round in a sweeping gesture which included the whole western horizon. 'There!' she cried. 'O comme elles sont tristes et sauvages, ces collines! But I have flowers here. You will give me water, will you not? They will wither else.' She gathered her treasures into her lap, and a moment later we heard her light springy footfall upon the stair.

So she had been out all night, this strange woman. What motive could have taken her from her snug room on to the bleak wind-swept hills? Could it be merely the restlessness, the love of adventure of a young girl? Or was there, possibly, some deeper meaning in this nocturnal journey?

I thought, as I paced my chamber, of her drooping head, the grief upon her face, and the wild burst of sobbing which I had overseen in the garden. Her nightly mission, then, be it what it might, had left no thought of pleasure behind it. And yet, even as I walked, I could hear the merry tinkle of her laughter, and her voice upraised in protest against the motherly care wherewith Mrs Adams insisted upon her changing her mud-stained garments. Deep as were the mysteries which my studies had taught me to solve, here was a human problem, which for the moment at least was beyond my comprehension.

I had walked out on the moor in the forenoon; and on my return, as I topped the brow that overlooks the little town, I saw my fellow-lodger some little distance off among the gorse. She had raised a light easel in front of her, and with papered board laid across it, was preparing to paint the magnificent landscape of rock and moor which stretched away in front of her. As I watched her, I saw that she was looking anxiously to right and left. Close by me a pool of water had formed in a hollow. Dipping the cup of my pocket flask into it, I carried it across to her. 'This is what you need, I think,' said I, raising my cap and smiling.

'Merci bien,' she answered, pouring the water into her saucer. 'I was indeed in search of some.'

'Miss Cameron, I believe,' said I. 'I am your fellow-lodger. Upperton is my name. We must introduce ourselves in these wilds if we are not to be for ever strangers.'

'Oh then, you live also with Mrs Adams,' she cried, 'I had thought that there were none but peasants in this strange place.'

'I am a visitor, like yourself,' I answered. 'I am a student, and have come for the quiet and repose which my studies demand.'

'Quiet indeed,' said she, glancing round at the vast circle of silent moors, with the one tiny line of gray cottages which sloped down beneath us.

'And yet not quiet enough,' I answered, laughing, 'for I have been forced to move farther into the fells for the absolute peace which I require.'

'Have you then built a house upon the fells?' she asked, arching her eyebrows.

'I have, and hope within a few days to occupy it.'

'Ah, but that is triste,' she cried. 'And where is it, then, this house which you have built?'

'It is over yonder,' I answered. 'See that stream which lies like a silver band upon the distant moor. It is the Gaster Beck, and it runs through Gaster Fell.'

She started, and turned upon me her great dark questioning eyes with a look in which surprise, incredulity, and something akin to horror seemed to be struggling for a mastery.

'And you will live on the Gaster Fell?' she cried.

'So I have planned.—But what do you know of Gaster Fell, Miss Cameron?' I asked. 'I had thought you were a stranger in these parts.'

'Indeed, I have never been here before,' she answered. 'But I have heard my brother talk of these Yorkshire moors; and if I mistake not, I have heard him name this very one as the wildest and most savage of them all.'

'Very likely,' said I carelessly. 'It is indeed a dreary place.'

'Then why live there?' she cried eagerly. 'Consider the loneliness, the bareness, the want of all comfort and of all aid, should aid be needed.'

'Aid! What aid should be needed on Gaster Fell?'

She looked down and shrugged her shoulders. 'Sickness may come in all places,' said she. 'If I were a man, I do not think I would live alone on Gaster Fell.'

'I have braved far worse dangers than that,' said I, laughing; 'but I fear that your picture will be spoilt, for the clouds are banking up, and already I feel a few raindrops.'

Indeed, it was high time we were on our way to shelter, for even as I spoke there came the sudden steady swish of the shower. Laughing merrily, my companion threw her light shawl over her head, and, seizing the easel, ran with the lithe grace of a young fawn down the furze-clad slope, while I followed after with camp-stool and paint-box.

Deeply as my curiosity had been aroused by this strange waif which had been cast up in our West Riding hamlet, I found that with fuller knowledge of her my interest was stimulated rather than satisfied. Thrown together as we were, with no thought in common with the good people who surrounded us, it was not long before a friendship and confidence arose between us. Together we strolled over the moors in the morning, or stood upon the Moorstone Crag to watch the red sun sinking beneath the distant waters of Morecambe. Of herself she spoke frankly and without reserve. Her mother had died young, and her youth had been spent in the Belgian convent from which she had just finally returned. Her father and one brother, she told me, constituted the whole of her family. Yet, when the talk chanced to turn upon the causes which had brought her to so lonely a dwelling, a strange reserve possessed her; and she would either relapse into silence or turn the talk into another channel. For the rest, she was an admirable companion—sympathetic, well read, with the quick piquant daintiness of thought which she had brought with her from her foreign training. Yet the shadow which I had observed in her on the first morning that I had seen her was never far from her mind, and I have seen her merriest laugh frozen suddenly upon her lips, as though some dark thought lurked within her, to choke down the mirth and gaiety of her youth.

It was the eve of my departure from Kirkby-Malhouse that we sat upon the green bank in the garden, she with dark dreamy eyes looking sadly out over the sombre fells; while I, with a book upon my knee, glanced covertly at her lovely profile, and marvelling to myself how twenty years of life could have stamped so sad and wistful an expression upon it.

'You have read much,' I remarked at last. 'Women have opportunities now such as their mothers never knew. Have you ever thought of going farther—of seeking a course of college or even a learned profession?'

She smiled wearily at the thought. 'I have no aim, no ambition,' she said. 'My future is black—confused—a chaos. My life is like to one of these paths upon the fells. You have seen them, Monsieur Up-perton. They are smooth and straight and clear where they begin; but soon they wind to left and wind to right, and so mid rocks and over crags until they lose themselves in some quagmire. At Brussels my path was straight; but now, mon Dieu, who is there can tell me where it leads?'

'It might take no prophet to do that, Miss Cameron,' quoth I, with the fatherly manner which twoscore years may show toward one. 'If I may read your life, I would venture to say that you were destined to fulfil the lot of woman—to make some good man happy, and to shed around, in some wider circle, the pleasure which your society has given me since first I knew you.'

'I will never marry,' said she, with a sharp decision which sur-prised me and somewhat amused me.

'Not marry; and why?'

A strange look passed over her sensitive features, and she plucked nervously at the grass on the bank beside her. 'I dare not,' said she, in a voice that quivered with emotion.

'Dare not!'

'It is not for me. I have other things to do. That path of which I spoke is one which I must tread alone.'

'But this is morbid,' said I. 'Why should your lot, Miss Cameron, be separate from that of my own sisters, or the thousand other young ladies whom every season brings out into the world?—But perhaps it is that you have a fear and distrust of mankind. Marriage brings a risk as well as a happiness.'

'The risk would be with the man who married me,' she cried. And then in an instant, as though she had said too much, she sprang to her feet and drew her mantle round her. 'The night-air is chill, Mr Upper-ton,' said she, and so swept swiftly away, leaving me to muse over the strange words which had fallen from her lips.

I had feared that this woman's coming might draw me from my studies; but never had I anticipated that my thoughts and interests could have been changed in so short a time. I sat late that night in my little study, pondering over my future course. She was young, she was fair, she was alluring, both from her own beauty and from the strange mystery that surrounded her. And yet, what was she, that she should turn me from the high studies that filled my mind, or change me from the line of life which I had marked out for myself? I was no boy, that I should be swayed and shaken by a dark eye or a woman's smile, and yet three days had passed, and my work lay where I had left it. Clearly, it was time that I should go. I set my teeth, and vowed that another day should not have passed before I should have snapped this newly-formed tie, and sought the lonely retreat which awaited me upon the moors.

Breakfast was hardly over in the morning before a peasant dragged up to the door the rude hand-cart which was to convey my few personal belongings to my new dwelling. My fellow-lodger had kept her room; and steeled as my mind was against her influence. I was yet conscious of a little throb of disappointment that she should allow me to depart without a word of farewell. My hand-cart with its load of books had already started, and I, having shaken hands with Mrs Adams, was about to follow it, when there was a quick scurry of feet on the stair, and there she was beside me all panting with her own haste.

'Then you go, you really go?' said she.

'My studies call me.'

'And to Gaster Fell?' she asked.

'Yes, to the cottage which I have built there.'

'And you will live alone there?'

'With my hundred companions who lie in that cart.'

'Ah, books!' she cried, with a pretty shrug of her graceful shoulders.—'But you will make me a promise?'

'What is it?' I asked in surprise.

'It is a small thing; you will not refuse me?'

'You have but to ask it.'

She bent forward her beautiful face with an expression of the utmost and most intense earnestness. 'You will bolt your door at night?' said she, and was gone ere I could say a word in answer to her extraordinary request.

It was a strange thing for me to find myself at last duly installed in my lonely dwelling. For me, now, the horizon was bounded by the barren circle of wiry unprofitable grass, patched over with furze bushes, and scarred by the protrusion of Nature's gaunt and granite ribs. A duller, wearier waste I have never seen; but its dullness was its very charm. What was there in the faded rolling hills, or in the blue silent arch of heaven, to distract my thoughts from the high thoughts which engrossed them? I had left the great drove of mankind, and had wandered away, for better or worse, upon a side-path of my own. With them, I had hoped to leave grief, disappointment, and emotion, and all other petty human weaknesses. To live for knowledge, and knowledge alone, that was the highest aim which life could offer. And yet upon the very first night which I spent at Gaster Fell there came a strange incident to lead my thoughts back once more to the world which I had left behind me.

It had been a sullen and sultry evening, with great livid cloud-banks mustering in the west. As the night wore on, the air within my little cabin became closer and more oppressive. A weight seemed to rest upon my brow and my chest. From far away, the low rumble of thunder came moaning over the moor. Unable to sleep, I dressed, and standing at my cottage door, looked on the black solitude which surrounded me. There was no breeze below; but above, the clouds were sweeping majestically across the sky, with half a moon peeping at times between the rifts. The ripple of the Gaster Beck and the dull hooting of a distant owl were the only sounds which broke upon my ear. Taking the narrow sheep-path which ran by the stream, I strolled along it for some hundred yards, and had turned to retrace my steps, when the moon was finally buried beneath an ink-black cloud, and the darkness deepened so suddenly, that I could see neither the path at my feet, the stream upon my right, nor the rocks upon my left. I was standing groping about in the thick gloom, when there came a crash of thunder with a flash of lightning which lit up the whole vast fell, so that every bush and rock stood out clear and hard in the livid light. It was but for an instant, and yet that momentary view struck a thrill of fear and astonishment through me, for in my very path, not twenty yards before me, there stood a woman, the livid light beating upon her face and showing up every detail of her dress and features. There was no mistaking those dark eyes, that tall graceful figure. It was she—Eva Cameron, the woman whom I had thought I had for ever left. For an instant I stood petrified, marvelling whether this could indeed be she, or whether it was some figment conjured up by my excited brain. Then I ran swiftly forward in the direction where I had seen her, calling loudly upon her, but without reply. Again I called, and again no answer came back, save the melancholy wail of the owl. A second flash illuminated the landscape, and the moon burst out from behind its cloud. But I could not, though I climbed upon a knoll which overlooked the whole moor, see any sign of this strange midnight wanderer. For an hour or more I traversed the fell, and at last found myself back at my little cabin, still uncertain as to whether it had been a woman or a shadow upon which I had gazed.

For the three days which followed this midnight storm I bent myself doggedly to my work. From early morn till late at night I immured myself in my little study, with my whole thoughts buried in my books and my parchments. At last it seemed to me that I had reached that haven of rest, that oasis of study for which I had so often sighed. But alas for my hopes and my plannings! Within a week of my flight from Kirkby-Malhouse, a strange and most unforeseen series of events not only broke in upon the calm of my existence, but filled me with emotions so acute as to drive all other considerations from my mind.

CHAPTER III.—OF THE GRAY COTTAGE IN THE GLEN.

It was either on the fourth or the fifth day after I had taken possession of my cottage that I was astonished to hear footsteps upon the grass outside, quickly followed by a crack, as from a stick, upon the door. The explosion of an infernal machine would hardly have surprised or discomfited me more. I had hoped to have shaken off all intrusion for ever, yet here was somebody beating at my door with as little ceremony as if it had been a village alehouse. Hot with anger, I flung down my book, withdrew the bolt just as my visitor had raised his stick to renew his rough application for admittance. He was a tall powerful man, tawny-bearded and deep-chested, clad in a loose-fitting suit of tweed, cut for comfort rather than elegance. As he stood in the shimmering sunlight I took in every feature of his face. The large fleshy nose; the steady blue eyes, with their thick thatch of overhanging brows; the broad forehead, all knitted and lined with furrows, which were strangely at variance with his youthful bearing. In spite of his weather-stained felt hat and the coloured handkerchief slung round his broad muscular neck, I could see at a glance he was a man of breeding and education. I had been prepared for some wandering shepherd or uncouth tramp, but this apparition fairly disconcerted me.

'You look astonished,' said he, with a smile. 'Did you think, then, that you were the only man in the world with a taste for solitude? You see that there are other hermits in the wilderness besides yourself.'

'Do you mean to say that you live here?' I asked in no very conciliatory voice.

'Up yonder,' he answered, tossing his head backwards. 'I thought as we were neighbours, Mr Upperton, that I could do no less than look in and see if I could assist you in any way.'

'Thank you,' said I coldly, standing with my hand upon the latch of the door. 'I am a man of simple tastes, and you can do nothing for me. You have the advantage of me in knowing my name.'

He appeared to be chilled by my ungracious manner. 'I learned it from the masons who were at work here,' he said. 'As for me, I am a surgeon, the surgeon of Gaster Fell. That is the name I have gone by in these parts, and it serves as well as another.'

'Not much room for a practice here,' I observed.

'Not a soul except yourself for five miles on either side.'

'You appear to have had need of some assistance yourself,' I remarked, glancing at a broad white splash, as from the recent action of some powerful acid, upon his sunburnt cheek.

'That is nothing,' he answered curtly, turning his face half round to hide the mark. 'I must get back, for I have a companion who is waiting for me. If I can ever do anything for you, pray let me know. You have only to follow the beck upwards for a mile or so to find my place.—Have you a bolt on the inside of your door?'

'Yes,' I answered, rather startled at this sudden question.

'Keep it bolted, then,' he said. 'The fell is a strange place. You never know who may be about. It is as well to be on the safe side.—Goodbye.' He raised his hat, turned on his heel, and lounged away along the bank of the little stream.

I was still standing with my hand upon the latch, gazing after my unexpected visitor, when I became aware of yet another dweller in the wilderness. Some little distance along the path which the stranger was taking there lay a great gray boulder, and leaning against this was a small wizened man, who stood erect as the other approached, and advanced to meet him. The two talked for a minute or more, the taller man nodding his head frequently in my direction, as though describing what had passed between us. They then walked on together, and disappeared in a dip of the fell. Presently I saw them ascending once more some rising ground farther on. My acquaintance had thrown his arm round his elderly friend, either from affection, or from a desire to aid him up the steep incline. The square burly figure and its shrivelled meagre companion stood out against the sky-line, and turning their faces, they looked back at me. At the sight, I slammed the door, lest they should be encouraged to return. But when I peeped from the window some minutes afterwards, I perceived that they were gone.

For the remainder of the day I strove in vain to recover that indifference to the world and its ways which is essential to mental abstraction. Do what I would, my thoughts ran upon the solitary surgeon and his shrivelled companion. What did he mean by his question as to my bolt? and how came it that the last words of Eva Cameron were to the same sinister effect? Again and again I speculated as to what train of causes could have led two men so dissimilar in age and appearance to dwell together on the wild inhospitable fells. Were they, like myself, immersed in some engrossing study? or could it be that a companionship in crime had forced them from the haunts of men? Some cause there must be, and that a potent one, to induce the man of education to turn to such an existence. It was only now that I began to realise that the crowd of the city is infinitely less disturbing than the unit of the country.

All day I bent over the Egyptian papyrus upon which I was engaged; but neither the subtle reasonings of the ancient philosopher of Memphis, nor the mystic meaning which lay in his pages, could raise my mind from the things of earth. Evening was drawing in before I threw my work aside in despair. My heart was bitter against this man for his intrusion. Standing by the beck which purled past the door of my cabin, I cooled my heated brow, and thought the matter over. Clearly it was the small mystery hanging over these neighbours of mine which had caused my mind to run so persistently on them. That cleared up, they would no longer cause an obstacle to my studies. What was to hinder me, then, from walking in the direction of their dwelling, and observing for myself, without permitting them to suspect my presence, what manner of men they might be? Doubtless, their mode of life would be found to admit of some simple and prosaic explanation. In any case, the evening was fine, and a walk would be bracing for mind and body. Lighting my pipe, I set off over the moors in the direction which they had taken. The sun lay low and red in the west, flushing the heather with a deeper pink, and mottling the broad heaven with every hue, from the palest green at the zenith, to the richest crimson along the far horizon. It might have been the great palette upon which the world-painter had mixed his primeval colours. On either side, the giant peaks of Ingleborough and Pennigent looked down upon the gray melancholy country which stretches between them. As I advanced, the rude fells ranged themselves upon right and left, forming a well-defined valley, down the centre of which meandered the little brooklet. On either side, parallel lines of gray rock marked the level of some ancient glacier, the moraine of which had formed the broken ground about my dwelling. Ragged boulders, precipitous scarps, and twisted fantastic rocks, all bore witness to the terrible power of the old ice-field, and showed where its frosty fingers had ripped and rent the solid limestones.

About half way down this wild glen there stood a small clump of gnarled and stunted oak-trees. From behind these, a thin dark column of smoke rose into the still evening air. Clearly this marked the position of my neighbour's house. Trending away to the left I was able to gain the shelter of a line of rocks, and so reach a spot from which I could command a view of the building without exposing myself to any risk of being observed. It was a small slate-covered cottage, hardly larger than the boulders among which it lay. Like my own cabin, it showed signs of having been constructed for the use of some shepherd; but, unlike mine, no pains had been taken by the tenants to improve and enlarge it. Two little peeping windows, a cracked and weather-beaten door, and a discoloured barrel for catching the rain-water, were the only external objects from which I might draw deductions as to the dwellers within. Yet even in these there was food for thought; for as I drew nearer, still concealing myself behind the ridge, I saw that thick bars of iron covered the windows, while the rude door was all slashed and plated with the same metal. These strange precautions, together with the wild surroundings and unbroken solitude, gave an indescribably ill omen and fearsome character to the solitary building. Thrusting my pipe into my pocket, I crawled upon my hands and knees through the gorse and ferns until I was within a hundred yards of my neighbour's door. There, finding that I could not approach nearer without fear of detection, I crouched down, and set myself to watch.

I had hardly settled into my hiding-place when the door of the cot-

tage swung open, and the man who had introduced himself as the surgeon of Gaster Fell came out, bareheaded, with a spade in his hands.
In front of the door there was a small cultivated patch containing potatoes, peas, and other forms of green stuff, and here he proceeded
to busy himself, trimming, weeding, and arranging, singing the while
in a powerful though not very musical voice. He was all engrossed in
his work, with his back to the cottage, when there emerged from the
half-open door the same shadowy attenuated creature whom I had
seen in the morning. I could perceive now that he was a man of sixty,
wrinkled, bent, and feeble, with sparse grizzled hair, and long colourless face. With a cringing sidelong gait, he shuffled towards his companion, who was unconscious of his approach until he was close upon
him. His light footfall or his breathing may have finally given notice of
his proximity, for the worker sprang round and faced him. Each made
a quick step towards the other, as though in greeting, and then—even
now I feel the horror of the instant—the tall man rushed upon and
knocked his companion to the earth, then whipping up his body, ran
with great speed over the intervening ground and disappeared with
his burden into the house.

Case-hardened as I was by my varied life, the suddenness and
violence of the thing made me shudder. The man's age, his feeble
frame, his humble and deprecating manner, all cried shame against
the deed. So hot was my anger, that I was on the point of striding up
to the cabin, unarmed as I was, when the sound of voices from within
showed me that the victim had recovered. The sun had sunk beneath
the horizon, and all was gray, save a red feather in the cap of Pennigent. Secure in the failing light, I approached near and strained my ears
to catch what was passing. I could hear the high querulous voice of
the elder man, and the deep rough monotone of his assailant, mixed
with a strange metallic jangling and clanking. Presently, the surgeon
came out, locking the door behind him, and stamped up and down in
the twilight, pulling at his hair and brandishing his arms, like a man
demented. Then he set off, walking rapidly up the valley, and I soon
lost sight of him among the rocks.

When the sound of his feet had died away in the distance, I drew
nearer to the cottage. The prisoner within was still pouring forth a
stream of words, and moaning from time to time like a man in pain.
These words resolved themselves, as I approached, into prayers—

shrill voluble prayers, pattered forth with the intense earnestness of
one who sees impending an imminent danger. There was to me something inexpressibly awesome in this gush of solemn entreaty from the
lonely sufferer, meant for no human ear, and jarring upon the silence
of the night. I was still pondering whether I should mix myself in the
affair or not, when I heard in the distance the sound of the surgeon's
returning footfall. At that I drew myself up quickly by the iron bars
and glanced in through the diamond-paned window. The interior of
the cottage was lit up by a lurid glow, coming from what I discovered
to be a chemical furnace. By its rich light I could distinguish a great litter of retorts, test tubes, and condensers, which sparkled over the table and threw strange grotesque shadows on the wall. On the farther
side of the room was a wooden framework resembling a large hen-
coop, and in this, still absorbed in prayer, knelt the man whose voice I
heard. The red glow beating upon his upturned face made it stand out
from the shadow like a painting from Rembrandt, showing up every
wrinkle upon the parchment-like skin. I had but time for a fleeting
glance; then dropping from the window, I made off through the rocks
and the heather, nor slackened my speed until I found myself back
in my cabin once more. There I threw myself upon my couch, more
disturbed and shaken than I had ever thought to feel again.

Long into the watches of the night I tossed and tumbled on my
uneasy pillow. A strange theory had framed itself within me, suggested by the elaborate scientific apparatus which I had seen. Could it
be that this surgeon had some profound and unholy experiments on
hand, which necessitated the taking, or at least the tampering with the
life of his companion? Such a supposition would account for the loneliness of his life; but how could I reconcile it with the close friendship
which had appeared to exist between the pair no longer ago than that
very morning? Was it grief or madness which had made the man tear
his hair and wring his hands when he emerged from the cabin? And
sweet Eva Cameron, was she also a partner to this sombre business?
Was it to my grim neighbours that she made her strange nocturnal
journeys? and if so, what bond could there be to unite so strangely
assorted a trio? Try as I might, I could come to no satisfactory conclusion upon these points. When at last I dropped into a troubled slumber, it was only to see once more in my dreams the strange episodes
of the evening, and to wake at dawn unrefreshed and weary.

Such doubts as I might have had as to whether I had indeed seen my former fellow-lodger upon the night of the thunderstorm, were finally resolved that morning. Strolling along down the path which led to the fell, I saw in one spot where the ground was soft the impressions of a foot, the small dainty foot of a well-booted woman. That tiny heel and high instep could have belonged to none other than my companion of Kirkby-Malhouse. I followed her trail for some distance till it lost itself among hard and stony ground; but it still pointed, as far as I could discern it, to the lonely and ill-omened cottage. What power could there be to draw this tender girl, through wind and rain and darkness, across the fearsome moors to that strange rendezvous?

But why should I let my mind run upon such things? Had I not prided myself that I lived a life of my own, beyond the sphere of my fellow-mortals? Were all my plans and my resolutions to be shaken because the ways of life of my neighbours were strange to me? It was unworthy, it was puerile. By constant and unremitting effort, I set myself to cast out these distracting influences, and to return to my former calm. It was no easy task. But after some days, during which I never stirred from my cottage, I had almost succeeded in regaining my peace of mind, when a fresh incident whirled my thoughts back into their old channel.

I have said that a little beck flowed down the valley and past my very door. A week or so after the doings which I have described, I was seated by my window, when I perceived something white drifting slowly down the stream. My first thought was that it was a drowning sheep; but picking up my stick, I strolled to the bank and hooked it ashore. On examination it proved to be a large sheet, torn and tattered, with the initials J.C. in the corner. What gave it its sinister significance, however, was that from hem to hem it was all dabbled and discoloured with blood. In parts where the water had soaked it this was but a discoloration; while in others the stains showed they were of recent origin. I shuddered as I gazed at it. It could but have come from the lonely cottage in the glen. What dark and violent deed had left this gruesome trace behind it? I had flattered myself that the human family was as nothing to me, and yet my whole being was absorbed now in curiosity and resentment. How could I remain neutral when such things were doing within a mile of me? I felt that the old Adam was too strong in me, and that I *must* solve this mystery. Shutting the door of my cabin behind me, I set off up the glen in the direction of the surgeon's cabin. I had not gone far before I perceived the very man himself. He was walking rapidly along the hillside, beating the furze bushes with a cudgel and bellowing like a madman. Indeed at the sight of him, the doubts as to his sanity which had risen in my mind were strengthened and confirmed. As he approached, I noticed that his left arm was suspended in a sling. On perceiving me, he stood irresolute, as though uncertain whether to come over to me or not. I had no desire for an interview with him, however; so I hurried past him, on which he continued on his way, still shouting and striking about with his club. When he had disappeared over the fells, I made my way down to his cottage, determined to find some clue to what had occurred. I was surprised, on reaching it, to find the iron-plated door flung wide open. The ground immediately outside it was marked with the signs of a struggle. The chemical apparatus within and the furniture were all dashed about and shattered. Most suggestive of all, the sinister wooden cage was stained with blood-marks, and its unfortunate occupant had disappeared. My heart was heavy for the little man, for I was assured I should never see him in this world more. There were many gray cairns of stones scattered over the valley. I ran my eye over them, and wondered which of them concealed the traces of this last act which ended the long tragedy.

There was nothing in the cabin to throw any light upon the identity of my neighbours. The room was stuffed with chemicals and delicate philosophical instruments. In one corner, a small bookcase contained a choice selection of works of science. In another was a pile of geological specimens collected from limestone. My eye ran rapidly over these details; but I had no time to make a more thorough examination, for I feared lest the surgeon should return and find me there. Leaving the cottage, I hastened homewards with a weight at my heart. A nameless shadow hung over the lonely gorge—the heavy shadow of unexpiated crime, making the grim fells look grimmer, and the wild moors more dreary and forbidding. My mind wavered whether I should send to Lancaster to acquaint the police of what I had seen. My thoughts recoiled at the prospect of becoming a witness in a cause célèbre, and having an over-busy counsel or an officious press peeping and prying into my own modes of life. Was it for this I had stolen away from my fellow-mortals and settled in these lonely wilds? The thought of publicity was repugnant to me. It was best, perhaps, to wait and watch without taking any decided step until I had come to a more definite conclusion as to what I had heard.

I caught no glimpse of the surgeon upon my homeward journey; but when I reached my cottage, I was astonished and indignant to find that somebody had entered it in my absence. Boxes had been pulled out from under the bed, the curtains had been disarranged, the chairs drawn out from the wall. Even my study had not been safe from this rough intruder, for the prints of a heavy boot were plainly visible on the ebony black carpet. I am not a patient man at the best of times; but this invasion and systematic examination of my household effects stirred up every drop of gall in my composition. Swearing under my breath, I took my old cavalry sabre down from its nail and passed my finger along the edge. There was a great notch in the centre where it had jarred up against the collarbone of a Bavarian artillery-man the day we beat Van Der Tann back from Orleans. It was still sharp enough, however, to be serviceable. I placed it at the head of my bed, within reach of my arm, ready to give a keen greeting to the next uninvited visitor who might arrive.

CHAPTER IV.—OF THE MAN WHO CAME IN THE NIGHT.

THE night set in gusty and tempestuous, and the moon was all girt with ragged clouds. The wind blew in melancholy gusts, sobbing and sighing over the moor, and setting all the gorse-bushes agroaning. From time to time a little sputter of rain pattered up against the window-pane. I sat until near midnight glancing over the fragment on immortality by Iamblichus, the Alexandrian platonist, of whom the Emperor Julian said that he was posterior to Plato in time, but not in genius. At last, shutting up my book, I opened my door and took a last look at the dreary fell and still more dreary sky. As I protruded my head, a swoop of wind caught me, and sent the red ashes of my pipe sparkling and dancing through the darkness. At the same moment the moon shone brilliantly out from between two clouds, and I saw, sitting on the hillside, not two hundred yards from my door, the man who called himself the surgeon of Gaster Fell. He was squatted among the heather, his elbows upon his knees, and his chin resting upon his hands, as motionless as a stone, with his gaze fixed steadily upon the door of my dwelling.

At the sight of this ill-omened sentinel, a chill of horror and of fear shot through me, for his gloomy and mysterious associations had cast a glamour round the man, and the hour and place were in keeping with his sinister presence. In a moment, however, a manly glow of resentment and self-confidence drove this petty emotion from my mind, and I strode fearlessly in his direction. He rose as I approached, and faced me, with the moon shining on his grave bearded face and glittering on his eyeballs. 'What is the meaning of this?' I cried as I came up on him. 'What right have you to play the spy on me?'

I could see the flush of anger rise on his face. 'Your stay in the country has made you forget your manners,' he said. 'The moor is free to all.'

'You will say next that my house is free to all,' I said hotly. 'You have had the impertinence to ransack it in my absence this afternoon.'

He started, and his features showed the most intense excitement. 'I swear to you that I had no hand in it,' he cried. 'I have never set foot in your house in my life. Oh sir, sir, if you will but believe me, there is a danger hanging over you, and you would do well to be careful.'

'I have had enough of you,' I said. 'I saw the coward blow you struck when you thought no human eye rested upon you. I have been to your cottage, too, and know all that it has to tell. If there is a law in England, you shall hang for what you have done. As to me, I am an old soldier, sir, and I am armed. I shall not fasten my door. But if you or any other villain attempt to cross my threshold, it shall be at your own risk.' With these words I swung round upon my heel and strode into my cabin. When I looked back at him from the door he was still looking at me, a gloomy figure among the heather, with his head sunk low upon his breast. I slept fitfully all that night; but I heard no more of this strange sentinel without, nor was he to be seen when I looked out in the morning.

For two days the wind freshened and increased with constant squalls of rain, until on the third night the most furious storm was raging which I can ever recollect in England. The thunder roared and rattled overhead, while the incessant lightning flashes illuminated the heavens. The wind blew intermittently, now sobbing away into a calm, and then, of a sudden, beating and howling at my window-pane until the glasses rattled in their frames. The air was charged with electricity, and its peculiar influence, combined with the strange epi-sodes with which I had been recently connected, made me morbidly wakeful and acutely sensitive. I felt that it was useless to go to bed, nor could I concentrate my mind sufficiently to read a book. I turned my lamp half-down to moderate the glare, and leaning back in my chair, I gave myself up to reverie. I must have lost all perception of time, for I have no recollection how long I sat there on the borderland betwixt thought and slumber. At last, about three or, possibly, four o'clock, I came to myself with a start—not only came to myself but with every sense and nerve upon the strain. Looking round my chamber in this dim light, I could not see anything to justify my sudden trepidation. The homely room, the rain-blurred window, and the rude wooden door were all as they had been. I had begun to persuade myself that some half-formed dream had sent that vague thrill through my nerves, when in a moment I became conscious of what it was. It was a sound, the sound of a human step outside my solitary cottage.

Amid the thunder and the rain and the wind, I could hear it—a dull stealthy footfall, now on the grass, now on the stones—occasion-ally stopping entirely, then resumed, and ever drawing nearer. I sat breathlessly, listening to the eerie sound. It had stopped now at my very door, and was replaced by a panting and gasping, as of one who has travelled fast and far. Only the thickness of the door separated me from this hard-breathing, light-treading night-walker. I am no coward; but the wildness of the night, with the vague warning which I had had, and the proximity of this strange visitor, so unnerved me that my mouth was too dry for speech. I stretched out my hand, however, and grasped my sabre, with my eyes still bent upon the door. I prayed in my heart that the thing, whatever it might be, would but knock or threaten or hail me, or give any clue as to its character. Any known danger was better than this awful silence, broken only by the rhyth-mic panting.

By the flickering light of the expiring lamp I could see that the latch of my door was twitching as though a gentle pressure were ex-erted on it from without. Slowly, slowly, it rose, until it was free of the catch, and then there was a pause of a quarter minute or more, while I still sat silent, with dilated eyes and drawn sabre. Then, very slowly, the door began to revolve upon its hinges, and the keen air of the night came whistling through the slit. Very cautiously it was pushed open, so that never a sound came from the rusty hinges. As the aperture enlarged, I became aware of a dark shadowy figure upon my threshold, and of a pale face that looked in at me. The features were human, but the eyes were not. They seemed to burn through the darkness with a greenish brilliancy of their own; and in their baleful shifty glare I was conscious of the very spirit of murder. Springing from my chair, I had raised my naked sword, when, with a wild shouting, a second figure dashed up to my door. At its approach my shadowy visitant uttered a shrill cry, and fled away across the fells, yelping like a beaten hound. The two creatures were swallowed up in the tempest from which they had emerged as if they were the very genii of the beating wind and the howling rain.

Tingling with my recent fear, I stood at my door, peering through the night with the discordant cry of the fugitives still ringing in my ears. At that moment a vivid flash of lightning illuminated the whole landscape and made it as clear as day. By its light, I saw, far away, upon the hillside, two dark figures pursuing each other with extreme rapidity across the fells. Even at that distance the contrast between them forbade all doubt as to their identity. The first was the small elderly man whom I had supposed to be dead; the second was my neighbour the surgeon. For an instant they stood out clear and hard in the unearthly light; in the next, the darkness had closed over them, and they were gone. As I turned to re-enter my chamber, my foot rattled against something on my threshold. Stooping, I found it was a straight knife, fashioned entirely of lead, and so soft and brittle that it was a strange choice for a weapon. To render it the more harmless, the top had been cut square off. The edge, however, had been assiduously sharpened against a stone, as was evident from the markings upon it, so that it was still a dangerous implement in the grasp of a determined man. It had evidently dropped from the fellow's hand at the moment when the sudden coming of the surgeon had driven him to flight. There could no longer be doubt as to the object of his visit.

And what was the meaning of it all? you ask. Many a drama which I have come across in my wandering life, some as strange and as striking as this one, has lacked the ultimate explanation which you demand. Fate is a grand weaver of tales; but she ends them, as a rule, in

defiance of all artistic laws, and with an unbecoming want of regard
for literary propriety. As it happens, however, I have a letter before me
as I write which I may add without comment, and which will clear all
that may remain dark.

KIRKBY LUNATIC ASYLUM,
Sept. 4, 1885

SIR—I am deeply conscious that some apology and explanation is
due to you for the very startling and, in your eyes, mysterious events
which have recently occurred, and which have so seriously interfered
with the retired existence which you desire to lead. I should have
called upon you on the morning after the recapture of my father; but
my knowledge of your dislike to visitors, and also of—you will excuse
my saying it—your very violent temper, led me to think it was better
to communicate with you by letter. On the occasion of our last interview I should have told you what I tell you now; but your allusions
to some crime of which you considered me guilty, and your abrupt
departure, prevented me from saying much that was on my lips.

My poor father was a hard-working general practitioner in Birmingham, where his name is still remembered and respected. About
ten years ago he began to show signs of mental aberration, which
we were inclined to put down to overwork and the effect of a sun-
stroke. Feeling my own incompetence to pronounce upon a case of
such importance, I at once sought the highest advice in Birmingham
and London. Among others we consulted the eminent alienist, Mr
Fraser Brown, who pronounced my father's case to be intermittent in
its nature, but dangerous during the paroxysms. 'It may take a homicidal, or it may take a religious turn,' he said; 'or it may prove to be a
mixture of both. For months he may be as well as you or me, and then
in a moment he may break out. You will incur a great responsibility if
you leave him without supervision.'

The result showed the justice of the specialist's diagnosis. My
poor father's disease rapidly assumed both a religious and homicidal
turn, the attacks coming on without warning after months of sanity.
It would weary you were I to describe the terrible experiences which
his family have undergone. Suffice it that, by the blessing of God, we
have succeeded in keeping his poor crazed fingers clear of blood. My

sister Eva I sent to Brussels, and I devoted myself entirely to his case. He has an intense dread of madhouses; and in his sane intervals would beg and pray so piteously not to be condemned to one, that I could never find the heart to resist him. At last, however, his attacks became so acute and dangerous, that I determined, for the sake of those about me, to remove him from the town to the loneliest neighbourhood that I could find. This proved to be Gaster Fell; and there, he and I set up house together.

I had a sufficient competence to keep me, and being devoted to chemistry, I was able to pass the time with a fair degree of comfort and profit. He, poor fellow, was as submissive as a child, when in his right mind; and a better, kinder companion no man could wish for. We constructed together a wooden compartment, into which he could retire when the fit was upon him; and I had arranged the window and door so that I could confine him to the house if I thought an attack was impending. Looking back, I can safely say that no possible precaution was neglected; even the necessary table utensils were leaden and pointless, to prevent his doing mischief with them in his frenzy.

For months after our change of quarters he appeared to improve. Whether it was the bracing air, or the absence of any incentive to violence, he never showed during that time any signs of his terrible disorder. Your arrival first upset his mental equilibrium. The very sight of you in the distance awoke all those morbid impulses which had been sleeping. That very evening he approached me stealthily with a stone in his hand, and would have slain me, had I not, as the least of two evils, struck him to the ground and thrust him into his cage before he had time to regain his senses. This sudden relapse naturally plunged me into the deepest sorrow. For two days I did all that lay in my power to soothe him. On the third he appeared to be calmer; but alas, it was but the cunning of the madman. He had contrived to loosen two bars of his cage; and when thrown off my guard by his apparent improvement—I was engrossed in my chemistry—he suddenly sprang out at me knife in hand. In the scuffle, he cut me across the forearm, and escaped from the hut before I recovered myself, nor could I find out which direction he had taken. My wound was a trifle, and for several days I wandered over the fells, beating through every clump of bushes in my fruitless search. I was convinced that he would make an attempt on your life, a conviction that was strengthened when I heard that some one in your absence had entered your cottage. I therefore kept a watch over you at night. A dead sheep which I found upon the moor terribly mangled showed me that he was not without food, and that the homicidal impulse was still strong in him. At last, as I had expected, he made his attempt upon you, which, but for my intervention, would have ended in the death of one or other of you. He ran, and struggled like a wild animal; but I was as desperate as he, and succeeded in bringing him down and conveying him to the cottage. Convinced by this failure that all hope of permanent improvement is gone, I brought him next morning to this establishment, and he is now, I am glad to say, returning to his senses.—Allow me once more, sir, to express my sorrow that you should have been subjected to this ordeal, and believe me to be faithfully yours,

JOHN LIGHT CAMERON.

P.S.—My sister Eva bids me send you her kind regards. She has told me how you were thrown together at Kirkby-Malhouse, and also that you met one night upon the fells. You will understand from what I have already told you that when my dear sister came back from Brussels I did not dare to bring her home, but preferred that she should lodge in safety in the village. Even then I did not venture to bring her into the presence of her father, and it was only at night, when he was asleep, that we could plan a meeting.

And this was the story of this strange group, whose path through life had crossed my own. From that last terrible night I have neither seen nor heard of any of them, save for this one letter which I have transcribed. Still I dwell on Gaster Fell, and still my mind is buried in the secrets of the past. But when I wander forth upon the moor, and when I see the little gray deserted cottage among the rocks, my mind is still turned to the strange drama, and to the singular couple who broke in upon my solitude.

NOTES TO 'THE SURGEON OF GASTER FELL'

First published in *Chamber's Journal*, 6, 13, 20 and 27 December 1890.

1. The story is of some autobiographical interest in that Conan Doyle's own father, after years of increasing alcoholism, was certified as an epileptic and committed to a mental institution in 1882. He remained confined in various Scottish institutions until his death in October 1893. The story as published in *Chamber's Journal* included the following sentence 'My poor father's disease rapidly assumed both a religious and a homicidal run, the attacks coming on without warning after months of sanity. It would weary you to describe the terrible experiences which his family have undergone'; but this passage was omitted when the story was collected in 1925, and in all subsequent re-printings until a special edition published in 2000. Although the 'madman' in the story is shown as having ferocious homicidal tendencies, there is no evidence that Charles himself was ever violent or a danger to anybody.[1]

---

[1] See Daniel Stashower, *Teller of Tales*, pp. 24-25; Martin Booth, *The Doctor and the Detective*, pp. 91 and 185; *The Surgeon of Gaster Fell*, edited with an afterword by Daniel Stashower (Norfolk, Va.: Crippen and Landru, 2000).

THE RETIREMENT OF SIGNOR LAMBERT

Sir William Sparter was a man who had raised himself in the course of a quarter of a century from earning four-and-twenty shillings a week as a fitter in Portsmouth Dockyard to being the owner of a yard and a fleet of his own. The little house in Lake Road, Landport, where he, an obscure mechanic, had first conceived the idea of the boilers which are associated with his name, is still pointed out to the curious. But now, at the age of fifty, he owned a mansion in Leinster Gardens, a country house at Taplow, and a shooting in Argyleshire, with the best stable, the choicest cellars, and the prettiest wife in town.

As untiring and inflexible as one of his own engines, his life had been directed to the one purpose of attaining the very best which the world had to give. Square-headed and round-shouldered, with massive, clean-shaven face and slow deep-set eyes, he was the very embodiment of persistency and strength. Never once from the beginning of his career had public failure of any sort tarnished its brilliancy.

And yet he had failed in one thing, and that the most important of all. He had never succeeded in gaining the affection of his wife. She was the daughter of a surgeon and the belle of a northern town when he married her. Even then he was rich and powerful, which made her overlook the twenty years which divided them. But he had come on a long way since then. His great Brazilian contract, his conversion into a company, his baronetcy—all these had been since his marriage. Only in the one thing he had never progressed. He could frighten his wife, he could dominate her, he could make her admire his strength and respect his consistency, he could mould her to his will in every other direction, but, do what he would, he could not make her love him.

But it was not for want of trying. With the unrelaxing patience which made him great in business, he had striven, year in and year out, to win her affection. But the very qualities which had helped him in his public life made him unendurable in private. He was tactless, unsympathetic, overbearing, almost brutal sometimes, and utterly unable to think out those small attentions in word and deed which women value far more than the larger material benefits. The hundred pound cheque tossed across a breakfast table is a much smaller thing to a woman than the five-shilling charm which represents some thought and some trouble upon the part of the giver.

Sparter failed to understand this. With his mind full of the affairs of his firm, he had little time for the delicacies of life, and he endeavoured to atone by periodical munificence. At the end of five years he found that he had lost rather than gained in the lady's affections. Then at this unwonted sense of failure the evil side of the man's nature began to stir, and he became dangerous. But he was more dangerous still when a letter of his wife came, through the treachery of a servant, into his hands, and he realised that if she was cold to him she had passion enough for another. His firm, his ironclads, his patents, everything was dropped, and he turned his huge energies to the undoing of the man who had wronged him.

He had been cold and silent during dinner that evening, and she had wondered vaguely what had occurred to change him. He had said nothing while they sat together over their coffee in the drawing-room. Once or twice she had glanced at him in surprise, and had found those deep-set prey eyes fixed upon her with an expression which was new to her. Her mind had been full of someone else, but gradually her husband's silence and the inscrutable expression of his face forced themselves upon her attention.

"You don't seem yourself, to-night, William. What is the matter?" she asked. "I hope there has been nothing to trouble you."

He was still silent, and leant back in his arm-chair watching her beautiful face, which had turned pale with the sense of some impending catastrophe.

"Can I do anything for you, William?"

"Yes, you can write a letter."

"What is the letter?"

"I will tell you presently."

The last murmur died away in the house, and they heard the discreet step of Peterson, the butler, and the snick of the lock as he made all secure for the night. Sir William Sparter sat listening for a little. Then he rose.

"Come into my study," said he. The room was dark, but he switched on the green-shaded electric lamp which stood upon the writing-table.

"Sit here at the table," said he. He closed the door and seated himself beside her. "I only wanted to tell you, Jacky, that I know all about Lambert and the Warburton Street studio."

She gasped and shivered, flinching away from him with her hands out as if she feared a blow.

"Yes, I know everything," said he, and his quiet tone carried such conviction with it that she could not question what he said. She made no reply, but sat with her eyes fixed upon his grave, impassive face. A clock ticked loudly upon the mantelpiece, but everything else was silent in the house. She had never noticed that ticking before, but now it was like the hammering of a nail into her head. He rose and put a sheet of paper before her. Then he drew one from his own pocket and flattened it out upon the corner of the table.

"I have a rough draft here of the letter which I wish you to copy," said he. "I will read it to you if you like. 'My own dearest Cecil,—I will be at No. 29 at half-past six, and I particularly wish you to come before you go down to the Opera. Don't fail me, for I have the very strongest reasons for wishing to see you. Ever yours, Jacqueline.' Take up a pen, and copy that letter."

"William, you are plotting some revenge. Oh, Willie, if I have wronged you, I am so sorry——"

"Copy that letter!"

"But what is it that you wish to do? Why should you desire him to come at that hour?"

"Copy that letter!"

"How can you be so harsh to me, William. You know very well——"

"Copy that letter!"

"I begin to hate you, William, I believe that it is a fiend, not a man, that I have married."

"Copy that letter!"

Gradually the inflexible will and the unfaltering purpose began to prevail over the creature of nerves and moods. Reluctantly, mutinously, she took the pen in her hand.

"You wouldn't harm him, William!"

"Copy the letter!"

"Will you promise to forgive me, if I do?"

"Copy it!"

She looked at him with the intention of defying him, but those masterful, grey eyes dominated her. She was like a half-hypnotised creature, resentful, and yet obedient.

"There, will that satisfy you?" He took the note from her and placed it in an envelope.

"Now address it to him!"

She wrote "Cecil Lambert, Esq., 133B, Half Moon Street, W.," in a straggling agitated hand. Her husband very deliberately blotted it and placed it carefully in his pocket-book.

"I hope that you are satisfied now," said she with weak petulance.

"Quite," said he gravely. "You can go to your room. Mrs. McKay has my orders to sleep with you, and to see that you write no letters."

"Mrs. McKay! Do you expose me to the humiliation of being watched by my own servants!"

"Go to your room."

"If you imagine that I am going to be under the orders of the housekeeper——"

"Go to your room."

"Oh, William, who would have thought in the old days that you could ever have treated me like this. If my mother had ever dreamed——"

He took her by the arm, and led her to the door.

"Go to your room!" said he, and she passed out into the darkened hall. He closed the door and returned to the writing-table. Out of a drawer he took two things which he had purchased that day, the one a paper and the other a book. The former was a recent number of the "Musical Record," and it contained a biography and picture of the famous Signor Lambert, whose wonderful tenor voice had been the delight of the public and the despair of his rivals. The picture was that of a good-natured, self-satisfied creature, young and handsome, with a full eye, a curling moustache, and a bull neck. The biography explained that he was only in his twenty-seventh year, that his career had been one continued triumph, that he was devoted to his art, and that his voice was worth to him, at a very moderate computation, some twenty thousand pounds a year. All this Sir William Sparter read very carefully, with his great brows drawn down, and a furrow like a gash between them, as his way was when his attention was concentrated. Then he folded the paper up again, and he opened the book.

It was a curious work for such a man to select for his reading—a technical treatise upon the organs of speech and voice-production. There were numerous coloured illustrations, to which he paid particular attention. Most of them were of the internal anatomy of the larynx, with the silvery vocal cords shining from under the pink aretenoid cartilages. Far into the night Sir William Sparter, with those great virile eyebrows still bunched together, pored over these irrelevant pictures, and read and re-read the text in which they were explained.

★ ★ ★ ★ ★

Dr. Manifold Ormonde, the famous throat specialist, of Cavendish Square, was surprised next morning when his butler brought the card of Sir William Sparter into his consulting room. He had met him at dinner at the table of Lord Marvin a few nights before, and it had struck him at the time that he had seldom seen a man who looked such a type of rude, physical health. So he thought again, as the square, thick-set figure of the shipbuilder was ushered in to him.

"Glad to meet you again, Sir William," said the specialist. "I hope there is nothing wrong with your health."

"Nothing, thank you."

"Or with Lady Sparter's?"

"She is quite well."

He sat down in the chair which the Doctor had indicated, and he ran his eyes slowly and deliberately round the room. Dr. Ormonde watched him with some curiosity, for he had the air of a man who looks for something which he had expected to see.

"No, I didn't come about my health," said he at last. "I came for information."

"Whatever I can give you is entirely at your disposal."

"I have been studying the throat a little of late. I read McIntyre's book about it. I suppose that is all right."

"An elementary treatise, but accurate as far as it goes."

"I had an idea that you would be likely to have a model or something of the kind."

For answer the Doctor unclasped the lid of a yellow, shining box upon his consulting-room table, and turned it back upon the hinge. Within was a very complete model of the human vocal organs.

"You are right, you see," said he.

Sir William Sparter stood up, and bent over the model.

"It's a neat little bit of work," said he, looking at it with the critical eyes of an engineer. "This is the glottis, is it not? And here is the epiglottis."

"Precisely. And here are the cords."

"What would happen if you cut them.'"

"Cut what?'"

"These things—the vocal cords."

"But you could not cut them. They are out of the reach of all accident."

"But if such a thing did happen?"

"There is no such case upon record, but, of course, the person would become dumb—for the time, at any rate."

"You have a large practice among singers, have you not?"

"The largest in London."

"I suppose you agree with what this man McIntyre says, that a fine voice depends partly upon the cords."

"The volume of sound would depend upon the lung capacity, but the clearness of the note would correspond with the complete control which the singer exercised over the cords."

"Any roughness or notching of the cords would ruin the voice?"

"For singing purposes, undoubtedly—but your researches seem to be taking a very curious direction."

"Yes," said Sir William, as he picked up his hat, and laid a fee upon the corner of the table. "They *are* a little out of the common, are they not?"

* * * * *

Warburton Street is one of the network of thoroughfares which connect Chelsea with Kensington, and it is chiefly remarkable for a number of studios, in which it is rumoured that other arts besides that of painting are occasionally cultivated. The possession of a comfortable room, easily accessible and at a moderate rent, may be useful to other people besides artists amid the publicity of London. At any rate,

Signor Cecil Lambert, the famous tenor, owned such an apartment, and his neat little dark green brougham might have been seen several times a week waiting at the head of the long passage which led down to the chambers in question.

When Sir William Sparter, muffled in his overcoat, and carrying a small black leather bag in his hand, turned the corner he saw the lamps of the carriage against the kerb, and knew that the man whom he had come to see was already at the place of assignation. He passed the empty brougham, and walked up the tile-paved passage with the yellow gas-lamp shining at the far end of it.

The door was open, and led into a large empty hall, laid down with cocoa-nut matting and stained with many footmarks. The place was a rabbit warren by daylight, but now, when the working hours were over, it was deserted. A housekeeper in the basement was the only permanent resident. Sir William paused, but everything was silent and everything was dark, save for one door which was outlined in thin yellow slashes. He pushed it open and entered. Then he locked it upon the inside and put the key in his pocket.

It was a large room, scantily furnished, and lit by a single oil lamp upon a centre table. A gaunt easel kept up appearances in a corner, and three studies of antique figures hung upon unpapered walls. For the rest a couple of comfortable chairs, a cupboard, and a settee made up the whole of the furniture. There was no carpet, but the windows were discreetly draped. On one of the chairs at the further side of the table a man had been sitting, who had sprung to his feet with an exclamation of joy, which had changed into one of surprise, and culminated in an oath.

"What the devil do you mean by locking that door? Unlock it again, sir, this instant!"

Sir William did not even answer him. He took off his overcoat and laid it over the back of a chair. Then he advanced to the table, opened his bag, and began to take out all sorts of things—a green bottle, a dentist's gag, an inhaler, a pair of forceps, a curved bistoury, and a curious pair of scissors. Signor Lambert stood staring at him in a paralysis of rage and astonishment.

"You infernal scoundrel; who are you, and what do you want?"

Sir William had emptied his bag, and now for the first time he turned his eyes upon the singer. He was a taller man than himself, but far slighter and weaker. The engineer, though short, was exceedingly powerful, with muscles which had been toughened by hard, physical work. His broad shoulders, arching chest, and great gnarled hands gave him the outline of a gorilla. Lambert shrunk away from him, frightened by his sinister figure and by his cold, inexorable eyes.

"Have you come to rob me?" he gasped.

"I have come to speak to you. My name is Sparter."

Lambert tried to retain his grasp upon the self-possession which was rapidly slipping away from him.

"Sparter!" said he, with an attempt at jauntiness. "Sir William Sparter, I presume? I have had the pleasure of meeting Lady Sparter, and I have heard her mention you. May I ask the object of this visit?" He buttoned up his coat with twitching fingers, and tried to look fierce over his high collar.

"I've come," said Sparter, jerking some fluid from the green bottle into the inhaler, "to treat your voice."

"To treat my voice?"

"Precisely."

"You are a madman! What do you mean?"

"Kindly lie back upon the settee."

"You are raving! I see it all. You wish to bully me. You have some motive in this. You imagine that there are relations between Lady Sparter and me. I do assure you that your wife——"

"My wife has nothing to do with the matter either now or hereafter. Her name does not appear at all. My motives are musical—purely musical, you understand. I don't like your voice. It wants treatment. Lie back upon the settee!"

"Sir William, I give you my word of honour——"

"Lie back!"

"You're choking me! It's chloroform! Help, help, help! You brute! Let me go! Let me go, I say! Oh, please! Lemme—Lemme—Lem—!" His head had fallen back, and he muttered into the inhaler. Sir William pulled up the table which held the lamp and the instruments.

★ ★ ★ ★ ★

It was some minutes after the gentleman with the overcoat and the bag had emerged that the coachman outside heard a voice shouting, and shouting very hoarsely and angrily, within the building. Presently came the sounds of unsteady steps, and his master, crimson with rage, stumbled out into the yellow circle thrown by the carriage lamps.

"You, Holden!" he cried, "you leave my service to-night. Did you not hear me calling? Why did you not come?"

The man looked at him in bewilderment, and shuddered at the colour of his shirt-front.

"Yes, sir, I heard someone calling," he answered, "but it wasn't you, sir. *It was a voice that I had never heard before.*"

* * * * *

"Considerable disappointment was caused at the Opera last week," said one of the best informed of our musical critics, "by the fact that Signor Cecil Lambert was unable to appear in the various *rôles* which had been announced. On Tuesday night it was only at the very last instant that the management learned of the grave indisposition which had overtaken him, and had it not been for the presence of Jean Caravatti, who had understudied the part, the piece must have been abandoned. Since then we regret to hear that Signor Lambert's seizure was even more severe than was originally thought, and that it consists of an acute form of laryngitis, spreading to the vocal cords, and involving changes which may permanently affect the quality of his voice. All lovers of music will hope that these reports may prove to be pessimistic, and that we may soon be charmed once more by the finest tenor which we have heard for many a year upon the London operatic stage."

NOTES TO 'THE RETIREMENT OF SIGNOR LAMBERT'

First published in *Pearson's Magazine*, Vol. 6, 1898.

1. See the discussion in the notes to 'The Case of Lady Sannox'. The cutting of the vocal cords is a transparent metaphor for castration. The story is highly improbable in that a real operation of this kind would have been quite dangerous even when conducted by a team of surgeons in a hospital. The idea that an amateur could cut a person's vocal cords in such a way that the victim not only does not bleed to death or suffer gross injuries to his throat, but even retains his voice, however croaky, is implausible.

Nonfiction Medical Writings

EDITOR'S NOTE

In these nonfiction writings we can see Conan Doyle attempting to fulfil the program he had outlined in the letter to his mother in 1879—write for the *Lancet*, establish a reputation, go for a hospital consultancy. But we can also see that program being slowly abandoned as his mind turned from medicine to storytelling; and although nothing he contributed to the medical press was of any clinical significance, the letters make an interesting contrast with, and in some ways complement, his stories. Conan Doyle managed only a few contributions to medical journals—on the effects of gelseminum (the dried root of yellow jasmine, with an action similar to nicotine), on gout (which he seems to have regarded as potentially a hereditary disease) and on leukæmia (leucothyæmia). Articles and letters in the non-medical press further indicate the range of his interests: advances in bacteriology, the possibility of a cure for tuberculosis, and controversies such as compulsory vaccination and the Contagious Diseases Acts. In both these cases we see him taking a public health rather than a libertarian or laissez faire position.

Until Edward Jenner developed an effective and fairly safe vaccine, smallpox was one of the most serious of all diseases: highly contagious, killing thousands every year, and leaving many more horribly disfigured. Legislation passed between 1853 and 1874 had made vaccination of infants for smallpox compulsory, but the requirement sat uneasily with Britain's laissez faire traditions, and it ran into a good deal of resistance, especially in working class communities.[1]

The Contagious Diseases Acts were a reaction to the high incidence of venereal disease among the armed forces and the result of a conviction, based on the latest medical reports and advice, that the most important means by which it was spread was through prostitution. The unsatisfactory fitness and poor performance of British troops in the Crimean War had aroused fears that an epidemic of syphilis was sapping the nation's strength. After lengthy inquiries, Par-

---

[1] For details see Nadia Durbach, "'They Might as Well Brand Us': Working Class Resistance to Compulsory Vaccination in Victorian England', *Social History of Medicine*, Vol. 13, 2000, pp. 45-62 and her *Bodily Matters: The Anti-Vaccination Movement in England, 1853-1907* (Durham: Duke University Press, 2005).

liament responded with the Contagious Diseases Acts of 1864, 1866, and 1869, which provided that, in garrison towns, women deemed to be prostitutes could be apprehended, required to submit to a medical examination and detained in hospital if found to be infected. Because the aim was to control venereal disease in the armed forces, the acts applied only to named centres with large numbers of naval or military personnel, including Portsmouth. Although the acts were deplored by moralists, who saw them as condoning fornication, and by a smaller number of feminists who resented the way in which women had been singled out for blame and made liable for humiliating examinations, most medical authorities supported the legislation and believed that it had worked well and contributed to the decline of syphilis. In the second edition of his *Prostitution* (1870) William Acton wrote that the acts had 'been attended with the happiest results, both as regards the health of our army and navy, and the sanitary and moral improvement wrought in the unhappy women who have come within the scope of its provisions'.[1] So successful did Acton consider the acts that he made the fatal mistake of trying to get their scope extended from garrison towns to the whole population, an alarming suggestion which provoked a powerful moral backlash which succeeded in having the acts suspended and eventually repealed in 1883.

The campaign to repeal the acts represented the breakdown of the old medico-moral alliance and the rise of a new discourse in which medical science was to be subordinated to 'moral law' and personal decency, which really meant abstention from sex: as the leader of the campaign, Josephine Butler, put it at a congress in 1877, the essential basis for individual and national health was 'self-control in the relations between the sexes'.[2] The opponents of the Contagious Diseases Acts attacked male sexuality as the real origin of vice and disease: the Social Purity Alliance (established 1873) insisted that male desire was the origin of the immorality which led to prostitution and associated diseases, and that the 'new and final solution' to these problems was to impose the obligation of restraint on men.[3] The campaign

---

[1] William Acton, *Prostitution*, 2nd ed. (1870), edited and with an introduction by Peter Fryer (New York: Praeger, 1969), p. 21.

[2] Frank Mort, *Dangerous Sexualities: Medico-Moral Politics in England Since 1830* (London: Routledge, 1987), p. 89.

[3] *Dangerous Sexualities*, p. 93.

was waged by a coalition of diverse forces, but most of them did not aim at personal liberation, but rather to equalise the double standard by imposing on men the same puritanical rules of sexual propriety which already limited women. The tendency of the movement was expressed in Christabel Pankhurst's later slogan, 'Votes for women and chastity for men',[1] and her allies wrote consistently of the need to enforce social purity, and of venereal disease as 'the God-ordained consequences of his sin' and 'the bitter wages of sexual depravity'.[2]

The medical profession (including Conan Doyle) generally remained in favour of regulation and condemned its opponents as 'friends of contagion', but they were overwhelmed by the lobbying power of Butler's forces and by deserters from within their ranks, notably Jonathan Hutchinson, who denounced sex outside marriage as fornication and thus a sin that should never be countenanced. Instead of regulating the sexual services industry he proposed mass circumcision of boys.[3]

There is a considerable literature on Victorian prostitution and the campaign against the Contagious Diseases Acts, much of it written in a tone of virtuous indignation by feminist historians keen to denounce the 'double standard' and put forward Josephine Butler as the hero of the day; for classic statements of this perspective, see Judith Walkowitz, *Prostitution and Victorian Society: Women, Class and the State* (Cambridge University Press, 1980) and Lucy Bland, *Banishing*

---

[1] Christabel Pankhurst, *The Great Scourge and How to End It* (London, 1913).

[2] Joanne Townsend, *Private Diseases in Public Discourse*, p. 113.

[3] For details, see *A Surgical Temptation*, chap. 12, 'The Purity Movement and the Social Evil'. We can see a similar pattern emerging in sub-Saharan Africa today, where the prevalence of prostitution is a major factor in the spread of heterosexual AIDS, yet where government agencies have been extremely reluctant to regulate the industry or restrict the activities of the prostitutes in any way because such action might infringe their civil or human rights. At the same time, they have recommended and urged widespread circumcision of male infants and boys, whose own civil and human rights are thus treated as non-existent or of no account. It is of interest that in Senegal, one of the few African countries where the problem was faced early on and efforts were made to regulate the sex industry and ensure that prostitutes received regular health checks, the incidence of HIV infection is only around 2 per cent., compared with 30 or 40 per cent. in places such as Tanzania or Botswana. For Senegal, see Martin Meredith, *The State of Africa: A History of Fifty Years of Independence* (London: Free Press, 2005), p. 367. The sad fact is that little boys are an easier target.

the Beast: English Feminism and Sexual Morality 1885-1914 (Penguin, 1994). More recent studies have rather emphasised the anti-liberalism of the campaign, suggested that the so-called double standard (inspecting prostitutes rather than their clients) could be regarded as an early measure of consumer protection, and contrasted the British obsession to improve public morals with the less puritanical approach adopted on the Continent, where the emphasis was more on controlling disease and improving public health. The key text here is Peter Baldwin, *Contagion and the State in Europe* (Cambridge University Press, 1999).

GELSEMINUM AS A POISON[1]

SIR,—Some years ago, a persistent neuralgia led me to use the tincture of gelseminum to a considerable extent. I several times overstepped the maximum doses of the text-books without suffering any ill effects. Having recently had an opportunity of experimenting with a quantity of fresh tincture, I determined to ascertain how far one might go in taking the drug, and what the primary symptoms of an overdose might be. I took each dose about the same hour on successive days, and avoided tobacco or any other agent which might influence the physiological action of the drug. Here are the results as jotted down at the time of the experiment. On Monday and Tuesday, forty and sixty minims produced no effect whatever. On Wednesday, ninety minims were taken at 10.30. At 10.50, on rising from my chair, I became seized with an extreme giddiness and weakness of the limbs, which, however, quickly passed off. There was no nausea or other effect. The pulse was weak but normal. On Thursday, I took 120 minims. The giddiness of yesterday came on in a much milder form. On going out about one o'clock, however, I noticed for the first time that I had a difficulty in accommodating the eye for distant objects. It needed a distinct voluntary effort, and indeed a facial contortion, to do it.

On Friday, 150 minims were taken. As I increased the dose, I found that the more marked physiological symptoms disappeared. To-day, the giddiness was almost gone, but I suffered from a severe frontal headache, with diarrhœa and general lassitude.

On Saturday and Sunday, I took three drachms and 200 minims. The diarrhœa was so persistent and prostrating, that I must stop at 200 minims. I felt great depression and a severe frontal headache. The pulse was still normal, but weak.

From these experiments I would draw the following conclusions.

1. In spite of a case described some time ago in which 75 minims proved fatal, a healthy adult may take as much as 90 minims with perfect immunity.

2. In doses of from 90 to 120 minims, the drug acts apparently as a motor paralyser to a certain extent, causing languor, giddiness, and a partial paralysis of the ciliary muscle.

---

[1] From *The British Medical Journal*, 20 September 1879.

3. After that point, it causes headache, with diarrhœa and extreme lassitude.

4. The system may learn to tolerate gelseminum, as it may opium, if it be gradually inured to it. I feel convinced that I could have taken as much as half an ounce of the tincture, had it not been for the extreme diarrhœa it brought on.

Believe me,

Yours sincerely,

A.C.D.

Clifton House, Aston Road, Birmingham.

NOTES ON A CASE OF LEUCOCYTHÆMIA[1]

To the Editor of THE LANCET.

SIR,—As the causation of this rare and curious disease has been as obscure hitherto as its treatment has been futile, your readers may be interested by a case which seems to throw some light upon both points.

The patient, a well-built man, twenty-nine years of age, came to my friend Mr. Hoare complaining of a large tumour, which extended across his abdomen from the right costal border to the left anterior superior spine of the ilium. This proved upon examination to be an enormously hypertrophied spleen, the hilum being represented by a deep notch a little above the level of the umbilicus. The account of the patient was that some years before he had had a sharp attack of ague at Aspinwall, on the American coast, and that he had never entirely shaken off its effects. The swelling, however, had appeared recently, and attained its large proportions in the course of a few weeks. On examining the blood under the microscope we found that the leucocytes were enormously increased in number, almost filling up the interspaces of the rouleaux, while the coloured corpuscles were ill-formed, and diminished not only relatively, but also in the aggregate. The proportion of white to red was calculated at one to seven. None of the other blood glands were affected, and the only symptoms complained of were referable to pressure of the tumour, principally

---

[1] From *The Lancet*, 25 March 1882.

dyspepsia and vomiting from its interference with the stomach, and pain in the legs from compression of the lumbar plexus. The liver was slightly enlarged and tender, but the secretion of bile appeared to be unaffected. The heart was weak and had a well-marked functional murmur. Excessive marasmus was another leading feature of the case, the patient having fallen from fourteen to eleven stone in a few weeks. Having given both iron and quinine a fair trial, and found them equally inefficacious, we have now had recourse to arsenic in large doses, in combination with the iodide and chlorate of potash. This mode of treatment, combined with a liberal diet, and strict attention to the state of the bowels, has been remarkably efficacious. The tumour has already diminished in size, and some of the more distressing secondary symptoms have been alleviated. The principal interest of the case lies, I think, in the connexion to be traced between the malarious poison and the subsequent leucocythæmia, a connexion which seems to show that this obscure disease is intimately allied to ordinary "ague-cake," if not a mere modification of that pathological condition, determined by some idiosyncracy of constitution or temperament.

I am, Sir, your obedient servant,

A. CONAN DOYLE, M.B., C.M. EDIN.

Aston, March, 1882.

LIFE AND DEATH IN THE BLOOD[1]

HAD a man the power of reducing himself to the size of less than the one-thousandth part of an inch, and should he, while of this microscopic stature, convey himself through the coats of a living artery, how strange the sight that would meet his eye! All round him he would see a rapidly flowing stream of clear transparent fluid, in which many solid and well-defined bodies were being whirled along. These are the smooth straw-coloured elastic discs which act simply as mechanical carriers of oxygen and jostle through their brief existence without any claim to a higher function than that of a baker's cart, which carries round the necessaries of life, and is valuable not for itself, but for its burden. Here and there, however, on the outskirts of the throng, our

---

[1] Originally published in *Good Words* (1883), pp. 178-181.

infinitesimal spectator would perceive bodies of a very different character. Gelatinous in consistence, and irregular in shape, capable of pushing out long prehensile tentacles with which to envelop its food and draw it into its interior, this creature would appear from his point of view as a polyp of gigantic proportions and formidable aspect. No differentiated organs are to be seen in it, save a dark mass of pigment in its centre, which may represent some rudimentary visual or auditory apparatus. Digestion is its strong point, for it has the power of seizing upon any oily particle which may drift in its direction, and of introducing it into its interior by the simple method of surrounding it without any preliminary ceremony of swallowing. Small hope for our poor little mite of humanity should one of these floating stomachs succeed in seizing him in its embrace. They are slow, and ungainly in their motions, however, and drift glutinously along, clinging to the edges of the stream, and occasionally impaling themselves upon the projecting angle when the artery divides into two branches. Now and again they protrude an excrescence which gradually separates itself by a constriction at the base, and hurries away into the blood stream as an independent organism.

These creatures are the leucocytes, or white corpuscles, and in spite of their being very much less numerous than the carriers of oxygen, there are still several millions of them within the healthy human body. In certain diseased conditions they multiply enormously until they outnumber the straw-coloured discs. When removed and placed upon a surface, kept at the same temperature as that to which they have been accustomed, they are capable of carrying on an independent existence for some time. They have indeed a prototype, wandering at large, from which they are hardly recognisable, viz.: the tiny amœba which may be washed from damp moss and detected under the microscope.

This then is the only creature possessing the attributes commonly associated with life, which is found in healthy human blood; but in diseased conditions numerous others appear, differing from each other as widely as the flounder does from the eel, and presenting an even greater contrast in the effects which they produce. The existence of these little organisms, which lie upon the debateable ground between the animal and vegetable kingdoms, may have been suspected by our forefathers; but it is only in the last few years that their presence has been clearly demonstrated, and their relation to disease duly appreciated. I propose to glance at some of the work done of late in this direction—work which has opened up a romance world of living creatures so minute as to be hardly detected by our highest lenses, yet many of them endowed with such fearful properties that the savage tiger or venomous cobra have not inflicted one fiftieth part of the damage upon the human race.

There is a disease named seven days' fever, which, though rare in Britain, is not uncommon in the Emerald Isle, as well as in Russia, India, and other places where the fare of the lower orders is exceptionally poor and scanty. Let us go to the bedside of some poor fellow suffering from this complaint, and having once more assumed our microscopic proportions, let us inspect personally the condition of his circulation. We see again the transparent serum, the busy yellow discs, the languid omnivorous pieces of jelly; but what is this? Writhing their way among the legitimate corpuscles there are countless creatures, thin and long, with snake-like body and spiral motion. They are the spirilla of relapsing fever, discovered by Obermeier in 1872. Where have they come from, and why are they here? Ah, that is the question to which science is even now striving to give a definite answer. They were not in the blood before, but they are there now in all their grim obtrusive reality, and the fever was coincident with their appearance. In a week they die, and the fever passes away; but as Dr. Haydenreich, of St. Petersburg, has pointed out, they leave their young behind them, which take seven days to mature. After this short respite, then the patient is once again prostrated by a fresh brood, which in turn gives rise to another; and so the horrible process goes on until either the race dies away, or their victim is exhausted.

It was not a human ailment, but one common among cattle, which first drew the attention of the scientific world to the terrible power possessed by these tiny organisms. Splenic fever, since identified as one of the plagues of Egypt, has long been a bugbear of Continental farmers. The extreme virulence and infectiousness of this disease had often invited speculation, but it was not until about the year 1850 that Dr. Devaine discovered a very minute rod-like creature in the blood of the afflicted animals, which he conjectured to be the true cause of the disease, though he did not see his way to demonstrating the fact.

A young German, Koch, of Woolstein, a name which he has written for ever across the annals of medicine, took up the broken thread of Devaine's researches, and succeeded in proving what his French rival had surmised. Starting upon the supposition that these little creatures were not necessarily confined to the blood, but would live and multiply in any medium which was nutritious and warm, he made a suitable animal infusion, and introduced a small quantity of infected blood. In a few days the fluid which had been clear became turbid, and he found it to be swarming with countless millions of the *Bacillus anthracis,* as the organism is named, all derived apparently from the few which chanced to be in the original drop of blood. By taking a little of this fluid and introducing it into a second bowl of the cultivating medium he produced a second generation, and from that a third, each as virulent as the first. A drop injected into an animal brought on all the characteristic and deadly symptoms of splenic fever. In the course of these researches, Koch found that the organism appeared in three forms, as rods, as round spores, and as long branching filaments; and he made the extremely important discovery that while in the two former cases they were extremely poisonous, in the form of filaments they became absolutely innocuous. The first great step was won when Koch found himself able to cultivate the infection, as he might grow monkshood or any vegetable poison in the soil of his back garden.

This advantage was quickly followed up. If the young German had found the breach, there were many ready to rush into it. In England, Klein demonstrated the existence of an organism in the disease known as pig-typhoid, and succeeded in cultivating it apart from the body. In France, Toussaint, of Toulouse, extracted the cause of the epidemic among fowls, called "fowl-cholera," and bred it in an animal infusion. The time was evidently approaching when these countless myriads, who had maintained their independence so long, should at last be forced to acknowledge man as the lord of creation.

It was at this crisis that the great Pasteur brought his gigantic intellect to bear upon the subject. By his investigations on the parasites of silkworms, and the causes of fermentation, he had already proved himself to possess indomitable patience and a rare scientific intuition; but it was not until he had launched out upon this new and congenial field that he came out in his true light as one of the master minds of the century.

Turning his attention first to the organism discovered by Toussaint in fowl-cholera, he cultivated it in chicken broth, as Koch had done the *Bacillus anthracis*. He produced, as he had expected, a most infective infusion which rapidly caused the death of any animal inoculated. Upon leaving the fluid to stand for a month exposed to the air, however, he discovered that its virulent properties were very much decreased, and at the end of six months it became absolutely innocuous. And now he came upon his great discovery. *If a few drops of this innocuous material be introduced into an animal's system, it is protected for ever afterwards against the original disease.*

This was a gigantic step, as proving that vaccination as a preventive to smallpox was not a mere isolated eccentricity of nature, but part of an endless system, did we but know how to procure the antagonistic materials. Many a man might have rested upon his laurels, but the active brain of Pasteur hurried on to consider the analogous case of the organism cultivated by Koch in splenic fever. Again he made his infusion, again he allowed it to stand until it became weakened, or "attenuated," to use his expression, and again he found to his inexpressible delight that a healthy animal inoculated with this attenuated material was secured for ever against the disease. Here was a great commercial fact. The proofs were overpowering. Government took the matter in hand, and France will soon be a million per annum the richer, that sum representing the yearly loss from the ravages of the disease.

We have seen that for the extirpation of this pestilential little rod, three great men had to bring their minds to bear upon it. Devaine saw it, Koch isolated it, Pasteur tamed it. In this work of theirs they conferred a blessing upon men as well as on animals. The bacillus is a creature of cosmopolitan tastes. The butcher who cuts up the diseased carcase and gets one drop of its juices on to a raw surface of his body dies of malignant pustule—one of the most awful maladies that flesh is heir to. The tanner or wool sorter who works with the infected skin, and inhales air laden with the poisonous particles, is struck down by wool-sorter's disease. To these, as well as to cattle, the attenuated virus brings relief.

One great thinker stimulates the latent powers of many others. A troop of French worthies have followed in the steps of their chief, and made the last few years redound to the honour of their country. Arloing, Cornevin, and Thomas, of Lyons, have attenuated the organism of another deadly cattle disease, named the "Maladie de Chabert," after its discoverer, and have by inoculation demonstrated the possibility of stamping it out. Galtier and Pasteur himself have been working at hydrophobia, and their researches are most interesting. No doubt, by attenuating the poison, they will be able to inoculate for this malady too, so that from being the most intractable it will become the most docile of diseases; for remember that inoculation would in all probability be effective even if applied after the bite of the rabid animal.

Hitherto we have been considering organisms which affect animals rather than man, and it was natural that these should be the first to be brought under human control, for we have unlimited powers of experimenting upon them. Having established a certain number of facts as a working basis, *savants* were now able to turn their attention to our own diseases, content to reason by analogy where they were unable to demonstrate by experiment. It was but yesterday, as it were, that scientific investigation was directed into this channel, and yet enormous strides have been made. Toussaint and Koch have demonstrated the existence of a little rodlike creature in tubercle or consumption, which swarms in the diseased lungs, and which, if transferred to another body, will establish itself and breed, thereby proving the malady to be really an infectious one. Whether by inoculating with the weakened infusion they can ward off the disease in a family predisposed to develop it, remains to be seen, but is a perfectly feasible supposition.

Another interesting series of experiments has been undertaken by Klebs and Tomassi Crudelli, in the marsh lands of the Campagna. Suspecting the existence of an organism in the swamps which gave rise to ague and remittent fever when introduced into the blood, they examined the soil very carefully, selecting it from the most unhealthy situations. They soon found the creature not only among the damp earth, but also in the air which emanated from the marsh. This organism was also cultivated and showed itself to be amenable to human influences.

This is but a hasty glance at what has been done of late years towards subjecting the fishes of the blood. I have not even mentioned the researches of Chauveau, Burdon-Sanderson, and other eminent inquirers. All tend, however, towards the one object. Given that a single disease, proved to depend upon a parasitic organism, can be effectually and certainly stamped out, why should not all diseases depending upon similar causes be also done away with? That is the great question which the scientific world is striving to solve; and in the face of it how paltry do war and statecraft appear, and everything which fascinates the attention of the multitude! Let things go as they are going, and it is probable that in the days of our children's children, or even earlier, consumption, typhus, typhoid, cholera, malaria, scarlatina, diphtheria, measles, and a host of other diseases will have ceased to exist. It is true that in many of these cases the organism has not only never been cultivated, but has not been detected by the highest microscopic powers, yet we are almost as certain of its presence as if we saw it, and it is those very infinitesimal creatures which have proved to be the most virulent in their effects and the most difficult to destroy. All honour then to the men striving in generous rivalry to strike at the very root of the foul tree whose branches the physicians of other ages have been content to prune; not only for the energy and sagacity which they have displayed, but for the dogged courage with which they have worked for years among fluids, the inoculation with which meant in many cases a horrible and lingering death to the workman.

A. CONAN DOYLE.

THE CONTAGIOUS DISEASES ACTS[1]

SIR,—As an ounce of fact is proverbially superior to an indefinite quantity of theory, I think that I am justified in citing one or two instances of the effects of the present suspension of the Acts. Being in practice as a medical man in the town most affected by the measure, I am able to speak with some authority on the subject. Last week a large transport entered Portsmouth Harbour with time-expired men from India. Upon the same day several diseased women left the hospital presumably with the intention of meeting that transport, and there was no law to prevent it. I say that if an unfortunate soldier, coming home to his native land after an absence of years, and exposed to such temptations, should yield to them, and entail disease upon himself and his offspring, the chief fault should not lie at his door. It surely emanates logically from those hysterical legislators who set loose these bearers

---

[1] From *The Medical Times*, 16 June 1883.

of contagion, and their like, upon society. For fear delicacy should be
offended where no touch of delicacy exists, dreadful evils are to result,
men to suffer, children to die, and pure women to inherit unspeak-
able evils. Loose statements and vague doctrines of morality may impose upon hasty thinkers, but surely, when the thing is reduced to
its simplest terms, it becomes a matter of public calamity that these
Acts should be suspended for a single day, far more for an indefinite
period. The apostles of free trade in infection have worked to such
good purpose that within a few weeks the streets of our naval stations
have become pandemonia, and immorality is rampant where it lately
feared to show its face. Property has depreciated near all the public-
houses since the suspension of the Acts, on account of the concourse
of vile women whose uproar and bad language make night hideous. I
venture to say that, were the old laws enforced again to-morrow, there
would still in a hundred years' time be many living who could trace
inherited mental or physical deformity to the fatal interregnum which
the champions of the modesty of harlots had brought about.

A. Conan Doyle.

Southsea, 1883

AMERICAN MEDICAL DIPLOMAS[1]

Sir,—In ventilating the question of sham degrees and American diplomas you do the public a great service. In all other trades and pro-
fessions an incompetent man is a mere inconvenience, of more harm
to himself than to others. It is different, however, in medicine. There,
a blunder in diagnosis or an error in treatment means death to the unfortunate sufferer. It is obviously impossible for the poor and unedu-
cated to distinguish between a qualified practitioner and a quack who
has appropriated some high-sounding title. In order to protect them,
therefore, it is necessary that the law and the force of public opinion
should be brought into play.

The so-called "University of Philadelphia" might stand as a type
of these sham examining boards. The university consisted of a small
body of speculative parchment-mongers who did a roaring trade in

---

[1] From *The Evening News* (Portsmouth), 23 September 1884.

worthless diplomas until the Government of the United States dis-
countenanced them. They then established agencies in Europe and
continued their dishonest traffic. Anyone who could muster the necessary dollars was free to their degree and might then pose as the equal
of the *bona fide* practitioner, who had expended hundreds of pounds
and years of his life in obtaining his qualification. It is true that in
practising on the strength of their bogus degree they rendered themselves liable to the Apothecaries Act. This, however, is seldom put in
force, for the reason that the prosecutor too often finds his opponent
a man of straw, and has to bear the expense of the proceedings. There
is a body called the Medical Defence Association, which occasionally
comes down upon these gentry and gibbets one to act as a scarecrow
to the others. The public Press, however, is the best of all defences, for
by ventilating the question it opens the eyes of those who might become dupes. It is no question of the comparative merits of British and
American degrees. An M.D. of a good Transatlantic college is always
respected in England, and any man might be proud to hail from the
school of which Gross, Sayre, and Austin Flint are shining lights. It is
against sham degrees that we protest, which enable a man to cover his
ignorance by an imposing title, and to decide matters of life and death
without being competent to do so.

I remain, Sir, sincerely yours,

A.C.D.

THE REMOTE EFFECTS OF GOUT[1]
To the Editor of THE LANCET.

SIR,—I read with much interest the description of the relation of certain diseases of the eye to gout, as reported last week in THE LANCET.
Mr. Hutchinson has remarked in his lecture on the obscure non-ar-
thritic effects which gout may produce in the children of gouty parents, without any ordinary gouty symptoms. I have had two cases
lately in my practice which illustrate his remarks so well that I cannot
forbear from quoting them. A Mr. H— came to me suffering from
chronic eczema and psoriasis. He attributed it himself to the great
changes of temperature and profuse perspirations incidental to his

---

[1] *The Lancet*, 29 November 1884.

business. I put him on arsenic and afterwards on iodide of potash, without much benefit. He told me that he had never had any gouty symptoms in his life. Shortly afterwards his married daughter, Mrs. B—, consulted me on certain intense pains in her eyes, accompanied by temporary congestion and partial blindness, which attacked her whenever her digestion was deranged. Recognising this to be a gouty symptom, and bethinking me of the obscure skin disease which afflicted the father, I made somewhat minute inquiries into the previous family history. I then found that the grandfather of Mrs. B— and the father of Mr. H— had been a martyr to gout for many years, and had eventually died of a form of Bright's disease, which I have no doubt from the description was the "contracted granular kidney" so intimately associated with gout.

These cases are, I think, interesting as showing the protean character of the disease, extending over three generations. The grandfather was thoroughly gouty; the father had skin affections without any other gouty symptom; the third generation exhibited eye symptoms and nothing else. I may mention that both cases improved rapidly upon colchicum and alkalies.—Yours sincerely,

A. CONAN DOYLE, M.B., C.M.

Southsea, Nov. 24th, 1884.

COMPULSORY VACCINATION[1]

SIR,—From time to time some champion of the party which is opposed to vaccination comes forward to air his views in the public Press, but these periodical sallies seldom lead to any discussion, as the inherent weakness of their position renders a reply superfluous. When, however, a gentleman of Colonel Wintle's position makes an attack upon what is commonly considered by those most competent to judge to be one of the greatest victories ever won by science over disease, it is high time that some voice should be raised upon the other side. Hobbies and fads are harmless things as a rule, but when a hobby takes the form of encouraging ignorant people to neglect sanitary precautions and to live in a fool's paradise until bitter experience teaches them their mistake, it becomes a positive danger to the community at large.

---

[1] *The Evening Mail* (Portsmouth), 15 July 1887.

The interests at stake are so vital that an enormous responsibility rests with the men whose notion of progress is to revert to the condition of things which existed in the dark ages before the dawn of medical science. Colonel Wintle bases his objection to vaccination upon two points: its immorality and its inefficiency or positive harmfulness. Let us consider it under each of these heads, giving the moral question the precedence which is its due. Is it immoral for a Government to adopt a method of procedure which experience has proved and science has testified to conduce to the health and increased longevity of the population? Is it immoral to inflict a passing inconvenience upon a child in order to preserve it from a deadly disease? Does the end never justify the means? Would it be immoral to give Colonel Wintle a push in order to save him from being run over by a locomotive? If all these are really immoral, I trust and pray that we may never attain morality. The colonel's reasoning reminds me of nothing so much as that adduced by some divines of the Scottish Church, who protested against the introduction of chloroform. "Pain was sent us by Providence," said the worthy ministers, "and it is therefore sinful to abolish it." Colonel Wintle's line of argument is that smallpox has been also sent by Providence and that it becomes immoral to take any steps to neutralise its mischief. When once it has been concisely stated, it needs no further agitation.

In the second place is the mode of treatment a success? It has been before the public for nearly a hundred years, during which time it has been thrashed out periodically in learned societies, argued over in medical journals, examined by statisticians, sifted and tested in every conceivable method, and the result of it all is that among those who are brought in practical contact with disease, there is a unanimity upon the point which is more complete than upon any other medical subject. Homœopath and allopath, foreigner and Englishman, find here a common ground for agreement. I fear that the testimony of the Southsea ladies which Col. Wintle quotes, or that of the district visitors which he invokes, will hardly counter-balance this consensus of scientific opinion.

The ravages made by smallpox in the days of our ancestors can hardly be realised by the present sanitary and well-vaccinated generation. Macaulay remarks that in the advertisements of the early Georgian era there is hardly ever a missing relative who is not described as "having pock marks upon his face." It was universal, in town and in country, in the cottage and in the palace. Mary, the wife of William the Third, sickened and died of it. Whole tracts of country were decimated. Now-a-days there is many a general practitioner who lives and dies without having ever seen a case. What is the cause of this amazing difference? There is no doubt what the cause appeared to be in the eyes of the men who having had experience of the old system saw the Jennerian practice of inoculation come into vogue. When in 1802 Jenner was awarded £30,000 by a grateful country the gift came from men who could see by force of contrast the value of his discovery.

I am aware that Anti-Vaccinationists endeavour to account for the wonderful decrease of smallpox by supposing that there has been some change in the type of the disease. This is pure assumption, and the facts seem to point in the other direction. Other zymotic diseases have not, as far as we know, modified their characteristics, and smallpox still asserts itself with its ancient virulence whenever sanitary defects, or the prevalence of thinkers of the Colonel Wintle type, favour its development. I have no doubt that our recent small outbreak in Portsmouth would have assumed formidable proportions had it found a congenial uninoculated population upon which to fasten.

In the London smallpox hospital nurses, doctors and dressers have been in contact with the sick for more than fifty years, and during that time there is no case on record of nurse, doctor, or dresser catching the disease. They are, of course, periodically vaccinated. How long, I wonder, would the committee of the Anti-Vaccination Society remain in the wards before a case broke out among them?

As to the serious results of vaccination, which Colonel Wintle describes as indescribable, they are to a very large extent imaginary. Of course there are some unhealthy children, the offspring of unhealthy parents, who will fester and go wrong if they are pricked with a pin. It is possible that the district visitors appealed to may find out some such case. They are certainly rare, for in a tolerably large experience (five years in a large hospital, three in a busy practice in Birmingham, and nearly six down here) I have only seen one case, and it soon got well. Some parents have an amusing habit of ascribing anything which happens to their children, from the whooping-cough to a broken leg, to the effects of their vaccination. It is from this class that the anti-vaccinationist party is largely recruited.

In conclusion I would say that the subject is of such importance, and our present immunity from smallpox so striking, that it would take a very strong case to justify a change. As long as that case is so weak as to need the argument of morality to enforce it I think that the Vaccination Acts are in no great danger of being repealed.

Yours faithfully,

A. CONAN DOYLE, M.D., C.M.

Bush Villa, July 14th, 1887

COMPULSORY VACCINATION[1]

SIR,—Colonel Wintle's second letter appears to me to contain a jumble of statistics and quotations, some of which do not affect the question at all, while others tell dead against the cause which he is championing. If there is such a consensus of testimony that there was a marked diminution of pock-marked faces between the years 1815 and 1835, is it not a fact that these are the very years when the fruits of Jenner's discovery might be expected to show itself upon the rising generation? Colonel Wintle's argument appears to be that it was a mere coincidence that the disease should begin to diminish at the very time when the new treatment was adopted by a considerable section of the public. The medical profession holds that it was cause and effect—an explanation which has been amply borne out by subsequent experience.

The Colonel seems to think that because we still suffer from occasional epidemics of smallpox, that proves the system of vaccination to be a failure. On the contrary, the most clinching argument in its favour is furnished by these very epidemics, for when their results come to be tabulated they show with startling clearness the difference in the mortality between those who have and have not been vaccinated. The unvaccinated not only contract the disease more readily, but it attacks them in a far more virulent form. The Sheffield case recorded by "Common Sense" is a remarkable and recent example of this well-known fact.

The protection afforded by vaccination is in exact proportion to the thoroughness of the original inoculation. I suppose the most de-

---

[1] *The Hampshire County Times* (Portsmouth), 27 July 1887.

termined anti-vaccinationist would hardly venture to suggest that the statistics of hospitals are cooked in order to annihilate their particular fad. Here are Marson's tabulated results of the cases treated at the Smallpox Hospital during twenty years, and if Colonel Wintle can ignore them, I am puzzled to know what evidence would be accepted by him as conclusive. A glance at the subjoined table will show that there is a most exact correspondence between the degree of vaccination and the degree of mortality:

Of those with 4 vaccine marks	.5 per cent. died
3	1.9
2	4.7
1	7.7
With none, but professing to have been vaccinated	23.3
Non-vaccinated patients	37

Here it will be seen that the death-rate varies from less than one in a hundred among the well-vaccinated to the enormous mortality of 37 per cent. among Colonel Wintle's followers. These figures, remember, are taken from no single outbreak, where phenomenal conditions might prevail, but they represent a steady average drawn from twenty years of London smallpox. I might quote other corroborative tables of statistics, but I feel that if the foregoing fails to convince no other evidence is likely to succeed. Colonel Wintle remarks that London and Liverpool are more afflicted by smallpox than any other towns and deduces from that an argument against vaccination. The reason for the prevalence of the disease is of course that they have a larger floating population than any other English city and that therefore it is more difficult to enforce the vaccination acts. With all the zeal in the world a public vaccinator cannot eliminate smallpox in a large port with a constant influx of foreigners and seamen.

Anti-vaccinationists harp upon vaccine being a poison. Of course it is a poison. So is opium, digitalis, and arsenic, though they are three of the most valuable drugs in the pharmacopœia. The whole science of medicine is by the use of a mild poison to counteract a deadly one. The virus of rabies is a poison, but Pasteur has managed to turn it to account in the treatment of hydrophobia.

As to fatal cases following vaccination, medical men are keenly alive to the necessity of using the purest lymph, and no candid enquirer can deny that some deplorable cases have resulted in the past from the neglect of this point. Such incidents are as painful as they are rare. Every care is now used to exclude a possibility of a strumous or syphilitic taint being communicated, these being the only constitutional diseases which have been ever known to be conferred. As I said in my previous letter, there are some children who will fester and inflame if they are pricked with a pin, and these occasionally have their hereditary weakness brought out by the vaccination. Such stray cases, however, even if we allowed Colonel Wintle's extreme estimate of one a week, bear an infinitesimal proportion to the total amount of good done. At present if a child dies of any cause within a certain time of its vaccination the anti-vaccinators are ready to put it down as cause and effect. Convulsions, whether arising from worms, or teething, or brain irritation, are all ascribed to the pernicious effect of what the literature of the league terms "that filthy rite."

In conclusion, there is no reason why Colonel Wintle should not hold his own private opinion upon the matter. But he undertakes a vast responsibility when, in the face of the overwhelming testimony of those who are brought most closely into contact with disease, he incites others, through the public press, to follow the same course and take their chance of infection in defiance of hospital statistics. Only the possession of an extremely strong case can justify a man in opposing medical men upon a medical point, and this is of all points the one which should be most cautiously approached, as the welfare of the whole community is at stake. Should I put forward some positive and dogmatic views upon the rifling of guns or the trajectory of a shell, Colonel Wintle, as an Artillerist, would be justified in demanding that I should produce some good reasons for the faith which was in me. The tendency of the scientific world, if we may judge from the work not only of Pasteur and Koch, but also of Burdon-Sanderson, Toussaint, and others, lies more and more in the direction of preventive methods of inoculation to check zymotic disease. In opposing that tendency Colonel Wintle, however much he may persuade himself to the contrary, is really opposing progress and lending himself to the propagation of error.

To anyone who wishes to know exactly the evidence upon which the practice of vaccination is based I should recommend "The Facts about Vaccination," published by the National Health Society, 44, Berners-street, London.

Yours faithfully,

A. CONAN DOYLE, M.D., C.M.

Bush Villa, Southsea

DR. KOCH AND HIS CURE[1]

BY A. CONAN DOYLE.

To the Englishman in Berlin, and indeed to the German also, it is at present very much easier to see the bacillus of Koch, than to catch even the most fleeting glimpse of its illustrious discoverer. His name is on every lip, his utterances are the constant subject of conversation, but, like the Veiled Prophet, he still remains unseen to any eyes save those of his own immediate co-workers and assistants. The stranger must content himself by looking up at the long grey walls of the Hygiene Museum in Kloster Strasse, and knowing that somewhere within them the great master mind is working, which is rapidly bringing under subjection those unruly tribes of deadly micro-organisms which are the last creatures in the organic world to submit to the sway of man.

THE RECLUSE OF KLOSTER STRASSE.

The great bacteriologist is a man so devoted to his own particular line of work that all descriptions of him from other points of view must, in the main, be negative. Some five feet and a half in height, sturdily built, with brown hair fringing off to grey at the edges, he is a man whose appearance might be commonplace were it not for the vivacity of his expression and the quick decision of his manner. Of a thoroughly German type, with his earnest face, his high thoughtful forehead, and his slightly retroussé nose, he looks what he is, a student, a worker, and a philosopher. His eyes are small, grey, and searching, but so sorely tried by long years of microscopic work that they require

---

[1] Originally appeared in *The Review of Reviews*, Vol. 2, No. 12 (Dec. 1890), pp. 552-560.

the aid of the strongest glasses. A married man, and of a domestic turn of mind, his life is spent either in the complete privacy of his family, or in the absorbing labour of his laboratory. He smokes little, drinks less, and leads so regular a life that he preserves his whole energy for the all-important mission to which he has devoted himself. One hobby he has, and only one, derived very probably from the hereditary influence of a long series of mountain-dwelling ancestors. He is a keen mountaineer, and never more happy than when, alpinestock in hand, he is breathing in the invigorating air of the higher Alps. Visitors at Pontresina last year may have observed there a quiet little sturdy gentleman, tweed-suited and bespectacled, who vanished early from the hotel to reappear jaded and travel-stained in the evening; but few would have surmised that the energetic climber was none other than the renowned Professor of Berlin. It might perhaps be possible to trace some analogy between the clear and calm atmosphere of scientific thought and those still and rarefied regions in which Tyndall loves to dwell and Koch to wander.

THE KOCH LABORATORY.

To his own private sanctum few, as has already been remarked, can gain access, but in the Kloster Strasse there is his public laboratory, in which some fifty young men, including several Americans and Englishmen, are pursuing their studies in bacteriology. It is a large square chamber, well lit and lofty, with rows of microscopes bristling along the deal tables which line it upon every side. Bunsen burners, reservoirs of distilled water, freezing machines for the cutting of microscopic sections, and every other conceivable aid to the bacteriological student, lie ready to his hand. Under glass protectors may be seen innumerable sections of potatoes with bright red, or blue, or black, smears upon their white surfaces where colonies of rare bacilli have been planted, whose growth is watched and recorded from day to day. All manner of fruits with the mould and fungi which live upon them, infusions of meat or of sugar peopled with unseen millions, squares of gelatine which are the matrix in which innumerable forms of life are sprouting, all these indicate to the visitor the style of work upon which the students are engaged, and the methods by which they carry them out. Here, too, under the microscope may be seen the prepared slides which contain specimens of those bacilli of disease which have already been isolated. This one, stained with logwood, where little purple dots, like grains of pepper, are sprinkled thickly over the field, is a demonstration of that deadly tubercle-bacillus which has harassed mankind from the dawn of time, and yet has become visible to him only during the last eight years. Here, under the next object-glass, are little pink curved creatures, so minute as to be hardly visible under the power of 700 diameters which we are using. Yet these pretty and infinitely fragile things are the accursed comma-bacilli of cholera, the most terrible scourge which has ever devastated the microbe-ridden earth. Here, too, is the little rod-shaped filament of the Bacillus anthracis, the curving tendrils of the Obermeyer spirillus, the great spores of Bacillus prodigiosis, and the jointed branches of Aspergillus. It is a strange thing to look upon these utterly insignificant creatures, and to realize that in one year they would claim more victims from the human race than all the tigers who have ever trod a jungle. A satire, indeed, it is upon the majesty of man when we look at these infinitesimal and contemptible creatures which have it in their power to overthrow the strongest intellect and to shatter the most robust frame.

A special section exists in connection with the laboratory for experiments upon the effects which the bacteria have upon animal life, and here the action of all infusions and injections is checked by their use upon guinea pigs before being used upon human subjects.

THE EARLY DAYS OF DR. KOCH.

Professor Koch is forty-seven years of age. In 1843 he saw the light at Clausthal, where his father was an official in the employ of a mining company. From the age of nineteen to twenty-three he studied at Gottingen, where he was brought under the influence of the famous Jacob Henle. Henle was an all-round man of science, who had gained his laurels as an anatomist, but who held enlightened and advanced views on many medical points. Among other things, he held very strongly that the influence of plant life in its lower forms would be found to underlie many of the diseases to which the human frame is liable. It is more than probable that to Henle's suggestions may be traced that line of thought which in the case of Koch has led to such great results.

After taking his degree, Koch became assistant physician at the hospital of Hamburg, and shortly afterwards he started in private practice in the little town of Langenhagen, in Hanover. Thence he migrated to Wollstein, where, in a little village, he settled down to the humdrum life of a country doctor. He was then twenty-nine years of age, strong and vigorous, with all his great powers striving for an outlet, even in the unpropitious surroundings in which he found himself. To him it must seem but yesterday that he drove his little cob and ramshackle provincial trap along the rough Posen roads to attend the rude peasants and rough farmers who centre round the village. Never, surely, could a man have found himself in a position less favourable for scientific research—poor, humble, unknown, isolated from sympathy and from the scientific appliances which are the necessary tools of the investigator. Yet he was a man of too strong a character to allow himself to be warped by the position in which he found himself, or to be diverted from the line of work which was most congenial to his nature. Looking round, he saw that in one respect, at least, he might claim an advantage over his scientific brethren. If they had chemicals, laboratories, instruments, microscopes, he, at least, had cattle—nothing but cattle. To cattle, therefore, he turned himself, and soon proved that work of first-class importance might be achieved among these humblest of patients.

THE DISCOVERY OF THE BACILLUS ANTHRACIS.

Splenic fever, which has been surmised to have been one of the plagues of Egypt, has long been a bugbear of Continental farmers. The extreme virulence and infectiousness of this disease had often invited speculation, but it was not until about the year 1850 that Dr. Devaine discovered a very minute rod-like creature in the blood of the afflicted animals, which he conjectured to be the true cause of the disease, though he did not see his way to demonstrating the fact.

This was the broken enquiry which Koch now took in hand with the most successful results. Starting upon the supposition that these little creatures were not necessarily confined to the blood, but would live and multiply in any medium which was nutritious and warm, he made a suitable animal infusion, and introduced a small quantity of infected blood. In a few days the fluid, which had been clear, became turbid, and he found it to be swarming with countless millions of bacillus anthracis, as the organism is named, all derived apparently from the few which chanced to be in the original drop of blood. By taking a little of this fluid, and introducing it into a second bowl of the cultivating medium, he produced a second generation, and from that a third, each as virulent as the first. A drop injected into an animal brought on all the characteristic and deadly symptoms of splenic fever. In the course of these researches Koch found that the organism appeared in three forms—as rods, as round spores, and as long branching filaments; and he made the extremely important discovery that while in the two former cases they were extremely poisonous, in the form of filaments they became absolutely innocuous. A great step was won when Koch found himself able to cultivate the infection, as he might grow monkshood or any vegetable poison in the soil of his back garden. It is a matter of history how Pasteur enlarged upon Koch's results, how he found that a weaker infusion might be made, which would render the animal innocuous to the more virulent type of the disease, and how France has been millions of pounds the richer for the vast number of animals who have been inoculated against the plague. Here was indeed a worthy rivalry between France and Germany—a contest as to which should confer the greatest benefits upon mankind. Koch's paper upon anthrax appeared in Colin's "Communications on the Biology of Plants," and instantly drew widespread attention to the writer, as did a second paper shortly afterwards upon the preserving and photographing of bacteria.

AT THE UNIVERSITY OF BONN.

In the year 1880 Koch finally abandoned his country practice, and came to the University of Bonn, as assistant to Professor Finkelnburg. Before leaving Wollstein he had published a research over those micro-organisms which infest wounds. Lister's antiseptic system of surgery had been founded upon the presumption that such creatures exist, but Koch was the first to absolutely demonstrate it. His research was of importance not only for its results, but also on account of the additions which it made to our knowledge of the technical management of the microscope. Koch was the first to show the extreme importance of using certain staining agents, which enabled the bacteria to be more easily distinguished by the fact that they took a deeper tint than the tissues in which they lay. He was also the first to use oil immersion method, by which the object glass is screwed down upon a drop of oil which condenses the light upon the object which is being examined.

HE FINDS THE BACILLUS OF TUBERCLE.

In the scientific atmosphere of Bonn, Koch found himself at last in a thoroughly congenial situation, and was soon at work again with his microscopes and his solutions. In 1882 he announced and demonstrated the bacillus of tubercle. Important as this discovery has proved, by being the one end of the chain which led to the idea of inoculation, it was also of great service to physicians as putting into their hands an exact means of testing as to whether any given illness be tubercular or not. The presence of the little rod-like body is conclusive as a sign of true phthisis as distinguished from fibroid pneumonia, or any other wasting disease. In his recent report he complains, with some truth, that physicians have not sufficiently used this weapon which he has placed in their hands. He also was able to prove beyond all doubt that the condition known as scrofula and the skin disease known as lupus were both distinguished by the presence of the bacillus, and were therefore all different manifestations of the same disease. It is an affair of yesterday how brilliantly he has proved by the bedside what he had deduced in the laboratory.

AND THE CHOLERA BACILLUS.

In 1883 cholera, after a rest of ten years, hovered once more over the eastern portion of Europe. It appeared first in Damietta, whence it spread rapidly over Egypt. The German Government sent out a commission, with Koch at its head, to investigate the disease upon the spot. Before they had come to any definite conclusions, however, the cholera abated. With the thoroughness and patience which characterizes all Koch's work, he obtained leave to follow the cholera to India, where it is endemic, and to study it at its source. Here he succeeded in isolating and demonstrating the comma bacillus. Whether in this case also the finding of the cause of mischief may be the first step towards the discovery of its antidote time alone can show. It is at least well within the limits of reasonable hope.

AT BERLIN.

Honours now crowded thick and fast upon the discoverer, but even as poverty had failed to drive him from his life's work, so the greater trial of success was unable to relax his diligence. Appointed Professor of Hygiene and of Bacteriology in the University of Berlin, he quietly settled down to the investigation upon tubercle, which had been interrupted by his journey to India. For four years he pursued his silent studies, until he was able, at the recent medical congress at Berlin, to announce that they were almost complete, and that he would shortly give them to the world. The announcement was perhaps unfortunate, for it aroused such immense interest, and gave rise to so many circumstantial but fictitious rumours as to the efficacy of his treatment, that he was compelled, in order to prevent widespread disappointment, to give his discovery to the public rather earlier than he would otherwise have done.

And now as to the real value of that treatment—a question of the most vital importance to so many thousands of sufferers and so many hundreds of thousands of anxious relatives. Before entering into so grave a question, I may perhaps explain what grounds I have upon which to form an opinion. I had the good fortune to be the first English physician to arrive in Berlin after the announcement of Koch's discovery, and I had opportunities of seeing all the cases which are under treatment in Von Bergmann's wards, the clinical wards of Dr. Levy in the Prantzlauer Strasse, and under Dr. Bardeleben at the Charité Hospital. From these combined sources, I may fairly say that I had some material from which to draw a deduction.

THE COURTESY OF VON BERGMANN.

The stranger in Berlin is somewhat lost among the number of hospitals and clinical classes which make the city a great centre of teaching. My letters of introduction were to gentlemen who showed me the greatest kindness, but who were not medical men, and knew little, therefore, as to the means by which I might attain my end.

Hearing, however, that Professor Von Bergmann intended to give a lecture upon the Sunday night on the cases under his treatment, I adopted the course which seemed to me to be the most direct and the most likely to be successful. Putting myself in the position of a German medical man who was seeking information in London, I thought it best to go straight to the Professor and explain to him my difficulty. No doubt it would have succeeded in ninety-nine cases out of a hundred, but Von Bergmann unfortunately was the hundredth man. Never at any time remarkable for the suavity of his manners, he is notoriously gruff to our fellow-countrymen, and sees a Morell Mackenzie in every travelling Briton. No one can come in contact with him without at once seeing the difficulty which any colleague would have in working with him, and understanding where the blame lay in the painful controversy which followed the late Emperor's decease.

"There's no place," he shouted, in answer to my modest request that after travelling 700 miles I might be admitted to his lecture. "Perhaps you would like to take my place. That is the only one vacant." Then, as I bowed and turned away, he roared after me, "The first two rows of my clinik are entirely taken up by Englishmen." As I happened to know that the only Englishmen at his lectures were Mr. Malcolm Morris, of St. Mary's, and Dr. Pringle, of the Middlesex Hospital, I was as little impressed by his accuracy as by his courtesy.

PATIENTS UNDER TREATMENT.

As it happened, however, there was among the knot of students who overheard the incident an American gentleman, Dr. Hartz, of Michigan, who, on the good old principle that blood is thicker than water, at once lent me his powerful aid. Through his kind assistance I was enabled next morning to turn the Professor's flank by seeing in his wards the same cases which he had lectured upon the night before. A long and grim array they were of twisted joints, rotting bones, and foul ulcers of the skin, all more or less under the benign influence of the inoculation. Some of the ulcers were nearly healed, and I was assured by the assistant surgeons, and by Dr. Hartz, that where I now saw a white cicatrix drawing over the gap, there had formerly been nothing but disease and putrescence. Here and there I saw a patient, bright-eyed, flushed, and breathing heavily, who was in the stage of reaction after the administration of the injection; for it cannot be too clearly understood that the first effect of the virus is to intensify the symptoms, to raise the temperature to an almost dangerous degree, and in every way to make the patient worse instead of better.

DR. LEVY'S CLASS ROOMS.

From Von Bergmann's wards we made our way to Dr. Levy's Clinik, where again a similar series of cases were presented to us. The rooms were small, and, what with the press of the doctors, the crowd of patients seeking admission, and the number of sufferers who already occupied the beds, it was a somewhat trying atmosphere. The same scene was to be witnessed at the Charité Hospital, save that it was to the students rather than to the doctors that the teaching was addressed.

WHAT THE REMEDY DOES.

As to the efficacy of the treatment, the scepticism with which it has been encountered in some quarters is as undeserved as the absolute confidence with which others have hailed it. It must never be lost sight of that Koch has never claimed that his fluid kills the tubercle bacillus. On the contrary, it has no effect upon it, but destroys the low form of tissue in the meshes of which the bacilli lie. Should this tissue slough in the case of lupus, or be expelled in the sputum in the case of phthisis, and should it contain in its meshes all the bacilli, then it would be possible to hope for a complete cure. When one considers, however, the number and the minute size of these deadly organisms, and the evidence that the lymphatics as well as the organs are affected by them, it is evident that it will only be in very exceptional cases that the bacilli are all expelled. By the cessation of the reaction after injection you can tell when the tubercular tissue is all cleared out of the system, but there are no means by which you can tell how far the bacilli themselves have been got rid of. If any remain they will, of course, cause by their irritation fresh tubercular tissue to form, which in turn may be destroyed by a new series of injections. But, unfortunately, it is evident that the system soon establishes a tolerance to the injected fluid, so that the time must apparently come when the continually renewed tubercle tissue will refuse to respond to the remedy, in whatever strength it may be applied. Here lies the vast difference between Koch's treatment of consumption, and the action of vaccine in the case of small-pox. The one is for a time at least conclusive, while in the other your remedy does not treat the real seat of the evil. It continually removes the traces of the enemy, but it still leaves him deep in the invaded country.

ONE OF ITS DANGERS.

Another objection, though a much lighter one, is that the process stirs into activity all those tubercular centres which have become dormant. In one case which I have seen, the injection, given for the cure of a tubercular joint, caused an ulcer of the eye, which had been healed for twenty years, to suddenly break out again, thus demonstrating that the original ulcer came from a tubercular cause. It may also be remarked that the fever and reaction after the injection is in some cases so very high (41 deg. Cent, or nearly 104 deg. Fahr.) that it is hardly safe to use it in the case of a debilitated patient.

So much as to the more obviously weak points of the system. Others may develop themselves as more experience is gained. On the other hand, its virtues are many, and it represents an entirely new departure in medicine.

ITS ADVANTAGES.

There can be no question that it forms an admirable aid to diagnosis. Tubercle, and tubercle alone, responds to its action, so that in all cases where the exact nature of a complaint is doubtful, a single injection is enough to determine whether it is scrofulous, lupous, phthisical, or in any way tuberculous. This alone is a very important addition to the art of medicine.

Of its curative action in lupus there can be no question, though I have heard Dr. Koeler, the Berlin specialist upon skin affections, express a doubt as to the permanency of the cicatrix. This point, however, will be very shortly settled in England by the outcome of the case which Mr. Malcolm Morris, the well-known specialist, took over to Berlin. As far as this case has progressed there can be no doubt that the result has been astonishingly successful.

In the case of true phthisis of the lungs, which is of more immediate importance in these islands, the evidence is so slight that we can only regard it as an indication and a hope, rather than a proof. It is obvious that the difficulty of getting rid of the tubercular matter is enormously increased when the diseased products are buried deeply in a vital organ. It may prove that even here the specific action of the remedy may triumph over the degenerative process, but it would be an encouraging of false hopes to pretend that this result is in any way assured.

THE DEMAND FOR THE LYMPH.

Lastly, as to the obtaining of the all-important lymph, I called upon Dr. A. Libbertz, to whom its distribution has been entrusted, and I learned that the present supply is insufficient to meet the demands, even of the Berlin hospitals, and that it will be months before any other applicants can be supplied. A pile of letters upon the floor, four feet across, and as high as a man's knee, gave some indication as to what the future demand would be. These, I was informed, represented a single post.

Whatever may be the ultimate decision as to the system, there can be but one opinion as to the man himself. With the noble modesty which is his characteristic, he has retired from every public demonstration; and with the candour of a true man of science his utterances are mostly directed to the pointing out of the weak points and flaws in his own system. If anyone is deceived upon the point it is assuredly not the fault of the discoverer. Associates say that he has aged years in the last six months, and that his lined face and dry yellow skin are the direct results of the germ-laden atmosphere in which he has so fearlessly lived. It may well be that the eyes of posterity, passing over the ninety-year-old warrior in Silesia, and the giant statesman in Pomerania, may fix their gaze upon the silent worker in the Kloster Strasse, as being the noblest German of them all.

DR. KOCH'S OWN ACCOUNT OF HIS REMEDY.

The following is Dr. Koch's own account of his discovery, entitled, "A Further Communication on a Remedy for Tuberculosis," translated from the original article published in the *Deutsche Medizinsche Woehenschrift*, November 14. The translation is that of the *British Medical Journal:*—

INTRODUCTION.

In an address delivered before the International Medical Congress I mentioned a remedy which conferred on the animals experimented on an immunity against inoculation with the tubercle bacillus, and which arrests tuberculous disease. Investigations have now been carried out on human patients, and these form the subject of the following observations.

It was originally my intention to complete the research, and especially to gain sufficient experience regarding the application of the remedy in practice and its production on a large scale before publishing anything on the subject. But, in spite of all precautions, too many accounts have reached the public, and that in an exaggerated and distorted form, so that it seems imperative, in order to prevent all false impressions, to give at once a review of the position of the subject at the present stage of the inquiry. It is true that this review can, under these circumstances, be only brief, and must leave open many important questions.

The investigations have been carried on under my direction by Dr. A. Libbertz and Stabsarzt Dr. F. Pfühl, and are still in progress. Patients were placed, at my disposal by Professor Brieger from his Polikninik, Dr. W. Levy from his private surgical clinic, Geheimrath Dr. Frantzel and Oberstabsarzt Kohler from the Charité Hospital, and Geheimrath von Bergmann from the Surgical Clinic of the University.

THE REMEDY.

As regards the origin and the preparation of the remedy I am unable to make any statement, as my research is not yet concluded; I reserve this for a future communication. Doctors wishing to make investigations with the remedy at present can obtain it from Dr. A Libbertz, Lueneburger Strasse, 28, Berlin, N.W., who has undertaken the preparation of the remedy, with my own and Dr. Pfühl's co-operation. But I must remark that the quantity prepared at present is but small, and the larger quantities will not be obtainable for some weeks. The remedy is a brownish transparent liquid, which does not require special care to prevent decomposition. For use this fluid must be more or less diluted, and the dilutions are liable to decomposition if prepared with distilled water; bacterial growths soon develop in them, they become turbid, and are then unfit for use. To prevent this the diluted liquid must be sterilized by heat and preserved under a cotton wool stopper, or more conveniently prepared with a half per cent. solution of phenol.

HOW TO USE IT.

It would seem, however, that the effect is weakened both by frequent heating and by mixture with phenol solution, and I have therefore always made use of freshly-prepared solutions. Introduced into the stomach the remedy has no effect; in order to obtain a reliable effect it must be injected subcutaneously. For this purpose we have used exclusively the small syringe suggested by me for bacteriological work; it is furnished with a small india-rubber ball, and has no piston. This syringe can easily be kept aseptic by absolute alcohol, and to this we attribute the fact that not a single abscess has been observed in the course of more than a thousand subcutaneous injections. The place chosen for the injection—after several trials of other places—was the skin of the back between the shoulder-blades and the lumbar region, because here the injection led to doubtful cases of phthisis; for instance, cases in which it is impossible to obtain certainty as to the nature of the disease by the discovery of bacilli, or elastic fibres, in the sputum, or by physical examination. Affections of the glands, latent tuberculosis of bone, doubtful cases of tuberculosis of the skin, and such like cases will be easily and with certainty recognised. In cases of tuberculosis of the lungs or joints which have become apparently cured we shall be able to make sure whether the disease has really finished its course, and whether there be not still some diseased spots from which it might again arise as a flame from a spark hidden by ashes.

ITS EFFECT.

Of much greater importance, however, than its diagnostic use is the therapeutic effect of the remedy. In the description of the changes which a subcutaneous injection of the remedy produces in portions of skin changed by lupus, I mentioned that after the subsidence of the swelling and decrease of redness the lupus tissue does not return to its original condition, but that it is destroyed to a greater or less extent, and disappears. Observation shows that in some parts this result is brought about by the diseased tissue becoming necrotic, even after one sufficient injection, and, at a later stage, it is thrown off as a dead mass. In other parts a disappearance, or, as it were, a melting of the tissues seem to occur, and in such case the injection must be repeated to complete the cure.

IT KILLS THE TUBERCULOUS TISSUE.

In what way this process occurs cannot as yet be said with certainty, as the necessary histological investigations are not complete. But so much is certain that there is no question of a destruction of the tubercle bacilli in the tissues, but only that the tissue enclosing the tubercle bacilli is affected by the remedy. Beyond this there is, as is shown by the visible swelling and redness, considerable disturbance of the circulation, and evidently in connection therewith, deeply-seated changes in its nutrition, which cause the tissue to die off more or less quickly and deeply, according to the extent of the action of the remedy.

THE LIMITS OF ITS ACTION.

To recapitulate, the remedy does not kill the tubercle bacilli, but the tuberculous tissue; and this gives us clearly and definitely the limit that bounds the action of the remedy. It can only influence living tuberculous tissue; it has no effect on dead tissue, as, for instance, necrotic cheesy masses, necrotic bones, &c., nor has it any effect on tissue made necrotic by the remedy itself. In such masses of dead tissue living tubercle bacilli may possibly still be present, and are either thrown off with the necrosed tissue, or may possibly enter the neighbouring still living tissue under certain circumstances. If the therapeutic activity of the remedy is to be rendered as fruitful as possible, this peculiarity in its mode of action must be carefully observed. In the first instance the living tuberculous tissue must be caused to undergo necrosis, and then everything must be done to remove the dead tissue as soon as possible, as, for instance, by surgical interference. Where this is not possible, and the organism can only help itself in throwing off the tissue slowly, the endangered living tissue must be protected from fresh incursions of the parasites by continuous application of the remedy.

THE DOSE.

The fact that the remedy makes tuberculous tissue necrotic, and acts only on living tissue, helps to explain another peculiar characteristic thereof—namely, that it can be given in rapidly increasing doses. At first sight this phenomenon would seem to point to the establishment of tolerance, but since it is found that the dose can, in the course of about three weeks, be increased to about 500 times the original amount, tolerance can no longer be accepted as an explanation, as we know of nothing analogous to such a rapid and complete adaptation to an extremely active remedy. The phenomenon must rather be explained in this way—that in the beginning of the treatment there is a good deal of tuberculous living tissue, and that consequently a small amount of the active principle suffices to cause a strong reaction; but by each injection a certain amount of the tissue capable of reaction disappears, and then comparatively larger doses are necessary to produce the same amount of reaction as before. Within certain limits a certain degree of habituation may be perceived.

As soon as the tuberculous patient has been treated with increasing doses for so long that the point is reached when his reaction is as feeble as that of a non-tuberculous patient, then it may be assumed that all tuberculous tissue is destroyed. And then the treatment will only have to be continued by slowly increasing doses and with interruptions, in order that the patient may be protected from fresh infection while bacilli are still present in the organism.

Whether this conception, and the inferences that follow from it, be correct, the future must show. They were conclusive as far as I am concerned in determining the mode of treatment by the remedy, which, in our investigations, took the following form.

FOR LUPUS.

To begin with the simplest case, lupus; in nearly every one of these cases I injected the full dose of 0.01 cubic centimètres from the first. I then allowed the reaction to come to an end entirely, and then, after a week or two, again injected 0.01 cubic centimètre, continuing in the same way until the reaction became weaker and weaker, and then ceased. In two cases of facial lupus the lupus spots were thus brought to complete cicatrization by three or four injections; the other lupus cases improved in proportion to the duration of the treatment. All these patients had been sufferers for many years, having been previously treated unsuccessfully by various therapeutic methods.

Glandular, bone, and joint tuberculosis was similarly treated, large doses at long intervals being made use of; the result was the same as in the lupus cases—a speedy cure in recent and slight cases, slow improvement in severe cases.

FOR CONSUMPTION.

Circumstances were somewhat different in phthisical patients, who constituted the largest number of our patients. Patients with decided pulmonary tuberculosis are much more sensitive to the remedy than those with surgical tuberculous affections. We were obliged to lower the dose for the phthisical patients, and found that they almost all reacted strongly to 0.002 cubic centimètre, and even to 0.001 cubic centimètre. From this first small dose it became possible to rise more or less quickly to the same amount as is well borne by other patients.

Our course was generally as follows:—An injection of 0.001 cubic centimètre was first given to the phthisical patient; on this a rise of temperature followed, the same dose being repeated once a day until no reaction could be observed. We then rose to 0.02 cubic centimètre, until this was borne without reaction; and so on, rising by 0.001, or at most 0.002, to 0.01 cubic centimètre and more. This mild course seemed to me imperative in cases where there was great debility. By this mode of treatment the patient can be brought to bear large doses of the remedy with scarcely a rise of temperature. The patients of greater strength were treated from the first, partly with larger doses, partly with rapidly repeated doses. Here it seemed that the beneficial results were more quickly obtained.

CURE CERTAIN AT EARLY STAGES.

The action of the remedy in cases of phthisis generally showed itself as follows:—Cough and expectoration generally increased a little after the first injection, then grew less and less, and in the most favourable cases entirely disappeared; the expectoration also lost its purulent character, and became mucous.

As a rule, the number of bacilli only decreased when the expectoration began to present a mucous appearance; they then from time to time disappeared entirely, but were again observed occasionally until expectoration ceased completely. Simultaneously the night sweats ceased, the patients' appearance improved, and they increased in weight. Within four to six weeks patients under treatment for the first stage of phthisis were all free from every symptom of disease, and might be pronounced cured. Patients with cavities, not yet too highly developed, improved considerably, and were almost cured; only in those whose lungs contained many large cavities could no improvement be proved objectively, though even in these cases the expectoration decreased, and the subjective condition improved. These experiences lead me to suppose that phthisis in the beginning can be cured with certainty by this remedy. This sentence requires limitation in so far as at present no conclusive experiences can possibly be brought forward to prove whether the cure is lasting. Relapses naturally may occur; but it can be assumed that they may be cured as easily and quickly as the first attack. On the other hand it seems possible that, as in other infectious diseases, patients once cured may retain their immunity. This, too, must, for the present, remain an open question.

EFFECT IN ADVANCED CASES.

In part this may be assumed for other cases when not too far advanced; but patients with large cavities who almost all suffer from complications caused, for instance, by the incursion of other pus-forming micro-organisms into the cavities, or by incurable pathological changes in other organs will probably only obtain lasting benefit from the remedy in exceptional cases. Even such patients, however, were benefited for a time. This seems to prove that, in their cases too, the original tuberculous disease is influenced by the remedy in the same manner as in the other cases, but that we are unable to remove the necrotic masses of tissue with the secondary suppuration processes.

The thought suggests itself involuntarily that relief might possibly be brought to many of these severely afflicted patients by a combination of this new therapeutic method with surgical operations (such as the operation for empyema), or with other curative methods. And here I would earnestly warn people against a conventional and indiscriminate application of the remedy in all cases of tuberculosis. The treatment will probably be quite simple in cases where the least local reaction—generally none at all—and was almost painless.

ITS EFFECT ON GUINEA-PIGS.

As regards the effect of the remedy on the human patient, it was clear from the beginning of the research that in one very important point the human being reacts to the remedy differently from the animal generally used in experiments—the guinea-pig—a new proof for the experimenter of the all-important law that experiment on animals is not conclusive for the human being, for the human patient proved extraordinarily more sensitive than the guinea-pig as regards the effect of the remedy. A healthy guinea-pig will bear two cubic centimètres and even more of the liquid injected subcutaneously without being sensibly affected. But in the case of a full-grown, healthy man 0.25 cubic centimètre suffices to produce an intense effect. Calculated by body weight the 1,500th part of the quantity, which has no appreciable effect on the guinea-pig, acts powerfully on the human being.

HOW YOU FEEL UNDER THE TREATMENT.

The symptoms arising from an injection of 0.25 cubic centimètre I have observed after an injection made in my own upper arm. They were briefly as follows:—Three to four hours after the injection there came on pain in the limbs, fatigue, inclination to cough, difficulty in breathing, which speedily increased. In the fifth hour an unusually violent attack of ague followed, which lasted almost an hour. At the same time there was sickness, vomiting, and rise of body temperature up to 39.6 deg. C. After twelve hours all these symptoms abated. The temperature fell until next day it was normal, and a feeling of fatigue and pain in the limbs continued for a few days, and for exactly the same period of time the site of injection remained slightly painful and red. The lowest limit of the effect of the remedy for a healthy human being is about 0.01 cubic centimètre (equal to 1 cubic centimètre of the hundredth solution), as has been proved by numerous experiments. When this dose was used, reaction in most people showed itself only by slight pains in the limbs and transient fatigue. A few showed a slight rise of temperature up to about 38 deg. C. Although the dosage of the remedy shows a great difference between animals and human beings—calculated by body weight—in some other qualities there is much similarity between them. The most important of these qualities is the specific action of the remedy on tubercular processes of whatever kind.

ITS SPECIFIC ACTION.

I will not here describe this action as regards animals used for experiment, but I will at once turn to its extraordinary action on tuberculous human beings. The healthy human being reacts either not at all or scarcely at all—as we have seen when 0.01 cubic centimètre is used. The same holds good with regard to patients suffering from diseases other than tuberculosis, as repeated experiments have proved. But the case is very different when the disease is tuberculosis; the same dose of 0.01 cubic centimètre, injected subcutaneously into the tuberculous patient caused a severe general reaction, as well as a local one. (I gave children, aged from two to five years, one-tenth of this dose—that is to say, 0.001 cubic centimètre; very delicate children, only 0.0005 cubic centimètre, and obtained a powerful but in no way dangerous reaction.) The general reaction consists in an attack of fever, which, generally beginning with rigors, raises the temperature above 39 degs., often up to 40 degs., and even 41 deg. C.; this is accompanied by pains in the limbs, coughing, great fatigue, often sickness and vomiting. In several cases a slight icteric discoloration was observed, and occasionally an eruption like measles on the chest and neck.

The attack usually begins four to five hours after the injection, and lasts from 12 to 15 hours. Occasionally it begins later, and then runs its course with less intensity. The patients are very little affected by the attack, and as soon as it is over feel comparatively well, generally better than before it.

BEGIN WITH LUPUS.

The local reaction can be best observed in cases where the tuberculous affection is visible; for instance, in cases of lupus—here changes take place which show the specific anti-tuberculous action of the remedy to a most surprising degree. A few hours after an injection into the skin of the back—the is, in a spot far removed from the diseased spots on the face, &c.—the lupus spots begin to swell and to redden, and this they generally do before the initial rigor. During the fever, swelling and redness increase, and may finally reach a high degree, so that the lupus tissue becomes brownish and necrotic in places. Where the lupus was sharply defined we sometimes found a much swollen and brownish spot surrounded by a whitish edge almost a centimètre wide, which again was surrounded by a broad band of bright red.

After the subsidence of the fever the swelling of the lupus tissue decreases gradually, and disappears in about two or three days. The lupus spots themselves are then covered by a crust of serum, which filters outwards, and dries in the air; they change to crusts, which fall off after two or three weeks, and which, sometimes after one injection only, leave a clean red cicatrix behind. Generally, however, several injections are required for the complete removal of the lupus tissue. But of this more later on. I must mention, as a point of special importance, that the changes described are exactly confined to the parts of the skin affected with lupus. Even the smallest nodules, and those most deeply hidden in the lupus tissue, go through the process, and become visible in consequence of the swelling and change of colour, whilst the tissue itself, in which the lupus changes have entirely ceased, remains unchanged.

TUBERCULOSIS OF JOINTS, ETC.

The specific action of the remedy in these cases is less striking, but is perceptible to eye and touch, as are the local reactions in cases of tuberculosis of the glands, bones, joints, &c. In these cases swelling, increased sensibility, and redness of the superficial parts are observed. The reaction of the internal organs, especially of the lungs, is not at once apparent, unless the increased cough and expectoration of consumptive patients after the first injections be considered as pointing to a local reaction. In these cases the general reaction is dominant; nevertheless, we are justified in assuming that here, too, changes take place similar to those seen in lupus cases.

ITS VALUE IN DIAGNOSIS.

The symptoms of reaction above described occurred without exception in all cases where a tuberculous process was present in the organism, after a dose of 0.01 cubic centimètre, and I think I am justified in saying that the remedy will therefore, in future, form an indispensable aid to diagnosis. By its aid we shall be able to diagnose the beginning of phthisis and simple surgical cases are concerned, but in all other forms of tuberculosis medical art must have full sway by careful individualization, and making use of all other auxiliary methods to assist the action of the remedy. In many cases I had the decided impression that the careful nursing bestowed on the patient had a considerable influence on the result of the treatment, and I am in favour of applying the remedy in proper sanitoria as opposed to treatment at home and in the out-patient room. How far the methods of treatment already recognised as curative—such as mountain climate, fresh-air treatment, special diet, &c.—may be profitably combined with the new treatment cannot yet be definitely stated, but I believe that these therapeutic methods will also be highly advantageous when combined with the new treatment in many cases, especially in the convalescent stage. As regards tuberculosis of brain, larynx, and military tuberculosis, we had too little material at our disposal to gain proper experience.

TAKE IT EARLY.

The most important point to be observed in the new treatment is its early application. The proper subjects for treatment are patients in the initial stage of phthisis, for in them the curative action can be most fully shown, and for this reason, too, it cannot be too seriously pointed out that practitioners must in future be more than ever alive to the importance of diagnosing phthisis in as early a stage as possible. Up to the present the proof of tubercle bacilli in the sputum was considered more as an interesting point of secondary importance, which, though it made diagnosis more certain could not help the patient in any way, and which, in consequence, was often neglected. This I have lately repeatedly had occasion to observe in numerous cases of phthisis which had generally gone through the hands of several doctors without any examination of the sputum having been made. In future this must be changed. A doctor who shall neglect to diagnose phthisis in its earlier stage by all methods at his command, especially by examining the sputum, will be guilty of the most serious neglect of his patient, whose life may depend on this diagnosis, and the specific treatment at once applied in consequence thereof. In doubtful cases medical practitioners must make sure of the presence or absence of tuberculosis, and then only the new therapeutic method will become a blessing to suffering humanity, when all cases of tuberculosis are treated in their earliest stage, and we no longer meet with neglected serious cases forming an inextinguishable source of fresh infections. Finally, I would remark that I have purposely omitted statistical accounts and descriptions of individual cases, because the medical men who furnished us with patients for our investigations have themselves decided to publish the description of their cases, and I wish my account to be as objective as possible, leaving to them all that is purely personal.

THE LATEST REPORTS OF EXPERTS.

Since Mr. Conan Doyle, to whom I am indebted for the foregoing sketch, left Berlin there have been numerous reports by various medical societies and others as to the value of Dr. Koch's treatment. One thing is quite clear, and that is that while there have been apparently good results following the application of the alleged remedy in certain cases of lupus, there is absolutely no proof as yet that the Koch inoculations have cured a single case of consumption, even in its earliest stages, while it is admitted by Dr. Koch himself to be useless whenever consumption has made much progress.

The following are some of the reports which have been drawn up on the subject, which may be taken to represent the last word which medical science could say upon the alleged discovery up to the end of November:—

A distinguished member of the medical faculty in England, who came to Berlin to make a study of Dr. Koch's new cure for tuberculosis in all its forms, reported as follows to the *Times:*—

The value of the remedy, as an aid in diagnosis, is thus very great, and would alone serve to stamp its discovery as one of the first importance. It will be found especially useful in enabling the surgeon to detect the existence of tuberculosis in bones and joints.

Professor Billroth, at Vienna, on November 26th, said, unless the greatest caution is used in the application of the powerful medicine internal complications may arise which in certain cases may do immeasurable harm. He has known consumptive patients who had tubercular disease of the brain, and these might be absolutely killed if the remedy were applied in the dose prescribed by Dr. Koch. He hopes, however, that the remedy when carefully used may arrest the progress of consumption, but believes it will never heal it.

Dr. Kowalski, chief of the Bacteriological Institute for Army Physicians in Vienna, who was sent to Dr. Koch by the War Office a fortnight ago to study the new treatment, is most guarded where disease of the lungs or throat tuberculosis comes in question; but he is enthusiastic in his praises of the action of the remedy in external diseases. He has seen cases of diseased spine treated with most extraordinary results. Lupus, he says, is already beyond discussion, and may be considered as good as done with once for all. As a diagnostic test, the remedy works miracles.

At a special meeting, on November 25th, of the Medical Society of Cracow, the following resolutions were adopted:

(1) That Dr. Koch's lymph is a more effectual specific against external tubercles than any other known remedy. (2) That the therapeutic quality of the lymph and the mode of its application require further experiment before anything about them can be positively affirmed. (3) That the whole discovery is still in the stage of observation. (4) That the therapeutic value of specially selected health resorts for cases of tuberculosis remains unaffected, the climates of these places serving to fortify the system against the invasion and ravages of bacilli.

Dr. Désiré Schmitz, an eminent Antwerp clinical practitioner, reports November 23rd:—

The remedy acts against the living tubercular tissue, and slowly cures lupus; till now not a single case has been cured completely. As regards pulmonary phthisis, the remedy is still doubtful, and the experiments are only commencing.

After making an adequate grant to Dr. Koch, the State will, according to the *Börsen Zeitung*, undertake the production of his lymph on its own account. The number of patients treated by Dr. Koch's method in Berlin city was estimated at from seven to eight hundred up to the end of December.

THE ROMANCE OF MEDICINE[1]

I BELIEVE that the opening address of your Session is usually delivered by some medical man of distinction. You can imagine, therefore, how highly honoured I feel in being asked to occupy so exalted a position. You can also, I am sure, sympathise with me in my difficulties, since I have no possible claim to be regarded as a successful medical man. An unkind chairman in America once remarked that the most sinister feature of my career was that no *living* patient of mine had ever yet been seen. As a matter of fact, I could point to a few survivors, but I admit that they are not a numerous band. But though my actual practice of the profession was never either very profitable or very glorious, I think I may claim that at least it was very varied, and that I have seen it from several points of view. My experiences go back to the days of the unqualified assistant—a person who has now been legislated out of existence, with I have no doubt, an excellent result upon the death rate. I served in that legion of the lost before I ever attained to the regulars. I have been an assistant in country practices of rural England. I have served in the slums of Sheffield and of Birmingham. I have been the unqualified surgeon of an Arctic whaler, and the qualified one of a West African mail-boat. I have taken temporary military duty at Portsmouth. I have been for eight years in general practice in Southsea. I have migrated to the exalted neighbourhood of Cavendish Square, where I started a waiting-room—which is a room where a doctor waits for something to come along. The only thing which came along to me was the rent collector, so I left my profession, only to return to it for six months of South African service. There is my humble record, and it will serve to show you what poor credentials I have for standing here. At the same time it will also show you that I am not an amateur, and that there are few phases of medical life, from the sixpenny dispensary to the two-guinea prescription, of which I have not had personal experience. So perhaps if I bring but little learning, I may at least bring a fresh point of view to this task of addressing you today.

---

[1] This address to medical students was first published in *St. Mary's Hospital Gazette*, Vol. 16, 1910, pp. 100-106.

This fresh point of view comes from the fact that though I am of the medical profession, I am not in it. But I can testify how great a privilege and how valuable a possession it is to be a medical man, and to have had a medical training, even though one does not use it. It might seem that the thousand pounds which went to a man's education, and the long years of hard work, with an examination like a steeple-chase jump at the end of each, were wasted in a case where he did no work. Not a bit of it. It tinges the whole philosophy of life and furnishes the whole basis of thought. The healthy scepticism which medical training induces, the desire to prove every fact, and only to reason from such proved facts—these are the finest foundations for all thought. And then the moral training to keep a confidence inviolate, to act promptly on a sudden call, to keep your head in critical moments, to be kind and yet strong—where can you, outside medicine, get such a training as that? Believe me, the man who has a competence and never means to do any work in life would be very wise none the less to undergo the medical curriculum, for he would emerge with qualities which neither the classics nor the higher mathematics are ever likely to give him.

And then there is another way in which it acts. It sets a very high standard of strenuous work. You may not consider this altogether an advantage while you do it, but it remains a precious heritage for life. To the man who has mastered Grey's Anatomy, life holds no further terrors. To remember that huge catalogue of attachments and ganglia and anastomoses is, I think, the most arduous task any of you will ever be called upon to do. But it is worth doing, for it leaves you with that ideal. In after life, when you are confronted with any task, you may say to yourself, "Well, I will do it as thoroughly and accurately as I did my anatomy at College," and if you do it in that spirit I can assure you that nothing and nobody can stand against you. All work seems easy after the work of a medical education.

There are, perhaps, some dangers which come from a medical training, but there is a great postgraduate course called Life, and in that course one learns to correct these weaknesses. One is an undue Materialism. I think that I was educated in a materialistic age, before psychical research, scientific hypnotism, telepathy and other such agencies emphasised the possibilities which lie outside the things that we can see, handle, and explain. We looked upon mind and spirit as

secretions from the brain in the same way as bile was a secretion of
the liver. Brain centres explained everything, and if you could find and
stimulate the centre of holiness you would produce a saint—but if
your electrode slipped, and you got on to the centre of brutality, you
would evolve a Bill Sikes. That was, roughly, the point of view of the
more advanced spirits among us. I can clearly see now as I look back,
that this frame of mind was largely a protest and a reaction against
transcendental dogmas which had no likelihood either in reason or
in science. Swinging away from dogma, we lost all grip upon spirituality, confusing two things which have little connection with each
other—indeed, my experience is that the less the dogma the greater
the spirituality. We talked about laws, and how all things were done by
immutable law, and thought that was profound and final. Only more
mellow experience and riper thought make a man realise that there
must be a law-maker at the back of a law, and that if every dogma
were banished from earth, there still remain the ordered Universe
without, and the conscious Soul within to testify to forces, call them
by what name we will, which must break down the barriers of any
purely materialistic philosophy.

I would ask you then, gentlemen, in your studies of matter, not to
be precipitate in your conclusions as to spirit. Keep your minds open
on the subject. And besides an undue materialism there is another
danger upon which I would warn you. It is intellectual priggishness.
There is a type of young medical man who has all his diseases nicely
tabulated, and all his remedies nicely tabulated, the one exactly fitting the other—you produce the symptom, and he will produce the
tabloid—who really is a very raw product. Life may turn him into a
more finished article. Each generation has thought it knew all about
it, each generation has in turn discovered its limitations, and yet with
invincible optimism each fresh lot still thinks that they really *have* got
to the bottom of the matter. Not only have we never got to the end
of any medical matter, but it is only the truth that we have never got
to the beginning of it. What we have done is to come in in the middle
of it, with more or less accurate empirical knowledge. It will help to
keep you humble if you remember how largely the very words we
use, Life, Matter, Spirit, and so on, are mere symbols of the real meaning of which we know little. There is a true story of Lord Kelvin, how
he visited some electrical factory, and was shown round by a smart

foreman who explained everything very glibly, not knowing the identity of the illustrious visitor. Lord Kelvin listened in silence, but when he was leaving he said to the learned foreman, "By the way, what *is* electricity?" There again, you see, empirical knowledge has broken in upon the middle, while neither the source nor the end is known. As the philosopher said, "We are but children picking up pebbles on the shores of an illimitable ocean." There is no shame in being children before such forces, but a priggish child is not a pleasant object.

There is another fact which life will teach you, which is the value of kindliness and humanity as well as of knowledge. That is exactly the point which the intellectual prig has missed. A strong and kindly personality is as valuable an asset as actual learning in a medical man. I do not mean that trained urbanity which has been called "the bedside manner," but the real natural benevolence which may be slowly cultivated in the character, but cannot be simulated by any forced geniality. I have known men in the profession who were stuffed with accurate knowledge, and yet were so cold in their bearing, and so unsympathetic in their attitude, assuming the *rôle* rather of a judge than a friend, that they left their half-frozen patients all the worse for their contact. While, on the other hand, I have known—and who has not—men who were of such exuberance of vitality and kindliness that however humble their degrees the mere clasp of their hand and light in their eyes have left their patient in a more cheery and hopeful mood. Above all, no doctor has a right to be a pessimist. If you are conscious of that temperament, you should fly the profession. A reasoned optimism is essential for a doctor. He must believe the best, and so he goes half way to effecting it. We have known for all time that the cheery man was the healing man, but now in hypnotic suggestion, we come upon the physical explanation of the fact. If you can convey the expectation of cure, you have served your patient well. You need not go the lengths of a doctor I knew, who used to say to his neurotic and hysterical cases, "Now, Miss So-and-So, you will take three doses of the medicine, and then watch the clock till it is quarter past five, and at that instant all your troubles will disappear." It is true that his prophecy was often fulfilled, and yet the method was perhaps a little crude for general use.

With a knowledge of medicine you will find that you continually, in your general reading, bear with you a little private lantern which throws a light of its own. It illuminates many an incident which is dark to the layman. In every transaction of the world you are likely to find medical facts down at the root of it, influencing its origin and growth. I know few more interesting lines of thought than this, and there is a wide field for the writer who will explore the influences of medical facts upon social customs and upon historical incidents. To take an obvious example of what I mean, for centuries mankind beautified themselves by means of wigs. You go into any picture gallery and you see your bewigged ancestors, full wigs, and tie wigs, and bob wigs, staring arrogantly at your cropped modern pate. Whence came such a custom, unknown to antiquity and absurd in its nature? Medical, of course. A skin disease on the top of the head of Francis the First of France, which induced alopecia, or bald patches, compelled him to cover himself with artificial hair, his courtiers all followed suit, exactly as they all whispered when the same monarch got laryngitis, and so, the custom enduring after the true cause of it was passed, you find the explanation for all your tow-headed ancestors. It is a very typical instance of the influence of a medical fact upon social manners.

But when you come out into the wider field of history, what an enormous and fascinating range of thought lies before you, one almost untouched by the lay historian, and seldom explored by the medical writer. The association of certain diseases with certain characters is an extraordinary problem. To take an example, I suppose there are few men who have influenced history more deeply than Julius Cæsar and Mahomet. They were both epileptics. Is not that a most remarkable fact? Many other great men, including Napoleon, Saint Paul, and Alexander the Great, may be said to be under suspicion, but these two were undoubted. Julius Cæsar was, I believe, at all times of his life subject to fits, although it is on record that the open-air life which he led with the legions during the Gallic war had a very favourable influence upon his health. But to the end he was an epileptic. You will note that Shakespeare was aware of the fact, for at the beginning of "Julius Cæsar" comes the following morsel of dialogue:—

Cassius: What, did Cæsar swoon?

Casca: He fell down in the market-place and foamed at m o u t h and was speechless.

Brutus: 'Tis very like. He hath the falling sickness.

Plutarch says, "Concerning the constitution of his body he was lean, white and soft skinned and often subject to headache and other while to the falling sickness." Then as to Mahomet, we know that he also had sudden trance-like fits, quite apart from his religious visions, so that even the most pious Mahomedan must admit them to have been symptoms of disease.

Such conjunctions of the highest human qualities with a humiliating disease has surely both its pathological and its moral interest. Pathologically, one might suppose that there is a limit to the point to which the keenness of the spirit can drive the body; that at last the strain tells and they tear away from each other, like a racing engine which has got out of control. Morally, if the human race needed anything else to keep it humble, surely it could find it in the contemplation of the limitation of its own greatest men.

I have mentioned Napoleon, and I would further adduce him as an example of the sidelights and fresh interests which a medical man can read into history. One can trace for many years, certainly from 1802, the inception of that disease which killed him at St. Helena in 1821. In 1802, Bonncierre said:—

"I have often seen him at Malmaison lean against the right arm of his chair, and unbuttoning his coat and waistcoat exclaim, 'What pain I feel!'"

That was perhaps the first allusion to his stomachic and hepatic trouble; but from then onwards it continually appeared, like Banquo at the Banquet. He could scatter the hosts of Europe and alter its kingdoms, but he was powerless against the mutinous cells of his own mucous membrane. Again and again, he had attacks of lethargy, amounting almost to collapse, at moments when all his energy was most required. At the crisis of Waterloo he had such an attack, and sat his horse like a man dazed, for hours of the action. Finally, the six years at St. Helena furnish a clinical study of gastric disease which was all explained in the historical *post mortem*, which disclosed cancer covering the whole wall of the stomach, and actually perforating it at the heptic border. Napoleon's whole career was profoundly modified by his complaint. There have been many criticisms—not unnatural ones—of his petty, querulous and undignified attitude during his captivity; but if his critics knew what it was to digest their food with an organ which had hardly a square inch of healthy tissue upon it, they would perhaps take a more generous view of the conduct of Napoleon. For my own part, I think that his fortitude was never more

shown than during those years—the best proof of which was, that
his guardians had no notion how ill he was until within a few days
of his actual death. History abounds with examples of what I have
called the romance of medicine—a grim romance, it is true, but a
realistic and an absorbing one. Medicine takes you down to the deep
springs of those actions which appear upon the surface. Look at the
men, for example, who were the prime movers in the French Revolution. How far were their inhuman actions dependent upon their own
complaints? They were a diseased company—a pathological museum.
Was Marat's view of life tainted by his loathsome skin disease, for
which he was taking hot baths when Charlotte Corday cut him off?
Was the incorruptible, but bilious, Robespierre the victim of his own
liver? A man whose veins are green in colour is likely to take a harsh
view of life. Was Couthon's heart embittered by his disfigured limbs?
These are the problems where medicine infringes upon history, and
these are the illustrations of the philosophy which is only open to the
medical thinker.

How many times do the most important historical developments
appear to depend upon small physical causes? There is, for example,
the case of the Revocation of the Edict of Nantes. By this measure
the whole history of France has been profoundly modified, because
by that action there were driven forth the Huguenots, who were
the most stable and Teutonic portion of the nation—I say Teutonic,
because religion is a great test of race—and the result has been to
destroy the balance of the nation, and to leave France as brilliant as
ever, but without a certain solidity which she possessed before. On
the other hand, it reacted profoundly upon surrounding nations, giving us and others a fresh accession of the most valuable strain which
has prospered greatly ever since. Now, how came Louis XIV, who had
always held out upon this point, to give way at last to the pressure of
Madame de Maintenon and his clerical advisers? The answer lay in
one of his molar teeth. It is historical that he had for some months
had toothache, caries, abscess of the jaw, and finally a sinus which
required operation; and it was at this time, when he was pathologically abnormal and irritable, that he took the step which has modified
history. Great results may depend upon a King's jaw or a statesman's
digestion. That is one thing which may be said of those terrible com-
petitive examinations which are called Parliamentary elections, and

which give us our rulers. No one who is not physically fit is ever likely to get through them. I fear that I have wearied your patience in these discursive remarks, but I will get back now to something a little nearer the question at issue, which is medical life and medical education. It is nearly thirty years since I graduated, and it is a wonderful thing to me to note the progress which those thirty years have effected. As to how you stand in the present I will say a few words presently; but I have a very keen recollection, and perhaps a more accurate appreciation, of how we stood in the past. I am talking now of medicine, not of surgery. Someone described our condition as that of a blind man with a club, who swung it at random. Sometimes he hit the disease and sometimes the patient. The club consisted, of course, of our very copious and hard-worked pharmacopœia. There were noble prescriptions in those days—I don't know if they are quite extinct now—which were about as long as a fashionable restaurant's bill-of-fare, with the usual invocation to Jupiter at the top, which the patient might well echo. Wondrous was the science which combined so many powerful drugs, and yet so accurately balanced them that they never modified the action of each other. I suppose it was really based on the same principle as that of a country practitioner, whom I knew, who dispensed his own medicines. He used to empty all the bottles which had not been claimed into one huge jar, from which he occasionally dispensed droughts for his more obscure cases. "It's like grape-shot," he explained. "If one misses, another may hit." The patient's constitution could be trusted to pick out what was best for it in the splendid selection which the old physicians used to lay before it.

It cannot be denied that medicine was at that time an empirical science. Iron was good for anæmia; podophyllin for the liver; squills for the bronchi, and so on. But why it should be so, or what the real sources of a disease was, had not, as a rule, been very clearly made out. To show how wide of truth were some of the surmises of the day, I can remember, when I was a young graduate, reading an article in which the writer insisted that the mosquito was largely composed of what he called animal cinchoidine, and that when the creature bit you it was really giving you a subcutaneous injection which would protect you against the fever. The idea of little hypodermic syringes upon wings flying to your succour, seemed an admirable example of the benevolence of Nature, and under this pleasing delusion I have watched anopheles with a smile of gratitude while he buzzed at the end of my nose. I don't know whether I owe to this bit of science the sharp attack of coast fever which nearly left my bones at Lagos, but it was certainly an example of the danger of false explanations of cause and effect.

In surgery, Professor Lister had just brought out his antiseptic system, and when I was a young student the wards of the infirmary were divided between the antiseptic people and the cold-water school, the latter regarding the whole germ theory as an enormous fad. One sardonic professor of the old school used to say, as he was operating, "Please shut that door, or the germs will be getting in." On the other hand, the Listerians seem to have been almost unnecessarily scrupulous in keeping the germs out. Every operation was conducted amid clouds of carbolic steam, which often made the details invisible to the spectator. We should have been very much surprised to learn that the Puffing Billy could be done away with, and yet that complete antisepsis could be maintained.

I think that our educational tendency—as is natural in all clinical courses—was to expend undue attention upon rare diseases, and to take the common ones for granted. Many men who were quite at home with strange pathological lesions found themselves in practice without ever having seen a case of scarlatina or measles. I have no doubt at all that it was our own fault, and not that of my old University, which has always had the highest reputation for practical teaching. I found it much the same in men from other schools. They all came forth with much to learn. It is not possible in five years to cover every branch of medicine, especially if allied subjects such as botany, chemistry, and zoology are added to the curriculum. A young medical man who had just entered practice said to me once, speaking of his unfortunate patients, "When they are alive I don't know what is the matter with them, and when they are dead, I am not sure they are dead." The same practitioner is reported to have said to a sorrowing widow, "Your husband appears to be dead, madam, and no doubt he *is* dead, but I have no objection to meeting anyone in consultation."

I have said that our weakness thirty years ago was due to the vagueness of our knowledge. We never knew why. But this generation has, as it seems to me, brought about a greater change in medical science than any century has done before. At last there is some attempt to make it exact instead of empirical. Great results have been obtained, and even greater ones have been promised for the future. We fought a hidden enemy. You have brought him out into the open. It is true that the microbic origin of zymotic disease was taught thirty years ago, but we could hardly hope at that time that so many of these minute organisms would be actually separated, and that we should be able to artificially cultivate these lowly vegetable growths with the same certainty as we grow watercress or sweet peas. This would indeed have seemed to us to be a most far-fetched chapter in the romance of medicine.

In every literary or dramatic romance, you will observe that from the time that the villain is unmasked he is innocuous. It is the undiscovered villain who is formidable. So it has been in this wonderful romance of medicine. All this work of late years has been in the direction of exposing the villain. When once this is done, be he micrococcus or microbe, and be his accomplice a mosquito or a rat-flea, the forces of law and order can be turned upon him and he can be broken in to that human system which he has so long defied.

The story of how these forces of evil were exposed, how one by one their machinations were traced, is, I think, one of the most wonderful, and certainly one of the most eventful in Science. It is one also which we, as Britons, can regard with a peculiar satisfaction, for our fellow-countrymen have been protagonists in the battle. That great line which honours British medicine since the days of Harvey, has never had a more brilliant group than that which contains the name of Manson, Ross, Bruce, and Wright.

Each of these makes a story by himself, and it is one in each case which young aspirants to medicine should know, for it is always one which should arrest their attention and excite their emulation. They should learn, for example, of the untiring patience of Manson in his pursuit of the methods by which filaria gets from one human body to another. It is a fine instance of the fact that knowledge and good work are never thrown away, and that often they find their fruition in a manner never contemplated by the worker. Another fellow-countryman of ours, Timothy Lewis, had discovered the filaria in the blood of great numbers of Orientals. Manson took up the question of how it got there. His experiments necessitated the testing of the blood of literally thousands of Chinamen. Then, his suspicion as to the mosquito being aroused, he was able to show microscopically that the stomach of the mosquito, instead of digesting and so destroying the filaria, when it was taken in with a sip of human blood, actually strengthened and invigorated it, so that it passed through the stomach wall, made its way up to its head, and then sat expectant inside the sheath of its proboscis, all ready to spring into the blood-stream of the next victim. What dream of romance could be more extraordinary than that?

As I have said, great work leads to great work, and there is no end to its ultimate results. In this case, the immediate practical result of Manson's work was not great, as the filaria is not one of the chief pests of the human race, but it set Ross looking, on similar lines, for the methods of conveyance of malaria poison. In 1897 he conducted his classic investigation at Secunderabad. The parasite of Laveran was already known as the cause of the disease. The question was, how it got into the body. Heat and moisture had from time immemorial been taken as the answer. Ross showed once for all that neither heat nor moisture had anything to do with it. He worked on the lines of Manson, examining microscopically a long series of mosquitoes and other insects which had bitten malarious patients, in the hope of finding that with the blood they contained undigested parasites. For weary months the search was negative. The work was carried on under most exhausting conditions. He says himself, "The work, which was continued from 8 a.m. to 3 or 4 p.m., with a short interval for breakfast, was most exhausting, and so blinding that I could scarcely see afterwards, and the difficulty was increased by the fact that my microscope was almost worn out, the screws being rusted with sweat from my hands and forehead, and my only remaining eye-piece being cracked, while swarms of flies persecuted me at their pleasure as I sat with both hands engaged at the instrument. As the year had been almost rainless (it was the first year of plague and famine) the heat was almost intolerable, and a punkah could not be used for fear of injuring the delicate dissections. Fortunately, my invaluable oil-immersion object-glass remained good.

"Towards the middle of August I had exhaustively searched numerous grey mosquitoes, and a few brindled ones. The results were absolutely negative; the insects contained nothing whatever."

Finally his attention became drawn to some small brindled mosquitoes of innocent appearance. Then, at last, the villain stood revealed. No one could improve upon his own vivid description of the climax of his labours.

"On August 20th I had two remaining insects, both living. Both had been fed on the 16th instant. I had much work to do with other mosquitoes, and was not able to attend to these until late in the afternoon, when my sight had become very fatigued. The seventh dappled-winged mosquito was then successfully dissected. Every cell was searched, and to my intense disappointment nothing whatever was found, until I came to the insect's stomach. Here, however, just as I was about to abandon the examination, I saw a very delicate circular cell, apparently lying amongst the ordinary cells of the organ, and scarcely distinguishable from them. Almost instinctively I felt that here was something new. On looking further, another and another similar object presented itself. I now focussed the lens carefully on one of these, and found that it contained a few minute granules of some black substance, exactly like the pigment of the parasite of malaria. I counted together twelve of these cells in the insect, but was so tired with work, and had been so often disappointed before, that I did not at the moment recognise the value of the observation. After mounting the preparation I went home and slept for nearly an hour. On waking, my first thought was that the problem was solved, and so it was."

The discovery was at once confirmed by experiments. Among many other final demonstrations, anopheles was brought to London and there bit Professor Manson's son, who at once developed malaria. But the practical consequences were enormous. At once war was made upon anopheles. He was found very open to attack, for he breeds in such a way that his larva can be easily destroyed. Already, in ten years, he has ceased to exist where he used to be common. Italy, Greece, Ismailia, the West Coast, the West Indies, and many other places, have had their whole conditions of life profoundly altered by the discovery. When we think of all that has come from Ross' investigation, I feel that the rusted microscope of which he speaks should be erected in a place of honour as one of the proudest relics of this nation—a more glorious one, surely, than any warlike trophy ever can be.

And here is the Romance of Medicine at its highest. In 1807 we sent a force of 40,000 men to Flanders. No finer force ever left these shores. They returned beaten, decimated, and disorganised, and yet they had never seen the enemy. Who had beaten them? They did not know themselves. And now we know. Just a little grey gnat, a tiny insect buzzing up from the marshes of Walcheren. All the brigades and all the guns were powerless before its little proboscis. We know it now, and could meet it now, but then it was our conqueror. And so through all the ages, in the history of Africa, in the history of Central America, even in the history of such European districts as Greece and the Campagna of Italy, you will find the whole course of history altered by this fantastic and absurd little insect, whose chief physical characteristic is that he prefers to stand on his head with his tail almost perpendicular in the air above him.

I have not the knowledge, nor is this the occasion for me to enlarge upon the many other romances of science which have in recent times cleared some pathways in what used to be one confused jungle. One can only allude in passing to Bruce's splendid work at Malta, where, by the demonstration of the micrococcus of Maltese fever, and by the proof that the milk of the goats was the chief medium of infection, he was able to practically abolish a disease which used to prostrate thousands of people every year. Another great triumph of the new medicine was won by Reed and his fellow Americans when they proved that the stegomyia mosquito was the carrier of yellow fever, and by acting upon their discovery they have reduced the death-rate of the workmen at the Panama Canal until it is little higher than London. It is indeed a remarkable fact that upon our relations with a single species of mosquito should depend the possibility of joining the Pacific to the Atlantic. To the doctors rather than to the engineers is the triumph due.

I cannot pass from these stories—stimulating stories, as I hope—of modern medicine without referring to that most remarkable of all, the opsonic researches of Professor Wright, with which this hospital is so closely associated. This transcends romance and seems rather to approach the fairyland of science. It is presumptuous of me to describe it among so many who have such intimate knowledge of it, but I should leave my address very incomplete if I did not give some crude description of it. It was a familiar thought, even in my student days, that the leucocyte or white corpuscle was the guardian of the body, and that he devoured and digested every microbe which penetrated into the blood-stream. He floated in the clear fluid or blood plasma always ready to destroy the intruder, and it was only when the intruder was too numerous or too virulent to be destroyed that the blood became contaminated and our health in danger. Now, the starting point of the Opsonin investigation was when it was shown that a white corpuscle taken out of the blood plasma would not digest microbes, and would only renew its activities when it was moistened with that fluid. This experiment showed that in that fluid there was suspended some invisible stuff which increased the activity of the white corpuscle, and made it devour microbes—some sort of sauce, in fact, which made the microbes more attractive to it. This substance was named Opsonin.

The next stage was to prove that the normal man has a fixed quantity of opsonin, and therefore a fixed power of resisting any disease. What that fixed point is, could be actually shown by counting how many microbes one of his white corpuscles could destroy. This normal resisting power is called the Opsonic Index. If certain complaints—localised tubercle for one—have established themselves in a man, it means that his white corpuscles have been conquered. You would expect, therefore, to find that the Opsonic Index had fallen, that his power of destroying microbes was lessened, and this you would find to be so, and the fact would aid you in your diagnosis of the disease. But now comes the question of cure. In order to effect this, you want to raise the opsonic index—in other words, to stimulate the activity of the white corpuscles to a point above the normal, so that they may make unusual exertions and destroy the microbes. It has been found—and this part of the discovery lies with Koch—that an injection of dead microbes of the sort which causes the disease—is the most effective means to this end. With every injection the leucocytes work harder, the living intruders are more rapidly destroyed, and the cure comes nearer. Only one point Koch did not know, and it was an essential one for the clinical use of his discovery. It was that the first effect of such an injection was to *decrease* the opsonic index, then it went up; but after a time it reacted and come below the normal again. The whole point of the treatment is, not to allow it to do so—for in that case the last state of the patient must necessarily be worse than the first—but to arrest the decline by a fresh injection, always keeping the white corpuscles at their best until they have destroyed all the invaders. Such, in a nutshell, is the opsonic treatment, and surely one could not desire a clearer illustration of the strange romance of modern medicine. Now I have spoken long enough. Let my last words be personal to yourselves. The great Abernethy, when he was asked to give such an opening address, and when he saw the lines of students before him, cried out: "Good God, gentlemen! what is going to become of you all?" I think that under modern conditions one can say: What will become of you all? You will find your work ready to your hand. Some will find their way into the great Services, some into the Over-sea Empire, many into private practice. For all of you life will offer hard work. To few of you will it give wealth. But a competence will be ready for all, and with it that knowledge which no other profession can give to the same extent, that you are the friends of all, that all are better for your lives, that your ends are noble and humane. That universal goodwill without, and that assurance of good work within, are advantages which cannot be measured by any terms of money. You are the heirs to a profession which has always had higher ideals than the dollar. Those who have gone before you have held its reputation high. Unselfishness, fearlessness, humanity, self-effacement, professional honour—these are the proud qualities which medicine has ever demanded from her sons. They have lived up to them. It is for you youngsters to see that they shall not decline during the generation to come.

CPSIA information can be obtained
at www.ICGtesting.com
Printed in the USA
LVHW030842010223
738313LV00003B/218